THE DETACHMENT

Gary Reilly

Running Meter Press
Denver

The Detachment
by Gary Reilly

Published by

Running Meter Press
2509 Xanthia St.
Denver, CO 80238
Publisher@RunningMeterPress.com
720-328-5488

Cover art and book design by Nick Zelinger

ISBN: 978-0-9908666-3-3
Library of Congress Number: 2015951428

First edition, 2016
Printed in the United States of America

Also by Gary Reilly:

The Asphalt Warrior Series:
The Asphalt Warrior
Ticket to Hollywood
The Heart of Darkness Club
Home for the Holidays
Doctor Lovebeads
Dark Night of the Soul
Pickup At Union Station

Also:
The Enlisted Men's Club

FOREWORD

The Detachment, by the late writer Gary Reilly, is the second novel in a trilogy featuring Private Palmer, a U.S. Army draftee during the Vietnam War. The first in the series, *The Enlisted Men's Club*, followed Palmer while he was stationed at The Presidio awaiting orders to deploy to the war zone.

This book picks up where *The Enlisted Men's Club* left off. It covers Palmer's year-long tour in Vietnam, serving as an M.P. in a traffic unit—an experience shared by the author. Reilly captures the frustration, boredom and capricious nature of military life. And the fear.

In the first, war on the other side of the world loomed for Private Palmer. In *The Detachment*, the war gets a whole lot more personal. How does Palmer cope? With beer. With a wily sense of how to turn the system to his advantage. And by finding ways to detach himself from reality.

Survival will require Palmer to dig deep into the scariest place of all—himself.

That the book you hold would ever see print is the result of some minor sleuthing, mind reading and a great deal of luck. When Gary died in 2011, he was an unpublished novelist. He left behind at least 25 complete manuscripts and a few others that had to be pieced together. *The Detachment* is one of the latter.

Reilly's trove fell into the hands of two of his friends: Mark Stevens and me. Just before he died, he included a statement in his three-line will that granted us custody of his work, to do with as we saw fit.

We knew his writing. After he finished a book, he would print and hand-bind one or two copies to be passed around a small circle of people he trusted. Mark and I were among the lucky ones. We marveled at the quality and clarity of his words and could not imagine leaving Gary's novels sitting idle—and unread—in a box.

As soon as we got the files, we began publishing his work. It was a no-brainer.

Running Meter Press was established to bring Gary's talent to the public. We began with The Asphalt Warrior series, 11 comic novels about a Denver cab driver named Murph. To date, seven have been published, all landing among the top three on *The Denver Post* bestseller's list. Two of those were named finalists for The Colorado Book Award.

On NPR's Weekend Edition Saturday in December, 2014, host Scott Simon interviewed Londoner Will Grozier, his annual guest book critic, who picked The Asphalt Warrior series as his favorite fiction of the year. "Huge fun," said Grozier.

The Private Palmer trilogy invokes an altogether different mood. Yes, there is humor. But this is soul-baring, serious material. And, unlike the Murph novels, which were well-organized and easily retrieved, the Palmer material, created much earlier, was in disarray. Written with long-obsolete software, stored on ancient drives and floppies, some passages corrupted and with multiple versions here and there, we were not sure we could piece it together. In addition, it seemed that Reilly had not decided whether *The Detachment* was one book or three. Mark remembers reading the first and second parts of *The Detachment* as stand-alone affairs.

Then, a stroke of fortune: a single Reilly-bound copy turned up at the bottom of an old box of his belongings. The spine was broken, pages flapping, whole chapters tucked in loosely. Most likely it was one of his first efforts with home printer, paper cutter and rubber cement. It was in bad shape. But it became our Rosetta Stone. With technical help from Anita Austin and Justine Chapel, editing by Mike McClanahan, Joanne Krieg and Karen Haverkamp and spiritual guidance from Sherry Peterson, the book came together.

Beautifully-structured and complete, we are confident *The Detachment* is the novel that Gary intended.

Mike Keefe
August, 2015

PART ONE

CHAPTER 1

There he is. The tall soldier standing by himself aloof from everybody else. He has been standing aloof ever since he realized he no longer had any interest in being a soldier. This loss of desire began to occur in early February, when he was a trainee at the Military Police School in Fort Gordon, Georgia.

"Is your name Palmer?"

Private Palmer is standing at the magazine rack in a small PX in the Oakland Army Replacement Depot, flipping through the pages of a magazine called *Slammer*, a pulp monthly which offers softcore photos of women in skimpy lingerie. At the mention of his name, a feeling of depression engulfs his heart in the way that mists of adrenaline grip his neck bone whenever anything resembling danger or responsibility intrudes on his life. He doesn't want to talk to anyone, knows no one here in this clearinghouse for men going to Vietnam, and can only assume that he has been tracked down by the military authorities for having dodged KP the previous evening.

Still holding the magazine open to a grainy black-and-white photo of a woman in panties and bra which looks like it might have been snapped in the early Fifties, Palmer turns his head and looks at a PFC who is studying his face with as much intensity as Palmer has been giving the photo. Palmer doesn't recognize him, but the man is wearing jungle fatigues and is obviously headed for Vietnam, so Palmer feels safe in saying, "Yes."

"I thought I recognized you," the man says, his freckled face becoming animated, grinning, his bulging cheeks and slightly crooked teeth throwing into soft focus something familiar—Palmer knows this man from somewhere. His name tag has not yet been sewn onto his fatigues, just as Palmer's name has not been stitched on by a military seamstress. That will happen when he arrives at whatever duty station the army has waiting for him across the Pacific, beyond the longitudes that his own father had endured thirty years earlier: New Guinea; Manila; The Solomon Islands. "Krouse!" the man says, his face lighting up, his eyes bright behind his black army-issue glasses. "You and me were in basic training together!"

Krouse. The name pops like a subscription insert from the pages of *Time* magazine and falls to the floor at Palmer's feet. He glances down at the scuffed PX tiles, frowns as if trying to remember. But he remembers. Krouse was one of the Michigan trainees, he had arrived with a group of National Guardsmen who were fulfilling their NG requirement by taking eight weeks of basic before heading back to the Upper Peninsula to get on with their lives, though Krouse was a regular army draftee. The one thing that stands out in Palmer's memory concerning the Michigan NGs is that half of them were complete assholes.

"Oh...yeah...Krouse," Palmer says, trying to imbue his voice with as much disinterest as he can muster while still maintaining a modicum of military courtesy. "Good to see you again."

Krouse seems ecstatic. But why not?

Oakland is a lonely place. Even Palmer feels a brief tug inside his chest at the sight of a familiar face. But he squelches it. Going to the war is something he wants to do alone, like taking a shit or staring at a skin magazine. Traveling to a foreign country where he will most likely die isn't a jolly lark or a trip to the flicks—it has the quality of an embarrassing miscalculation in judgment. He doesn't want to discuss it with anyone. He just wants to get it over with, get shot or get home safely, but get it over with.

"How long have you been here?" Krouse says as if resuming a conversation cut off almost a year earlier at the end of basic. But that's the army. You make friends fast, they disappear fast, and an old face is an old friend.

"Four days," Palmer says, closing *Slammer*, giving up on a moment's peace at the magazine rack. He tucks it among all the other thumbed rags arranged in lop-eared disorder. "I got here on Monday."

"I got here Tuesday," Krouse says. "Do you remember Tigler?"

Another vague name. Palmer nods. He doesn't remember the man.

"He showed up on Wednesday and they sent his ass to the CO. He got busted from PFC back to E2."

Palmer has heard this story before, from his brother Phil who had been here months ago, so it neither surprises nor interests him, the naive belief in the mythical day-of-grace bought into by amateurs and half-baked rebels. But Palmer lifts his chin and softly says, "Wow," because he knows he is stuck with Krouse for the rest of the day and thus has to act interested, but doesn't really mind. This is a lonely place.

"Brenner and Willerton are here too," Krouse says. "Do you remember them?"

More names from basic. Palmer decides to nod. He has

forgotten most of the names of the men he had served with in Fort Campbell. But now, apparently, they are back.

"Want to go get a beer?" Palmer says, feeling edgy about having this uninvited and uninteresting conversation with a near-stranger. It isn't that he finds it completely impossible to talk to another person while sober, it's just that booze makes it tolerable.

"It's a little early isn't it?" Krouse says, and just like that Palmer loses interest in him. Who made the rule that ten A.M. was too early to drink? Krouse seems like a little kid to him now. But Palmer leads him out of the PX and onto an asphalt street, giving a bit of thought to concocting an excuse to ditch him. Have to go to operations and check on my orders, or some other lie.

"What happened to your arm?" Krouse says.

Palmer rotates his left forearm and looks at the scars on the underside that will never disappear. "It was injured in an accident awhile back."

"Jesus, it looks awful. What happened?"

Palmer reaches for a pack of cigarettes with his left arm, pokes around in his breast pocket, the movement hiding the scars that draw people's attention like the face of a celebrity. He supposes he will be hiding it all his life under long-sleeved shirts. He doesn't want to talk about it. There are things in life that concern him more than this wound, such as potential wounds awaiting him in Vietnam.

"Got broken in a judo class. I'm an MP." He lights a cigarette.

Gazing at Palmer's forearm, Krouse raises his face, eyebrows arched, and looks at Palmer. "Really?"

"What do you do?" Palmer says.

"Clerk/typist. Me and Tigler got sent to clerk school at Fort Knox at the end of basic. We've been stationed at Fort Huachuca ever since then."

They walk as Krouse speaks, Palmer blowing smoke and leading him toward the enlisted men's club. Millions of milling men in green it seems are wandering just as they are, drifting around the Depot in search of something to do, each ticking off the five days in his mind until his name will be called to go to Vietnam. You arrive on the first day as baffled as a newborn, learn the ropes, the tricks, the shit details, and by the fifth day you are a veteran, resigned to your fate like folks in a nursing home. Palmer knows he will be called today, most likely this evening. That's the legend of this place, you are here for five days and then you are called.

"Guess what I did this morning," Krouse says, grinning at the ground as they walk along, Krouse a few inches shorter than Palmer, shoulders rounded, legs short, bowed but gangly in their manner, each boot seeming to lunge to find the asphalt, slapping it. He walks like a little kid, talks like one.

"What," Palmer says.

"I snuck out on a shit detail." He glances up at Palmer as he makes this announcement, his eyes momentarily shot white by the reflection of the sun off his glasses. The bay sky is clear today but had been gray with clouds all week, had dusted the troops with mists at morning reveille.

Palmer waits while Krouse's proud grin runs its course, waits for the facts. Krouse looks back at the ground and says he was sent to a warehouse to hand out uniforms to returning veterans—men who had served their year in Vietnam, who had come home alive decked out in the same dirty sun-blasted fatigues they were wearing when they departed their units to climb onto the freedom bird, the legendary freedom bird. Palmer knows there is a whole slew of jargon waiting for him in the war. He dislikes army jargon, feels like an idiot talking like a soldier who gives a shit, rapping like a cool cat in olive-drab.

"As soon as we got to the warehouse a sergeant grabbed eight of us and sent us to this gigantic room. It was like an airplane hangar. Right in the middle of it was this island of uniforms on racks. The sergeant was in a big hurry, so he forgot to take our ID cards from us."

This particular detail piques Palmer's interest. He exhales smoke and looks over at Krouse whose head is hung with a kind of abashed pride at the story he is telling.

"I didn't want to even be on the detail, you know what I mean? I hate this place. So anyway the sergeant was running back and forth telling us what to do and everything, and there was this long table set up in front of the uniforms and he told us that we were gonna have to work fast and stay on our toes and all that shit because the troops would be coming through any minute."

Krouse glances at Palmer as if to ascertain that his audience is enraptured, which it is in a way. Palmer is looking right at him, piqued.

"So you know what I did? While the sergeant was talking, I just sort of stepped backwards into this island of uniforms and started making my way between the racks. They were set real close together; it was like a jungle. I was invisible. I walked all the way through it. There was a loading dock on the far side of the hangar and the door was raised. I had thirty feet of open floor to cross to make it to the door. I just stood there for a minute getting up the nerve." He grins and shakes his head.

Palmer intuits what is going to happen next, pictures it, since Krouse has already told him the upshot: escape. Krouse standing hidden in the safety of the uniforms crowding him, Class A fabric nudging his nervous arms like fronds in a triple-canopy jungle. He makes his move. If you act like you're doing what you're supposed to be doing, nobody will question you. All escapes have a similarity about them, Palmer knows.

"I walked out of the racks and crossed the floor expecting to get yelled at, but nobody even saw me I guess because I got out on the dock and jumped down to the street and ran away."

Palmer can't help but grin, giving Krouse what he wants. All victory possesses a similarity too. Fifty million people dead at the end of World War II, but the living cheered.

Hearing this tale diminishes the likelihood of Palmer relating the details of his own military victory of the night before—escape from KP. The benevolence of elusive ID cards—it probably happens with frequency in this place, sergeants dealing with the minutiae of disorganized labor, although how many draftees would figure things out fast enough to make a run for it? You have to be exceptionally desperate. The upshot of the story makes Palmer like Krouse.

When they get to the EM club they find the door locked. It's usually open at this time of day, but the door won't budge. No polite explanatory note taped to it like you find on civilian bars, stores, 7/11s inexplicably shut down in the shank of the evening.

"Fuck," Palmer says softly, more to himself than to Krouse, who looks on with the indifference of all people to whom beer is just something you drink.

The alternative is to head back to the PX and buy a Coke, sit on an OD green bench in the sunlight and trade excruciating stories about where they've been and what they've done since the day they graduated from basic.

"Tigler and the other guys should be getting off their shit details by now," Krouse says. "Want to go see them? We always meet back in the barracks after the details are over."

Krouse's group has learned the ropes, the tricks. Palmer field-strips his cigarette, flicks the balled pebble of paper away, and lights up a fresh smoke. "Sure," he says. With any luck he'll never see them again anyway after his name is called at evening formation.

CHAPTER 2

Everybody grins in the barracks, Tigler and Brenner and Willerton reaching out to shake hands with Palmer. They look about the same, their hair a bit longer, basic training buddies crossing paths again in this small military world. Tigler and Palmer are the only E2s. Tigler is taller than Palmer, a bit horse-faced. He has a voice that could always be heard above the shouting of trainees in basic, deep and loud, has a brassy laugh that had the potential of becoming annoying except that he seemed to laugh only at things that actually were funny. Brenner is smaller than Palmer, his longish hair now revealed as dark black—everyone's hair had seemed blond it was so short in basic. He has a lean compact body, athletic, his head small, squared, his teeth slightly buck, had seemed back then always to be smirking. He had been a good sprinter as Palmer recalls, always at the head of the pack in the mile run. Willerton is the most like Palmer, same height, a brown-haired nonentity that Palmer can recall nothing in particular about. When Palmer was stationed at the Presidio across the bay he had seen a basic training acquaintance named Plamenski seated in the base cafeteria, wearing a Class A uniform and talking to another man. Plamenski was from New Jersey, talked like a hood, like a gangster in a movie but apparently really was like that—Palmer has never been east of Augusta. Plamenski looked like he might have been in-transit, maybe headed to Vietnam, but had been an especially obnoxious trainee, worse than the Michigan NGs, so Palmer hadn't approached him to grin and shake hands and share excruciating stories. The Presidio just wasn't lonely enough.

"Palmer's an MP," Krouse says, and the others look at him as if seeing him for the first time, look him up and down as if to ascertain whether his MOS has changed him in any tangible way since last they saw him. Everybody hates the MPs, but maybe these men have never been ticketed, rousted, busted by a man of their own or lesser rank enforcing laws that nobody takes very seriously because the army isn't real enough. They seem only curious, and ask him what it's like to be an MP.

Palmer shrugs. "I was stationed at the Presidio. We mostly drove around in MP vehicles, crappy old six-bangers. There wasn't much going on at the Presidio. What do you guys do?"

"I drive trucks," Brenner says, and Tigler laughs and says, "*Convoyyys,*" in a drawl that makes Brenner laugh too, apparently some running joke between them. Brenner could end up transporting supplies across the highlands of Vietnam, but then Palmer could end up escorting convoys. The instructors in MP school had told them about the V-100s that the MPs would be driving, tank-like vehicles with big rubber tires, armed and armored, and said the VC always tried to take out the V-100s with their rocket-propelled grenades. The instructors seemed to take pleasure in describing the death and destruction awaiting the draftees, and Palmer had wondered if infantry instructors were like that too.

Willerton is in the Signal Corps. Tigler and Krouse clerks. No infantry here. The final week of basic training had been rife with suspense as each trainee had waited to receive his random orders. Two buddies named Porter and Gomez, both from Wichita, had received orders for Infantry—11-Bravo. They had grinned sheepishly on the day they received their orders. Palmer sometimes wonders if either of them are already dead, but he doesn't ask these men if they know. The Michigan NGs had sat around the barracks at night laughing at the draftees and telling them that they were going to end up humping the boonies in search of Sir Charles. No stigma attached to what had seemed a wise decision to play week-end warrior. In high school the conversations among those not going to college, Palmer included, had focused on ways to stay out of combat. Reserves. National Guard. Dumb luck. Nobody talked about going to Canada, they discussed only the acceptable methods of dodging the draft, but Palmer had never doubted for a moment that he would end up in the war.

"What happened to your arm?" Brenner says.

Palmer turns the underside up to let everyone see, lowers it. "Broke it in a judo class."

"Do you know judo?" Willerton says, seemingly amazed.

"No," Palmer says. "We took it in MP school, but nobody got very good at it. It was like karate in basic." The men nod, remembering the hour given over to fake oriental hand-to-hand each afternoon in Fort Campbell. Palmer wonders if the EM club is open yet. "Tell them about your shit detail," he says to Krouse.

Krouse tells his story, Palmer not really listening, trying to remember anything else about these men from basic, whom he had never expected to see again. They had been in different platoons, had bunked in different barracks from Palmer, and became his buddies only when they were thrown together on KP or crawling under barbed wire. They laugh, are impressed with Krouse's tale, then tell dull tales of their own about mopping latrines, sweeping floors, carrying crates in warehouses.

"Where are you bunked, Palmer?" Willerton says.

"Another barracks," he replies, pointing with his right thumb in a random direction.

"Why don't you go get your shit and bunk here with us?" Willerton says.

Palmer shrugs. "I'll probably get called today," he says a little too quickly, almost as if he is lying. "I've been here since Monday."

They nod. They all will be headed for Vietnam soon.

Krouse suggests they drift over toward the mess halls in order to get in line early even though noon chow is more than an hour away, one of the learned tricks. There are hordes of men at Oakland to be fed, it isn't like the small companies they had come from, Brenner and Willerton having been stationed at Fort Polk, Tigler and Krouse at Huachuca, Palmer at the Presidio far across the bay. Tigler finally asks him why his hair is so short, "Do MPs always wear it that way?" So Palmer tells this story in lieu of the one that still waits inside him for an audience that hasn't already heard an elusive ID story, the escape from KP which raises his spirits so high that not even the thought of getting on an airplane— he hates flying—can put a dent in his joy.

"A sergeant ordered me to get it cut." He describes an incident involving a chubby E5 at the reception table who took one look at the hair tickling the tips of his ears and refused to process him in until he had been to the barbershop. "What an asshole," one of the men says behind Palmer as they emerge from the barracks into the light of a sky going pale behind a gathering sheath of clouds like gauze over the lens of a camera. They step onto the asphalt of the parade ground where formations are held, a vast field that looks like an airstrip. No matter what building you emerge from at Oakland, it always seems like you're walking out of a back door.

"So I told the barber to take it all off," Palmer says, finishing his story. He, among all these men, still looks like a basic trainee. His cap fits loosely on his head but he doesn't care, he likes short hair, had liked long hair only as a civilian.

With his story over, the men shake their heads with exasperation at one more layer of army bullshit that has accumulated like rising silt around their ankles during the past year, as if it had happened to them, for it could have happened to any of them. It creates a kind of unity that Palmer can feel as the group wanders along the sidewalk in the general direction of the many mess halls that serve the Depot, one of which is a man short on the roster because Private Palmer had gone AWOL last night.

Brenner begins describing a porno paperback that he recently read, a chapter that took place inside a spaceship with alien women having sex with control levers. The men laugh like high school kids. Brenner has a slight southern accent, and Palmer wonders what state he's from. In basic Palmer was the only trainee from Colorado. Quite a few were from Nebraska. One man was from California and had seemed a bit exotic to the others for that reason alone. The land of the surfers. He had a dark tan. All the other white guys were pasty white, were from the midwest, the east coast, the south. A lot of heavy southern accents in basic training.

All the black guys seemed to be from either Mississippi or Chicago.

Everyone in the group but Krouse lights up cigarettes. A Marlboro here, an Old Gold there. Willerton lights a Salem. Palmer has never met any GI who smokes Camels, his own brand, which is fine, since people tend not to want to bum nonfiltered smokes. Ever since he received his draft notice he had been trying to give up smoking, but doesn't give it any more thought now, since he's on his way to a war.

They come to a mess hall where a lot of men are milling around outside the door waiting for chow, and Palmer wonders if this is only because the EM club is closed. There are clusters of men like his own group, and it occurs to him that they are probably men waiting out their last day or two like himself. Old friends and acquaintances converging. Or maybe just new friendships forged quickly because isolation can be intolerable to young GIs in a situation like this, though Palmer prefers it, practically thrives on it. Other men stand off by themselves smoking cigarettes and gazing at the pale sky. New guys, Palmer decides.

He looks at his former basic buddies that he somehow has gotten attached to again, and doesn't know what to say to them. They stand silently puffing on cigarettes and gazing out across the tarmac, waiting. It's like being at the wedding of a friend and finding yourself having to make up conversations with people you don't know. He sometimes dreams he's back in basic, but does not recognize any of the men in those dreams. None of the faces had stuck. He finally asks Tigler about his getting busted from PFC to E2, an event that does not actually interest him. Tigler hisses with disgust, tosses his cigarette to the ground without field-stripping it, the stub flattening under his boot. He tells Palmer that he'd heard from a Spec Four in operations that he probably would get his rank back as soon as he arrived at his unit in Vietnam. "It's just harassment," Tigler says, but looks pleased to be able to pass on this bit of inside info which sounds highly probable to Palmer only because it's so chickenshit.

Palmer looks at Willerton. "My father was in the Signal Corps in World War II," he says. "He was stationed in New Guinea."

Willerton nods, has no response to this.

"Did you have to learn Morse code?" Palmer says.

"Oh yeah," Willerton replies. He doesn't elaborate upon his training. Maybe the conversation is too excruciating. Palmer looks away, studies the empty tarmac.

When the mess hall door finally opens, the waiting troops, mostly strangers to each other, herd inside politely, demonstrating the military courtesy instilled in them throughout the past year, or else four months. Some of them must have arrived here right out of advanced training, as had Palmer's older brother Phil who is now in Hawaii—Schofield Barracks. Probably it's infantry who are shunted immediately into the pipeline to the war, unlike Palmer who, to his surprise, had been sent to the Presidio at the end of advanced individual training. Two hundred men killed in one week in Vietnam, according to a *Life* magazine feature. Page after page of basic training photos, most of them probably infantry but Palmer hadn't known enough about the army when he'd read it to know. He was young enough then to believe that everybody who went to Vietnam died, and it really wasn't all that long ago.

CHAPTER 3

The mess hall is a big, bustling place, noisy with men who do not seem particularly morose about going off to the war, but then these are the men who had not turned their backs on the draft, had known what eventually would happen to them. Palmer had gone to a different mess hall each evening this week for no other reason than he has always tried to stay a moving target in the army, a nearly unconscious thing, a way to avoid shit details. Don't let anyone above the rank of corporal become familiar with your face. It's only a game, but one that Palmer cannot help but take seriously.

The tables in this mess hall are like those in basic and AIT and the Presidio, each one seating only four men. It occurs to Palmer to volunteer to be the fifth wheel and let the others sit together, he will find an empty seat somewhere across the room, but in fact there are plenty of empty tables all around. They've gotten here early thanks to Krouse's strategy. Krouse sits with Palmer at one table, and the others sit at a table adjacent.

Barbecued chicken is on the menu today, along with potato salad. Palmer dislikes barbecued chicken, dislikes the grubby feel of sauce on his fingers when he wipes them with a napkin. But he has never minded army food, recalling the jokes he had heard about army food mostly from the movies and a few novels: creamed chipped-beef on toast was shit on a shingle, but Palmer had found it tasty the first time he ate it in basic, the tastiest food to eat with a hangover. Spicy. But then those novels and movies were about World War II, so maybe the food really was bad in those days, except soldiers love to bitch about everything, as Palmer has discovered. Funny how some people seem to love oppression. Every minor inconvenience is the London Blitz. Palmer never has liked gripers, the verbal ones, the moaners, as if they're the only ones who feel like shit. The day he was sworn into the army, almost one year earlier, he had sat in a cafeteria in the US Customs Building in downtown Denver, staring at a tray filled with food that he couldn't eat. He had managed to drink only a glass of milk. He had lost his appetite when a man with yellow stripes on his sleeves informed the group of draftees that approximately ten of them would be inducted into the Marines. He said if your name is called, please go quietly with no kicking or screaming. Everybody laughed nervously. As the afternoon wore on, and one name was called, and then another, Palmer could feel the gloom in the large room where the men were seated at tables, slouched, silent, staring. Everybody felt like shit. The Marines ended up taking only six men from that group, and when the culling was over, Palmer's appetite returned, was robust, he was so goddamned happy to be in the fucking army.

The KPs working the chow line are kept busy by the influx of troops, some cracking jokes but most morose, probably about KP rather than Vietnam, Palmer supposes. Slapping potato salad and peas onto trays, handing out cake or ice cream, there isn't the sort of joking that Palmer always heard in the mess halls of basic and MP school. The one great promise of Vietnam is that GIs will not have to pull any KP. They have Vietnamese workers to do that, according to the Vietnam veterans whom Palmer had known at the Presidio, MPs with a few months left of their enlistments to serve out. The Vietnamese did everything for you, they said, house girls who shined your boots and washed and starched and ironed your fatigues and swept your barracks for a measly ten bucks a month from each resident GI. It had seemed to Palmer that the veterans were trying to make it sound paradisiacal, but who the hell wanted to live in a war zone just to get a cheap shoeshine? Still, the business about no KP has an appeal that Palmer cannot deny. He hates KP more than any job the army makes you do.

"Did any of you guys get stuck on KP yet?" he says apropos of nothing except that which rolls continuously through his mind like a film loop.

No, they all had lucked out, nobody had gotten nabbed for KP this week. Palmer looks at the KPs moving about changing the milk in the machines or policing fallen napkins or checking levels in the salt and pepper shakers, and he wonders if this is the mess hall that is shorthanded, wonders if dodging KP makes him one with Beetle Bailey or if he is just another buddyfucker. But he had learned as far back as the US Customs Building in Denver that when it comes to dereliction of duty, it's every man for himself.

Palmer sips coffee with his meal, has it at breakfast, lunch, and dinner, though he had never drank coffee as a civilian. The sugar containers are beveled glass jars with chrome lids as in civilian cafes, and in pouring sugar into his coffee he remembers a morning in basic when a KP had accidentally put salt into the sugar containers. The entire company had been pouring salt into their dawn coffee. Halfway through chow a Drill Sergeant strode through the mess hall with a coffee cup knuckled in one finger and began roaring at somebody back in the kitchen. A cook came out and told everybody what had happened. Palmer still recalls the fact that the coffee, strangely enough, had not tasted noticeably bad to him that morning. He asks Krouse if he remembers the incident. But no, Krouse doesn't remember. Palmer finishes his meal in silence. Nobody ever remembers anything.

Noon formation is a little less than an hour away when they exit the mess hall. Palmer thinks about asking the men if they want to go to the EM club for a quick beer or two, but then decides against it. There will be time for that after formation, if he doesn't get picked for a shit detail, mopping latrines or carting boxes of crap to dumpsters while a bit high on two or three beers. And there's also the other thing that has begun to creep up on him, now that it's Friday, the thing that takes the edge off his desire to drink: the grapevine says that once you enter Building 629, you are cut off from the rest of the world until you arrive in Bien Hoa. Drinking beer is something you do when you have nothing else to do.

Building 629 is a large place, looks like a factory off in the distance, surrounded by fences topped with barbed wire, almost as if the decor is designed to prepare the men for what they will be seeing for the next year: lots of barbed wire, lots of concertina wire, lots of fences and guard towers. But everyone here knows what the security around Building 629 is really all about: the army doesn't trust the men who hadn't turned their backs on the draft, doesn't trust them to pick up their duffel bags and come along as agreed so many months ago when they had entered basic. Doesn't trust them, as far as Palmer can tell, not to run off to San Francisco at the last moment and become dope-smoking hippie AWOLs. Building 629 reminds him of the Presidio stockade.

"What do you guys want to do now?" Krouse says as everyone stands around lighting up their favorite brands. Palmer again thinks about concocting some excuse, some lie, and abandoning these men, but the fact of Friday afternoon squelches it. Six hours from now he will be in Building 629.

"Want to go play some pinball?" he says.

This is another kind of high. Palmer became addicted to pinball in MP school, had played it as often as possible at the Presidio, and now leads his buddies to one of the snack bars where there is a pinball machine that he has become familiar with, had mastered during the previous four days when he was not seated in the EM club.

But to his disappointment these men are not very interested in pinball. It holds no more fascination for them than it had for Palmer himself before he went to MP school, before Gilchrest had taught him to read a pinball field. The men play it the way most people play miniature golf, laughing at their blunders, taking no pride in their lucky hits, feeling no shame at their ineptitude. But there is nothing else to do at Oakland so Palmer keeps feeding the machine quarters, and hearing an occasional metallic snapping thump from within the guts of the machine signaling a free game, which he lets his buddies play.

The snack bar begins emptying as the hands on a 24-hour clock above the snack counter near thirteen hundred. Time for the noon formation. Palmer wishes now he had checked to see if the EM club had opened its doors yet, rather than playing pinball with these duds who have shown little enthusiasm beyond that of entertained amateurs. He could have had three or four beers by now. He decides that after formation he will ditch these guys, make some excuse, head for the club and spend his last afternoon in America drinking Budweiser.

The group walks away from the pinball machine, emerges onto the asphalt backyard of Oakland where thousands of men in jungle fatigues are making a silent trek from all directions toward the parade ground like desultory ants returning to a nest empty handed. They fall into formation dressed-right and covered-down as enlisted strangers always do, with competence. The sergeants don't have to tell them how to do it. Palmer positions himself in a rank behind Krouse and the others because he has decided that he will simply slip away at the end of the formation without even speaking to them again, barring any shit detail he gets stuck on. The longest detail he has been on yet lasted an hour and a half, the sorting of used fatigues discarded by returning veterans. He doesn't know why the sergeant didn't tell the men to just throw the uniforms away. What good are used fatigues? But then, what good is questioning any decision made by the army?

It's like a clarion bell ringing across the heads of the formation, the single word "Palmer" drawing his attention away from thoughts of beer and a pleasant last afternoon. He realizes that the sergeant in the tower has called his name. His time has come. Not at evening formation but right now. He is on a roster of men scheduled to fly out of Travis Air Force Base at dawn. Just like that. Vietnam.

He steps out of the rank and begins edging toward the right side of the formation, but stops as Krouse and the others turn to him with eyebrows arched, reaching out to shake his hand, hey, maybe we'll see you over there, good luck Palmer, catch you later buddy. Palmer shakes hands with Krouse, with Tigler, Willerton, Brenner. He feels oddly lightheaded, as if he has been told to step onstage to perform a role in a badly-rehearsed play.

He emerges from the side of the formation and begins walking toward the barracks where he has been quartered all week, and the only thing he can think about is the fact that he won't be going to the EM club this afternoon. Once you enter building 629 you are cut off from the rest of the world until you arrive in Bien Hoa. Shit.

The barracks he enters is made of brick, is like a college dorm, all the rooms as large as classrooms, maybe they once were, the floors tiled, with bunks arranged in neat rows. His duffel bag is locked to an upper bunk, the strap looped through the frame. He unlocks the padlock, examines the canvas bag for tampering although he can't imagine a barracks thief in this place. Seems like there would be too much on a thief's mind, like death in a rice paddy, to practice his dirty craft. Palmer gets his shit together and leaves the building for the last time, heads across the asphalt toward a formation where the men going to Building 629 are gathered smoking, joking, grinning, waiting for someone to tell them what to do next.

CHAPTER 4

The interior of Building 629 is cavernous, huge like a place where the Air Force might once have built some secret monstrous bomber, the ceiling so high that voices from the GIs, as well as a PA system, echo like birds continuously gliding among the steel rafters. What did the Oakland Depot used to be anyway? Palmer wonders. Giant abandoned airstrips, giant buildings like this, classrooms turned into dormitory barracks. Did the Air Force used to run this place before the Vietnam War? He will never know. When he enters he sees hundreds of bunk beds arranged in rank and file on a floor of concrete, with hundreds of men hurrying to claim a bunk. There are plenty of bunks, he can see that, extending off to the left and right and out across the concrete in front of him. He feels a kind of disgust rising in him at the sight of men hurrying to grab a bunk. This is only a one-night gig in a spit-shined flophouse.

Men hurry past him as he walks into the island of bunks like Krouse's story of uniforms on racks, a rectangular island made of steel frames and mattresses. But then Palmer remembers—hurrying was what you did to combat the possibility of getting yelled at by Drill Sergeants. He strolls toward the center of the island, passing men tossing their duffel bags onto bunks as if staking claims in a gold rush. He finally angles toward one empty double-bunk but just before he arrives he sees out of the corner of his eye another man making for it. Palmer picks up his step because he wants the top bunk. In prison movies the men always fight for the bottom bunk but Palmer prefers the top, always took it in basic, AIT, the Presidio, he never liked having a body hovering over him in sleep like a roof sagging in a cloudburst.

He shoulders his duffel bag onto the top bunk a mere second or two before the other man arrives. The man stops and says, "You can have the bottom bunk if you want it," as though a dispute has erupted, has run its course, is being settled.

Palmer turns to look at the man that he has beaten in this small and meaningless race, and sees a PFC a head taller than himself, broad-shouldered, standing slightly stooped under the weight of his own duffel bag, a shy smile accompanying his offer. Maybe because he is tall he too prefers top bunks, but it's every man for himself now, and will be for the next year, Palmer has to assume.

"That's okay, you can have it," Palmer says affably, experiencing the excruciation of conversing with a stranger. He would be perfectly happy to spend the next year talking to no one at all. Words have become, finally, pointless in his life. He's always been good with words, excuses, lies, flattery, horseshit, and bullshit, but you can't bullshit a bullet. Everything that happens to him from now on will be real.

The PFC nods, shrugs his own duffel bag off his shoulder and leans it against the edge of the bottom bunk. He eases himself down onto the bare mattress, ducking his head as he sits. He begins fiddling with the padlock on his duffel bag. Seated there hunched over, his shoulders rounded from reaching, he looks like a football player, a large man used to dealing with rooms and furniture just a bit too small for his frame. Palmer now regrets having taken the top bunk. But that's the way you get in the army, always looking out for yourself, nobody is going to bust their ass looking out for your interests. If you want a promotion, you have to figure out who to impress. If you want to avoid a shit detail, you have to figure out when to duck. It's been a long time since Palmer has heard the phrase "Help your buddy" that he heard constantly in basic training when everybody was in the same shit, united by their bewilderment, their ignorance, their wariness of Drill Sergeants.

The PFC reaches into his duffel bag and pulls out a small black book. He leafs through it for a moment, then tucks it into a breast pocket and folds the duffel bag flap closed, hooks the strap around a bunk post and padlocks it shut. He stands up and looks at Palmer with that shy smile again. "Listen," he says, "I want to go make some phone calls. Would you watch my gear for me?"

The man is big but has a boyish face, his brown hair bordering on red with the curled bristly quality of a Brillo pad. His brows are raised as he asks this favor, giving his eyes a slightly exaggerated rounded quality that, for some reason, strikes Palmer as devoid of guile.

"Sure," Palmer says. "I'm not going anywhere."

"Thanks. I want to call my wife," the man says. He walks away, moves toward a long bank of phone booths, dozens it seems, at one end of the big room where men are already converging, making their last phone calls to their families, to the world, before they fly to Bien Hoa. Palmer watches the man stride across the room, his shoulders seeming hunched but actually rounded with muscle, the kind of guy who might have been nicknamed Moose by his high school football friends. A fullback, a reliable player. Wants to call his wife. Jesus. Easy to forget that not all soldiers going to Vietnam are single men untethered by anything resembling responsibility.

Palmer can still remember the news when the Selective Service dropped the marriage deferment. That was during freshman year of high school, or maybe eighth grade. The war has been going on for a long time. He remembers his mother making sympathetic remarks about all the youngsters getting married all over America just one day before the deferment was voided. Walter Cronkite did a story on the evening news. Get in under the wire, get married and stay out of the war. It had seemed comical to Palmer at the time. It hadn't occurred to him that the war would still be going on by the time he was old enough to get married.

He unlocks his own duffel bag and places his cap inside. No use carrying it around. From what he understands he will not be going outside again until tomorrow morning when the troops will get onto buses and ride to Travis. Lockdown. It's like being in a prison in a movie with all the noise, the bodies shuffling about, except there is none of the malevolence that you sense in prison movies. Shank in the ribs. Danger in the showers. Here it's like a multitude of high school kids leery about their futures but bearing up no differently than during the first week of basic. Warm bodies filled with vague hope, willing to give it a try and do their best over there in Vietnam. Unlike in prison though, over there they will get to carry rifles and drink beer.

After a while Palmer starts to regret his promise to watch the PFC's gear. He can no longer see the man over near the phone booths where long lines are beginning to form. Everyone wants to say a last goodbye. Palmer had said his in person in Denver, and there hadn't been all that many people to say goodbye to. His parents, younger sisters and little brother, his older brother Mike whose draft number is 355, a few friends from high school. In basic he had stood in a long line at an outdoor phone just to call home, then found that he didn't have much to say to his parents. It was only the romance of making a phone call from Fort Campbell, like a scene out of a WWII movie. He realized later that he was as forgotten as he himself had forgotten about Phil when his older brother went off to Fort Lewis for basic. In the end it was like going to the store for cigarettes and coming back two months later with a crewcut. Where ya been?

All around him men are getting their shit together for their one night in this place, and it occurs to Palmer that he ought to just grab his own duffel bag and walk to the other end of the island and find a new bunk and get set up. The PFC would never know who the E2 was who broke his promise. But Palmer remains. What if someone does steal the PFC's duffel bag, or tries to rifle it? Palmer is weary of the sour feeling that comes from being a perpetual buddyfucker.

When the PFC finally returns, he has a slightly grieved look on his face that comes as no real surprise to Palmer. The man has just spoken to his wife, will not see her again for a year. He's looking down as he approaches the bunk, holding the small black book in one hand and gently slapping it against his other palm like a man weighing the amount of cash left over from a bad purchase.

Palmer smiles at him, asks if he was able to get through, and the man nods, says thanks for watching my gear. A bit of life has gone out of his voice, and the shy smile is gone.

Palmer straps his duffel bag to his bunk, locks it. Everyone will be sleeping on bare mattresses tonight, no sheets or blankets to mess with. Making a perfect bed every morning for the past year had been a minor chore so annoying that it became funny to Palmer. Like little KP. He hadn't made a bed once after he left home at eighteen and moved into the basement apartment with his two older brothers. Every night he would hoist the wad of a blanket off his mattress and drape it over himself as he crashed.

His gear secured, Palmer looks around the big room. Nobody is lying on bunks, and he wonders if there is some rule about it like in basic, no sacking out in the daytime. Men are moving here and there, back and forth in groups, talking, going nowhere. He looks at the PFC who is fiddling with his duffel bag. When the man stands up, Palmer holds out his hand. "My name's Palmer."

The man looks at him and smiles, says his name is Carlson. They shake hands, and Carlson says thanks again for watching my gear.

"Want to go get something from the pop machines?" Palmer says.

Out at the formation on the tarmac prior to entering the building a sergeant had given the troops a brief orientation, told them what to expect during their stay, explained that there were phone booths, showers, a supply room, operations office, Red Cross, pop machines, everything a soldier needs to fill lockdown time.

Beyond the phone booths, over in one corner, are the machines where men are buying Cokes. "What's your MOS?" Palmer says as they approach a dispenser.

"Engineering," the man says. "What's yours?"

Palmer hesitates a fraction of a moment. This has become SOP for him, has been that way ever since he had graduated from MP school only to learn that everybody hates the MPs. He hadn't know that until afterwards. It was a learned thing.

"I'm a Military Policeman," he says, stifling the urge to explain that he had been drafted into the MPs, had not volunteered, had never in his life imagined that he would end up as anything in the army except an Infantryman. He waits to see if the man is going to ask about his arm. But Carlson seems to have other things on his mind.

They buy their Cokes, pop them open, head back toward their bunks. Palmer notices that a lot of men are sitting silently on bunks, doing a lot of staring at nothing in particular. A lot of men are wandering around the room with vacant looks on their faces, and Palmer cannot but assume that they are thinking the same thing he is thinking continuously in one segregated part of his mind: fatal misfortune. They're all in it now and there is no going back.

"Where are you from?" Palmer says, and Carlson replies Ohio.

There is nothing excruciating about this small talk. The bleak look that seems to reside just under the skin of Carlson's face takes Palmer's mind off his own pointless unease. He's curious about Carlson's phone call. What does a young man say to his wife before going off to war?

"Do you have any kids?" Palmer says when they get back to the bunk. The man smiles and shakes his head no, says that he's been married only six months. "We got married just before I got drafted."

Palmer feels something like a brief whirlwind circumvent his brain, questions, in amazement that any man would get married before entering the army in these times. But not everybody in the world thinks like Palmer. This was a learned thing too.

"How about yourself?" Carlson says, looking at him with his brows raised. "Are you married?"

"No, I'm single," Palmer replies with a slight chortle in his voice as if the question is ludicrous, which to him it is.

Then the man quietly says, "My wife was really upset when I talked to her."

Palmer stands perfectly still. His curiosity about the phone call now seems perverse, now that the conversation has taken this small turn in that direction, now that this stranger has confided in him. Palmer doesn't know what to say, how to respond, whether to nod his head or arch his eyebrows or just run away.

"Was she?" Palmer says quietly, ludicrously, his voice fading as he says it. At least he didn't say, "I'll bet."

Carlson nods two or three times, takes a deep breath and exhales, sits down on his bunk and seems to sag a bit like a football player on a bench waiting out the last seconds of a losing game.

Palmer looks right at him, doesn't flinch. The man wants to talk and who else is there to talk to? Soldiers aren't strangers, they're buddies no matter who or where they are. Help your buddy.

"It must be hard," Palmer says, dredging deeply into himself for something adult to say, reaching further than he has ever reached in his life, down to the silt of reality that has settled around his ankles like sludge because he never stirs it up, has never had any taste for reality, has avoided it all his life. "With you being married and everything," he continues, unsure that he is saying anything, unable to add anything more. He is unused to this.

Carlson looks up at Palmer, smiles briefly, shakes his head no, and says, "She doesn't want me to go to Vietnam." His Adam's apple bobs once. "When I was home on leave she told me she didn't want me to go. But I told her, you know, I said I had to go or they'd put me in jail."

Palmer nods, wants to look away but doesn't do it. He's taken men to jail.

"Then she told me I should go to Canada. But I told her I couldn't do that either. She cried all night."

There is shyness in Carlson's eyes, he's telling this E2, this stranger, a lot of personal things. But Palmer had watched over his gear.

"She told me the same thing on the phone just now," Carlson continues, a kind of hard resignation filtering into his voice. It's anger. Palmer recognizes it. Carlson's wife has made him angry, she won't let go of it. Palmer has made a lot of people angry in his life, so he recognizes the subtle hardness that signals that sadness or despair is changing into something that might get somebody hurt.

The conversation is interrupted by a loud voice coming over the PA, an echoing, almost incomprehensible voice telling someone to report to the operations office. It's repeated, then recedes, the ambient sounds of GIs going about their quiet business reemerging and drifting like smoke over Carlson and Palmer, who takes advantage of this hiatus to redirect the tone of the conversation, to take it back to more familiar ground. He shakes his head slowly as if in response to the things Carlson has been saying, then inhales deeply and says, "Do you suppose there's some place in here where I could buy you a beer?"

Carlson grins, an abbreviated laugh flying from his esophagus like a rounded cough, a laugh he might have perfected in a locker room. "Didn't you hear what the sergeant said when we were outside? There's no alcohol allowed in this place."

Leave it to an athlete to have the coach's rules memorized. Though maybe Carlson isn't an athlete, maybe he's just a big farm boy raised on the Bible, on walking the straight and narrow, on taking care of the business at hand. None of the subtle drawn and haggard signs of drinking mark his face as they do Palmer's when he looks back at himself in a latrine mirror. Carlson's face has the innocence of an eighth grader. And he's married. Fuck the Selective Service.

CHAPTER 5

Steam like a thin dawn fog fills the shower room. Palmer stands with his eyes closed beneath a hissing spray of hot water, inhaling the stink of soap and listening to the slap of wet feet wrought by other men who have risen early on this last morning in America. He had slept poorly all night, had arisen finally at four-thirty and walked across the silent dark cavernous bay in his skivvies, his shaving kit under one arm, a towel draped over a shoulder, and entered the latrine where lone men who could not sleep either were seated on benches undressing or dressing.

He twists the spigots. The pleasant stinging thin jets of water drop from his face to his chest and fall to a dribble. He steps out of the room and towels himself dry, puts on his skivvies, slips his feet into his rubber shower shoes (the trainee from California called them "flip-flops" and everybody laughed) and stands in front of the mirror examining the almost nonexistent whiskers on his young chin. Like a burgeoning goatee. He had never been able to grow decent sideburns as a civilian. Patchy. He squirts a puddle of Gillette Foamy onto his palm and works it across his cheeks and chin, and spends a minute scraping the stubble away.

His face clean, naked, pink, masked by steam, he looks almost like Carlson. Funny how the big guys always got shit on by the drill sergeants in basic. Back in high school the men who might have been nicknamed Moose were the favorites of the various coaches who came and went during those four endless years. If you weighed more than two hundred pounds you could do no wrong. Then in basic the Drill Sergeants were like lean hyenas who screamed at anyone who would have made a good lineman. Fat guys lying on their backs holding rifles above their heads yelling, "I am a dying cockroach!" while the Drill Sergeants hovered over them barking "Lose that goddamn lard or Charlie'll run right up your ass." By the end of basic the skin hung loose on all the men who had come in weighing more than two hundred pounds.

Palmer puts his shaving gear away, zips the kit closed, throws the towel over his shoulder and walks out to the big bay where troops are beginning to rise. Carlson is digging through his duffel bag, pulling out his shaving kit, a towel. He smiles, nods at Palmer, then heads across the floor toward the showers. He hadn't talked any more about his wife yesterday. Throughout the evening they had talked about army things, basic, engineering school, MP school, the things Palmer normally found excruciating but had taken a kind of refuge in. Palmer told Carlson about escaping from KP. Carlson laughed. The memory of that immaculate dodge still buoys Palmer's spirits.

He puts on his jungle fatigues, laces up his jungle boots which feel strange about the ankles because they are soft canvas and not leather. There's supposed to be a small square of steel or hard plastic or something embedded in each sole to protect the bottoms of the feet from punji stakes, but Palmer doesn't really know. You hear all kinds of things. He's mostly concerned about bullets.

During morning chow Palmer is surprised to find that his appetite has not diminished, not like that day in the Customs

Building. He eats his eggs, bacon, toast, drinks his coffee and milk with the same mild sensation of resignation that has preceded all his obligations throughout the past year. He had learned long ago that most of his apprehensions were unjustified, that there was very little you had to do in the army that was truly difficult, dangerous, or even challenging. But that was stateside duty. Men are dying in Vietnam. More than forty-thousand so far. He overheard a conversation this week between two GIs, one of whom was going back to Vietnam for his third tour. "Forty-thousand ain't so bad," the man had said.

When the time comes to leave Building 629 and go out to the buses, Palmer has things on his mind, feels lightheaded as he had when his name was called yesterday, and loses track of Carlson who is somewhere in the crowd of men moving out the doorway and into the muted dawn light, a thin mist covering the sky, fielding the reflective glare of the sun rising over the eastern ridges of Oakland. Waiting in a convoy outside the building, beyond the barbed-wire topped fences, are big blue buses just like the ones that had taken Palmer's group across the Golden Gate Bridge so many months ago for one day of Vietnam training. He hauls his duffel bag through the unlocked gate that has been swung open, hikes out to the asphalt where officers are standing around wearing shades and holding clipboards, seeming nervous and alert at this critical juncture, the loading of soldiers onto buses, as if the brass expects half the men to bolt across the tarmac and dive into the bay. It's an insulting scenario, but then Palmer has learned that few things in life aren't.

Names are called. Men step forward. Palmer looks around at the brick barracks far across the parade ground where he had bunked this week, where Tigler and the others still await their orders. Watery mirages emerge in low places here and there on the vast flat parade ground. A faint mist is in the air. It's cold outside, but no breeze. Palmer looks at everything, like taking photographs of a place he will never want to remember. He has a Kodak Instamatic in his duffel bag, has an 8mm movie camera, but didn't take either of them out this week to add to his record of the places he had been to in the army like the movies he took at the Presidio, MP school, basic. He feels that he ought to have done it, taken a few pictures of the Oakland Depot just for the record, but it hadn't seemed worth the effort. He'll remember this place.

He gets in line at one of the buses, moves forward a step at a time for the slow loading, finally climbs on and works his way down the aisle lugging the duffel bag in front of him, and grabs a seat by a window so he can see things. The window is covered with a metal screen on the outside like a prison bus. He sets the duffel bag upright on the floor nestled tightly between his knees and looks out at the men still shuffling toward their buses, and sees Carlson walking past headed toward a bus down the line, leaning against the weight of his duffel bag slung over a shoulder. Palmer thinks about tapping the window, waving, but doesn't do it. Carlson has a distant look on his face, slightly wide-eyed, going where he is told to go, probably thinking about his wife. He passes from view, and Palmer raises his eyes and looks out at the tarmac where thousands of men will be gathering in formation later today, and tomorrow, and next month, and next year.

The engine starts. Palmer leans his head against the glass and closes his eyes and lets the pleasant vibrations mute his thoughts until the bus is put into gear and the convoy begins moving. He raises his head and looks out the window at the landscape passing by, the brick barracks disappearing, the main gate where the MPs wear white gloves. They are rolling out into the civilian world now, but only long enough for the buses to work their way over to Interstate 80, the highway that leads north past Berkeley, and Richmond, and Vallejo, and Fairfield, to Travis Air Force base where a plane is waiting.

How many buses has he been on in the past year? How many planes? All of them leading toward this one trip which is what it's always been about. He doesn't know why he didn't just volunteer eight months ago to climb onto a plane and fly straight to Vietnam, given everything he's been through. He's no more qualified to be there now than he was then. What was that all about? MP school. What do they need cops for in Vietnam anyway, to give grunts speeding tickets? The Presidio was just marking time. He wishes now he'd gone to Vietnam straight out of MP school. His tour would be more than half over.

The bus skirts the San Francisco bay. They pass Berkeley where all the student radicals live. In high school the nuns had shown a movie about communist infiltration in the United States, footage of a student protest somewhere, and when he got older Palmer realized it had been part of a news-reel about the Free Speech movement at Berkeley. The nuns wanted the kids to know what communists looked like, how they acted, how violent they could be, the seductive nature of their false promises. There is no paradise on earth.

He looks off across the waters of the bay toward the Golden Gate Bridge, a tiny red link in the distance that he has crossed many times. He once walked that fucker. But he can't see the white smear of buildings on top of the hill where Company D is located. Everybody going about their business doing the things he himself did when he was stationed there, men plugged into jobs then unplugged and plugged in somewhere else, like Vietnam, or Germany, or Korea. Gilchrest is in Korea, the only man Palmer has kept in touch with from his training days. Gilchrest writes funny letters about hookers and Hong Kong suits that fall apart in the rain. He's a stockade guard. Beaudry is somewhere in Korea too. Palmer now wonders if his decision not to make any attempt whatsoever to shape or alter his two years in the army has turned out to be a bad decision after all. But he'd always been such a quitter, had never played sports in school, had avoided everything in life so much that when he got drafted he told himself that he would go wherever he was told to go and do whatever he was told to do and not try to weasel out of the war if that's where they told him to go so he wouldn't have to live the rest of his life with the sour feeling that he has lived with for the past twenty-one years. He wants to come out of this clean.

The landscape passes. He looks at everything, the misty dark green hills of Northern California, clusters of stores off the highway, civilians in cars that race past the convoy. When they arrive at Travis Air Force Base the buses roll right out onto an airstrip where a 727 is waiting.

The troops get off the buses and set their duffel bags on the tarmac to be collected and loaded into the belly of the plane. They climb up the mobile staircases, the officers entering first-class near the nose of the plane, the enlisted men entering coach. Palmer is amazed to see stewardesses greeting the GIs. It's a commercial 727. He hadn't really known what to expect, had assumed that the jet would be manned by military personnel. His father went to the Solomon Islands on a troop ship. Sailed beneath the Golden Gate Bridge. It took two months. This will take fifteen hours, according to the word at Oakland. Palmer hates flying so much that the thought of a year in Vietnam doesn't bother him as much as the thought of flying there, and then flying home again. It takes the joy out of the anticipation of his discharge. How can a machine stay in the air for fifteen hours?

The interior of the plane looks strange filling with OD green uniforms, all men, all hatless, all short-haired. The stewardesses are wearing blue uniforms, are smiling, and Palmer wonders what the deal is, do the stewardesses volunteer to make the Vietnam run? Do they get combat pay for stopping off in Bien Hoa? He will never know.

The plane taxis out to the runway, takes off, the part Palmer hates most. Like a rock in a slingshot. Hates it so much that he closes his eyes and tries to relax, waits to get airborne, waits for the odd unnerving thumps from under the belly to cease, waits until the change in air pressure pops his ears, waits until the plane levels off before he opens his eyes and glances out a window at an invisible medium tinted blue buoying these hundreds of tons of steel. Flying is a crock of shit. He can't wait to get to Vietnam.

CHAPTER 6

The plane begins its descent long before the continent appears, Palmer feels it in his gut, the gentle level dropping that makes the airline food seem to lift off a bit, trying to become weightless in his stomach, though maybe it's only butterflies. There had been an hour layover in Anchorage where the sky was absolutely black, no midnight sun, the airport appearing snowed in, but wasn't. He had wandered with all the other men around the terminal, looking at things in a gift shop, then climbed back onto the plane which thrust like a bullet into the blizzard. He didn't think they stood a chance. Then another stopover in Yokota, Japan, where the clerk in the gift shop had bronze skin, almond eyes, but an American skirt and blouse. Palmer had thought about buying a wristwatch since he had accidentally taken a shower wearing his own and ruined it, although it was his brother Phil's watch that he had borrowed because he lost his own after the judo accident. But he decided not to buy one here, too expensive and he's too cheap, though he would have liked to buy something in Japan just as a souvenir. His father's enemy. The father of a friend in Denver brought a bloodstained flag home from Iwo Jima which he had survived, Japanese words hand-printed on the corners by the dead Nippon soldier he had taken it off of. The flag still hangs tacked to a wall inside their garage.

The pilot makes the announcement, the shore of Vietnam coming into view, and because Palmer is seated on the starboard side of the plane, and because they are cruising down the wall of the world along the great polar route that he had studied in grade school, he does not have to leave his seat as do other men eager to see the place they are going to be stationed in for the next year as though seeing it as soon as possible will somehow protect them. It looks like Africa, Palmer thinks, tall jungle trees green and thick as giant bushes growing right to the edge of a thin strip of white sand along the shore, the Africa of movies shot in color. Ought to have carried his 8mm with him on the plane for a view like this that can never be recaptured.

The plane drops lower, the jungle thick for a while, then thinning with roads appearing between what must be rice paddies, what else could they be, rectangled sheets of greenish water reflecting sky and clouds.

Then Palmer sees something that hadn't occurred to him he might see, which is a shell hole in the middle of a barren patch of ground. He's seen enough WWII movies to know what it is, the starburst of earth surrounding a crater. The pilot announces that they will be landing in Bien Hoa in five minutes. Everyone returns to their seats, buckles up, and then something even stranger than a shell hole happens. The plane begins tilting, the pilot making a hard right turn in preparation for landing.

The body of the plane continues to tilt as the plane continues to turn, and Palmer looks down the long length of the wing reaching toward the shell-pocked earth, the entire landscape below looks like the moon, thousands of holes spread across the landscape the way neat furrows decorate farmland in America. And still the plane tilts until it is like an amusement park ride, as if the pilot is working up a barrel roll, hundreds of tons rotating in the atmosphere, the wing so low now, and seemingly vertical, that Palmer wonders if the tip is going to start dragging furrows into that mottled earth. Then the plane levels off and makes a quick landing at the airfield. The pilots must love this maneuver, Palmer thinks. Hamstrung by FAA regulations back home, they get to play ace in the war zone. But he just wants off this god-damn death bucket.

The plane taxis along the runway past concrete hangars shaped like Quonset huts, the green noses of F-4 Phantom jets poking from the darkness that is sliced by the stark sunlight now of Vietnam and not America. Air Force men in fatigue pants and boots but no shirts, their skin bronze, their eyes behind sunglasses, guide a squat rolling F-4 with semaphore, the streamlined wings hugged so tightly to the body that it appears to Palmer impossible that such a machine could stay airborne, except with the speed of a bullet.

His plane finally stops rolling and there is a civilian moment when the men are rising and looking around for their things, the door opening to a mobile staircase hurriedly rolled across the runway by busy Air Force men, the stewardesses at the exit saying goodbye sweetly, as if the GIs were stopping over in a resort. Palmer shuffles up the aisle slowly in line and looks right at a stewardess, perhaps twenty-five, svelte, bright-eyed, white-toothed, she smiles as she must have smiled at thousands of men and says, "Good luck" to him and then to the man behind him.

He steps out from the doorway of the plane and only now realizes how chilled the interior of the plane is by the curtain of heat that he steps into, thick, almost gelatinous in its shocking muggy presence, and containing a stink so strange that he cannot place it except that it reminds him vaguely of the rot odor of a city dump, though not quite as sickly sweet, almost metallic, it latches onto the back of his tongue as he descends to the bottom of the ramp and steps onto Vietnam.

Lots of people milling around the apron of concrete in all this ungodly heat and sunlight and stink, Air Force men but also people in civilian clothes. The men from the plane walk in an unmilitary line toward the terminal which is a big but simple wooden building, its doors open like the two doors to a furnace from which all this hot air might be rolling. Officers in shades with clipboards at their sides tell the men to go on inside and be ready to pick up their duffel bags when they're offloaded from the plane.

The fast landing, the forward motion of the line toward the terminal, the unstoppable momentum, reminds Palmer of the first day of the first real job he ever had, delivering furniture for an upholstery shop, only three years ago but fifteen thousand miles away, entering the shop that first morning with the sickly feeling that he was going to hate this worse than high school, and he was right. The interior of the terminal is shaded but no less hot, and Palmer wonders how anyone could fight a war for two seconds in this heat, not counting the natives, one of whom he sees for the first time, a woman sweeping the terminal amid the crowds of GIs wandering back and forth across the wide, boot-polished concrete floor.

Stooped, holding a foreshortened broom in one hand, the bundled bristles long like a witch's broom, she's slapping at the floor, left and right, seeming to sweep nothing at all. Palmer stares at her, a Vietnamese national, almost half a lifetime of TV and Walter Cronkite and here she is in person. She seems almost pretending to be of another culture in her black silk pants and white blouse and conical woven hat like a drum cymbal. Palmer has the urge to go up and talk to her as if asking for a familiar movie star's autograph. But even as he stares he knows what a rube he is—what rubes the soldiers of World War I must have been staring at mademoiselles, the rubes of his father's war staring at frauleins or geishas, reality revealing itself to be simply odd.

Palmer looks away, gazes around the terminal which is the least modern airport terminal he has ever been inside, everything made of wood, no chrome, no conveyor belts, primitive in its simple hollow structure and monochromatic gray. The duffel bags are hauled inside on dollies by Air Force EM and laid out on a long table, a fake conveyor belt, and the GIs from the plane search for their stenciled names, find them, and start looking around for the door that will lead them out to the buses that will haul them to the 90th Replacement Center in Long Binh, the Oakland of Vietnam.

Everyone is already sweating, their new green fatigues going black at the armpits and backs. They shuffle up onto the waiting buses which also have screened windows, the troops carrying their duffel bags in front of them and sitting down to look out the windows and wonder about the screens which are there to keep things out and not in. Doubtless hand grenades.

The road leading from Bien Hoa to Long Binh is asphalt and looks out of place, the only civilized artifact in this strange flat land, farmers far away in rice paddies, water buffalo, sparse trees, brown pocked earth, the two-lane

highway weaving across the countryside like a black sidewalk. But then Hondas appear zipping past, two to a bike,
sometimes men in black pajamas. They always said in basic
that you never knew who the enemy was. Someone would
tell you. In MP school they said the VC surreptitiously
dropped hand grenades down the gas-tank pipes of MP
jeeps, the handles held by rubber bands that dissolved in the
gasoline.

The main gate at Long Binh is surrounded by sandbags,
which Palmer had seen in training but which he now stares
at as he had stared at the woman in the airport terminal.
Reality sandbags. He senses he will always be a rube in this
country.

The compound at Long Binh is rocky earth, a bit hilly with
two-story green barracks, asphalt roads traveled by deuce-
and-a-halfs and jeeps. Vietnamese women wander to and
from the barracks on wooden sidewalks. The sky is overcast
here, hot, the air thick, and Palmer wonders how infantrymen
could last even one day fighting farther south in the Mekong
Delta. The men get off the buses and are led into a one-story
building where their orders will be processed.

When Palmer's turn comes he sits on a chair by a desk
where a clerk wearing fatigues faded to a pale pastel green
examines his orders and types new paperwork. On his desk
stands a small rectangled cardboard sign hand printed in red
Magic Marker that says, "9 days." Palmer asks him what that
means and the man says that he has nine days left in-country.
He has been here as long as Palmer has been in the army
which has seemed an eternity. This brings the weight of
Palmer's obligation bearing down on him harder even than the

fact of just being in Vietnam. Three hundred and sixty-five days.

The men are sent to a finance window where they are told to hand over their greenbacks and small change; American currency is illegal in Vietnam. They are given equivalent amounts in Military Payment Certificates, little bills that look like Monopoly money, the smallest ten cents. No nickels in Vietnam. The MPC has colorful pictures of jets or submarines, pink and blue and orange like pictures from a child's encyclopedia.

Afterwards the men line up outside in formation and are told where they can store their duffel bags, told that they must show up at evening formation at seventeen hundred hours, there are three mandatory formations a day, as at Oakland. The barracks off in that direction are transient, just go in and find yourself an empty bunk tonight. There's movies here in the evening. Red Cross is over there, the operations office. Palmer only half listens because nothing the man is saying will alter the fact that he is going to be here for three hundred and sixty-five days. Words have become meaningless, until the sergeant says "enlisted men's club" which gets Palmer's attention. He listens up but the sergeant is talking about other things now. Palmer failed to listen up as he has failed so many times in the army, and now he doesn't know where the beer is.

The troops are finally released, the men dispersing, talking, walking nowhere in the heat. They will all be here for three hundred and sixty-five days. Burdened by his duffel bag that he wants to get rid of as quickly as possible, Palmer looks around the compound wondering where the enlisted men's club might be. This is a vast place, a far rise in one direction with white buildings along a ridge, a bustling place with a strange smell different than out at the airfield. But he can see nothing that looks like an EM club, all the buildings looking the same, green and surrounded by low wooden bunker walls, or else fifty-five gallon oil drums topped with sandbags.

The storage depot is a barracks filled with shelves like a furniture warehouse, the men manning it apparently new men on shit detail wearing dark green fatigues, handing out tags like hat-check clerks in exchange for duffel bags. Palmer takes his tag and stuffs it into his pocket, steps outside the building relieved to get shut of the burden of that thing which he has been hauling around since Denver. He feels free. A copy of his orders tucked in his breast pocket, a billfold with seventy dollars in it, all he needs now is directions to the enlisted men's club.

CHAPTER 7

Palmer wanders back toward the building where the formation was held, continues along the rocky ground looking at the barracks on small rises in the distance, transient barracks where he will sleep tonight. He decides to look around this place a bit, steps to the edge of a road and has to wait for a deuce-and-a-half rumbling empty and bouncing along the asphalt with hollow, rattling chain sounds. He crosses over and steps onto a wooden sidewalk, another primitive thing, like something out of the old west, thinking of the airport terminal now like a train station in a cowboy movie. Everything cheap and cheesy, but not so unlike basic training where he'd lived in a white wooden barracks like the green ones here. The army itself is an old-fashioned thing.

A Vietnamese woman comes toward him in her silk and cymbal, walking with a slightly bowlegged waddle. Palmer glances at her curiously but looks above her head as she gets closer the way he wouldn't look too closely at a midget on the streets of America. There's something unreal, almost cartoonish, about people dressed this way, like they're faking it, that round hat and sandals, they must have dressed like this a hundred years ago, a thousand. She walks on by and Palmer comes to an intersection where a group of GIs wearing dark green fatigues like his own are standing around gazing at everything like the tourists they are. They remind him of Krouse and the others. And Carlson. He hasn't seen Carlson since Oakland, didn't see him on the plane when shuffling back toward the toilets every three hours, and knows that he will never see Carlson again. Engineer. Someday an MP will hassle him about something and he will forget he once confided in this E2, will hate MPs forever.

Palmer asks the men if they know where the enlisted men's club is, and they point off toward a building farther along the road and down a slight hill. Nothing is level here, though the landscape seems flat to the eye because it is so vast. He can see one edge of the perimeter of the 90th across a field demarcated by a fence with barbed-wire strung across the top, with coils of concertina wire like massive dangerous Slinkys stretched along the base on both sides and stacked three deep, vicious razor-blade teeth attached to the wires to keep the sappers out. The veterans at the Presidio said sappers got through all the time. Pop and beer cans dangle from the concertina wire like Christmas ornaments. Cheap and cheesy burglar alarms. Beyond the perimeter fence are shell holes.

The enlisted men's club is a one-story building, fairly long and wide, but then there's a lot of enlisted men at the 90th. Palmer walks around to the front entrance and sees a sign posted above the doorway, slightly psychedelic hand-printed words wrought with orange Day-Glo paint on a black wooden board: "Alice's Restaurant." He opens the door and steps inside, and a sergeant seated on a wooden stool near the door barks, "Uncover!" with a disdain that Palmer has become familiar with throughout the past year. Palmer removes his cap and curls the brim, shoves the thing into a back pocket and walks farther into the club.

The odor of cigarette smoke fills his nostrils, suppresses the sour tangy odor of the 90th that he is already starting not to notice. It's a big room, a long bar stretching to the far end on his right, on his left a wide floor filled with tables. Not too crowded at this time of day. He hears the muted ping of pinball machines, so rather than heading straight to the bar he follows the sound to a small room farther off to his left where men are standing braced in front of pinball machines. A game room. And there are slot machines here.

He has never seen a slot machine before, did not even know they were legal anywhere except in Nevada. He wanders toward a GI pulling a lever, stands and watches the cherries and lemons spinning, the final tally clicking into place. Coins spill from a metal mouth at the base of the machine. Slot machines. There are four set against the wall. A tingle of excitement passes briefly through Palmer. A new game, and one that pays off in cash rather than ego satisfaction. He looks around the unpainted wooden-walled room where men are playing foosball, pinball, and there's a booth like a teller's cage set into a wall where a Vietnamese woman in a pretty purple dress sits waiting to change MPC into coin. Palmer walks out of the room with a small grin that he cannot quite control. Pinball, beer, and slot machines, and in his youth he once thought men climbed off airplanes and dove into foxholes for their year in Vietnam.

He goes up to the bar and orders a tall can of Budweiser, waits while the bartender, a sergeant, dips an arm into a pop cooler and withdraws the familiar white and red can that takes Palmer home again. Then surprisingly the sergeant punches holes into the top with a church-key. No snap-tops in Vietnam. Maybe the army had learned that snap-tops burst during shipment overseas the way they had learned that

M-16s jammed with frequency at the beginning of the war. Palmer places ten cents in funny money on the bar, takes the sweating cold can in his fist and carries it to an empty table, sits down feeling right at home.

Before he takes a swig, he pulls out his pack of Camels, lights up, inhales deeply and exhales. Then lifts the can to his lips and sucks in a mouthful and is appalled because the beer tastes awful, almost rotten to his learned palate. Christ. This is not Budweiser, except it is, so he has to presume that shipment overseas, crates sitting on seaport docks or in airport warehouses in all this heat, has altered the chemical nature of the beer. He's no longer home, he's back in Vietnam where everything is revealing itself to be cartoonish.

By the time he has drunk half the can the beer is already warm, which serves only to intensify the wretched flavor. At least it has alcohol in it. When he returns to the bar he orders a twelve ounce can, calculating, in the way that he has always calculated his moves when it comes to satisfying his desires, that a twelve ounce can will be empty before it will be warm.

Within fifteen minutes he has drunk off two beers and is sitting down with his third, lighting his fifth cigarette and waiting for the furry feeling to begin sprouting in his brain the way dreams come when you're still awake enough to know you're falling asleep. Inebriation. It begins to pull him toward home again. The first time he ever got drunk he was at the house of a friend who owned a set of drums, sat drinking a tall Bud and watching while his friend accompanied a Beatles album pumping the bass with a frantic right foot and rattling off funny little solos on the sock-cymbal. By the time he had finished his second tall Bud he was plastered and went outside and vomited in his friend's backyard.

He rises and drifts toward the game room. He is a bit high and wants to try one of the slot machines. He steps up to the cashier's cage and buys a dollar's worth of slugs, like brass nickels, carries them to an empty machine and stands in front of it looking at the lemons, blueberries, cherries, having no idea how to read a slot payoff but knowing it doesn't matter. Just put the slug in and pull the handle and see what happens, like people who don't read the rules of board games.

He's pleased when a smattering of coins is pumped out of the guts of the machine with an oily slithering ring. Two clustered cherries and a black bar with the white word JACKPOT stenciled across it. He feeds his winnings back in, pulls the handle again, but there is no payoff. He goes again, standing in front of the slot winning and losing and sipping at his Bud with the knowledge that the seventeen hundred formation is looming and it would probably be best if he doesn't have a fourth beer. Men are picked for shit details after formation, as at Oakland.

At a quarter to five Palmer is on his third set of coins. The enchantment of slot machines is already beginning to fade. The math is vague to him, and he was never good at math anyway, but he can see that over the long run the machine is taking a little bit more than it is giving back. The intrigue of competition, of the control you have over a chrome ball on a pinball field, has been usurped by the simple electric thrill of pure luck. There is a small metal plate attached to the front of the machine with fruit symbols on it and which Palmer at first took to be nothing more than a decoration but which, when he looked a little closer, turned out to be a chart explaining the payoffs. The jackpot on this slot is eighteen dollars. Men are leaving the club. It's getting close to formation. Palmer continues to feed the machine, deciding to rid himself of the burden of slugs in the thin fabric of his rip-stop fatigue pockets. And then one, two, three jackpot bars line up in a dressed-right row. This is followed by a silence which not only surprises him but engulfs his heart with a frustration that he has known all his life. Nothing comes out of the metal mouth.

He looks the machine up and down, squints at the payoff plate, reaches up and gently shakes the lever, but nothing happens. "Shit." He takes hold of the machine and tries to shake it but it's a heavy cheating bastard. The club is emptying. Palmer stands there gazing at the three bars, feeling a bit of life go out of him. It's like every used-car he ever owned. Working fine until now, like every piece of mechanical junk that's ever fucked him over.

He pulls the last three coins out of his pocket and puts one in the slot, yanks the lever to see if the machine really is broken, and the sorry bastard spits out five slugs. He scoops them up saying to hell with it and turns to leave, glancing toward the woman in the teller cage. Then he notices a sign on the wall at the side of the cage which says "All jackpots will be paid off by the cashier." Livid, Palmer walks out of the room feeling blood gathering in his forehead and cheeks. A lesson learned: know your game rooms.

A few men are still seated at tables, finishing their cans of Bud or Schlitz or Carling Black Label. Palmer goes up to the bar and asks the sergeant where the latrine is.

Leaning to stack fresh cans into the pop cooler, the man stands erect and looks at Palmer with his chin raised a bit as if to deflect a question he has been asked too many times. "The piss tube is around back," he says.

Army jargon, Palmer thinks with disgust as he heads past the stool that is empty now where the other sergeant had barked at him. He steps outside wondering if the EM club actually closes when it's time for a formation. He goes around to the back of the club and encounters a group of men in dark green fatigues standing near a small wooden structure, three sided, the plywood walls shoulder high. The ground is damp, trammeled, one man backing away from the walls so that Palmer sees a metal tube jammed into the ground at a forty-five degree angle. Another man steps up to the tube working at his zipper, takes his stance shielded by the wood. Piss tube.

When his turn comes Palmer steps into the shelter of this odd outhouse and unzips, aims at the mouth of the hole, and stands gazing out across the landscape of the 90th Replacement Center. GIs moving toward the area where formations are held. Vietnamese women walking here and there. No American women that he can see. Buzzed on beer and pissing, gazing at the world with a new perspective, Palmer finally zips up and steps away from the walls. Other men have queued up behind him. He joins the drift of GIs making their way toward the seventeen hundred formation.

CHAPTER 8

It's similar to Oakland, a small parade ground, earthen and not asphalt, with a short wooden tower where a sergeant stands ready to begin calling the names of men who are going to be leaving the 90th and heading for their permanent duty stations. Palmer takes a place at the back of the formation, knowing that he will not be leaving for a few days. Five, he heard at Oakland, but who knows? It doesn't matter. There is no suspense. He is in Vietnam now, will be here for three hundred and sixty-five days and in fact would like to hear his name called, to get it over with, to put some momentum into time.

The calling of names takes half an hour, and when it's over the sergeant tells the troops to close up the ranks. It's shit detail time. A bit of suspense returns because Palmer is itching to get back to the EM club. He wants to redeem his blunder at the slot machine. Surprising that he hit a jackpot, but then maybe the machines are rigged to pay off more frequently than slots in Nevada. Give the enlisted men a break. Alice's Restaurant. Who are they trying to kid? But mostly he wants to get back to the beer, his high seemingly sapped from his brain, drawn from his ear canals by all this muggy heat.

"Last ten men in this file," the sergeant says, his face shaded by the roof of the tower, his arm extended into sunlight, his finger pointing at the line where Palmer is standing. Jackpot. A sergeant steps up to the men and tells them to follow him. There are sergeants standing all around the formation, as at Oakland.

Palmer embraces his resignation, something he has gotten good at though never used to since being in the army. Something beginning in childhood, like doing homework that holds no interest when there's a TV waiting. He follows along at the end of the line, disgusted but a bit curious about the type of shit details they make you pull in Vietnam.

The sergeant looks to be in his mid-thirties, a lifer with possibly five years left of his enlistment, who leads them around behind a wooden box of a building, a latrine, then turns and gives them a smile which holds no disdain. There's a youngish look to his face. Maybe he doesn't drink.

"All right, men, this isn't hard work but it's gonna take about an hour. You don't have to hurry it. You're gonna be in this country for a whole year, so you don't have to hurry anything." He steps up to the back wall of the latrine, bends down and lifts a small door hinged at the top, raises it so the detail can see a tin washtub resting beneath the hole of a latrine seat. The tub is half filled with turds and toilet paper. "You're gonna burn this shit. That's how we get rid of it. We got pikes and diesel fuel for you."

Long wooden poles with slightly hooked metal ends are leaning against the back wall of the latrine. On the ground is a gallon tin can which the sergeant picks up. He tells two of the men to drag the tub out into the open. Palmer watches with resigned distaste, remembering the drill sergeants of basic snarling at the trainees to get in there with those scrub brushes and really attack those urinals. Conquer and shine. Basic training had dwindled to eating, running, shitting, and sleeping.

The sergeant unscrews the cap, pours diesel fuel into the tub, sprinkling it around the white and brown mess volcanic in shape. "It takes a while for diesel fuel to catch," he says. He caps the can, sets it on the ground, then asks who has a lighter. Palmer, it seems, is the only smoker in the squad. He pulls out his Zippo and holds it out to the sergeant, who grins and says you know what to do.

Palmer squats beside the tub and holds the flame against a loose stream of toilet paper which catches quickly, but burns out when it reaches the diesel fuel. He does it again, setting fires here and there, then standing back and waiting. It takes a while for the fuel to catch, and when it does it burns with low flames.

The rest of the men go about dragging tubs from under the latrine, there are six, though one is left for last in case any wandering GI needs it. The men stand around in the failing sunlight with their pikes stirring the tubs, sprinkling diesel fuel, grinning foolishly and making wisecracks. The massive bedpans begin to give off an odor that Palmer finally recognizes, the odor that has hovered over the 90th unlike the overwhelming stink out at the airport. Flaming diesel fuel and shit. A gritty odor. It, too, latches onto the back of his tongue.

After the contents of the six tubs have turned to ash, the job inspected and approved by the sergeant, after the tubs have been replaced and the doors closed down, the detail is released from duty. Palmer hurries back to the enlisted men's club. Dusk has come. But because he had been collared for a detail, the club is packed when he enters, his cap already removed because he could spend his entire tour annoying sergeants—not much of a skill but more a petty act of powerlessness that he has learned to use with discretion.

It takes almost ten minutes to get up to the bar. One of the few nice things about the army, the pushing and shoving of impatient civilians is bred out of soldiers, replaced with a respect for the rights of the man ahead of you, a form of military courtesy that Palmer would just as soon breach by cutting in line, which not only is impossible but risky. He orders two tall Buds, abandoning his calculations about lingering chill in favor of instant gratification. It will take too long to get back up to the bar.

He carries his open Buds to the game room but all the slot machines are occupied. The pinball machines too, and he has never played foosball. He's heard that helicopter pilots are good at foosball. He peers over the shoulders of men gathered around a pinball game, watches the chrome ball batted across the wooden rise dotted with bumpers that flash on revealing their worth in pale silhouette. The urge to place a quarter on the edge of the machine simmers inside him, but he would rather learn the nuances of the playing field before he performs in front of an audience. He moves on to the other pinball machines and looks them over, then stands watching the men playing the slots. Everybody is hooked. Nobody is leaving. Palmer drops his first empty into a trash can, starts on his second, and finally goes to the door of the game room and looks out across the heads of the men seated at the tables. He knows no one here.

The stink of diesel oil and shit has been erased from his nostrils, from the back of his tongue. He is hungry now. He hasn't eaten since the meal on the plane, all of which he ate. Vietnam hasn't affected him as did the Marines. He didn't shit for three days when he first entered basic, though he tried. It was something the other trainees admitted, joked about, even announced when victorious, the crude bastards.

Palmer finishes off the beer and decides to leave the enlisted men's club and look for a snack bar. They sell hamburgers at the EM club, but it would take too long to get up to the bar, and anyway he is beginning to feel leery standing inside this building. Don't the Viet Cong always attack at night? Maybe if he knew someone to drink with he would stay. He steps outside. The air seems thicker in this darkness. Hotter. His uniform is already sticking to his back and thighs. He wanders across the compound, then stops when he hears a rumble in the distance. Silence. He moves on, veering toward a small building where GIs are crowded around drinking pop from paper cups.

He sees a notice on a bulletin board that says a movie will be shown this evening in Building 1124. He goes into the snack bar where the line is short, where the men who don't drink booze are standing at tall tables that have no chairs, picking through bags of potato chips or French fries. It's like a snack bar at a drive-in movie theater. A railing to guide the customers past the awful but edible food. Ice cream in foggy freezers. Potato chip bags clipped to metal racks. Palmer buys a soft drink and two oven-warmed hamburgers wrapped in tinfoil, prepackaged with an American logo stamped on one side. Somebody is making money off this war, Coca-Cola and Anheuser-Busch leading the pack, he would think.

He asks strangers if they know where Building 1124 is, and they point off into the darkness toward a barracks. Palmer crosses the barren ground listening for rumbles in the distance, chewing on a hamburger. Flavorless, but at least he has something in his gut. He tosses the second burger into a trash barrel and enters Building 1124, follows a group of men up the stairs to the second floor which is empty, no bunks, no folding chairs, just a man fiddling with a movie projector set on a table. A sheet is nailed to a wall. Porno perhaps? But the cadre wouldn't post that on a bulletin board.

It turns out to be a movie about a million-dollar heist. Palmer sits on the floor in the swelter of bodies and daytime air trapped by the tin roof, until he feels he cannot breathe. Gold bullion is being transferred from a Brinks truck to a getaway car when he rises and makes his way politely through the cluster of bored bodies gazing at the flickering sheet.

It is not yet eight o'clock, but he is tired. He had slept on the plane an hour here and an hour there, but does not know how many hours he has slept since awakening in Oakland today, or yesterday, whenever it was, he has no grasp of the International Dateline. What time is it in Denver? He wants to go back to the EM club, but because the residue of the few beers that he has already drunk has left him weary he decides to make the trek to the top of one of the rises where the transient barracks are located, and find a bunk. End this day. Subtract one digit from the tally of his tour, three hundred and sixty-four.

He walks slowly along a wooden sidewalk that follows the rise of a sandy hill. He hears in the distance a soft popping sound which is probably an automatic rifle but he doesn't recognize it, cannot fit the sound to any weapon he had heard in basic or MP school. It ceases. Maybe that rumbling had been thunder. It's so muggy here it seems like it should always be raining.

He enters a barracks where a single lightbulb dangles at the far end giving off just enough light for the transients to make their way through the room without stumbling, to find an empty bunk, as Palmer does. Only bare mattresses, as at Oakland, and when Palmer climbs onto a top bunk and lies down fully-clothed but for his cap resting at his side, he discovers sand on the mattress. Everything cheap and cheesy, as if the army, the world, life itself has stopped pretending, has given up and is revealing everything to be rather mediocre, functional at best. But the army has always been that way. Palmer rolls onto his left side, closes his eyes and tries to calculate what time it must be in Denver. He has no wristwatch. Should have bought one in Yokota. What's he saving his money for anyway? He knows he's going to die in this country.

CHAPTER 9

At dawn a man comes through the barracks telling the troops to get up but there is no shouting as in basic, no hammering of garbage-can lids. Palmer doesn't even know if the man is a sergeant, he's already passed through and out the door, possibly a Spec Four, a clerk whose job it is to wake the newbies in this place where no one is in a hurry. Like Mexico, everything mañana according to the books and movies. Maybe the hurrying is saved for firefights.

He is glad not to have a hangover. If he hadn't been so suddenly tired last night he would have stayed at the enlisted men's club until it closed at ten. Apparently everything closes early in the war, but then the 3.2 bars in Denver close at midnight. He had drunk in real bars when he was home on leave. Two A.M. Went to one strip joint.

He eats in the 90th mess hall this morning, seated at a table with an audience of strangers chewing bacon and scooping scrambled eggs. The chow is no better or worse than stateside chow, but Palmer's attention is on the KPs, young Vietnamese women in colorful clothing, not the black pants and white blouses of the women he already has seen. And they are all cute in the face. He wonders if the mess sergeants in charge of hiring female KPs make this a qualification. Probably. Lifer sergeants overseeing fiefdoms. The memory of his dodge at Oakland returns, though the good feeling has never left him, hovers at the back of his mind always like something valuable that the army can never take away from him. It feels good to be in a place where there is no KP.

After morning formation he is again picked to burn shit, this time at a larger latrine, a twelve-holer. It doesn't seem to take much longer than the other detail, the men silent at their dawn labor, Palmer smoking a cigarette to mute the stink. When the men are released from duty Palmer decides not to go to the enlisted men's club but rather walk around the 90th, to look the place over. There is little else to do here, just wait for the daily formations and hope that he hears his name called soon. He approaches a perimeter fence and peers through the tin-can strung razor wire, looks out over the torn landscape wondering how long ago those shell holes appeared, whether they were all made by the Viet Cong, or if there are American hits out there, aftermath of duels.

He wanders the perimeter. There is nothing to see here, it's all the same, flat land beyond the fence, a few trees. He passes a truck with POTABLE WATER printed in white on the side. Like Mexico they say, don't drink the water. The pure drinking water comes in big rubber bags. He saw water coolers in the office when he was processed in, the same big inverted glass jugs where Dagwood kills time. No paper-cup dispenser, the clerks shared tan-colored mess hall cups on a tray. Half an hour later Palmer is back in the enlisted men's club, this time playing a pinball machine but drinking a Coke. Prior to getting drafted he rarely drank alcohol before noon, though not from a pretense at discipline, a false ritual, he just couldn't stand the taste of booze on awakening.

At noon formation he waits impatiently, hopefully, to hear his name called, then stands with a practiced resignation as the troops tighten up the ranks and the shit details are doled out. When it's over and he has not been picked, he stands for a moment on the parade ground as the men disperse, wondering whether to go retrieve his duffel bag and dig out his 8mm to collect a few scenes of the 90th as he had failed to do at Oakland. Then he hears a familiar voice say, "Palmer?" and he turns and sees Krouse approaching, his head cocked querulously, his slightly-crooked teeth clenched in a wide-lipped grin.

"Krouse," Palmer says softly, as if in warning to himself. There's something about seeing people whom he never thought he'd see again that makes him feel cautious, something tinged with guilt. "When did you get here?"

"This morning," Krouse says, holding out his hand as if it has been a year and not two days, three, whatever, since last they saw each other. But that was in another country, across a baffling dateline. "We're all here, Brenner and Tigler and Willerton. We got called the morning after they called you."

Palmer grins, begins chuckling softly as if he has just gotten the punchline of a vague joke, but it's only life's endless ribbing. He's not unhappy at all to see Krouse, looks forward to seeing the others. This is a lonely place.

Krouse tells him that the others had gotten picked for a shit detail. "I said I'd meet them at the enlisted men's club later. Do you want to go there now?"

They walk side by side, Krouse with his head slightly bowed as he fills Palmer in on things that ought to be excruciating, his last night in Oakland, a shit detail he couldn't dodge, his plane trip over here. Palmer listens as if hearing a letter from home read aloud, the minutiae of things he's familiar with. Krouse's booted feet slap the barren ground ahead of him, his sweat stained, untucked jungle fatigues making him look more slouched and slightly slovenly. Imagine what wrangles must have taken place in the Pentagon when these uniforms were being designed. Infuriated Generals, hard-liners, veterans of the brown-boot army disgusted by shirts like skirts, while concerned underlings who'd actually been to Southeast Asia tried to explain the heat.

Palmer and Krouse pass between two buildings and come out on an expanse of barren earth not far from the EM club piss tube, the landscape strangely crowded with men. Palmer hears shouting, and sees that the crowd is arranged in a kind of broken circle, the men watching something. It's like coming onto the scene of a traffic accident, an event dropped out of the sky into your eventless life, so that you stop, alert and cautious, to make sense of what you're seeing.

A tall black GI is yelling at someone, walking slowly backwards with his fists clenched. Might be a fight. Palmer and Krouse move in a little closer, but then an MP jeep rolls around the corner of the club and stops, and two MPs with shiny black helmets, nightsticks, pistols on their hips, get out and stride toward the man, who turns to them with his fists still clenched.

A black sergeant wearing no cap, a strange sight, emerges from the crowd, a lifer it would appear, his fatigues faded from the Vietnam sunlight. He approaches the yelling GI whose words are garbled. The sergeant tries to calm the man, tries to put a hand on his shoulder, says things to him, but the GI twists away. Another MP jeep rolls in, and another, three 90th Replacement MP jeeps converging on this scene, the tall GI yelling, "Naw, man, naw!" Drunk maybe, but looking mostly angry. Other black GIs have joined the sergeant, they are all trying to calm the man. One of the MPs, a short man, a sergeant, goes up to the group to find out what's going on. The other MPs encircle the angry man, cut him off from his buddies, from the crowd. "I'll talk to him, I'll talk to him," the hatless sergeant says as the MPs pull the man's hands behind his back. Palmer now hears the GI clearly, "Not the handcuffs, naw man, don't put no handcuffs on me!"

The crowd has grown larger, everyone wearing dark green fatigues, everyone silent like rubberneckers at a traffic accident, observing the MPs as they try to control the situation. The tall GI doesn't fight back, but keeps twisting away from the MPs saying, "Naw man, not the handcuffs," while the black sergeant pleads with the MP in charge, "Let me talk to him, I'll calm him down, you don't have to put the cuffs on him."

But the MP Sergeant isn't having any of it. He ignores the black sergeant. He steps up to the GI who is weeping as he twists away, grabs him, swings him around and shoves him against the fender of a jeep. The other MPs grab him, force his head down against the hood as the sergeant cuffs him. The six of them walk him around the jeep, put him in the backseat. Three MPs get in, two guarding him, the driver putting the jeep into gear and guiding the jeep across the yard and out onto a street. The other MPs drive off.

It's over just like that, but now the hatless sergeant, the black lifer, stands alone in the circle with his fists clenched, enraged at what has just happened. Palmer senses that it was the putting the cuffs on the man, the sergeant's request ignored by the MPs, that has set him off. He begins shouting at the crowd, telling everyone to move out, go on goddamnit, get the hell outta here!

The men drift away. Palmer and Krouse make a circle around the lone sergeant whose fists are shaking he is so angry, and head toward the entrance to the EM club. Krouse glances up at Palmer from his slouch, his glasses glinting quickly in the noon sunlight, and says, "That was weird, wasn't it?" which makes him sound like a kid again. But it's something that Palmer himself is thinking. He'd never seen anything like that vicious bit of rousting at the Presidio. The Presidio had been cruising around in cheesy six-bangers and writing parking tickets. MP duty in Vietnam portends to be real. A war zone where lawbreakers will likely be infantrymen as anybody else, men who've had to kill, to whom the law might be viewed as excess baggage they leave in their wall lockers when they go out on patrol. "Did you know any of those MPs?" Krouse says as they reach the door beneath the Day-Glo sign.

The question seems stupid to Palmer, who glances at Krouse with a smile of ridicule beginning to lift one corner of his lips, but then he realizes that it is not such a stupid question. The army is a small world. He hadn't looked closely at the MPs to see if he knew any of them. "No," he says, yanking the door open. He might have known one or two of them from MP school, from the Presidio, might have recognized a face as surprising as Krouse's own at Oakland.

"Uncover!" the sergeant barks as Palmer and Krouse walk inside.

Palmer removes his hat, irritated at this bit of forgetfulness. Things on his mind, Krouse's questions. He hates it when somebody else causes him to break a rule.

The air is almost unnoticeably cooler inside the club. Palmer and Krouse order sixteen ounce beers and select a table that they will save for their buddies. Krouse tells him that he and Tigler and the others had been in here earlier this morning, and Palmer asks if they had played the slot machines.

"No," Krouse says. "I don't have the money to play slot machines. I didn't bring very much with me. I'll have to wait until payday to try that."

Palmer decides to go ahead and tell Krouse about his jackpot blunder, even though he dislikes telling people about his foolish mistakes. They are legion. But this is too ripe, a greenhorn in Miss Kitty's saloon. And anyway, he's passing along a bit of worthwhile information to someone who hasn't got enough cash on him to afford foolish mistakes. "I brought seventy bucks with me over here," Palmer says at the end of his tale. "I could have had almost ninety."

The others arrive an hour later and their eyes light up in greeting. How long have you been here, Palmer? Itineraries are compared and contrasted. It's only a little bit excruciating. They shake hands, order beers, sit down at the table. Krouse tells them about the MPs outside the club, the black GI weeping, begging not to be handcuffed. Brenner glances at Palmer, who feels an unspoken insult reigned in: MPs are assholes.

Willerton reaches into a pocket of his fatigue shirt and pulls out a deck of cards. "Do you guys want to play Hearts?"

Palmer admits that he does not know how to play Hearts. He's never had any interest in card games, not even poker, has never been able to grasp the subtle math of odds.

"That's okay, we'll teach you," Tigler says.

Palmer would rather not play at all, would rather just observe, knowing how he himself feels when someone who doesn't understand a new game has to be shepherded along. But the men seem eager to teach him, and appear pleased when they are able to pass along some detail involving an obscure tactic or clever finesse, though maybe they're just happy to have a fifth player.

They are ten minutes into the game when a large black sergeant strolls over and leans down and puts one splayed hand on the table. "You gentlemen aren't playing poker, are you?"

The men look up at him wide-eyed. "No Sergeant, we're playing Hearts," Willerton says.

The sergeant nods slowly, looks around at the fanned hands. "Because it's against the rules to play for money in this room."

"It's just Hearts, Sergeant," Brenner says. "We're playing for points."

The sergeant nods, stands up straight. "Okay. All right. As long as you're not playing for money. You men enjoy yourselves."

He drifts away. The men look back to their hands, grinning, shaking their heads. The army and its rules. Palmer begins to get a feel for Hearts, but his confidence wanes after Brenner remarks, "You sure do make some unorthodox openings, Palmer." It's too much like algebra. You have to keep track of every damn thing. When Brenner suggests a game of Bridge, Palmer just laughs and tells them he's going to the game room and play pinball. Bridge is four-handed anyway, and Palmer is tired of learning.

That evening, as they walk toward the seventeen hundred formation, Palmer considers suggesting to his buddies that they not stand together in line, to spread out through the formation so they won't all be picked for a detail. High from beer, he is eager to share with them the knowledge that he has gained from every obscure tactic and clever finesse he has mastered as a Private E2. But in the end he remains silent. Krouse might understand his motives, but Palmer had learned long ago the futility of trying to include other people in his goldbricking. It can get complicated. After the formation ends, Palmer and his buddies spend an hour sweeping and mopping the floor of a latrine, and replacing rolls of toilet paper on short sections of broomstick nailed to the long wooden bench.

CHAPTER 10

At noon formation the following day, Palmer and Krouse are picked to pull a detail in Saigon. They climb onto a bus with five other nabbed men, as well as a sergeant who is in-transit like themselves and who is in charge of the detail, and are driven twenty miles along a road that is packed with Vietnamese walking or traveling on Hondas or bicycles, or small buses that hold only six people. Palmer peers out a window that is covered with a screen, looks at the flat landscape rushing by, green paddies beneath a gray sky. The driver of the bus speeds along the road, hits the brakes, accelerates, swerves to avoid collisions. The bus is carrying other GIs, some in jungle fatigues, a few in stateside Class A greens or khakis. The ride is so violent, the passengers thrust left right, forward, back, that Palmer stops trying to sight-see and peers ahead along the road wondering what it is that makes the driver so manic.

The driver's head swivels, he's looking everywhere as he guides the bus among, between, around, past the streams of people driving or walking on the road, and it occurs to Palmer that the driver is afraid. He's driving fast because he doesn't want to get shot at, doesn't want his vehicle fielding a tossed grenade. Must drive this route every day, maybe he already has been shot at. Drives like he's panicked, at one point slamming on the brakes and throwing the passengers forward in their seats, they grab hold to brace themselves. A man whose rank Palmer cannot see but who is wearing a green Class A uniform finally snarls, "Hey man, how about slowing this thing down? I want to come home from Vietnam alive."

The driver glances back, sweat on his forehead, his jungle fatigues neither dark nor pale. He looks like a kid. He mumbles something that Palmer can't hear, but slows his driving. The bus enters an American compound, the gate manned by MPs, Palmer glances at them as the bus passes through. No white gloves in Vietnam. The driver lets them off outside a warehouse.

The detail involves raking gravel outside the living quarters of a high-ranking officer. Palmer and the others are given rakes, they shuffle along under the hot sun combing the gravel, the sergeant standing by watching them and smoking a cigarette. He's young, probably twenty-three or twenty-four, he doesn't want to be here either. He tells them to take their time, don't hurry, this'll be over in a few hours. He makes small jokes, but not to the point of becoming buddies with the men. We're all in this together but I'm still in charge. It's not a bad detail, just pointless motion, making the landscape pretty for the brass. White painted stones border the gravel yard. Palmer wonders why they had to travel twenty miles on a bus just to rake gravel, are there no enlisted men on this compound? But he squelches it. You can make yourself physically ill trying to analyze army decisions. Best to think about other things. Beer. Three hundred and sixty-three days. If they all turn out to be as pleasant and pointless as this day, that would be all right with Palmer.

On the ride back to the 90th a different driver is at the wheel and takes it slowly. It is after five. The sun is low, golden. Palmer looks out the window and observes the people as the bus passes through the streets of Saigon. Hordes on Hondas, people walking, where are they going? Driving down Interstate 25 in Denver one afternoon, the traffic heavy, a friend of Palmer's hammered the steering wheel of his car and barked, "Where are all these people going? Why don't they stay home?" Inconceivable to two unemployed eighteen year olds that anybody else in the world could possibly have anything to do. But now Palmer wonders, where are these people going, what are they doing, thousands of people on the streets, are they all unemployed? What kind of jobs are there anyway in this smelly furnace of a city? And how often does the war make it into Saigon? Tet of '68. MPs took part in firefights at the American embassy. All the grunts were out in the bush, the men in the rear had to do some shooting. An MP at the Presidio had been a guard at the American embassy, though not during Tet. He said it was the best duty he ever pulled.

When the bus arrives at the 90th, it parks behind another bus that is loading with troops lined up with duffel bags, and there stand Tigler and Brenner and Willerton, fists on hips, their duffel bags resting on the ground. Palmer and Krouse climb off the bus and call to them, and the men turn and shout, "Your names were called!"

A sinking feeling, a familiar feeling, engulfs Palmer's heart. "What do you mean?" he says, approaching his buddies, looking at their duffel bags that have been retrieved from the storage barracks, are packed and ready to go.

"Our names were called at formation," Tigler says. "We're flying up to Qui Nhon right now. They called your names too and you guys weren't there. You better go check with operations."

The men say goodbye, shake hands all around, and afterwards, as Palmer hurries across the spot where formations are held, he feels as he had felt many times as a kid late for school. Calamity. Doors closing, locking, the world moving on without him. He knows it doesn't matter, three hundred and sixty-three days to go. But Jesus he wants to get the hell out of the 90th and go anywhere else. A place where they don't hand out shit details every five hours.

The operations building has a kind of open-air office built onto one side, a counter like the clubhouse at a Putt-Putt golf course, where Specialist Fourth-Class clerks are kept busy continuously answering questions. Palmer works his way up to the counter indifferent to who might be ahead of him, and explains to the clerk what had happened, we were on a detail in Saigon, our names were called, we're not AWOL, we were on a detail.

The clerk doesn't seem too concerned. Probably a common occurrence in a world where high-ranking officers need their gravel spruced up. He tells Palmer and Krouse not to worry, to just wait until tomorrow morning's formation and listen up for their names. No big deal.

Palmer is a bit mollified. He trusts Spec Fours. They have come through for him on other occasions during his time in service. But the man's reassurance doesn't lessen the odd feeling of being cut off from the world, from his orders, from his fate. He wishes like hell he was leaving on that bus.

"Feel like going to the EM club?" he says to Krouse, not really caring if Krouse wants to go with him, because the club is where Palmer plans to wait out the arrival of his misplaced fate. Jesus but this is a crock of shit.

"I don't have enough money for beer," Krouse says in a slightly mournful voice which may be real or simply a standard tactic to cadge from a buddy. Either way, Palmer recognizes it.

"That's okay, I'll buy, I've got money," Palmer says, still indifferent. Beer costs ten cents a can here. He's got enough money to buy six hundred beers, if it comes down to it.

"I think I'm gonna go to the mess hall," Krouse says. "I'll meet you there later."

Palmer walks toward the EM club trying to suppress his disgust, resignation sometimes a tough call. He enters the club with his cap off and heads for the bar. The club has not yet filled, most of the men at the 90th converging on the mess hall. Palmer has decided to try one of the EM club hamburgers, potato chips, beer, all this heat affecting his appetite. He's not very hungry, though maybe it's just the disgust having already filled his belly.

He's on his third tall Bud when Krouse enters the club with his cap off. His eyes seem large behind his glasses, searching, head pivoting to spot Palmer, who raises a hand to signal him. His disgust has abated. He's a bit high, and not displeased to have someone to talk to. Share the bullshit, spread it thin. He gives Krouse twenty cents worth of funny money, one for himself. After Krouse has sat down and taken his first drink, Palmer asks if he wants to play pinball.

Krouse doesn't respond right away, looking down at his can of Bud, elbows on the table, holding the rim with five fingers hovering splayed like a gripping spider's legs. "Say Palmer," he says, looking up with mournful eyes, "do you think you could loan me five dollars until payday?"

Something catches in Palmer's throat when he hears this

request. A mistake to have mentioned that he had brought seventy dollars with him to Vietnam. Now he is cornered.

Krouse continues. "I'll pay you back as soon as I can. I'm just kind of broke right now."

Well. Palmer's been broke in his lifetime. He's been unemployed and down to his last quarter. You feel cornered. He pulls out his billfold, removes a five. The fact that it looks like Monopoly money does nothing to lessen the sense that he is sacrificing a part of his safety net. Fifty beers.

"That's all right," he says. "Pay me back when you can."

Payday is almost two weeks off, and the two men will likely never see each other again. Palmer knows this, but he has been broke all his life.

Palmer cuts the evening short, leaving around eight, not expecting Krouse to use any of the five for beer and pinball, but not wanting to dig further into his own money. He has descended into the limbo of lost orders, and the two of them might be here for the next two weeks.

At dawn formation Palmer listens closely for his name, and when the sergeant ceases reading from his list Palmer sighs, sags, with resignation. The sergeant tells the formation to close the ranks. It's shit detail time. Krouse is standing directly in front of Palmer, but he suddenly steps out of line and walks over to the tower and stands looking up at the sergeant. He glances around at Palmer, gives his head a little twist that says come with me. Palmer stares at Krouse, not certain what the guy is doing. It's dangerous to talk to sergeants charged with handing out shit details.

Krouse gives another jerk of his head, and Palmer steps out of line and goes up to the tower and stands beside him, listens to what he has to say. He starts talking to the sergeant who leans down to hear, explains about being on a detail in Saigon yesterday, that both of their names were called, and he wonders what they ought to do.

The sergeant reaches out of the tower and points off to his right, tells the two men to go check with operations. As they trudge seemingly depressed toward the Putt-Putt counter, the sergeant hollers, "Last ten men in this file!"

Palmer is elated. Krouse is a genius. They step up to the operations counter and explain their plight to a Spec Four, who tells them the same thing the other Spec Four had told them yesterday. Then they go to the EM club.

At noon formation Palmer does not hesitate to follow Krouse up to the tower. It is the same sergeant, who says the same thing, leaning from the tower and pointing to his right. At evening formation Palmer and Krouse do not even make a pretense of stopping at the operations office. They go directly to Alice's Restaurant.

It lifts Palmer's spirits to be with a man of his own ilk, who apparently can think on his feet faster even than Palmer who had let the vicissitudes of army bullshit cloud his mind when he needed it most. This tower scam is equivalent to his weaseling out of KP, so much so that he finally tells Krouse about his own desperate dodge on that Thursday night less than a week ago when he was picked with fourteen other men to pull KP in one of the Oakland mess halls. "I didn't sign the KP roster when it was handed to me." Couldn't bring himself to sign it, he tells Krouse. "Then the sergeant handed back all the ID cards so we could get into the enlisted men's club that night. As soon as I got my card I ran like hell." He watches Krouse's face for signs of doubt during the telling. Nothing quite as demoralizing as relating a personal victory only to detect disbelief in a listener's eyes. But Krouse laughs, is a believer. He has dodged his share of details too. They are both one with Beetle Bailey.

The goldbrick beauty of the tower scam helps to alleviate the frustration that wells up when Palmer again does not hear his name called at the subsequent dawn and noon formations. His orders rest upon a slowly moving olive-drab conveyor belt. Krouse goes off somewhere by himself after the noon formation, and Palmer doesn't see him again until four-thirty.

Krouse enters the EM club hatless, and spots Palmer at a table in a corner of the room. He has a pleased look on his face. He goes to the bar and buys his own beer, comes to the table and sits down.

"Guess what I did?" he says, his voice muted, a bit conspiratorial.

"What?" Palmer says, wondering if Krouse has pulled out all the stops, has managed to slip their orders onto the top of some Spec Four clerk's OUT tray.

"I went to a massage parlor." His lips crease tightly, he grins with his cheeks.

Something catches in Palmer's throat when he hears this statement. He takes a sip of beer and sets the can on the table. "A massage parlor?" he says, not trusting his voice to say anything else.

"Yeah. You know those white buildings along the ridge near the perimeter?" pointing with a thumb. "One of them is a massage parlor. I went in and got a massage from a Vietnamese woman."

Words hang momentarily on the tip of Palmer's tongue, then emerge like a stream of smoke. "How much did that cost?"

"Five bucks."

Palmer stares with disbelief as Krouse describes his half-hour in the parlor. "It's all legal," Krouse says. "It's run by the army." Krouse is just a kid, oblivious to his own audacity, proud of lying naked on a table while a sexy stranger kneaded his freckled American flesh, he wants to tell the world about the mademoiselles, the frauleins, the geishas.

Palmer decides to ditch Krouse after this evening, in spite of the fact that Krouse is the one who engineered the tower scam and kept Palmer off five shit details so far, who has in effect paid off his loan, one buck per detail. There was no condition set on what he might do with that money. But Palmer will find another transient barracks, and avoid the man in formations even if it means ending up on shit details. Palmer no longer relishes the idea of hanging out with someone just like himself.

CHAPTER 11

Handing his hat-check stub to a harried man in dark green sweat-stained fatigue pants and stripped to a T-shirt, Palmer taps his knuckles lightly on the counter top, impatient to get going. His name was called at morning formation. He didn't hang around to listen up for Krouse's name, and prays that Krouse will not be on his bus, his airplane, his compound for the next year. Clerk/typist. They can get stationed anywhere. The bitter Screaming Eagle was a clerk/typist. His duffel bag is eased onto the counter, and he gives it a quick check for tampering. But this is a safe storage depot. Would take a lot of guts to be a barracks thief in a country where your victims have access to guns. But he will probably learn the details of that after he becomes an active-duty cop.

He stands beside his duffel bag, smoking a cigarette and gazing around at the other men waiting for the bus that will take them to the airport at Bien Hoa and then up to Qui Nhon, where the army will decide where to station him. He doesn't see Krouse anywhere, and as the bus pulls in he doesn't ever expect to see him again. He lifts his duffel bag off the ground, clutches it like a tackling dummy and wades onto the bus, finds a seat not near a window so that Krouse will not see him, leap onto the bus, beg for another loan. The man is not a pro, is not one with Beetle Bailey. If Krouse had confessed that he had blown it on the slots Palmer would have been less disgusted, probably would have laughed. If he had confessed that he drank fifty beers, Palmer would have given him another five.

When they arrive at the airfield Palmer sees that the plane scheduled to take him north is a C-130 transport, an appalling squat toad of a prop job, blotched green and brown. Duffel bags are dumped onto baggage dollies. The troops walk onto the plane through the open squared mouth of the belly's rear where supplies can be shoved off under unfurling parachutes, where men jumped off in Fort Campbell Airborne training, a night jump into a nearby field when Palmer was on bivouac, the silent spooky chutes drifting across the black sky like giant toadstools. All the gung-ho trainees wanted to go Airborne. Imagine dropping out of the sky onto a Vietcong bivouac. Good luck. Palmer hates the idea of flying across Vietnam. What if there's an emergency landing in the boonies? He doesn't even have a rifle yet.

The troops sit along the sides of the plane on net seats, with cheesy little seatbelts buckling like pistol belts. A joke of a safety device but one that Palmer clings to, buckles tightly, he has no faith whatsoever that this thing will make it off the ground, will last two minutes in the air, will not get shot down by the Vietcong like something out of a grade-B jungle movie, the hollow shell cradled like a steel balloon in the triple-canopy leaf that he's been hearing about ever since Kennedy was assassinated. With his luck he would probably live through it. Would have to revive all those survival skills from basic that he has forgotten. Eat bugs. Garrote Charlie. Good luck. He closes his eyes as soon as the plane starts taxiing down the runway. He has no idea how long the flight will last. An hour maybe. Vietnam is not very big. Seven hundred miles from Saigon to Hanoi, like Denver to Oklahoma City.

He tries to put himself to sleep, blanking his mind during the vibrating liftoff and swaying dive into the sky. It's a noisy sonofabitch. Four propellers grinding through all this damp Asian air. He drifts into a kind of half-sleep, random thoughts roaming as if in meditation shepherded by the humming sounds, the air-pockets that drop the plane bringing him briefly toward full consciousness. He opens his eyes now and again and looks up at the mountain of crates strapped tightly a foot or two away from him. Supplies. Primary cargo. The troops seem mere extras, like the thermos bottles you stow at the sides of a station wagon on a family vacation.

The plane lands at the airfield in Nha Trang but the troops who do not have written orders to get off here are told to stay put by a member of the crew wearing headphones, in contact with the pilot, Palmer supposes. A bustling man. This is his fiefdom.

When the plane takes off again, Palmer closes his eyes, his whole body sensitive to the altitude gained. He feels it peak, then start to go down, feels it in his stomach, Otis elevator, he opens his eyes to see the crewman with the headphones standing on a web seat at the rear of plane hollering something and pointing toward the front of the plane.

Shit! Palmer turns to a stranger seated next to him and asks what's happening. The man turns his bored eyes on Palmer and says we're landing in Qui Nhon.

This really is a small country. It seems they've been in the air barely ten minutes. All it takes is these few words to fill Palmer with relief. Words are meaningless, but for their power to delude. He's happy. The plane lands and rolls to a stop, and Palmer unlatches his buckle, tosses aside the soiled white web-belt, and stands up.

The sky is clear in Qui Nhon, cloudless, the air noticeably cooler. They have left the true heat and mugginess in the southern part of this country shaped like a ragged quarter-moon. Palmer steps out into the bright sunshine, his pupils shrinking, he follows the line of troops across the tarmac toward an opening in the cyclone-fence that appears to surround the small airfield. The runway barely looks long enough to accommodate a takeoff. There's a closed-in feel about this place, a smallness, with a dark range of mountains hovering over the city to the west, he can't tell how far away. The airfield is surrounded by one-story buildings, there is none of the vastness that made Long Binh seem like a rocky desert, no pockmarked fields. An asphalt road runs adjacent to the airfield fence, and across the road from the gate is a one-story building with big windows. The terminal, Palmer discovers, as he passes through the doors.

His written orders end here at Qui Nhon. He will have to find the Military Police battalion to learn how much farther he will be traveling before all this is over. Five days at Oakland, five days at the 90th, he wants to find a bunk, a wall locker, get settled. He dislikes being in-transit as much as he had come to dislike being a trainee.

The terminal isn't very big. It has a small cafeteria, with tables set near the big windows that look out on the airfield where a green and white airplane is landing. Vietnam Airlines painted on the side. Palmer goes up to a counter and shows his orders to a Spec Four, who says he will phone the MP battalion to come get him. Tells him to wait outside by the door as soon as he gets his duffel bag.

The duffel bags appear in a small room adjacent to the cafeteria. Palmer searches through the stenciled names, finds his own, carries it outside into the bright sunlight and sees that Vietnamese civilians are climbing down the short stairway that has been rolled up to the door of the green and white airplane. Civilians are wandering all around the terminal. A shared airport, just as the Vietnamese are sharing their war with us. He can see Huey helicopters parked in military rank and file farther down the airstrip, beyond the fence which is topped with barbed-wire as all fences probably are in Vietnam. Large white Huey-shaped objects wrapped in white like mummies, minus the rotors, are lined up down there too.

Civilians and Americans soldiers, Vietnamese men in uniform, ARVNs, wandering all around outside the terminal, there's a kind of busy cheerfulness emanating from the crowd at Qui Nhon, unlike the other places he's been so far. Heavy vehicle traffic moves along the road, jeeps and deuce-and-a-halfs and three-quarter ton trucks. Everybody talking. Beyond the airfield off to his right shines a corner of the ocean, the bay shore bordered by a road and trees and white sand. F Boats out there, large Navy ships at anchor, with motorboats and sailboats gliding past them across the bay. The NVA does not have a navy that Palmer knows of. Wouldn't be bad to be stationed in a place with an ocean at your back. One less field of fire to worry about. He's glad they don't have an air force either.

He spots two black GIs with duffel bags standing at the edge of the sidewalk that leads into the terminal. He goes over to them, dragging his duffel bag behind him.

"Are you guys MPs?" he says.

They turn to him with their eyebrows raised, both men bigger though not taller than Palmer. They look him up and down, at his newbie uniform, at his clean boots. One of them is eating ice-cream from a small paper cup, scooping it with a tiny wooden spoon. "MPs?" he says, both frowning and grinning, revealing a gold-capped tooth with a hollow star exposing white enamel. Both men laugh. They're buddies. Their uniforms are not dark green, but not so faded that the two might have only nine days left in-country. They look like they've been here awhile.

"Naw man, we're infantry," the other man says.

"Are you an MP?" the first man says, poking at his cup with the spoon.

Palmer nods.

"Yeh? Where you gonna be stationed?"

"Qui Nhon, I guess," Palmer says. He doesn't know. His orders go no further.

"You gonna be stationed here?" the man says, setting the spoon in the cup and pointing one long black pink-nailed finger down at the sidewalk.

"Yeah."

Both men bust out laughing, their eyes strafing the sky, their shoulders shaking. Palmer has no trouble understanding the joke. They are 11-Bravo. They will never live in a city as long as they are in Vietnam.

"Oh man, you got it dicked," the GI with the ice-cream says, plucking the spoon from the cup.

"Sheeit," the other man says. They are still chuckling when an MP jeep rolls up to the curb, but the man driving is not wearing a shiny helmet, a nightstick, a pistol. He is a Spec Four, probably a clerk-typist whose job it is to check the airport for MP cherry boys in dark green fatigues.

"MP?" he hollers from the driver's seat.

Palmer nods.

"Throw your gear in the back and get in."

Palmer stows his gear, climbs into the jeep and looks over at the two black GIs standing on the sidewalk watching him with grins. The man with the ice-cream raises one empty hand and makes the peace sign, V for Victory in their fathers' war. "Good luck, man," he says, then throws his head back revealing again that gold-capped tooth polished by his laughter.

As the jeep pulls away, Palmer hears the other man's fading voice saying "Sheeit" again. Palmer has no trouble at all understanding the source of their amusement. Qui Nhon will surely be nothing compared to the bush. He might get sent somewhere else though, up to Danang, or to a unit across the highlands, might get assigned to escort convoys, but he wants to stop moving, to get his permanent assignment. Motion never got him anywhere except here.

The driver is a Spec Four named Webber, his name sewn above his jacket pocket. His fatigues look new, but his arms and face are tanned. Palmer asks how long he's been in Vietnam.

"Seven months," Webber says, glancing over at him with a smile and saying, "How long have you been in Vietnam?" but it's a joke question, Palmer can tell.

"Ten days," he answers anyway.

Webber gives his head a shake as if he cannot believe anybody has been in Vietnam for only ten days. Stationed right here in Qui Nhon, the man has it dicked.

The jeep follows the curving asphalt road toward a cluster

of two story white buildings, an evacuation hospital Palmer sees by a sign posted at the entrance to a parking lot where gray ambulances with white crosses painted on the sides and hoods are parked. A Huey is resting on a circular pad far across the lot. No one around it. Webber slows at the main gate, is waved through by a man with an SP insignia on his black armband.

They are out of the airfield compound, Webber turning left onto a Qui Nhon road, a civilian road, following it past a motor pool compound crammed with vehicles, then turning right and heading down a long straight road which looks like it leads right up to the mountains hovering over the city. Full of VC with mortars, Palmer has to assume. To have it dicked is a relative concept. They travel a quarter-mile down the road, then Webber hangs a left into a compound guarded by two MPs in a small gate shack. He slows only to let them see him, then drives down a dirt road and turns right at the corner of a large building like all the buildings on this compound, green, two-story. A softball field lies farther out, the screened backstop hovering over a foot-trammeled diamond. Beyond the softball field is a one-story building of reddish stone, and beyond that, beyond the barbed-wire topped fence, the glimmer of the ocean.

"A group of new men came in earlier this morning," Webber tells him. "They're waiting to have a meeting with the battalion commander. You'll be going in with them."

He pulls around the building and into a small dead-end where four MP jeeps are parked, radio aerials shaped in thin arcs that rise from the rear of each vehicle, bend over the roofs, are locked down near the hoods. "That's the MP station,"

Webber says as he parks the jeep, pointing to a building on their left, a set of double-doors opened to the station itself. Palmer can see MPs without helmets wandering around in there. "This is battalion headquarters," pointing at the building they just drove around. "Leave your duffel bag on the ground with those others. It'll be safe."

Palmer climbs out of the jeep, grabs his duffel bag from the rear and carries it over to a row of four bags lying on the rocky parking lot. He sets it down, then looks at the names stenciled on each bag. He feels the odds are fair that he might recognize a name, but he doesn't. Doesn't see the word "Krause" either, thank goodness.

"Let's head upstairs," Webber says. "They're waiting on you."

This makes Palmer laugh to himself, not five minutes at his unit and he's already holding things up, grinning with the Vietnam sunlight flattening against his back as he follows Webber up a wooden staircase and into battalion headquarters.

CHAPTER 12

The room is like the movie room at the 90th, a big space filled with desks where men in pale fatigues are working at typewriters. A busy place. Not much talking here, but a lot of noise from the machines. Four men are sitting on folding chairs near an open doorway that leads into another part of the building, two PFCs, a Spec Four, and one buck sergeant with a smidgen of a mustache. He has a name tag on his jacket that Palmer can't quite make out. The other men look just like Palmer in their new fatigues. No names on their jackets.

"All right, this is everybody," Webber says. "Let's go see the colonel."

The men stand up and follow Webber through another office where only a few men are seated at desks. He knocks on a closed door, and a voice hollers at them to enter.

Palmer is struck immediately by the sight of the Colonel, who is seated slouched casually at the edge of a big wooden desk, his hands clasped on one knee. He looks just like the E8 who had helped Palmer so many months ago when he had gone to Oakland to get his brother's orders changed. Silver hair. Deep tan. He's grinning, white teeth perfect like the uniform he's wearing, impeccable starched fatigues, squared cuffs rolled above his elbows, and for some reason he's wearing a pistol belt though no weapon.

The Colonel rises from his desk and tells the men to stand at ease. "I always like to personally welcome the new men who arrive in battalion so I can get to know my people," he says. "Unfortunately I'm going to be leaving battalion in a few days, I'm headed home. So this is probably the only time I'll get to talk to you men."

The men stand almost at attention. At ease means so little in the presence of anyone above the rank of Major, and this man is a full bird-colonel.

"We got us a good battalion here, good MP duty, and I know you men are gonna like it." He peers at the buck sergeant's name tag. "Sergeant Lattimore, where you from?"

Lattimore grins, his teeth a bit crooked like Krouse's. Black-haired, with his mustache he resembles Warren Oates. A Drill Sergeant in Fort Campbell had held a vague resemblance to Paul Newman, the longish nose and angular face, pale eyes, but the resemblance ended there. He was a prick who loved to harass the dying cockroaches. "I'm from Duluth," Lattimore says.

"This your first tour?"

"Naw sir, my second, I was stationed down in Tuy Hoa last year in the 926." A Midwestern accent, he chews his words, says shiksh for six.

"The 926th. A good unit. Welcome back."

"Thank you, sir."

"How about you, troop?" the colonel says, looking right at Palmer. Palmer hates talking to officers. A sort of conditioned guilt always simmers inside him. "I'm from Denver, sir."

"Say I'll bet you ski, right?"

"No, sir, I've never skied."

"Never skied and you're from Denver?"

Palmer feels himself grinning like an idiot. Maybe it's time he started lying about this. "I've just never tried it, sir."

"My home is Vermont," the colonel says. "We have hills compared to the Rocky Mountains. You gotta get yourself up on those slopes, troop."

Palmer smiles with forced enthusiasm, says, "I plan to give it a try someday, sir."

The colonel nods, turns to the other men, learns their names, where they're from. "Do any of you men have any hobbies?" he says. "It's good for a man to have a hobby of some sort to fill up his free time. To be perfectly frank, there's not a hell of a lot to do around here when you're off duty. How about you, Palmer. What do you do when you're not skiing?"

Palmer hesitates a moment, then tells the colonel he takes home movies.

"All right," the colonel says. "I take home movies too. Do you have one of the new Super-8 cameras?"

"No, sir, just a regular 8."

"Ooooh," the colonel growls. "You got to move on up to Super-8, Palmer. The picture quality is outstanding."

Palmer smiles. This is excruciating. "Yes, sir."

The other men have normal hobbies. Softball. Swimming. One man collected stamps in his youth but doesn't anymore.

The interview with this man whom they will never see again comes to an end. He wishes all of them good luck, shakes their hands, a firm grip. The men file out of the room, led by Webber who tells them that it's lunch hour and they might as well head for chow because they can't be processed in until thirteen hundred.

"The mess hall is down the block," he says. "Or you can go to the enlisted men's club. They've got hamburgers, steaks, chicken dinners. Everything costs a buck."

"I know the place," Lattimore says. "I come through here last year." A kind of hard rock sound underlying his chewed words. He's a sergeant. You probably get used to talking like you're giving orders, Palmer supposes. Thrust your words like a bullet into a blizzard. "The EM club is down yonder by the edge of the ocean," Lattimore says as the men step down the stairway and onto the parking lot where their duffel bags lie fading in the tropical sunlight.

Lattimore might be twenty-six, twenty-seven. He's got the settled-in look men have who are going to be in the army for a long time. Palmer had seen it at the Presidio, basic, MP school. Not necessarily lifers, but men who won't be deciding what to do with their futures until they get into their thirties and the charm of the annual PT tests begins to fade. Of all the men in the group Lattimore looks the most comfortable, most natural, in his new green fatigues. The other men still look like they're faking it, pretending to be soldiers in Vietnam. Maybe it's because Lattimore already has his name tag sewed on.

Palmer had not paid attention to the names of the other men during the interview with the colonel, so he doesn't address them as they walk past the softball field toward the Camp Quincey enlisted men's club. A wooden sidewalk borders the ball field, but they walk on the dirt road. Lattimore is telling the men that he had passed through here more than a year earlier before he was shipped down to Tuy Hoa. Palmer looks across the softball field, sees beyond the backstop a grove of evergreen trees surrounding a small concrete patio with picnic tables on it. Evergreens like in the Rockies, tall and seeming out of place. Isn't Southeast Asia supposed to have nothing but palm trees? Isn't everything in the world only the way he thinks it's supposed to be?

The reddish building turns out to be the EM club, flagstone, modern architecture like a house in the suburbs, one-story, flat-topped, bushes growing along the front, with cement steps leading up to double-doors emitting faint music. Lattimore leads them into the place, a big room, high-ceilinged, dim, a few GIs sitting around at tables eating lunch. It's cool in here, air-conditioned, big as a barn, it looks like a dancehall. A jukebox is feeding a quiet country/western ballad through speakers hiked high at the four corners of the room. In the middle of the wide tiled floor stands a U-shaped bar where a Vietnamese woman is busy mixing drinks for a few GIs seated with their elbows resting on the padded edge of the countertop. Padded stools with backs. Palmer looks around with a kind of evergreen amazement. A large stage stands off to his left as in a high school auditorium, the red curtain drawn. He looks around for pinball machines but doesn't see any. Pinball is a noisy game. Maybe the men of Camp Quincey want peace and quiet when they eat their dollar steaks. I want to be stationed here, Palmer thinks as Lattimore leads them across the floor to a table. They pull an extra chair up. A Vietnamese waitress comes over and takes their orders, she's wearing black silk pants, a white blouse, no hat.

Palmer orders the chicken dinner. He's never liked steak. It's never tender enough and the gristle lodges between his teeth for hours, immune to toothpicks.

"Damn but this is nice," one of the men says. "I wouldn't mind getting stationed here."

Lattimore grins, his lips pulling back from long teeth. He

really does look like Warren Oates. Eyes dark, squinting as he grins. "Well hell, maybe you will, boy. I was shootin' the shit with one of them clerks back at battalion and he told me they need a warm body over at the 109th MP. The rest of us are going west."

"What's the 109th MP?" Palmer says.

Lattimore turns his head, fixes his dark eyes on Palmer, grins, his whole face diving into it. "That's the MP company what runs this town like the 926 runs Tuy Hoa. I was in the 109 when I first come to Vietnam but I asked for a transfer outta there. I didn't care much for the CO. He was kind of an asshole. I reckon they got a new one by now."

Another man shaping his army destiny, like Beaudry transferring to Korea. But Palmer's plan is to take whatever the army gives him and sit on it for a year. Any move you make to alter that which God has decreed will just end in disaster. He's never needed the Catholic Church to tell him that.

The food arrives, steak for Lattimore, hamburgers for the strangers. Palmer's chicken dinner tastes just like Chicken Delight back in Denver. French fries, cole slaw, all on a thick paper plate. Lattimore advises them not to order beer, they've still got their processing at battalion at thirteen hundred. Palmer wants to know why Lattimore came back to Vietnam for a second tour, but doesn't ask. Palmer wouldn't come to Vietnam for a first tour in the best of all possible worlds. But even as he thinks this he knows that there's a small part of him, no bigger than a fleck of cigarette ash, that had wanted to come to Vietnam ever since Kennedy was assassinated, an urge with no greater force than curiosity. The big adventure. A kid thing. But the government had to make him do it.

When lunch is over Lattimore leads them outside to a back patio built of wood stained red, a big porch with two picnic tables shaded by large metal umbrellas. "The South China Sea," he says like a pronouncement. "Charlie sends sappers out to plant satchel charges on the ships unloading over at Delong Pier," pointing vaguely off to his left. "They blew a hole under the waterline of a big boat when I was stationed here last year. A supply ship. The thing listed in the bay for a month before they got her patched up."

Frogmen. The communists do have a navy. Palmer looks out past a barbed-wire fence with dark sea garbage cluttered at its base. There's a wide beach, white sand stretching down to the edge of the water where low waves are rolling in, breaking with a soft sound, thinning on the sand.

"Looka them kids," Lattimore says. Two Vietnamese boys are wandering along the edge of the surf, stooping to examine things the way Palmer once examined smelly treasures on the banks of Clear Creek flowing from the Coors factory in Golden. "Lemme show you something," Lattimore says. He goes to the doorway of the club, calls to a waitress wiping a table. "Mamasan, two Coke."

When the woman brings the Cokes, Lattimore pays her and carries the red cans to the edge of the patio.

"Yo! Boysan!" he yells. He takes one can in his right fist, hauls back and chucks the thing in a high arc over the fence. The boys stand up and look at him, watch the tumbling sunlit flight of the can. It splashes into a breaking wave. The boys run to it, dig around in the surf. One of them comes up with it.

"Yo!" Lattimore shouts, and tosses the other can farther out. Both boys hop-step into the waves, scramble for it.

Lattimore stands grinning at the edge of the patio.

"How are they going to open them?" Palmer says, taking the long view of things.

"Shit," Lattimore says, glancing at Palmer. "Those dinks'll get 'em open."

Dinks. Part of the jargon that Palmer knows is waiting for him.

The boys clutch their treasures, start walking toward the patio, but Lattimore waves them off. "Finny!" he shouts. "Didi!"

The boys stop and study the GIs gathered on the patio, then turn and walk back the way they had come. Palmer lights a cigarette, looks at the kids, looks at the bay, looks up at the blue sky, at the harsh sun shining down on Qui Nhon. I want to be stationed here, he thinks. Three hundred and fifty-eight days left in Vietnam. He has been here six days, and each day feels like a coin won, clutched in his hand, stuffed in his pocket, banked, it can never be taken away from him. The feeling is as solid as the future is nebulous.

CHAPTER 13

The man who processes Palmer in is a Specialist Fifth-Class named Archer who looks like he might be in his early thirties but has a haggard face, like an aging drinker, or even an athlete who has spent too much time out in the sun and rain and wind. Something drawn and tired-looking as he smiles at Palmer and says, "Welcome to Vietnam" in a voice like a disk jockey, deep, friendly, the greeting seeming both practiced and corny. Palmer smiles. He's seated on a folding chair beside Archer's desk. This isn't like having a conversation with an officer, or even a sergeant. Palmer has never understood what differentiates the specialist ranks from the others, the corporals and sergeants. If he ever makes E4, which seems unlikely to him with only a year left of his time in service and still an E2, he will be wearing Specialist Fourth-Class pips on the corners of his fatigue collars and not the double stripes of a corporal. He has no chance of ever making sergeant.

The Spec Five looks over Palmer's travel orders, rolls a sheet of paper through the platen of his Remington and begins typing fast with all ten fingers, something Palmer has never been able to do even though he took a semester of typing in high school. He cheated in typing class, got straight A's, and the teacher, a lay teacher, a cute blonde, never called him on it even though he was sure she knew he was full of shit. But who in his lifetime hasn't known he was full of shit? The teacher was young and newly-married, and toward the end of senior year she was bulging at the belly, a strange sight in a Catholic school. Palmer had expected the nuns to gang up on the monsignor and make him fire her.

"It looks like you're going to be staying here with us, Palmer," Archer says, rolling the sheet of paper from the typewriter and handing it to him. "The 109th MP Company needs an E2 to fill a slot in their roster, and since you're the only E2 in today's group, it looks like you'll be going to the 109."

Palmer takes the piece of paper and looks it up and down, indecipherable orders. "Will I be stationed here at Camp Quincey?" pointing a finger toward the ground of this dream compound, this island in the war where everybody has it dicked.

"No, the 109 is located on the other side of the airfield," the man says, leaning back in his chair and folding his arms. "It's a nice compound. They have their own enlisted men's club over there." A quick smile. "Off-duty MPs generally are not welcome at any of the other EM clubs in this city." He speaks like a college-educated man, his words chosen slowly, unlike most of the inarticulate E5s Palmer has encountered during the past year. He can't figure out why this guy is still in the army. Archer seems like he ought to be doing something in civilian life, something successful. Junior exec. Moving up, making his mark.

"Where are the other men going?" Palmer says, wanting to know the nature of his near-miss. At least he's staying in Qui Nhon, even if it isn't Camp Quincey. A private EM club for Military Policemen.

Archer leans forward and looks at a piece of paper on his desk. "Let's see here...they need one man in An Khe. There's

two slots for men in Pleiku, and they also need a man to pull
V-100 duty escorting convoys."

He leans back in his chair and looks at Palmer with a faint
smile easing the tired lines running from the edges of his
nostrils to the corners of his lips. He knows how lucky
Palmer is. Knows how lucky he himself is, Palmer can see
that. The war is beginning to ebb.

Palmer walks out of battalion headquarters along with the
other men, the brief descent down the stairs feeling like the
last leg of the journey that he has been on for ten days, or a
year, or since Kennedy's death. Final duty station. He will be
getting a ride to the 109th from one of the Military Policeman
inside the station. Jeeps will be coming for the other men,
whose names Palmer at last learns as they stand in the parking lot smoking cigarettes and waiting for their ride. Now
that he is no longer a part of this group, he becomes interested
in who they are, who they were. Wright will be going as far
as An Khe. Nelson, Donley, and Sgt. Lattimore will be going
on to Pleiku where Lattimore will join the V-100 unit. "I love
driving them babies," he says, chewing gum with his mouth
open, the wad dancing around his tongue. "Last year I was
headed down a road outside Tuy Hoa in a V-100 when I come
on this water buffalo blocking the road. This ol' papasan was-
n't doing nothing to get his cow outta the way, so I trained
my M-60 on the buffalo and I says to papasan, I says, 'You
got five seconds to get that got-damn animal outta my way
or I'm gonna blow his ass right off the road.'" He grins as he
tells this story, a war story. Palmer wonders what kind of war
stories he himself will end up boring people with if he ever
gets home alive. Papasan is struggling to lead the water

buffalo off the road when two jeeps pull into the parking lot, the drivers wearing helmets and flak jackets.

"You the men going to Pleiku?"

This is their ride. There are flak jackets and helmets in the backseats, and one M-16 that Palmer can see. He knows little about the M-16, has never even disassembled one. He had trained in basic on the M-14 and still doesn't know why. He will have to ask someone at the MP company to give him a remedial course on the nomenclature and proper handling of an M-16, how to disassemble and reassemble it, how to clean it. He hasn't fired one of those weapons with live ammo since he was at the Presidio, a day of record fire, a day of fraud. Everybody was cheating on their scorecards.

Wright, Donley, and Nelson put on their flak jackets with a kind of joking reluctance. What do we need these for? Sgt. Lattimore slips quickly into his, puts on a helmet, tugs the brim low to his eyes. Back in harness. He might never have left Vietnam, is at home here. He turns to Palmer with a grin and holds out a hand. "All right, you lucky sonofabitch, I guess I'll be seeing you again when I pass through on my way home." They shake hands. Palmer knows he'll never see Lattimore or any of these men again. It's like the Mandatory Buddy Lie. Nice knowing you, pal, be sure to write. Palmer shakes hands all around, and sees in the eyes of Wright, Donley, and Nelson a bit of envy, or maybe only thinks he does. He gets to stay here. They will be driven across the Central Highlands in open jeeps, and who knows whether Charlie is out there waiting with an AK-47 or rocket-propelled grenades? They know.

Palmer picks up one of their duffel bags and stows it in the rear of a jeep. The men climb in, there's a bit of waving, grins, then the jeeps start up and head around the corner of battalion headquarters and out of sight forever. Palmer stands alone in the parking lot, finishing his cigarette and feeling as if he is shedding a skin, the in-transit husk that falls away when you know your bunk is waiting just around a corner.

He looks up at the mountains to the south, the range ending at the edge of the sea, the hillsides blue in afternoon shadow. Looming above the city, they remind him of the foothills of the Rocky Mountains looming over Golden, these hills dwindling northward, maybe all the way past the DMZ and right up to Hanoi. He doesn't know. He has never studied a map of Vietnam, does not even know where he really is. He was the only E2 in the group, and for that reason alone he is standing here waiting for a ride around the airfield to the 109th. That afternoon at the Presidio when he was denied a promotion to PFC by Sgt. Sherman he was livid. Left behind, the only E2 in the first platoon. Men who had come to Company D out of MP school after he did were promoted over him. So livid that he hiked across the Golden Gate Bridge, smoking cigarettes furiously, just to shed his rage. And now, all these months later, here is his reward for being a total fuckup: he has an ocean at his back. It's the manifestation of a truth he had learned as early as basic—if you want a dick job in the army, just screw up. They'll pull you off the line and plant you in some harmless job, like mail-clerk, that everybody else in the company would kill for. Screw up badly enough and they'll give you a promotion. But Palmer hasn't experienced that one yet.

An MP steps out of the station placing his black helmet onto his head with both hands. "Are you the man I'm supposed to drive over to the company?"

Palmer nods, retrieves his duffel bag, hoists it into the
jeep. He climbs in shotgun and looks at the driver's starched
fatigues, armband, the pistol belt and holster as shiny as black
plastic. Soon to be his uniform.

"Did you just graduate from MP school?" the man says
as he puts the jeep into gear and pulls out. His name tag says
Bowen.

"No. I was stationed at the Presidio of San Francisco for a
few months," Palmer says.

The man glances at him. "Yeah? That's good. They'll
probably put you on road patrol right away."

"Did you graduate from Fort Gordon?" Palmer says.

The man shakes his head no, guiding the jeep out the
main gate, glancing to his left for traffic, turning right onto
the road and heading back toward the airfield. "OJT. I came
over here 11-Bravo. I was out in the field for a week filling
sandbags. Next thing I knew I had orders to get on a chopper
and come here."

"Why did they transfer you?"

The man shifts into third, keeps staring straight through
the windshield. "I didn't ask. I was just glad as hell to get out
of that LZ."

Palmer can't tell if the man is irritated by the question, but
he seems so. Palmer has a lot of questions he wants to ask. Do
men die with frequency around here? The kinds of questions
he knows intuitively not to ask. It's too late for answers. He'll
get them eventually. He has a whole year to learn it all.

They enter the airfield compound, drive past the evacuation hospital, past the terminal, past the mummy choppers,
follow the two-lane asphalt all the way to the end of the airfield

and swing around it the way you can swing around Stapleton Airport runways in Denver, park your car at the fence, watch the underbellies of 707s lifting into the sky. Beyond the perimeter fence lie jumbles of slums, Vietnamese houses, Palmer has to assume. Nothing military about their disorder.

Bowen points out the TMP, the site where all the US vehicles in the city gas up. Fuel pumps for jeeps and diesel trucks are spread out on a vast concrete apron. "It's all free. Just pull in and fill up and sign for it in the shack." Somebody is making money off this war.

They skirt the airfield for a few hundred yards, then Bowen turns left and negotiates a series of asphalt streets, passing small American units, signal and quartermaster, finally turning right and driving along a dirt road that dead-ends at the 109th company area, a small compound segregated from all the other units in Qui Nhon. It's situated not far from an airport runway, Palmer notes, and is privileged to have its own enlisted men's club, because everybody hates the MPs.

CHAPTER 14

"Welcome to the 109th." The operations sergeant has a slight European accent, Palmer doesn't know which country, except it doesn't sound German. It reminds him of the voice of a man in MP school who had escaped from Czechoslovakia with his parents when he was a child, and joined the army to gain American citizenship. The sergeant's head is shaved so that, combined with the odd accent, he holds a faint resemblance to Yul Brynner, combined with the odd accent. Deep, bubbling from his throat. He sits casually behind his desk, his eyes flitting again and again to Palmer's hatless head where the hair is almost as bald as a basic trainee's. Palmer is aware of this, sees the man's focus rising, settling momentarily on that rare mown crop. How many men come from their furloughs in America with their hair crowding their ears because the draftees, doubtless always draftees, are pissed about being sent to Vietnam, about being in the army at all? Palmer believes he has inadvertently scored some points here. He knows how much sergeants hate long hair, hate the whole 60's scene, hate the hippies back home spitting on soldiers walking off airplanes. He had told the barber to take it all off at Oakland almost as an after-thought, and only because he was sick and tired of getting hassled over something as stupid as hair.

The operations sergeant, an E7 named Wesser, focuses on Palmer's eyes. He seems pleased to be welcoming someone who actually resembles a soldier, the same mistake Sgt. Sherman had made when Palmer arrived at the Presidio.

Appearances mean too much in the army. "How long have you been in the service?" Sgt. Wesser says, and Palmer tells him just over a year.

"Why are you still an E2?" Wesser says, but there is the hint of a smile on his lips. A lot of men go up and down the ladder during their time in service, and don't always want to talk about it. But Wesser needs to know what kind of men come into his unit, duds, or just victims of ill-fortune.

Palmer explains about the mass-promotion at the Presidio, and how his sergeant had told him that his name had fallen at the bottom of the list and there were no more slots but had said he was at the top of the next promotion list—all lies of course. Palmer was left off the list because he was a dud. "Then I got orders for Vietnam, so I missed out on the next round of promotions."

Sgt. Wesser nods, says, "Don't worry about it," his R's sounding like a soft and single D. Maybe he's Yugoslavian. Where does Yul Brynner hail from? "You'll get your PFC stripes in the next week or two. The Old Man doesn't like anyone below the rank of PFC pulling road patrol."

Like that, that's how Palmer will get promoted, like picking up his bedding at supply. He was so pissed at the end of basic when he didn't get his E2 stripe after working so hard to do everything right except brown-nosing the Drill Sergeants. He hadn't been in the army long enough to know how it really worked.

"What happened to your arm?" the sergeant says.

Palmer has been holding his left arm turned slightly to hide the scar on the underside, a habit now, possibly a liability. He wants to pull road patrol. He describes the judo accident.

"Is it in good shape?" Wesser says. "Any problems?"

"The doctors told me it's stronger now than before the accident," Palmer says, repeating what he believes is another lie.

Wesser nods, sits forward in his chair and tells Palmer that he will be assigned to the third platoon. "You'll be going out on the road two days from now. You'll be riding with two men who've been here for a while. Do you have your radio codes memorized?"

Palmer says yes, the codes that he had begun memorizing back in MP school, ten one-one, ten one-six, the private language of MPs. The instructor asked the trainees if they knew why MPs used codes, and nobody could give him a satisfactory answer. "Because you're gonna have prisoners in your vehicles someday," the instructor finally said, "and it isn't any of their goddamn business what you're saying over the radio." An obvious answer, simple, too simple to be easily divined, like everything else in the army.

Sgt. Wesser hands Palmer a sheet of paper with additional codes used by the 109th. "Get these memorized." Wesser tells Palmer to requisition his web gear from supply, tells him to take his fatigue jackets to a seamstress shop just down the road from the MP company. A Vietnamese woman will sew his name above the pockets. He gives Palmer two dollars' worth of Vietnamese piasters in exchange for two dollars' worth of MPC, and tells Palmer that he will have to pay his house girl with piasters, will eventually have to exchange his MPC at the battalion finance office because it's illegal to give the Vietnamese MPC.

After Palmer steps outside the operations office he walks along a concrete sidewalk to one end of the green building and looks out across the compound to the airfield not so far away. There is no fence between the compound and the airfield, he could walk right onto the nearest runway where a C-130 is taxiing. He looks beyond the airfield toward Camp Quincey, less than a mile away, a cluster of silver-topped buildings, peers beyond that to the mountains which now appear safely distant. Out of range of mortars? The blue crests had seemed to lean right over Camp Quincey.

He shoulders his duffel bag, walks along the sidewalk fronting three buildings, operations and two barracks. Sgt. Wesser had told him to find an empty bunk in the second barracks down, top floor. He climbs the stairs hearing rock music rolling faintly from the enlisted men's club, a one-story building near the unfenced perimeter of the airport. He stops on the landing and looks down at the EM club, which is accessed by a narrow concrete sidewalk crossing the barren ground, rising two or three inches out of the dirt like on the grassless front yard of his house when his family moved to the suburbs of Denver in 1956. His father rototilling that quarter acre of Colorado earth and battling to grow grass from seed with children sneaking across it while he was at work. The lawn came in looking kind of shabby, not like the putting greens of the houses farther along the block. Palmer left home at eighteen, and assumed that the neighbors were relieved when the rest of the family moved to Nebraska. The Palmers were a noisy bunch.

He enters the third platoon barracks. It's an open bay with men sleeping on bunks along both sides. Sgt. Wesser had told him that MP shifts at the 109 lasted twelve hours, oh six-hundred to eighteen hundred. There was tower-guard duty, which was usually reserved for new men, but since Palmer already had road experience he would be going out right away. There was hospital duty, wounded Viet Cong POWs to be guarded, Palmer would probably do a little of that. Also something called PBRs, MP duty in a boat patrolling waterways. Wesser didn't go into much detail about it. Palmer walks halfway down the bay and spots an empty bunk, the mattress rolled to one end. A wall locker with its door hanging open, a footlocker at the end of the bunk. Almost like basic training, except the bunk has a thin metal frame for a mosquito net, which he will have to pick up at supply. Each sleeping man is lying behind a haze of netting boxed like a green coffin, like something out of a WWII movie. The Bridge Over the River Kwai, men lying in the infirmary while the colonel rallies them to labor. William Holden rapping like a cool cat in khaki. There are things about some movies that Palmer has come to loathe. The only army movies that even come close to being realistic are the comedies.

At the far end of the room, Vietnamese women are squatting near the open screen door folding laundry. Their voices are muted in deference to the sleeping GIs, their words rapid, throaty, tumbling, interesting, it could be Latin or Yugoslavian for all Palmer knows.

He stows his gear in the locker, uses the padlock from his duffel bag to secure the door, an old-fashioned narrow locker, not like the fuckers Company D had to assemble that week at the Presidio. He goes downstairs to the supply room adjacent to the operations office, introduces himself to the supply clerk, a smiling young GI in a green T-shirt, his blond hair longish on top but cropped neatly above the ears. He informs Palmer that he also acts as mail-clerk, and hands Palmer a sheet of paper explaining the APO addresses. No postage stamps needed on mail from Vietnam. It's paradisiacal. Palmer carries his bedding up to his barracks and dumps the sheets, blanket, pillow and netting onto the bare square-linked springs.

A woman rises from the group and walks with rapid short steps toward Palmer and starts speaking to him, he can barely make out her words, "I hasgir." She is telling him that she will be his house girl. Sgt. Wesser had mentioned this, the business that the Presidio MPs had talked about, the house girls who do everything for you, wash your clothes, iron them, polish your boots. They make your bunks too. Palmer feels foolish nodding to this woman who looks maybe eighteen though Palmer has no way of judging the ages of Asians. He's never known an Asian person in his life. During his senior year of high school, a black student entered the freshman class, the first black ever at the school, whom he never got to know. Palmer had never known a single black person until he entered the army.

"I do," she says, unrolling his mattress and setting about making the bunk. Palmer feels like an idiot standing there watching her. Servant. He feels like an impolite fraud. Nobody has ever made his bed for him, not even his mother after he was old enough to wrestle the elastic corners of a sheet onto a mattress. Little KP. It's over.

He walks out of the barracks and stands again on the landing and looks off at the mountains from this higher perspective. He can see more of the buildings of Camp Quincey from here, can see the corner of the bay that he had seen when he was across the airfield. It's off to the far left, he can barely make out a strip of white sand, part of the beach that borders the EM club, demarcating the ocean from the land in a crooked line that runs up the coast and disappears into a pale greenish mist where the last mountain seems to plunge straight down into the bay two or three miles distant. It's pretty. The coast was pretty, the landscape between Long Binh and Saigon was pretty but had been overshadowed by the uneasiness he had felt at being in a country where a part of his mind was continually wondering if one form of projectile or another might arrive with a suddenness that they can't really prepare you for in basic training. An uneasiness that he is beginning to think might be with him for a long time, maybe his whole tour. At least he's not Infantry like Phil. He himself could have ended up kneeling on the ground filling sandbags in an LZ, tightening those drawstrings right at this very moment. Charlie anywhere around. Everything within mortar range. Well. He took his chance like everybody else. Lying on his bed at two in the afternoon, unemployed and asleep from partying, he awoke when he heard the basement door open. Phil came down the stairs, passed his bed, and Palmer felt the soft pat of an envelope land on the blanket bundled around his legs. He sat up and opened the envelope. "Greetings from President Nixon." He knew it was coming. When he took his army physical, a man with yellow stripes on the arms of his green uniform had told him to expect the letter within three months. He had timed quitting his last shit-job perfectly, had quit one month earlier and spent his nights in the 3.2 bars of Denver, waiting. He stuffed the letter back into the envelope and lay down, pulled the blanket over his head to block out the afternoon sunlight as well as the knowledge that he was going to be dying in Vietnam sometime during the next two years. And now here he stands with an ocean at his back and wishing he could go into the EM club to compare the quality of the beer in Qui Nhon with that of Long Binh. But Sgt. Wesser had told him to expect to be called to the CO's office within the next couple hours for a brief interview. Captain Metzler likes to personally welcome the new men to the 109th Military Police Company.

CHAPTER 15

Sgt. Wesser preps Palmer, inspects him, tells him to make sure all his pockets are buttoned. Palmer is standing near the door of the CO's office which is down a short hallway from operations. Wesser looks at the dull but clean black gloss of Palmer's jungle boots, looks again at the haircut that Palmer is now glad he had gotten at Oakland, glad he did not come here looking like a sullen draftee.

"After you knock on the door, the captain will call you inside," Wesser says like a man giving backstage instructions, which he is. "Walk up to his desk, salute, and report." Wesser probably does this with all the new men, but there is a satisfied air in Wesser's demeanor that Palmer has never sensed in any other sergeant he's ever encountered, barring the misplaced glee that Sgt. Sherman had demonstrated the day he plucked Palmer from the group of newbies at the Presidio. Wesser nods toward the door, then eases back into the operations office leaving Palmer alone.

Palmer hates this. He stands in front of the door and gives it two firm knocks and hears a muted voice say come in. He opens the door, enters, shuts it behind him, and walks up to the desk near the far wall where a young captain is seated with his fingers intertwined on the desktop, his shoulders hunched slightly, like a ready lineman.

Aside from performing MP duty, Palmer's salute is really the only thing he has ever taken any conscious pride in. Upper arm horizontal to the floor, palm flat and held at a forty-five degree angle, the tip of his index finger grazing his right eyebrow. For some reason that he has never understood, he despises sloppy salutes, the flop-handed quick whip that he has received from so many men with gold braid on their uniforms. "Sir, Private Palmer reports."

Captain Metzler returns the courtesy with a brisk commanding-officer karate chop. "At-ease, Private Palmer. Have a seat."

A clerk's chair has been set in front of the captain's desk, gray metal, padded. Palmer sits down with his spine erect and looks the captain right in the eye—officers seem to like this—and keeps his focus fixed on the captain's face throughout the entire interview.

"I want to start off by asking you a straightforward question, Palmer, and I expect an honest answer." The captain's fingers are again intertwined on his desk, his shoulders hunched in an almost aggressive posture. He leans a bit forward and says, "Have you ever smoked marijuana?"

Palmer is both startled by the abruptness of the question and relieved by it. He raises his chin and returns the captain's inquisitive stare feeling as if he has never looked anyone so full in the face in his entire life. The captain's eyes are as penetrating as father eyes searching for a lie.

"No, sir, I have never smoked marijuana," Palmer says, this truth emerging untinged with guilt. It feels good to be able to tell a truth for once. An unnatural, exhilarating feeling.

The captain comes out of his slight lean, his clasped hands sliding as he sits back in his chair as if satisfied by what he has heard and seen. He might be in his late twenties, he's tanned, has a kind of Hollywood-handsome face, his hair neither long nor especially short, razor-cut. Palmer has always wondered about officers who are not infantry. Wouldn't that be the career goal of all men who go through academies or OCS? Do MP officers feel self-conscious talking to Infantry officers at cocktail parties?

"I understand you pulled MP duty at the Presidio," Captain Metzler says.

Palmer nods, feeling like a bug under a microscope, a STRAC bug so far, drug clean and baldheaded, looking the captain right in the eye and using the voice that he uses only when talking to anyone above the rank of sergeant, crystal-clear and seemingly interested in the excruciating subject at hand.

"There wasn't a lot of action at the Presidio, sir," Palmer says, though the captain probably knows how quiet stateside duty is. "I primarily wrote speeding tickets," using an adverb he almost never uses.

"Were you ever required by circumstances to draw your weapon in the line of duty?" the captain says.

"No, sir."

"Well, you're going to find MP duty here in Vietnam a lot different than stateside," the captain says. "The army has a big drug problem right now, and you're going to find yourself apprehending men using dope. The 109th has dealt with murder, rapes, and robberies. This is a different world than the Presidio, Palmer."

Palmer wants to say it sounds like New York City, but he hasn't quite got the nerve to crack wise with the captain. You can never tell about officers. Best to tip-toe at all times.

The captain asks a few personal questions about Palmer, as did the departing colonel, where he's from, but doesn't ask if he skis. Palmer tells him a little bit about his family, has a brother at Schofield Barracks, then the CO brings the interview to an end by welcoming Palmer to the 109th, like the last step in a process, as if there might have been an alternative outcome, which there could have been, Palmer knows. The army can pluck you out of an LZ and drop you down on an island in the war, or do the opposite. They both stand up, and the captain shakes Palmer's hand. Palmer wonders if this is the same man that Lattimore had made reference to, the asshole CO. He seems all right, but then Palmer probably does too.

When Palmer gets back to operations, Sgt. Wesser smiles and asks how it went, doubtless wondering about the pot question that the captain asks everybody. "It went fine," Palmer says. "We had a good conversation." Palmer never talks like this. The army makes him feel like even more of a fraud than he actually is. Wesser tells him he ought to hit the sack and get some rest, he'll be pulling twelve-hour shifts soon. Palmer says he plans to do just that, and as he walks out of the office he thinks what a burden it will be if he has to go on talking like this for the next year.

The shadows are starting to get long out in the company area. Palmer stands for a moment gazing off toward the mountains, trying to get a feel for whether or not he's tired. He doesn't feel tired, but sometimes it seems travel generates a constant small flow of adrenaline that makes him think he's wide awake when it's just stretched nerves. What he wants is a beer.

Men are coming out of the two barracks now, some of them in their skivvies with towels over their shoulders, shaving kits clutched in their hands, headed toward a building to the left of the EM club, a big tin shed that stands beneath a water tower like something out of a western, a metal tank on wooden struts that would hang over a waiting, chuffing train. Other men are crossing the sidewalk to the EM club. A silence hovers over the compound. There are no friendly greetings, shouts, conversations, it's not like the end of a high school day, kids gathered in the parking lot to smoke cigarettes out of sight of the nuns and talk bullshit loud senior talk. Palmer doesn't know why he should expect this place to be like that, but he does. Too many movies probably. Army movies are noisy, always cadence being chanted in the background, sergeants yelling, shots from the rifle ranges. But there are men sleeping here, always someone asleep in a company that has twelve-hour shifts. Palmer remembers now—the Presidio was like this when they finally got around to pulling road duty instead of the chickenshit details that ultimately drove Beaudry off to Korea.

Palmer follows two men along the narrow sidewalk and enters the EM club behind them, and is surprised by the chilled air as he steps inside, surprised by the whole layout, which is bathed in red and purple light. The walls are painted black, there are booths with seats upholstered in red oilcloth, the booths themselves painted black, everything wooden painted black, the purple glow of black-lights illuminating images on psychedelic posters, lifting the images an inch off each paper, but only a few of these, just enough to remind the men that they are not a part of the brown-boot army. Tables in the middle of the floor. Off to the left, the click of pool balls. It's like a cheesy lounge in America except cheesy in a good way, a two-in-the-morning way, with rock music playing but not loudly. Palmer can see no jukebox, no slot machines, it's not a very big building, but big enough. It serves only the 109th. Off to the right is the bar itself, you have to go up a step to get to it. Somebody who likes bars designed this place, Palmer can feel it as he takes that step up to the next level where a few men are seated at a counter that can serve a dozen men, including a couple of men seated at the short leg of the L where the counter turns toward the back wall. A door is cut into the counter, rises on hinges so the bartender can get out of the wooden cage that surrounds him all day, the heart of his fiefdom. Palmer pulls out ten cents' worth of funny money and orders a Bud from the barkeep who is wearing a gray sweatshirt, has a trim mustache, a young guy but big, his hair long on top but cropped close above the ears and neck like all MPs will be, Palmer knows now. Captain Metzler had struck him as the kind of CO who wouldn't put up with any rebel shit for one second. A record is revolving on a turntable behind the bar, feeding music through thin wires that Palmer follows with his eyes toward speakers planted in corners in the main room.

He takes a studied drink of his Bud and finds that while the beer is colder than down in Long Binh, it tastes about the same. He wonders if the hard liquor, the scotches and bourbons, have been ruined by shipment too. He will try that sometime, but he has never really been into hard stuff. He loves the taste of beer, the Germans call it liquid bread. Maybe he could get his brother Mike to mail him some real Budweiser.

He steps down onto the main floor and carries the can

across the room toward the sound of pool balls, through a doorway where the decor is different, the walls pale green and lit by naked lightbulbs. Two men are playing pool on a table that looks a bit dusty under the bumper overhangs. There are booths in here too, but plain wooden and painted green, like cafe booths where men who don't desire the ambience of a late-night lounge might bring their Cokes and oven-warmed burgers, might give up their oilcloth booths to men who need that.

Palmer opens a door thinking it might lead to a latrine, looks in and sees a small table, octagonal, covered with green felt. It's a poker table. Empty chairs around it. The room is tiny, and serves only one purpose. He closes the door and goes over to a booth beneath a window that gives a view of the barracks and operations building. He sits down and sips at his beer. He has decided not to get drunk on this first night at his final duty station, has decided that his nerves are simply stretched by travel and by the uneasiness of wondering if one form of projectile or another might arrive with suddenness. After finishing the rancid beer he decides to lay off drinking altogether until he has been here at least a week, just to avoid fucking up until he has gotten settled in, has established his presence, has deluded Sgt. Wesser to the fullest extent.

More men are coming into the club. MP jeeps are parking outside operations, and Palmer realizes that it must be getting close to time for shift change. That's when the barracks came alive back at Company D. The compound is waking up, there will be inspections of the graveyard shift, men taking over the jeeps from the day shift, a flurry of activity, and then the compound will quiet down again, but for the laughter and noise that is already starting to erupt at the bar, off-duty MPs doing what soldiers have always done at the end of a work day regardless of MOS. They look like everybody Palmer went through basic training with, like Krouse and Tigler and Brenner and Willerton. But for the small insignia that they wear on their breast pockets—a green clover-shaped MP battalion crest—you wouldn't even know they were hated by everybody else in the army.

CHAPTER 16

"Palmer, wake up." A stranger's voice pulling him from a hard sleep, Palmer opens his eyes and sees a Spec Four through the haze of mosquito-netting that has done little to stop the winged leeches from zeroing in on him. Bites on the backs of his hands, he rubs at them as the man speaks.

"I'm on CQ. Sgt. Wesser sent me to get you. He wants to see you down in operations right away."

It's dim in the barracks, the light from a far telephone pole faintly illuminating the other bunks where men are still sleeping. Palmer raises himself on his elbows and looks up at the CQ. "What time is it?"

"Getting toward oh five-hundred. Better hop to."

The man walks away without further explanation. Palmer lifts the netting, it gets tangled on his shoulders, he worms his way out of the bunk and unlocks the padlock on his wall locker thinking, a phone message from home. Somebody died. He can never stop thinking things like this, he hates telephones.

Slapping his cap onto his head as he walks out the door, he descends the stairway looking out across the dark city, lights here and there like any American city, even lights on the mountain like Lookout Mountain west of Denver, a string of them at the very top. Other men are walking around the compound, coming from the showers, getting ready for inspection of the guard for the day shift. Palmer wonders if he will be put on road patrol right away. He removes his cap and enters operations where Sgt. Wesser is just setting a phone in its cradle. The man looks up at him from his chair, a small smile shaping his lips. "Sorry to have to roust you on your first full day here, Palmer, but it's money-change day and all the Vietnamese help have been barred from the American compounds, so you're going to have to pull KP."

Palmer gazes at the sergeant speechless. Money change? "Yes, Sergeant," he finally says as if he understands, which he doesn't.

"All the new men will be pulling KP today. The executive officer will be bringing in a money pouch this afternoon. The KPs will be given time off to go change their MPC."

"What does money-change mean, Sergeant?" Palmer says, leery of sounding impolite but already beginning to bristle.

"The old MPC is going to be exchanged for new bills. Nobody knew this was coming, the army always keeps it a secret. They do it every six months to control the MPC going into the black market. Make sure you bring all your cash with you so you won't have to go back to the barracks." The smile on Sgt. Wesser's face appears slightly apologetic, but only in the sense that someone getting fucked over can be funny in its way—a mission is a mission. "They need you at the mess hall ASAP," Wesser says. "This caught the cooks by surprise too."

Palmer gathers in his umbrage and smiles at the sergeant. Would I rather be filling sandbags? He has all his money on him, tucked into his billfold which, ever since basic, he has made a practice of keeping under his pillow while sleeping. A Drill Sergeant suggested that the men slip their billfolds into their skivvies at night because if they caught someone digging around down there the thief probably wasn't interested in money anyway. Palmer's smile turns into a polite grin which is not so forced. He nods, walks out of operations, and slaps his cap onto his head, releasing his umbrage with this slight gesture. Fuck the army. He decides not to make a race out of it to sign up for pots-and-pans as he had done at his other duty stations during the past year. He will sign up for whatever is available. Nothing that he does or does not do will alter the fact that he will be in Vietnam three hundred and fifty-six days. And anyway it's too hot in this place to stand around all day in a steamy pots-and-pans alcove.

The mess sergeant gathers the KPs in the dining room after they all arrive, and gives them a little pep talk. He knows that GIs come to Vietnam expecting never to pull KP, and he asks that they simply do their job without griping. Another slightly insulting scenario, anybody who has made it as far as Vietnam knows that you just do your job and keep your griping for those times when the sergeants are out of earshot. The mess sergeant looks costumed for a play about the army, a clean white apron tied above the bulge of his belly, green T-shirt underneath, a white cook cap planted on his head. His face is plump, rounded from nibbling, Palmer supposes. A lifer for certain.

Palmer signs the roster to work out front in the dining room, filling salt and pepper shakers, sugar jars, sweeping the floor, scrubbing the green vinyl tablecloths with the 109th emblem planted square in the middle. He had eaten here last night, had expected that mess halls in Vietnam would look like mess halls in the movies, long tables like in a high school cafeteria, but these are like the tables in basic, AIT, Presidio. The food served on plates and not on divided metal trays. Is this a part of the New Action Army? Lure young men into enlisting by letting them stuff their gullets at a civilized place-setting. Palmer had come into the army expecting everything to be hard-core forever, but so far it's been like one long stint at a cheesy summer camp. It's probably hard-core out in the bush.

The men of the 109th come and go at breakfast and lunch, grinning at Palmer as he works his way around the room filling the milk machine or replacing napkins in the metal holders. They say friendly things, "You must be a new guy, huh?" with everybody knowing that they could as easily have been nabbed for KP if their circumstances had been different, like his brother Phil nabbed by the Infantry after he'd gone ahead and volunteered for the draft. But it's amusing to watch someone who has been fucked over, though nobody sticks it to the KPs. Palmer doesn't know if this is due to maturity, or the fact that everyone here has access to a gun.

On-duty MPs come in at different times, their lunch breaks staggered so there will always be enough men on the road, just as at the Presidio. Some of the MPs have holsters as shiny as black glass, the white stitching stark at the edges. Palmer used to think you weren't supposed to wear shiny stuff in a war zone, but then he used to think a lot of things.

At noon he takes a half-hour break for chow and to hike down to the seamstress shop where a woman who looks ninety years old hands him his jackets squared away with his name tags and battalion crests sewed on. He gives her the piasters that Sgt. Wesser had given him.

At three in the afternoon, after the cleanup from noon chow has been completed, after the dishes have been run through the machine, after the pot-and-pans man has scoured his last cauldron, the mess sergeant calls the KPs together and tells them that they will be allowed to go in pairs to the operations office where the XO is exchanging money. It's like a little big-deal. The KPs stand around outside the mess hall smoking cigarettes and watching as one pair and then another hikes across the parking lot to operations. Most of the KPs have been here less than a month, Palmer the newest newbie. He tries to make conversation and jokes the way he did in basic when nobody knew anybody. Men bum smokes but nobody wants a Camel, which is fine with Palmer. When his turn comes he hikes across the parking lot with another man. They enter operations where the XO is seated behind a desk which is covered with brand-new funny money, flanked by Sgt. Wesser and an armed MP in full uniform but for a helmet.

The company executive officer looks like a kid. Not skinny but lean, he has a baby face, handsome like a Disney teen star. He's a second lieutenant and looks no more like an officer than Palmer looks like a sergeant. He frowns as he does his job, counting out the money, making the men sign for it. There are the faintest of dark circles under his eyes, like that of a drinker, or else a man with a lot of responsibilities. He seems irritable, and Palmer wonders if it sticks in his craw knowing that second lieutenants are the butt of half the jokes in the army. Beetle Bailey gets more respect than Lieutenant Fuzz.

When sixteen-thirty rolls around, the mess sergeant calls the KPs together and tells them they are being relieved of duty. Another crew of KPs is coming on, newbies who have been given the day off so they can pull graveyard KP. MPs work twenty-four hours a day, and the men on road patrol who get off work at dawn sit in the EM club until ten A.M. when the booze is cut off for a couple of hours. Palmer now understands why the inside of the bar is painted black: nighttime ambience twenty-four hours a day.

When he gets back to the barracks that evening he pulls his web gear from his locker and lays it out on his bunk which is neatly made, the house girl having folded the mosquito-netting up over the frame so Palmer won't have to wrestle with it until he hits the sack. Seems worthless anyway. Bites on his neck flared up during KP. He took his first malaria pill when he was still at Oakland, just to get a jump on the yellow fever, and it scoured his intestines out. Sat on a commode for half an hour wondering if malaria itself could be any worse.

The holster that he requisitioned from supply is dull black, but has no scrapes or tears that would have to be repaired before standing inspection. He digs out his can of Kiwi, removes the stained and folded cotton cloth, and applies a tiny dab to the holster leather. He rubs in just enough to create a patina of clean black, not as shiny as the holsters that some of the MPs wear with the white stitches glowing. He wants to look good for inspection tomorrow morning. It's been a long time since he's put to use those two months of training at Ft. Gordon. Disassembled and reassembled a .45 in nine seconds flat. Disassembly was easy once you got the barrel bushing twisted aside, the weapon practically fell apart in your hands. Reassembly took longer, the instructor standing there with a stopwatch clutched in his palm while the troops fit the parts together like contestants on Beat the Clock. A trainee across from Palmer gave up and sat gazing around the room completely lost. "Time!"

Palmer attaches the holster to a green pistol belt and wraps the belt around his waist, adjusts it for his skinny frame. He weighs 170 now. He was 160 when he entered basic. Graduated from high school weighing 129 and stood six-foot two. The gym coach was always asking him if he was gaining any weight from using the school barbells, and Palmer would grit his teeth after saying no. "What the fuck does it look like to you?" he wanted to say, but who talks that way to coaches? Grownups drove him insane.

He takes hold of the holster and tugs down on it approximating the weight of a pistol, and adjusts the slack on his web belt. The pistol will weigh three pounds when he loads it. Funny how a .45 seems to change when you put a magazine of bullets into it. After you slip the pistol into your holster you're always aware of its presence, like a rabid cat clinging to your hip. In MP school he tied with Gilchrest for the highest score on the day they qualified with the .45, the two of them as amazed as everybody else, since he and Gilchrest had been known up to then as buddies who spent an inordinate amount of time at the small EM club down the block from the fifth platoon barracks, getting plastered and playing pinball. But Palmer has a theory about his good showing on that day: he didn't tense up when he stood on the firing line because he didn't have one ounce of faith that he was going to hit anything. It seemed a joke to him, there was no drama to qualifying with the pistol as there had been to qualifying with the M-14 in basic. As a consequence he was loose that day, relaxed, expecting nothing at all, not even taking it seriously, and scored 480 out of 500 points. His .45 jammed while he was lying in the prone position shooting at a silhouette target, and a range NCO came out and fiddled with it. The NCO stepped back from the firing line and told him to expend the remaining bullets. Palmer put five slugs into the man shape in less than three seconds, thinking erroneously that the hits weren't going to count since everyone else had finished firing. Poked a rising line across the target's belly, then found out all five holes were worth ten points each. In another round of target shooting he hit two bull's-eyes and put four bullets through the ring surrounding the bull's-eye, but the range NCO couldn't find his seventh and last hit, and so didn't give him credit for it. Palmer wanted to suggest that the last bullet had passed through the large rip in the bull's-eye itself, but decided to remain silent. Logic had never gotten him anywhere in the army.

CHAPTER 17

A t oh five-hundred hours the MPs going on day-shift fall
into formation outside operations. The sky above the
compound is no longer black at this hour, is grayish, the mess
hall and enlisted men's club and water tower slowly emerging like images in a Polaroid as the sun works its way across
the wall of the Pacific. The men are standing at ease, waiting
for the Officer of the Day, the Provost Marshal, to arrive in
his jeep to perform the inspection. The Sergeant of the Guard,
an E5 named Bennell, a young man, walks up and down the
ranks looking the men over, giving them a pre-inspection
inspection, the only one that really counts. He stops in front
of Palmer and looks at his black helmet with the 109th decal
on the front, looks at his web-gear, his pistol belt, his bloused
fatigue pants, the toes of his jungle boots.

"Did you sleep in those fatigues?" Sgt. Bennell says.

"No, Sergeant."

"How long have you been in this company?"

"Three days, Sergeant."

Bennell looks Palmer up and down, his jaw moving like
he wants to say more, then he turns and walks farther along
the line inspecting the rest of the men.

Palmer looks down at his new green fatigues, looks at the
men standing next to him. Their fatigues have been tailored,
probably at the seamstress shop down the road. Some of the
jackets and pants are form-fitting, pegged, they look sharp
compared to Palmer's ballooning rip-stop. His house girl
had washed and ironed his uniforms yesterday while he

was on KP, but just wearing them outside this morning, in this growing heat and humidity, has left them looking like they have been slept in. "They were issued to me looking like this," he wants to say, but doesn't. He has failed his first inspection for all practical purposes. He feels like he's back at the Presidio.

The Provost Marshal's jeep pulls into the company area, driven by a PFC. The Provost Marshal is a young man, a captain. He climbs out of the jeep and lifts his black helmet off his head for a moment, begins adjusting the headband. He combs his hair in a sweep across his forehead like Glen Campbell. Not a lifer. He's wearing web gear, a pistol, the toes of his jungle boots shined to a gloss. His tailored dark green starch-pressed fatigues look better than anyone's. He places the helmet square on his head, then walks up to the Sergeant of the Guard, who salutes. The PM performs the ritual of inspection without gigging anyone, not even Palmer, then climbs back into his jeep where the driver has been waiting. Dick job. Palmer wonders what it takes to become the Provost Marshal's personal driver.

After the captain is gone, Sgt. Bennell of the Guard takes his place in front of the squad and says, "All right, at ease. I've got an announcement to make. Omar is on the loose again. He escaped from a hospital in Phu Tai."

The other MPs laugh a bit. Even the sergeant grins. "He might be headed this way, so if you spot Omar, apprehend him."

"How did he escape, Sergeant?" one of the MPs says.

"He was handcuffed to his hospital bed, but they think he had a key hidden on him, probably in his mouth. His guard went to take a leak and when he got back Omar was gone."

This evokes more laughter, which makes Palmer feel like he is not a part of this group. Who is Omar?

It is full daylight now, though the sun has not yet risen above the ocean. Palmer is assigned to Unit 1 where he will be riding in the rear of a jeep with two Spec Fours, Hillis and Dobnik, big men, taller than Palmer's six-two, Hillis a black GI who wears sunglasses all the time—Palmer saw him in the EM club on his first night, seated in a booth. Maybe prescription lenses, or maybe the regulations about shades are lax here in Vietnam. In basic training anyone who was spotted wearing dark lenses had to hand them over to a Drill Sergeant so he could look through them to make sure they were prescription. Palmer took it to be a private scam, the men pretending to need shades for their tender eyes when they just wanted to look cool. Dobnik is white and looks like a cop from a big city, has a gut on him, looks like the sort of man who might join the LAPD when his time in service ends. MPs at the Presidio were always yakking about joining the LAPD.

The graveyard partners in the Unit 1 jeep pull into the company area and climb out, tugging at the hems of their jackets which bunch up under the pistol belts the way Class A greens did when Palmer was pulling patrol at the Presidio. Soldiers look good only when standing up. The pistol belt with its holster and nightstick holder and ammo pouch and first-aid kit and handcuff pouch at the back is bulky like Batman's utility belt. It's awkward to sit down with all that gear. Did the cartoonist who drew Batman serve in the MPs? Or maybe he was a telephone lineman.

"You'll be riding in the rear today, Palmer," Dobnik says in a sergeant voice even though he's only a Spec Four. He looks like he might be twenty-four, twenty-five, must weight two-fifty at least, has a plodding gait as he strides toward the jeep. "Climb in."

The canvas top is up on the jeep. Palmer ducks and works his way past the shotgun seat and sits on the long canvas seat in the rear, next to the radio which quietly hisses and clicks at random moments. He's a trainee again, won't be allowed to ride with a partner until he's seen how it works in Vietnam. Dobnik climbs into the driver's seat, the jeep rocking with his bulk. Hillis sits shotgun and picks up the mike and reports to the radio operator at the MP station across the airfield that Unit 1 is on the road.

Neither of the men say anything to Palmer until the jeep arrives at the TMP. Dobnik swings their vehicle across the road and onto the apron of concrete, pulls up at a big olive-drab gas pump.

"Do you know how to fill a gas tank on a jeep, Palmer?" Dobnik says, a bored sound to his voice, as if he isn't happy at having a trainee along.

"Yes," Palmer says.

"Then you gas up our vehicle and go sign for it in the shack," Dobnik says, not looking at him, gazing toward the airfield where a C-130 is landing at the far end.

Hillis climbs out and yanks his seat up giving Palmer room to exit. Eyes hidden behind the shades, jaw stoic, he looks like Linc on The Mod Squad. Palmer gasses up the jeep, then steps into a small shack where a sloppy-looking PFC is overseeing the TMP alone, wearing his cap indoors, seated on a high stool and reading a copy of The Pacific Stars and Stripes. Everyone hates the MPs, so Palmer isn't surprised when the man doesn't say a word to him, just taps on a space on a roster where he has to sign his unit name and the amount of gas pumped into the tank. It's all free. Palmer wonders if any gasoline from this place ends up on the black market.

Unit 1 follows the road around the airfield past the terminal, past the evac hospital, and out onto the civilian road. Dobnik asks Palmer how much MP experience he has, and Palmer tells him about his one month of road patrol at the Presidio.

"One month?" Hillis says without turning his head.

"Did you ever fill out a 1208?" Dobnik says. A standard Military Police incident report.

"Only in MP school," Palmer replies. "I was never involved in an incident at the Presidio that called for a 1208."

"How about a 2418?"

Accident report. "I never investigated any traffic accidents," Palmer says.

Dobnik gives up a small laugh, little more than a breath, a shake of the shoulders.

Palmer is beginning to get what the hippies call bad vibes from Dobnik and Hillis. Maybe it's because the sergeant had made that crack about his fatigues at inspection. Who wants a dud as a partner? They ride along in silence after this brief interrogation, Dobnik slowing the jeep and turning left into Camp Quincey, lifting a finger in acknowledgement to the two men pulling gate guard.

He drives around battalion headquarters into the dead-end and backs the jeep up to the bunker wall near the open double-doors of the MP station. Dobnik and Hillis climb out, and before Palmer has a chance to move Dobnik leans down and wiggles his index finger saying, "Let's go, Palmer," as if he's holding up the show, as if Palmer is an E1 and not an E2.

Palmer climbs out and follows them into the station. The desk sergeant is seated behind a high wall of wood on the left, on a platform that gives him an aerial view of the entire station including the three detention cells along the back wall. They are vacant right now. The radio operator is sitting on a chair behind the desk sergeant with headphones on, taking calls from road units. A Dagwood cooler with a single brown cup stands in one corner of the room.

"This is Private Palmer, he's a new man," Dobnik says in that bored voice. The word condescension passes through Palmer's mind. Palmer has begun to think of Dobnik as The Dude. Mister Cool. Supertroop. He has encountered other men like this, GIs who seemed destined to be lifers.

The desk sergeant grins at Palmer. He might be thirty-five but looks younger, has the clear bright face of a non-drinker, his longish black hair trimmed and combed neatly. There's a fastidious air about him, a lifer air. "Welcome to the 109th," he says.

"Thanks, Sergeant," Palmer says, returning the man's smile.

Then it's all business, the desk sergeant telling Dobnik and Hillis that a sergeant from the PX reported a break-in that took place during the night. Unit 1 has to check it out. Dobnik nods, tells the sergeant that he has to show Palmer around the PMO. The break-in can wait. It took place during the night, so Palmer senses that this is routine, that there will be no suspects collared.

Dobnik points at the D-cells. "Did you ever handcuff a prisoner?"

Palmer nods. "When I transported prisoners to the Presidio stockade."

Dobnik points to a small room through a doorway, the report room, furnished with a table and some chairs. "That's where you'll be writing up your 1208s, Palmer. Don't ever leave your weapon lying unattended in there or the desk sergeant will confiscate it and you'll have to go to the old man to get it back."

He leads Palmer through a doorway into the rear of the building, a long room divided into offices. File cabinets line one wall in the first office. "That's where your 1208s will end up, Palmer." Through the doorway into the next office, three men are sitting erect at desks working at typewriters. "These men will be typing up your handwritten 1208s, Palmer. Make sure your printing is legible." Dobnik seems miffed that Palmer has never filled out a 1208 on duty. Palmer is becoming tired of him, and hopes he doesn't have to ride with Unit 1 again.

Dobnik steps into a tiny office off the second room where a Spec Four is seated at a desk typing a report. The man grins, his eyes brighten when he sees Dobnik. "Hey!"

"What's happening, Shappler?"

"Gettin' short."

"This is Private Palmer, a new man," Dobnik says, pointing at Palmer with a thumb. "Palmer, this is Specialist Fourth-Class Shappler. He's the traffic man. You'll be giving your 1480s to him after you get around to investigating traffic accidents and I guarantee that you will be investigating traffic accidents."

Shappler smiles at Palmer, nods. There are two desks in this crowded room, and at one of them sits a pretty Vietnamese woman in a tight red dress, also typing a report, doubtless a 1208.

"Let's go, Palmer," Dobnik says, edging past him. At the end of the long room is another office where two men are seated at typewriters. "The Provost Marshal's private office is behind that door," Dobnik says, pointing at a closed and unpainted door that has a brass knob. Every wall and door in this place is painted pale green except that door. "All right, you've seen it all, let's get out on the road," Dobnik says, walking back through the long room and into the MP station proper, Palmer following in his wake.

Hillis is already outside, standing beside the jeep with the seat yanked forward. As Dobnik and Palmer step out of the MP station, Hillis lifts a finger and points at the backseat, jams his finger toward it like a Drill Sergeant giving a man an unspoken order. The hard-core act that seems to have been perfected by these two partners like two vaudevillians is beginning to grate on Palmer's admittedly thin skin. He stops and looks at the backseat, then looks at Hillis. "Will I get to drive the jeep today?" he says, even though he knows he won't be driving. He says it only to bug the man. But Linc doesn't say a word, just stands there slowly shaking his head no. Palmer climbs into the rear and settles back for a long day.

CHAPTER 18

The PX is a mile west of Camp Quincey, toward the mountains which rise steadily as the jeep moves along the road. The hillsides are green now and not blue as when he first saw them, the sunlight flush against their flanks which roll and dip like curtains, like the hills west of Denver, revealing patchy spots where the earth might have been hit by rockets or mortars. He can see a vehicle traveling along a road that rises at a slight angle, probably a truck, can see only its top moving up the hillside, tiny, looking so vulnerable, as vulnerable as Palmer feels in Unit 1 as it moves down the road bordered on both sides by Vietnamese. Old men walking, women squatting at the side of the road cooking things on small fires, children racing around, chickens clucking and pecking, fowl carcasses hanging from bamboo poles. It's only now that he realizes he hasn't seen a single bird on the wing since he arrived in Vietnam.

The PX is a large building, like a K Mart back home, painted white, a perfect target, an easy shot from the mountains which are more like the colonel's Vermont than the Rockies. Dobnik drives down an access road bordered by hiking American soldiers, half of them in dirty fatigues and floppy boonie hats instead of caps, their boots dusted orange with dried mud. A few M-16s here and there held by the handle on top, so unlike the M-14. Palmer wonders what genius at the Pentagon had designed that convenient grip. He feels an affinity for whoever it was. Probably pissed-off the brown-boots, a gun like a briefcase.

Dobnik turns left into the PX compound which is bordered by a cyclone-fence and concertina wire. The parking lot is like that of a K Mart too, white lines painted on asphalt, but Dobnik parks the jeep in front of the doorway. Official business. Palmer is starting to feel foolish being with these two poseurs, the way Hillis keeps his right hand hiked on the butt of his pistol as he strides through the doorway like he's prepared for a fast-draw.

The interior of the PX is exactly like a K Mart, vast aisles selling the same things you'd find at home, perfume and lamps, fans and cigarettes. It's air-conditioned, Palmer breathes deeply after he steps inside. He hopes the investigation will take a while. He loves this place already.

The man who had made the complaint about the break-in is a sergeant E7 who leads the MPs out back of the building and shows them a spot along the perimeter fence cut by somebody with an efficient tool. Links snipped creating a slit, whoever did it had gotten inside last night and stolen canned goods from a small storage shed nearby.

The E7 points at a guard tower fifteen meters away. "The guard claims he didn't hear anything. That fucker was probably asleep. I'll tell you what I'd like to do the next time this happens. I'd like to plant an AK-47 next to the hole and let those tower guards see it. That'd keep the bastards on their toes at night."

He's pissed. His fiefdom has been breached, though probably only by ordinary thieves and not VC. Dobnik writes things down in a notebook, but that's all MPs can do, take a report, there will be no sleuthing, no tracking of footprints, the rounding up of suspects. Dobnik tells the E7 he'll pass the report along to the CID. A security breach is a significant event, but Palmer can tell from Dobnik's attitude that nothing will come of it.

They walk back through the PX to get to their jeep, Palmer inhaling the chilled air and looking around at all the customers who but for their green fatigues could be suburban shoppers at his favorite mercantile back home. There is a long magazine rack near the front of the store where a score of GIs stand leafing through skin magazines. There are two rotating paperback racks. There's an entire aisle running from the front of the store to the rear stocked only with beer.

When they get outside Palmer slows down to see if Linc will reach in and raise the seat for him, but he doesn't. Palmer raises it, climbs in, sits back, and wonders what it takes to become the Provost Marshal's personal driver. Dobnik drives out onto the road that leads to Camp Quincey, but turns right toward the mountain. In less than three minutes they are nearing the base of a foothill which rises as abruptly as Lookout Mountain above Golden. "There's an AFVN transmitting station at the top of this mountain," Dobnik says, and Palmer thinks of the string of white lights he had seen from the 109th compound yesterday morning. The asphalt road makes a hairpin turn to the right at the base of the mountain, but a dirt road veers off the main road at the apex of the curve and weaves up the side of the hill, disappearing behind one of the earthen folds of what Palmer now knows for certain is a Viet Cong domain because Dobnik mentions that Camp Quincey was hit by mortars two weeks earlier, the VC poking a neat line of mortar strikes across the softball field from a position on the mountain.

"Did you hear Clermont got a Purple Heart?" Hillis says, turning his head to Dobnik.

Dobnik glances at him. "He was hit?"

"Piece of flying concrete cut his thumb."

"Shit," Dobnik says, giving up another breathy chuckle, a single shake of the shoulders.

"Who's Clermont?" Palmer says, and for one moment he thinks neither of the men is going to answer. He's about to repeat his question just to bug them with newbie persistence but Dobnik says, "Supply captain at battalion," in that bored voice.

Palmer loses interest altogether in his day of training, sits silently in the rear of the jeep as Dobnik travels the backroads surrounding Qui Nhon, pointing out the places that all MP newbies need to know about, the ammo dump beyond a single mountain to the north of the city, the T intersection that leads up to Phu Tai where the 638th MP company is located, then driving to a place called The Mariner's Club, a bar located on a compound where merchant Marine ships are docked. Dobnik tells him that occasionally MPs are called to the club to apprehend drunk GIs. He drives past a building downtown where the Vietnamese military police, the TC, are headquartered. MPs pull combined patrols with Vietnamese partners. Qui Nhon is a bustling city like Saigon though not as big, and doesn't smell like much of anything at all. The city rests on a vast triangular chunk of land that juts out into the South China Sea. Maybe the sea breeze combs the shit smell out of the air constantly. Not even a fish smell, but he might be used to it by now. He wonders what it's like in An Khe and Pleiku where Lattimore and the others are stationed, out where the war is.

At noon they eat in the 109th mess hall, but Palmer sits at a table with three off-duty men, one of whom smells like beer. It reminds Palmer of his half-baked promise to himself that he would avoid drinking until he had been here at least a week, but he knows now that when he gets off duty at eighteen-hundred he will be heading for the EM club. Nothing he does or does not do will alter the fact that he has three hundred and fifty-four days left in Vietnam. The era of making personal vows has ended and he knows it. He remembers how he had struggled to give up smoking at the Presidio, thinks about it as he steps outside the mess hall and lights up a Camel, waiting for Dobnik and Hillis to finish chow. He can't wait for this dull day to end. Sitting in the rear of the jeep like a sack of potatoes reminds him of MP school. He wants his own partner and his own jeep. He wonders how soon he will get his PFC stripes.

During the afternoon there are no calls over the radio for Unit 1, the day flowing by as quickly as it had at the Presidio. Palmer likes MP duty a lot, likes having a little bit of power, the authority to handcuff a sergeant if a situation starts to get out of control, though that has never happened yet. And ticketing officers, he looks forward to doing that someday. Never got the opportunity at the Presidio. The highest ranking man he ever ticketed was a Spec 6 at Ft. Chronkhite across the Golden Gate Bridge. But that ticket was pulled.

Toward the end of the shift Palmer decides to go ahead and ask a question that's been bugging him, even though he would just as soon never speak to these two guys again.

"Who is this guy Omar that the sergeant mentioned this morning?" he says.

Dobnik and Hillis glance at each other and grin, then Hillis tosses a glance back at Palmer and says, "He's this fucking dud infantry dude that went AWOL a couple years ago. He's been caught a bunch of times but the asshole keeps escaping."

Palmer decides not to ask any more about Omar, but then Dobnik says, "He lives with the Vietnamese. He moves around the country a lot, trying to avoid getting caught." He tosses Palmer a glance too and says, "He's a black guy."

Palmer ponders this information. An AWOL who lives among the Vietnamese. Sneaking around Vietnam trying not to get apprehended, court martialed, jailed. What a life. He wonders if the man is a drug addict or something, but doesn't ask.

Unit 1 returns to the MP station at seventeen-thirty. Palmer is told to stand and watch while Dobnik sits at the table in the report room and fills in the information on a 1208 concerning the PX break-in. At the above time, date, and location, etc. Cops on TV shows always complain about the avalanche of paperwork. They want to be out on the street busting hippie pot pushers. After Dobnik finishes he scoots his chair back and stands up, taps the 1208 with his pencil and says, "That is how you fill out a 1208," as though a running argument has been irrefutably resolved. Not condescension but contempt. Palmer doesn't nod, doesn't say a word, just hopes he never has to ride with supertroop again.

The Unit 1 day-shift goes off-duty as soon as Dobnik wheels the jeep into the 109th company area. Palmer climbs out and walks to the arms room, clears his .45 over the sand barrel, turns it in, then heads up to his bunk to get out of his web gear. He thinks about taking a shower as he shoves his pistol belt into his locker, then decides to wait until after he's had a few beers. He will be going on the road tomorrow again, so cannot do any heavy drinking tonight, a six-pack at the most. Small cans. As a civilian he rarely drank twelve ounce Buds, only sixteen, and always kept at least two six-packs in the refrigerator in the basement apartment where his brother Mike is probably drinking right now and watching TV, unless he's at work. What time is it in Denver?

Palmer steps into the EM club. Not too many men in here right now, MPs are still coming off duty. He takes that small step up to the bar where the barkeep is placing beers into a pop cooler. The same man Palmer saw on the first night, wearing a sweatshirt with the word "Purdue" stenciled across it.

"Small Bud, please," Palmer says, and the man fishes through the cooler for a cold one, hands it to Palmer, his upper lip disappearing beneath his thick mustache as he smiles.

"You're new here, aren't you, Palmer?" the bartender says, glancing at Palmer's nametag.

"I got here three days ago."

The man goes back to work, talking as he stacks cans. "Where you from?"

"Denver, where are you from?" Palmer replies quickly to avoid ski talk.

"Phoenix," the man says with a groan, lifting a case of beer to the counter, then pulling out cans.

"What's your name?" Palmer says.

"Kennimere." The man has that slightly husky, naturally

hoarse voice that some people have that makes you want to clear your throat when they talk to you.

Palmer asks why there's a record player on the shelf against the wall, did they ever have a jukebox in here? Kennimere tells him that the player belongs to him, that they had a radio in here to pick up AFVN before he took over as bartender. "I pick the records I want to hear," he says, smiling with his lips clamped together, his cheeks bulging. Sounds to Palmer like The Moody Blues flowing quietly from the speakers. Acid rock bores him.

"Can you tell me something?" Palmer says.

"I'll try."

"Do you know anything about an AWOL named Omar? Sgt. Bennell told us he just escaped from a hospital in Phu Tai."

A grin stretches Kennimere's cheeks. "Omar," he says, shaking his head. "Yeah, he's a black GI that went AWOL a long time ago. Deserted his unit I guess. He lives out in the countryside. The Vietnamese help him get by. He's a nut case. Every time the MPs catch him he manages to escape."

"Is he...like...a criminal or something?" Palmer says.

Kennimere shakes his head no. "He's just an AWOL. They've been trying to catch him for years. He keeps getting away. He just doesn't want to be in the army I guess."

"Have you ever seen him?"

"Nope. He's never been caught in Qui Nhon. Not while I've been here anyway."

"Why do you suppose he was in a hospital in Phu Tai?" Palmer says.

"I don't know," Kennimere says, then laughs. "Maybe he

got bit by a snake and came in for treatment. I guess he knows he's always gonna get away."

Palmer smiles, and tries to imagine what it would be like to roam free in a war zone, hiding out from the authorities, hating the army so much that you would rather live in Vietnam than fight in its war. Like a draft dodger back home, running to Canada, or just plain running.

By the time Palmer has finished his third beer, the creep of alcohol has smothered the day's minor disgusts like small flames being extinguished leaving him floating serenely in a nighttime ambience. He's interested in knowing how Kennimere got this job, like the PM's personal driver, but waits until he has drained his fifth beer. "How did you get assigned to this bartending job?" he says, leery of saying dick job, since you never know how touchy a lockout might be.

Kennimere wipes his hands on a rag, grins at Palmer, and says he used to be the turnkey at the MP station but a prisoner stole his keys. They had to use a torch to cut the lock off a D-cell. They found the keys hidden inside the man's skivvies. Strip search.

"It wasn't Omar was it?" Palmer says, even though Kennimere told him he's never seen Omar.

The question makes Kennimere laugh softly, then he frowns and says, "Naw, just some white guy. The battalion commander fired me and demoted me to PFC after that. So Captain Metzler took me off the line and made me the company bartender. I'd like to go up to the battalion commander someday and shake that man's hand. He changed my life."

Some men don't like to talk about their travels up and down the ladder, but Kennimere doesn't seem to mind. His eyes sparkle, his grin muffled by his thick mustache after he finishes his story. He's a satisfied man, another manifestation of that army truth: just screw up. He has the air of a college student, though maybe it's just the Purdue sweatshirt he's wearing. Palmer has always liked college students, liked the idea of them, the casual, intellectual air of those he has met personally, friends of his brothers back in Denver mostly, though even the GIs he has met who've been to college have something easygoing and articulate about them. While he knows that he himself could go to college on the GI Bill after the army, he has no intention of doing so. He hates school. Even seated at desks in the classrooms at Ft. Gordon he had experienced that murky, trapped feeling that had tormented him during his four years of high school. If he were to go on to college after the army, he doesn't doubt for a second that the teachers would drive him insane.

CHAPTER 19

Palmer pulls MP duty the next day with a partner named Gosnell, a quiet PFC whom Palmer has trouble drawing out in conversation. The man doesn't seem to want to talk about much of anything, but his reticence does not make the day last any longer. There are no incidents to investigate, and they write no traffic tickets. They drive around the city waiting for something to happen, and the day is over almost as soon as it has begun, it seems. On Palmer's third day of work Sgt. Wesser assigns him to gate guard duty at Camp Quincey, and tells him to get some sleep because he will be pulling the grave-yard shift. After that he will have to pull hospital guard.

In a small way it is like duty at the Presidio where Company D had pulled one month of road patrol followed by a month of classroom training followed by a month of shit details, policing the landscape of Sixth Army Headquarters, a sched-ule that Palmer hated. But he doesn't mind this rotation very much because he is interested in learning the different jobs that will be required of him in Vietnam, just as he was interested in learning everything about being a soldier when he entered basic, before he found out how the army really worked.

On the night that Palmer pulls gate guard, the Viet Cong on the mountains fire mortars that strike somewhere to the north of the city, too far away for Palmer to feel the impact of the explosions either in his boots or in the air. When he hears the first rip of artificial thunder in the distance, it seems odd to be so near the true source of the sound-effects of Hollywood movies. Boom. His partner, a Spec Four named Mundt, tells him that the VC are probably trying to hit the ammo dump in order to make the stored bombs explode.

"They hit it every two months or so," Mundt says. "If they hit a big enough bomb, the ARVN barracks next door fall down."

Adjacent to the western perimeter of Camp Quincey is a small compound occupied by the South Vietnamese Army. Their one-story barracks appear to be made of bamboo and woven straw mats, like ridiculous miniature imitations of American barracks, and which cannot withstand the impact of the detonations of the larger bombs on the far side of the mountain north of town. Mundt tells him that sometimes after a VC attack you'll see ARVN out there rebuilding their barracks.

Palmer grins at this, looks off to the north. There is nothing to do inside this small wooden shack except sit on a high stool and listen, and hope that a bomb doesn't come this way. Be ready to duck below the sandbagged walls, but by the time you've decided to duck it will probably be too late—the muzzle velocity of a .45 caliber bullet is 830 feet per second, so he can imagine how fast mortar fragments dissipate into air, wood, flesh. He has discovered that pulling gate guard causes him to dwell upon minutiae, as though a kind of safety resides in analyzing each particle of the things he fears, because there isn't much else to do on gate guard.

The stuttering thump of Hueys comes from the airfield. Palmer looks down the road toward the evac hospital and sees white lights gathering, five or six helicopters slowly coming this way, as if using the road that runs adjacent to Camp Quincey as their guidon in the night, the headlights on

their noses pointed downward, tracing the asphalt. Palmer
steps outside the shack to watch them pass overhead. He
can't see their rotors, sees only the underbellies of the
choppers lit by streetlights as they drift past at treetop level
like a school of olive-drab whales floating west.

"This is going to be good," Mundt says.

The sounds of the choppers fade as they fly toward the
PX, cross over it, then separate and begin spreading out in a
combat formation, their fantails easing back and forth, the
Hueys now like tiny fish idling against a river's current. A
circle of light suddenly appears on the mountainside, a white
disk that must cover twenty square acres, and at first Palmer
thinks it has come from a helicopter. The circle probes the
hillsides, slithers along its rills and gullies in search of VC,
moves as rapidly as if Palmer himself were twitching the beam
of a hand-held flashlight across the far ranges, thousands of
meters swept in less than a second. Palmer raises his eyes to
the sky and sees the beam that casts the light, like a spotlight
you would see outside a movie theater at a premiere, though
he has never seen one in person but has seen them in the
movies.

"What's that light?" he says, looking over at Mundt who
is standing beside him with a smile of anticipation on his
compressed lips, his arms folded, studying the practiced
choreography of the Hueys. Before Mundt can reply, one of
the choppers fires a rocket, Palmer hears the roaring hiss,
hears the impact on the mountainside and looks back to see
the fading of the detonation, its white smoke boiling, and
another rocket is fired, flashes on the hillside, the sound
delayed like the crack of a baseball bat arriving after the white

flash has disappeared. Boom. He feels it through his boots, a soft single shudder. Tracer bullets streak toward the side of the mountain, the Hueys now like angry spiders spinning endless red threads, raking the gullies, the rills, the folds as the circle of white light stops, creating a bull's-eye target for the bullets tearing up the earth.

"That's a spotlight they got set up on top of the mountain over there," Mundt explains, pointing off to his right, although Palmer already has traced the beam across the sky toward the source, the very tip of the mountain north of town, beyond which lies the ammo dump.

Palmer hears voices behind him. He turns and looks across the compound and sees GIs standing in the dirt road, standing on the balconies of barracks, standing with towels wrapped around their waists, standing in T-shirts or bare-chested, holding cans of beer or Coca-Cola or nothing at all, watching the light show on the mountain. Men are drifting toward the main gate, so Palmer and Mundt move back inside the small shack where their view of the one-sided battle is not as good, but you never know, an officer might walk by and demand to know why you aren't positioned inside your duty station five feet away.

The battle sounds cease, the faint pulse of the earth no longer throbbing at irregular intervals through Palmer's soles. The massive spotlight begins to drift slowly north along the hillsides, its shape changing as it traces every mound and crevice like a flattened liquid cat in a cartoon sliding off a chair.

A dozen GIs have edged up toward the fence adjacent to the main gate, their chins lifted as they watch the Hueys silently hovering around their area of operations. One man steps away from the fence and strolls toward the gate shack with his arms folded, nods at Palmer and stops to take another look at the show before speaking. "I hope that's all that happens tonight," he says casually, glancing at Palmer but seeming almost to be speaking to himself. Palmer nods in agreement. The man's name tag says "Aldhoff." He's a Spec Four. He unwinds one of his arms, points a finger at the formation hanging in the sky and says, "They might send some Phantom jets from Phu Bai. They did that the last time the ammo dump got hit."

"Where's Phu Bai?" Palmer says.

The man drops both arms and steps closer to the shack. "About forty miles north of here. It only takes a minute for the jets to get here." He looks at the mountain, then says, "I got guard duty down at the motor pool at ten o'clock."

Palmer is a little bit surprised by the man saying ten o'clock instead of twenty-two hundred. Since basic training almost every GI he has met has glommed onto army jargon and used it as if to distance himself from any taint of civilian status. Everything is done ASAP. A truck is the little ball on top of a flagpole. Everyone wants to give up his identity and fit in fast, like hippies talking in whispers and saying everything is groovy and a gas. Palmer knows he himself is enough of a fraud without embracing other people's fraud.

Aldhoff lights up a cigarette and watches the sky. No Phantom jets show up, and there are no more explosions, though the Hueys continue to prowl above the hillsides, now like rangy and frustrated hunting hounds vexed by the lingering odor of rabbit. Aldhoff nods as if satisfied that the action is over for tonight, and he begins field-stripping his half-smoked cigarette. "Well...I guess I'll be seeing you around ten," he says, grinning at Palmer. "Will you still be on duty?"

"Until six A.M.," Palmer says.

"Catch you later," Aldhoff says, turning and strolling down the dirt road toward a dark cluster of barracks where the battalion MPs stationed on the compound live. Farther down the road stand more barracks where a quartermaster unit is located. Mundt had told him earlier that most of the quartermaster men work at the motor pool just down the road, adjacent to the airfield, where Aldhoff will be standing guard tonight.

The Hueys slowly congregate in a flight formation and return to the airfield, their white lights again tracing the road, the treetops battered by their passing, and after they are gone the GIs wander back toward their barracks. The night grows quiet, leaving Palmer to gaze at the mountains now black and indistinguishable from the sky, and to ruminate upon the minutiae that he knows will grow more refined as his tour tediously progresses toward his discharge.

A few minutes before ten P.M. Aldhoff emerges from the darkness of the clustered barracks wearing a steel helmet, a flak jacket, a pistol belt, and carrying an M-16 like a briefcase. He doesn't appear to have any ammunition, no bandoleer, but maybe they keep the ammo down at the motor pool. Aldhoff gives Palmer and Mundt a flicker of a wave with his empty hand. Mundt raises his chin and grins at him, gives him the go ahead with a quick wave. Aldhoff steps out through the open gate and trudges down the road toward the motor pool.

An hour later Palmer sees a man coming toward the main gate from the direction of the motor pool, and when he passes beneath a streetlight he sees that it is Sp/4 Aldhoff.

The man steps through the main gate and raises his hand in greeting to the two guards, but says nothing. He goes on down to his barracks.

"That was short guard-duty," Palmer says to Mundt. Guard duty in basic had lasted two hours, two-on and four-off, and gate-guard here lasts twelve hours. Palmer is amazed that there is one-hour guard duty in Vietnam.

Mundt seems reluctant to make any reply. He glances toward the motor pool, then finally says "Aldhoff wasn't going on guard duty."

Palmer absorbs this information, but doesn't quite know how to respond to it. Finally says, "Well...where did he go?"

"To see Madame K," Mundt says, a smile shaping his lips.

"Who?"

"Prostitutes," Mundt says. He speaks softly, though there is no one else around to hear this conversation. "We let MPs go off compound to visit the prostitutes that work down by the motor pool. We never let quartermaster men go outside the fence at night. Aldhoff works in the MP station. He's a clerk-typist."

Mundt looks away then, as if to indicate that this conversation is over. But something has been communicated to Palmer, something about a bond between MPs like the bond that once existed among the trainees back in basic: help your buddy. Rules, regulations, laws, they all bend in the presence of power, like rays of starlight passing near the gravitational field of the sun. No wonder everybody hates the MPs.

CHAPTER 20

The next night Palmer is given a ride over to the evac hospital by an MP unit just going on duty, two men whom he hasn't met before. They let him off in the hospital parking lot not far from the Huey pad, then point at a door on the second floor, Ward 2, where wounded POWs are kept under surveillance by MPs.

All the sidewalks around the hospital have wooden roofs, like long carports, probably to protect men on stretchers being evacuated to bunkers during mortar attacks. Must be terrible to have to stay in a bed in a war zone, unable to run to a bunker, have to wait for the medics to help you, or your buddies, if you have any. Hate to be a wounded MP in a ward full of infantry, but then maybe the wound itself would forge a bond. You have something in common: strangers have tried to kill you.

Palmer climbs a wooden stairwell to the second floor. The entrance to Ward 2 is at the northwest end of the building, he can see the mountains from here but not the bay. The hospital wards stand at the south end of the airfield where he had first arrived, the north-south runway like a vertical leg of the triangle that is Qui Nhon reaching into the sea. He opens the door and removes his MP helmet and steps into the ward, and it is like stepping off the airplane when he arrived in Vietnam, except that he is plunging into a curtain of chilled air and not the gelatinous city-dump stink of Bien Hoa. It's almost stunning the relief he feels as he walks into the ward, sweat seeming not to evaporate but simply disappear from his body, as if he has left Vietnam altogether and has stepped out onto a mountain peak in Colorado. Except there is a distinctly medicinal odor in the air, not especially unpleasant, but he could do without it. The ward is lined on both sides with beds, and in each bed that he passes there is an unconscious American soldier with a bandaged or plastered limb, or an affliction that Palmer cannot see but which brings him back from a mountain peak and sets him down in Vietnam.

The man that Palmer is relieving is Spec Four Bowen, the MP who had driven him to the 109th on his first day in Qui Nhon. Bowen shows him the POW, who is lying unconscious on a bed at the very end of the ward, segregated from the Americans. Palmer's job will be to see to it that nobody harasses or harms the POW, and see that he doesn't escape. "Other than that, the job is pretty boring," Bowen tells him. "They've got some paperback books on a shelf over there," he says as he gathers up his gear and prepares to leave the ward. He shows Palmer a sheet of paper with special orders written down, what to do in case of an emergency, the phone number of the MP station. Palmer's duty station is a table and a chair situated ten feet from the POW's bunk. That's all there is to the job.

While Bowen speaks, Palmer thinks about the POW, whose eyelids are not completely shut even though he is unconscious. Palmer wants to take a closer look at him in the way he had wanted to walk up to the first Vietnamese women he saw in Bien Hoa. Half a lifetime of Walter Cronkite, and now here's a communist. The face of the enemy. Bowen finally says catch you later and walks down the aisle between the beds, the MP unit waiting to take him back to the 109th.

A few wounded men are sitting up in bed now, one of them opening a newspaper, but none of them say anything to Bowen. He pushes through the door, steps outside, and Palmer looks around at his prisoner, whose mouth is hanging half open, whose breathing is shallow, whose eyes are not fully closed. Palmer thinks of Omar. Escaped from a hospital in Phu Tai with a key hidden in his mouth. But this man doesn't look like he can even stand up.

Palmer walks over to the bed and looks into the man's half-lidded eyes, sees a tiny glimmer, the reflection of a light at a nurse's station on the other side of the room. Head shaved bald, jaundiced chest naked, his fingers motionless but curled as if trying to clutch something, the man seems barely to be breathing. His legs are covered with a sheet. Captured somewhere out beyond the city limits of Qui Nhon, wounded, but Palmer can see no scars, no bandages. Bowen told him men from Military Intelligence are waiting for the POW to regain consciousness so they can interrogate him. What will they learn? Palmer turns and looks down the length of the ward where nurses in green fatigues are beginning to make bed checks. White women, almost as big as him, first lieutenants and second lieutenants. What motivates women to join the army?

He goes to the table and pulls the chair out and sits down. He glances at his wrist. He needs a watch, but then as he looks around the ward he sees a clock on the wall above the nurse's station, big enough for all the wounded men to see, to mark their time. Twelve hours for Palmer. Who knows how long for all these grunts? He assumes they are grunts. Who else gets hospitalized in a war? Traffic accident victims maybe. Engineers hurt in construction accidents. Men falling down in showers.

He again looks at the POW who has not moved, then realizes he should have brought a paperback book along. He almost never goes anywhere without a paperback to kill time, had read a part of *Dracula* on the flight across the Pacific. He had always wanted to read *Dracula*, since it was a classic like Frankenstein which he'd read for a class in high school, and he figured he might as well tackle Bram Stoker before he dies. He gets up and walks down the aisle to the hallway that leads to the latrines, and examines the bookshelf that Bowen had pointed out, begins reading the spines. James Bond. Matt Helm. He picks up a promising book and reads the back blurb, *Sherlock Holmes meets Jack the Ripper*, but it is not by Conan Doyle so he puts it back. He's a purist about some things, recognizes fraud when he sees it. He picks up another book, *The Liveliest Town in the West*, by the author of *The Hallelujah Trail* a blurb tells him. A comic novel, something light and funny, this is what Palmer wants. He carries the book back to the table thinking about *The Hallelujah Trail*, supposedly set in Denver, an epic farce like *Cat Ballou*, Hollywood always putting out these must-see comedies. *The Russians Are Coming, Dr. Strangelove, 2001*, which wasn't a comedy but was must-see, wasn't even very interesting, except the part where Keir Dullea breaks back into the spaceship. That was cool, something finally happening in a movie that was all talk talk talk, although the photography was great. But he could see through the phony ending, visual gibberish like the lyrics of a Bob Dylan song that's supposed to impress you with its profundity. His brother Mike loves

Bob Dylan. Palmer likes the sound, the melodies, the voice, *Positively Fourth Street*, *Like a Rolling Stone*, but shit, anybody could write gibberish lyrics, like the visual gibberish at the end of *2001*. He saw Keir Dullea in David and Lisa when he was fifteen and it made him feel like an intellectual.

The building shivers as a soft boom rolls across Qui Nhon, across the evac hospital, across the airfield, and the 109th, and beyond. Palmer sets the paperback down and sits absolutely motionless, waiting for another explosion. The VC must be tossing mortars again. He suddenly wants sky over his head, wants to be able to see everything around him, feels trapped inside this box of a room and wants to get out, to be able to see if there's somebody he has to shoot at. He's glad he's good with the .45. Barely made sharpshooter with the M-14, but then he might be better with the M-16, a crazy spring in its butt to absorb the kick, probably thought up by the genius who designed the briefcase handle. Palmer scoots his chair back and stands up, casually turns and begins strolling down the aisle between the beds where men are sleeping. Nobody but himself seems to have noticed the boom. Maybe it takes more than the gentle shiver of a building to alarm infantrymen. Probably more attuned to real danger than Palmer ever will be.

He pushes the door open and the humidity almost takes his breath away, the heat and stink, the metallic odor that he had smelled at Bien Hoa coming back to him. The medicinal air of the ward must have washed out his sinuses or something. He steps out onto the long balcony and closes the door and looks off toward the mountains. No more bombs, just the soft sounds of the city, the putter of Hondas on the nearby civilian road. He would rather pull his twelve hours standing right here where he can see everything, except the ward air is dry and cool. Everything is a tradeoff. If a mortar hits the hospital, what difference will it make if he's inside or outside?

After a minute he goes back inside, walks up the aisle and sits down on the chair and looks back along the aisle at the door, and imagines VC bursting in and spraying the ward with bullets. He'll never make it through this year if his brain doesn't shut up. He opens the paperback and tries to concentrate, tries to ignore the sensation that at any moment something is going to thump the back of his head.

A male aide comes into the ward to check on the POW, a semi-noisy man who cracks jokes with the nurses though not loudly. His hair is short but the same length all over, sticks up like the hair on the head of a red monkey, his upper-lip long like that of Joe E. Brown, simian too. The nurses smile at his quips, but Palmer can't tell if he amuses them or if he is just a pain in the ass. He looks like a lifer. A Spec Five, his fatigues are rumpled and unpegged. It seems to Palmer that most non-MPs are slovenly in some small way, but maybe their lack of pride is their pride. Maybe doing their duty is all that matters. That's how he felt at the Presidio, but he's always surprised whenever he encounters someone like himself. Puts things into an embarrassing perspective.

He is relieved after six hours by a road MP so he can go down to the hospital mess hall for chow. On the walk to the mess beneath the carports he notices huge webs up in the rafters where the wooden supports meet the roof. Bloated yellow spiders crouch motionless in the webbing, which is like dirty cotton candy stuffed into the corners. There are webs all along the roof, and dozens of spiders on every web, though no dangling spiders. It's like something out of the awful dreams that Palmer had when he was a kid, trapped in a basement filled with dangling insects. Too many monster movies, and he was scared shitless of basements when he was a kid anyway. His bedouin family had lived in a lot of old houses, his father always being transferred to another city by the Woolworth Company. He hasn't had one of those dreams in years, but he supposes now they will return.

The mess hall is not very big. The cooks serve roast beef and potatoes. There aren't too many people eating on the graveyard shift, slovenly medics and doctors in white smocks wandering down the chow line choosing food for their trays. None of the nurses looks slovenly. One of them is a blonde with a hell of a tan, looks like a *Playboy* centerfold but for the fatigues. Palmer eats quickly to get back and relieve the MP who had relieved him. He has half-an-hour to eat, but that's only official. Help your buddy. The man will want to get back on the road.

Palmer walks back beneath the long carports looking up at the spiders and wondering why the other people on the sidewalk returning to their posts aren't looking up. Must be used to it. What a thing to have to get used to. He enters Ward 2 and relieves the MP who is sitting at the table reading nothing, just staring at the floor. After the MP leaves, Palmer walks over and looks at his POW who has not changed positions in the past six hours. He wonders if this Viet Cong ever killed any Americans. Looks like he might be older than forty. Hard to tell. Might have killed French soldiers a long time ago.

Palmer goes over to the table, sits down and opens his comic novel and tries to lose himself in it. If he had a TV he would watch that instead, the effort of reading more fragile than staring at a moving picture. When he was a kid he could lose himself in Huckleberry Hound oblivious to his mother's vacuuming.

"Your prisoner escaped."

Palmer is following the antics of a town drunk when he hears these words behind his head. He looks around quickly and sees the male aide, his lips spread in a big-toothed grin, his eyes squinting below his high forehead and red bristles.

"What?" Palmer says.

"Your prisoner escaped," the aide says, and Palmer twists his head further and sees the POW lying on the bed.

"He's dead," the aide says.

Palmer sets the book down and stands up, goes over to the bed. The POW looks the same to him, same clutching posture, same half-lidded eyes, but when Palmer bends down to examine the eyes they no longer reflect the light from the nurse's station. There is nothing there at all. Opaque.

Palmer stands erect and looks at the aide, who is still grinning like a happy kid or a drunk at a party waiting with anticipation to hear laughter or applause at a joke memorized from a magazine.

Must be an old joke, escape, and jokers never tire of repeating themselves, but Palmer perceives that this is what this obnoxious man must say because he deals with death all the time. Palmer has seen one dead man before, lying in a coffin, a suicide named Thorpe, his face waxy, shining, but Palmer had never thought to joke about it.

"What should I do?" he says, the words springing from his mouth before he thinks not to say them. He knows what to do. Call the MP station and report it.

"Nothing you can do," the aide says, smiling, and for the first time Palmer notices that the man is holding a rolled bandage in one hand, flesh-colored, like an Ace bandage that a basketball player might wrap around his knee. "Your job is over, MP. Just sit back and take it easy." Then the aide goes to the bed and strips away the sheet and begins doing something so peculiar that Palmer cannot bring himself not to watch.

The aide wraps a bandage around the top of the POW's head and under his jaw, cuts the bandage and ties it off so the man looks like someone with a toothache in a cartoon. Binds the corpse's hands together, binds his ankles. With a piece of string he attaches a thin piece of cardboard to the dead man's right big toe, like a luggage tag, and writes something on it. Then he walks out of the ward.

Palmer goes to the nurse's station and tells a first lieu- tenant seated at the desk filling out paperwork that his POW has died and he needs to call the MP station, and asks if he can use her phone. She pushes it toward him with the tip of a finger. The desk sergeant says he will send a unit over to pick him up and take him back to the 109th.

The aide returns carrying a body-bag which he unfolds and spreads out on the bed next to the inert form. Palmer sits down at the table to wait for his ride, and to watch the aide do his job, deftly slipping the bag around the corpse, rolling the shoulders and hips this way and that until the rubber fabric is beneath the body. Zips it up. A quick and efficient piece of work. He's done this often enough to get good at it. The smile never once leaves his face.

CHAPTER 21

There's something bleak about this place, but while he does not especially like the atmosphere of the 109th, he has no intention of putting in for a transfer in the way that Lattimore had done when he was here, in the way that Beaudry transferred from the Presidio to Korea. This is where he ended up in the war, and he will stay here for his year among men like Dobnik and Hillis with their subtle hostility, and when his time in service ends he will go home and try to forget this place.

And then one afternoon Sgt. Wesser sends for him. It is Palmer's day off, a Wednesday. He is seated on his bunk cleaning his web gear and listening to the house girls gossiping at the doorway where they are squatted spray starching and ironing fatigues, folding them and placing them on wire hangers that will be looped through wall locker handles. His house girl is named Linh. She rarely speaks to him, but she smiles when she hooks his fatigues to his locker or sets his polished boots on the floor beneath his bunk. He would like to talk to her, to ask her things about herself, to find out how she feels about the fact that she will have to live in Vietnam all her life when he can barely stand to wake up every morning in this country.

"Palmer, they want you down in operations."

Palmer looks up from his web gear. Sp/4 Bowen is in charge of quarters today. Palmer hasn't pulled CQ runner yet and doesn't know if he ever will. He knows he will never pull PBR duty. He found out from the company bartender that

Cpt. Metzler sends pot smokers to the detachment that pulls river patrol. Metzler doesn't want any dopers in his company.

Palmer doesn't ask what they want him for in operations. He puts his web gear into his locker and walks out of the barracks tugging at his cap which fits tighter now because his hair has grown longer. Instead of a basic trainee he looks simply like a well-groomed GI.

When he enters operations he finds Sgt. Wesser seated behind his desk smiling as he had smiled on the day Palmer was put on KP.

"There's a job opening up at the Provost Marshal's Office," Wesser says. "Specialist Fourth-Class Shappler's DEROS is coming up next week and they're going to need a new traffic man to run the section. I'm offering you the job."

Palmer doesn't respond right away, a wariness engulfing him at the thought of being transferred to a clerk job. He likes being an active-duty MP, likes the freedom of roving around the city in a jeep, of carrying a .45, of not having any supervisors hovering over him twelve hours a day, of being his own boss during working hours. "The traffic section?" he says, stalling, trying to get his thoughts together.

"They want somebody who has a lot of time left in country," Wesser says. "I recommended you to Captain Metzler. He okayed it."

Palmer's hesitation is obvious. Sgt. Wesser raises his chin and says in an almost confidential tone of voice, low, throaty bubbling, "You should take the job, Palmer. It's a good job. Promotions come faster to clerks."

Palmer was promoted to PFC last week. There was a small ceremony. He had to report to the CO's office. He stood at attention while Captain Metzler handed him his orders and two black PFC pips for his collars.

Palmer begins to nod, recalling the vow he had made to himself long before he was ever drafted, that he would go wherever the army told him to go and do whatever the army told him to do so that he would come out of these two years clean. "All right, sergeant, I'll take the job," he says, feeling nevertheless as if he is volunteering, which is not a good feeling.

Sgt. Wesser sits forward with a pleased expression. "The Provost Marshal wants to interview you for the job this afternoon. I told him we'd have a new man at the PMO by eighteen hundred hours." He pauses a moment, his eyes flickering up and down Palmer's uniform of the day, examining his short, neat, GI haircut. "When you go in to speak with Major Wilhelm," he says in that Yul Brynner brogue, "just relax and answer his questions honestly. You've already got the job. He just wants to get a look at you. Make sure all of your pockets are buttoned."

Last minute backstage instruction. Palmer will miss Sgt. Wesser. The man has taken more of an interest in him than had any Drill Sergeant or any other sergeant that Palmer has ever met, but then as Palmer well knows, appearances mean too much in the army.

Sp/4 Bowen drives him to the PMO. As they round the airfield Palmer looks at everything with a new perspective. He is leaving the 109th just as he had arrived, with Bowen at the wheel and with that threadlike tingle in the spine that accompanies all new moves, new jobs, new duty stations, the concern that it might not work out, that he may blow it as he has blown so many things during the past year. There is already a new Provost Marshal. The captain who combs his hair like Glen Campbell has returned to the United States, so Palmer will be interviewed by a man who himself is a newbie, Major Wilhelm. Palmer feels that this might work in his favor, in the sense that the PM might be a bit too burdened by his new responsibilities to be able to see through Palmer, to realize that Sgt. Wesser has delivered a fraud to his doorstep. Palmer feels completely unqualified to be a clerk/typist.

Bowen drops him off outside the MP station. Palmer goes inside and walks through the doorway to the PMO, passes through the room filled with filing cabinets and into the second room. To his left is the doorway to the traffic section, the small room where Sp/4 Shappler is seated slouched on his chair holding a cup of coffee and not doing much of anything. No report plugged into his typewriter. He looks up as Palmer walks in, grins at him, says, "Hey, Palmer."

Palmer has not yet investigated any traffic accidents, hasn't given Shappler any reports to process, but they have gotten to know each other from brief encounters in the MP station.

"I'm supposed to report to the Provost Marshal for an interview," Palmer says. "Sgt. Wesser recommended me to replace you."

"My replacement!" Shappler says, setting his cup down, standing up and reaching out to shake Palmer's hand, but it's really a joke shake. Shappler is a happy man, intoxicated by the arrival of his DEROS and his ETS, a state of mind that is totally foreign to Palmer and which waits for him over a far horizon, a circumnavigation of the sun itself.

"Come with me."

Palmer follows Shappler through the PMO, past clerks seated erect at their desks typing reports. He looks at them now with new eyes—his new buddies, members of the small PMO Detachment. Shappler leads him into the office at the far end of the building, tells him to wait outside, he will go in and tell the PM that the new man is here.

He disappears through the unpainted doorway, and Palmer looks around the office. Two desks, two men silently typing. A small refrigerator up against one wall, an open cigar box on top of it with MPC scattered around inside. An open doorway leads outside to the rear of the PMO, he can see a volleyball court, a net with the metal poles grounded in the rims of big rubber tires. A jeep is parked near the door. And farther away, over near the fenced corner of the compound, a guard tower.

Shappler steps out of the PM's office and closes the door. "The major's ready for you. Just go on inside and report."

Palmer asks a clerk if he can leave his cap on the man's desk, and the man grins at him and says, "Sure." Palmer positions himself in front of the door and quickly runs his hands over the flaps of his breast pockets, and the jacket pockets near his waist, and on his thighs, the ritual checking-of-buttons before speaking to an officer, like making the sign of the cross.

He opens the door and steps inside and again meets a curtain of cold air as in the hospital, the PM's private office air-conditioned and air-tight, Vietnam has been banished from this place. The Provost Marshal is a big man, as big as a professional football player. He is seated behind his desk smiling like Sgt. Wesser, his flat-topped hair cropped at the sides so the planes of his skull rise to a shock of erect follicles like a squared cap on his head. His eyes are watery and pale like Paul Newman's, like a prick Drill Sergeant's. Palmer goes up to his desk, salutes and reports.

"Have a seat, Private Palmer." The PM's voice is mellow, smooth like an appliance salesman's. When he's not speaking his smile is pinched affably, there is something collegiate about this man who looks to be in his mid-thirties. Career officer. Anybody who goes as high as major is probably going all the way, as high as he can go anyway. It must be hard as hell to become a general. "I spoke with Sgt. Wesser on the phone a while ago and he told me a little bit about you, said you served as a Military Policeman at the Presidio of San Francisco."

Palmer smiles not too broadly and says, "Yes, sir. I was in Company D of the 127th MP Battalion. I served there for five months." He doesn't mention the fact that he had worked only thirty days as a road MP. Now that he has, in effect, volunteered for this job, he wants it, doesn't want to leak any information that might lessen his chances of getting it.

"Have you ever investigated a traffic accident?" the major says.

This could be the stickler. Palmer purses his lips ever so slightly, gives his head a little shake as a preemptive denial, preparing the major for the worst, and says, "I was trained to investigate traffic accidents in MP school at Ft. Gordon, but I've never investigated an accident in the field." It's sapping all his energy to talk this way. Major Wilhelm is the second-highest ranking officer that Palmer has ever had an extended conversation with. The highest ranking officer was the CO of the 127th at the Presidio, a colonel who had grilled him about his film making ambitions a long time ago.

Major Wilhelm smiles that pinched smile, nods with understanding. The army is a morass of amateurs. "Well, this job does not entail any actual investigation. That will be performed by the men out on the road. This is primarily a clerk/typist job and will involve the processing of traffic accident forms. Do you know how to type, Pvt. Palmer?"

Another potential stickler, possibly the greater one. It's all Palmer can do to stop himself from inhaling with a hiss. "I took a semester of typing in high school, sir," he says, a virtual lie, and then to cover his ass says, "but my typing skills are a little rusty."

The PM's pinched smile broadens. His gray eyes sparkle. "Hunt-and-peck like the rest of us around here, eh?"

Palmer gives up a breathy chuckle and says, "Yes, sir." This is excruciating, but he wants this job. He wants a transfer out of the bleak and hostile 109th.

The job aspect of the interview begins to recede, as if the major's quip has served as a kind of hump that the two of them have gotten over in this affable exchange. The major asks Palmer where he is from, and Palmer says Denver thinking that he ought to lie and say Kansas where he was born, or else lie and say he does ski, but the major doesn't ask. Palmer wouldn't lie anyway, not here, not today. Seated on the edge of the chair in front of the major's desk he feels like an acrobat balanced on a high wire, poised on the tip of a single toe, the slightest breeze can topple things. He's familiar with the feeling, has felt it all his life.

The major raises his chin slightly and smiles. "Specialist Shappler will start you on your training as soon as we get your orders written up detaching you from the 109th."

A knot that Palmer did not even know was there begins to loosen below his breastbone, intestines unraveling like shoelaces. Jackpot. His smile never once leaves his face.

Shappler is standing with his arms folded by the desk where Palmer had left his cap, he and the clerk laughing about something when Palmer exits the PM's office. Shappler looks up quickly. "How'd it go?"

"Good," Palmer says. "I'm your new replacement."

Another notch on the gun handle of his leaving, Shappler's grin gets bigger. He will have to outprocess, Palmer knows this, just as Palmer had outprocessed from the Presidio so many months ago but only to come here. The finance office, the hospital, the RE-UP office, like the raising of so many anchors. Shappler points at the clerk and says, "This is Specialist Aldhoff."

Palmer reaches out to shake his new buddy's hand and in doing so recognizes him. Aldhoff is the man who had gone outside the fence to visit a prostitute on the first night that Palmer had pulled gate guard at Camp Quincey. That old feeling of caution, tinged with guilt, that always comes over him when he encounters someone he never expected to see again emerges, as if he had been a part of a conspiracy, which he had. His reach slows a bit as this memory wells up, but then he leans in and takes Aldhoff's hand, shakes it, smiles and waits for recognition, but Aldhoff doesn't know him from Adam.

"Come on, I'll introduce you to your secretary," Shappler says.

They return to the traffic office, Palmer already feeling completely separated from the 109th, exploring his new bailiwick, the faces of the typists seated at their desks coming into a new kind of focus. He will be with them for the next year. Exactly how many days does he have left in Vietnam? He had stopped making that addictive calculation a couple weeks ago.

They enter the traffic office and Shappler steps up to the desk where his secretary is seated typing a report, wearing a tight electric-blue dress that Palmer has come to learn in the past weeks is not a dress but an au dai, a silk blouse with a skirt split at the sides from the waist to the ankles, with long black silk pants underneath. Did women dress like this hundreds of years ago, or is this a 60s fad in Southeast Asia?

"Anh, this is Palmer. He's your new boss."

The woman leaves off typing and sits back in her chair, folds her arms, looks up at Palmer with a smile on her painted crimson lips. A pale moon-face, she's pretty, her black hair swept down across her forehead not unlike Glen Campbell's, but long at the sides and back, almost to her waist, cascading over the back of her wheeled secretary chair.

"This is Missy Anh," Shappler says.

"Ann?" Palmer says.

The woman gives him a slight though amused frown, as if she has had to do this many times before. "Not Ann," she says, rhyming her name with ran, "Anh," rhyming with gone, correcting his pronunciation like every American Palmer has ever known, everybody is an English professor, Palmer himself has done that, probably still does, but then what else are you supposed to do with all the garbage they made you memorize in school?

Anh reaches out to shake his hand, her wrist, palm, fingers slightly limp, languid. It's like shaking hands with a feather.

"Anh's job is to type up traffic accident reports," Shappler says, plucking a 1408 from the IN file on his own desk and handing it to Palmer. Palmer takes it and looks it over, the blanks spaces that had confronted him in MP school now filled in with an almost indecipherable scribble wrought by a road MP.

"You'll have to go through the reports and make them legible," Shappler says, grinning at the burden descending upon Palmer's shoulders. "Some of these MPs are illiterate," he finishes in a muted tone of voice.

Anh goes back to work typing, and Shappler pulls open a drawer on his desk and shows Palmer a stack of traffic tickets. "You'll have to process 1208s and send copies out to commanding officers of the men who got tickets. There's other things, I'll explain all that shit to you later. Let's go over to the barracks. You can pick out a cubicle."

They leave the PMO by a side door, not through the MP station double-doors, and cross the gravel parking lot where Palmer had once stood watching two jeeps drive off with his temporary buddies, with Sgt. Lattimore grinning and riding shotgun truly like a man on a stagecoach. They go around the end of battalion headquarters and cross the dirt road that leads to the main gate.

"This is pretty good duty," Shappler says. "You have to pull tower guard twice a month, a weekday and a weekend. Friday or Saturday is counted as the weekend. It's only six hours though, six to midnight, or midnight to six. We share guard with battalion personnel." The tower that Palmer had seen earlier, beyond the volleyball court, is where he will be pulling guard.

"The mess hall is down the road there," Shappler says, pointing toward a long green one-story building along the main road. "Once in a while you'll have to pull duty in the officers' mess. You sit at a card table and collect money from the captains and ell-tees. They have to pay for their meals."

Shappler leads him into a short dead-end road, the same cluster of buildings that Aldhoff had emerged from on the night the ammo dump got hit. There are three barracks buildings along the left side of the road, and the PMO Detachment bunks in the middle barracks. Shappler points out the movie theater on the right side of the road, a former truck bay roofed over and converted into a theater with long benches, a white screen painted onto a wooden wall.

"Those barracks belong to the quartermaster battalion," Shappler says, pointing at the buildings on either side of the theater. There are more quartermaster buildings lined up in rank and file extending all the way to the fence that borders the South China Sea.

Shappler opens the screen door of the PMO Detachment barracks and steps inside. Palmer follows, and is surprised that the interior is not an open bay but rather has a kind of hallway running down the middle with empty doorways to rooms along both sides, except they are not rooms but cubicles as Shappler had said, sheets of plywood nailed to support posts with a space of two feet above and below each board, offering a modicum of the privacy that Palmer has never seen in the army, not counting toilet stalls, which they vaguely resemble.

Some of the doorways have plastic streamers covering them, white and blue or red or green strips hanging to the floor, and from one of them emerges a man in a T-shirt and fatigues wearing the sandals that all GIs seem to wear, "Ho Chi Minh" they are called, fashioned from truck tires. The man grins at Shappler, nods at Palmer.

"This is PFC Doukas," Shappler says, glancing back at Palmer, then says to Doukas, "this is the new traffic man, PFC Palmer."

Doukas is wearing glasses, wire-rimmed, not thick-framed army issue. He smiles and shakes hands with Palmer, says, "Welcome to the cave," then goes on about whatever business he is involved in. Must be off duty. Palmer doesn't ask. He will get his answers. He finds out why Doukas refers to the place as a cave when Shappler takes him to the far end where there are no cubicles, just a large space, a television set resting on a table, and a couple of overstuffed chairs and folding chairs placed out around it. There is no doorway to the outside at this end of the building. Beyond the wall is the operations sergeant's room, Shappler tells him, an E7 named Ancil. Palmer has seen Sgt. Ancil in the MP station but has never spoken to him, a dark-featured man, maybe Italian, who combs his black hair a bit like a Fifties greaser, swept back at the sides though acceptably GI in length. Palmer isn't sure he likes the idea of living inside a building with only one doorway. He likes to have plenty of exits around him at all times.

"There's three empty cubicles in here," Shappler says. "Take your pick. You'll probably be moving in tomorrow morning."

Palmer looks down the aisle, at three doorways without plastic curtains, and realizes these must be the vacant cubicles.

"You can hang out in here and fuck off if you don't want to go back to the 109th right away," Shappler says like a man who has learned the tricks, the ropes. "Or you can head down to the EM club and have a few beers." Too bad Palmer is replacing him. He likes GIs who speak so casually of gold-bricking. Men after his own heart. "I have to get back to the office," Shappler says, finishing up the brief tour. "I'll start training you tomorrow. There's nothing to this job. After you learn everything I plan to make myself scarce around here." Bird of a feather. Palmer says he'll take a look around and find a bunk.

Shappler leaves, and Palmer peers into each of the empty cubicles, picks one in the middle of the barracks, halfway down the aisle. An empty wall locker hanging open, an empty footlocker. The army will never get rid of wooden footlockers as he had once thought back at the Presidio when the men of Company D were required to bolt together those double-wide fuckers like drafted factory-workers. A mattress is rolled to one end of the bunk, and he unrolls it and sits down, hears the slack springs squeak.

He looks around at the walls of his cubicle, at the section of screened window above his head that runs the length of the barracks. He hears the faint pocks of a ping-pong ball coming from the building next door. Probably a day room. He will look in on that later, will look all around Camp Quincey with new eyes. This is where he will be living for the next three hundred plus days. He will have to check a calendar and count the number of days he has been in Vietnam, and note this singular occasion, mark it as a new day one. He realizes now that he was wrong when he stood in the parking lot on the first day he arrived here and watched Lattimore and the others—he has already forgotten their names—ride off in jeeps toward An Khe and Pleiku. The ocean at his back is not his reward for being a total fuckup. The traffic section is his reward: fiefdom.

PART TWO

CHAPTER 22

Palmer rattles the last captured bits of alcohol socketed in the crevices of cube ice stacked in the bottom of his twenty-cent mixed nightcap, tips it up to finish it off, and realizes that the only person who had ever spoken to him about his drinking was a head. The man had given him an unsolicited lecture on the benevolence of drugs, pot and heroin, but Palmer had told him that heroin is addicting, and had said with a kind of smugness, "I don't need to be addicted to anything."

The current dominant image in his mind is the tip of the letter A, a graphically-defined turning point leading to a downslope, for he has been on the downslope of his tour in Vietnam as of noon this day, and will again be as of midnight, if he thinks of noon as the exact center of the center of a year, and midnight as the end of the center of that year, which this coming midnight will be, so he imagines himself poised on the tip of the letter A. He had drunk in the barracks at noon, and he is priming himself now to celebrate again at midnight, at the end of this day and this center, this turning point toward his downslope. From here on out, the number of days behind him will be larger than those ahead of him.

Reluctant to leave bought booze sponged into cubes, he picks up the cup and lets the ice slip between his teeth and sucks on its contained depressive as he stands up from the padded barstool and clutches the scarred wood elbow-rest to make certain of his balance, even though he's had only five mixed drinks in the past hour-and-a-half since chow, three rum-and-Cokes, two scotch-and-sodas (he can't count the noon drinks worn off during the afternoon), burdened by the high-school fear of awkward walking. He is not drunk enough to not care if he stumbles.

He peels fresh cellophane from an uncracked pack of Camels and taps out a virgin tube, spins the serrated wheel of his Zippo, and sucks life into these leaves born in the States. He makes his balanced way across the floor of the EM club and out the door into a night air humid with the stink of diesel fuel and rotting barracks wood.

The darkness makes him feel less drunk, and his thoughts begin traveling ahead of him down the block into the dim yellow light of his barracks where he has a small refrigerator stocked with Budweiser purchased at the main PX at noon for this blessed occasion. As he walks along he looks down at the sidewalk to gauge its tripping tilt, an old engineering-fashioned walk built before Tet. He flicks ash in front of him thinking of the strategies of this night and wondering how much beer it will take to effect his scheme, understanding that part of the beauty of alcohol is that it makes you do the things you want to do.

Because the barracks is at the end of a dead-end where there is very little traffic even in the daytime, he walks down the center of the road, past the dark mass of parked quarter-ton trucks, jeeps, and a deuce-and-a-half outside the supply room which is shut down for the night. The arms room is locked, the racks of M-16s inaccessible, and he turns his mind away from a thought which has grown stale in six months: if the compound were ever overrun, the only available defensive weapons would be found by the VC in one single, locked, room.

Though it hadn't entered his mind earlier, Palmer begins toying with the idea of scoring a joint as he approaches the cannabis halo which surrounds the upper story of his barracks. He looks at his wristwatch, as though any decision tonight must now be appended to time, and sees that it's a quarter to eight. Already the evening seems accelerated, three drinks at noon, five drinks just now, the plan was conceived more than a week ago, and now H-hour is almost here. But pot slows time down. His heart begins to beat fast as he looks up the stairs to the second floor of the barracks. All the enlisted men who bunk up there are below the rank of sergeant, and many of them are dopers. He is glad he does not live up there. He wants to go home in-rank and with an Honorable Discharge. There might even be a Good Conduct Medal in the deal, if he never gets caught. Eighteen months in the army, six months in Vietnam, never been caught yet.

He goes into the barracks comforted by the idea that the pot is upstairs and available whenever he wants it, just as beer is available whenever he wants it, as long as he keeps on top of things and doesn't let his supply run low. Just try to cadge a few beers on a Saturday night from anyone around here, especially from a GI in another battalion. This, then, is the achievement which boosts his morale more than any job well-done at the office or any compliment from the Provost Marshal or his First Sergeant. That little icebox in his cubicle never holds less than two six-packs of beer after five in the afternoon. And there is always a carton of Camels on the top shelf of his wall locker.

He walks down the fluorescent-lit center aisle feeling tight and sure as a balled fist with the glow of alcohol pumping through his veins and the vague thought of pot bought later on. He walks past the thin abbreviated plywood walls of the cubicles, there's a two-foot space above and below each partition like a men's room stall, each room just big enough for a bed and a wall locker and a footlocker, the size and privacy ungenerous compared to a skid-row hotel room, but never so bleak.

At the far end of the barracks is a large empty space which serves the same function as the demarcated kick-back space of the dayroom, or the informal but restrained ambiance of the EM club. Places where men gather to drink and shoot the shit and watch TV and eat oven-defrosted box pizza, or in the case of Sp/4 Gerlach, to drive gripped iron toward naked rafters. Palmer does not know or want to know the nature of the void this activity must fill in Gerlach's life. Palmer prefers the activity of the man on the other side of the room, Sp/4 Mueller, sunk in the sprung cotton ruins of a Naugahyde chair watching reruns of Hee-Haw.

Gerlach is now in his third week of not speaking to anyone. Palmer does not understand the wellspring of this ostracism, but does not resent it. He is in fact intrigued by it, though a soldier's fierce silence gives an edge to barracks life he would willingly forego. He had watched with covert fascination three weeks earlier when Gerlach entered the barracks one rainy night hauling a stack of lumber stolen from outside the supply room. Gerlach emptied beers as he sawed and hammered those wooden lengths into a crude, serviceable, and to Palmer's eyes dangerous-because-slightly-crooked bench press. Gerlach's beer drinking ended and he proceeded with an unaccountable self-improvement program. He has two months left until his discharge, which means he is in another frame-of-reference altogether from Palmer, for to be a two-month man is almost inconceivable to a six-month man trapped by that amber bitch Time.

Palmer steps through cheap knotted plastic-straw curtains strung across his doorway and enters his cubicle listening to Gerlach's steady iron huff and groan beneath the down-home yuks erupting from the TV. He squats in front of the icebox, and when he opens it an avalanche of electricity-chilled air plows across him in a brief and ghostly wave. The cans of beer are lying butt-end toward him, stacked like cannonballs in irregular peaks on two shallow shelves. Among them lies a single can of Star-Kist tuna. The sight of his stash fills him with a greater sense of security than does the envelope of twenties on the top shelf of his wall locker which he will check as soon as he has punched triangles into the top of a can and wetted his tongue.

The disappointingly stale metallic taste of the beer is assuaged by its sheer iciness, having been stored almost twenty-four hours in the refrigerator. Everything grows so hot so fast here. That first sip is always coldest, best, but already the beaded walls of the red-and-white can are succumbing to humidity. Before it's half-empty, that jarring cold will be diminished to the temperature of lukewarm water.

He keys the padlock off the wall locker and opens it to his unworn khaki uniforms, and the wintergreen uniforms he supposes he will never wear again. You arrive at Oakland in wintergreens, arrive in Vietnam in jungle fatigues, and go home in khaki. He has six months to haul the khakis over to the seamstress at the small PX and have his rank sewn on. Six months during which those symbols of situation may change in ways good or bad. No point in rushing it.

He reaches to the top shelf of his wall locker, steps close to the coffin-like chamber with his back to the screened window and grabs a fat envelope. He opens it and peeks in at a stack of fifty purple pieces of toy currency proscribed as twenty-dollar bills by the army. In six months he has accumulated one thousand dollars, meaning he will go home with two thousand. A man can drink a long time in a cheap American apartment with two thousand dollars.

It's a superstition perhaps, and a form of arrogance, and possibly even fatalism, which prevents him from opening an account at the Chase Manhattan Bank on the finance compound and depositing this money. A superstition born of the idea that should he make even the feeblest attempt to plan for his future, he will never return home, he will die in Vietnam. It is the arrogance of the long-shot horse-player—I won't lose this money because God loves me.

He tucks the envelope closed and chucks the padded stack onto the top shelf as though it were nothing more significant than a tennis shoe.

He sits on his bunk and reaches for the fan standing on his footlocker with its blue plastic blades aimed at his pillow. He turns it on, and though the spiraling breeze itself is not chilly, the warm air thrown across his face and arms cools his moist skin, gives it an unpleasant but preferable ruddy feel. His mind no longer drifts to vague images of men humping trails in the Mekong Delta as it did when he was first assigned to this duty station. How can they possibly stand to sleep in the heat of a jungle? he used to wonder, his face pressed into the wind of his fan. But he has long since stopped speculating upon the misery an infantryman must endure in these latitudes. The infantry has become for him unfathomable.

When he strips, his fatigues roll off his arms and legs rumpled and dark with sweat, depleted of the shiny spray-starched creases ironed into the fabric by his house girl. He puts on a clean pair of OD shorts which feel cool against his skin, and grabs a clean folded towel and his shaving kit and slips into his rubber Ho Chi Minh sandals for a stroll to the shower shack behind the quartermaster barracks across the street.

This walk in a darkness lit by the single white light of a bulb affixed to a telephone pole half a block away, a walk he takes each night, gives rise through the swell of inebriation in his brain to a notion he frequently considers, the bedrock oddness of walking out of doors half naked, the sort of situation which, in a dream, begets bizarre duress. You're running down the corridors of your high school or dashing between incomprehensible suburban homes wearing only your glowing briefs, unable to grasp where your pants, at least, are.

He walks along the wooden sidewalk to the showers smiling about this neo-nudist camp milieu when it occurs to him that out of the three hundred dollars basic pay per-month he receives, he has already spent nearly a hundred on alcohol, in a place where the standard price of a drink is twenty cents.

Stripped and standing beneath the icy spittle of a half-inch shower pipe, he attempts to list his buys of necessity each week: soap, toothpaste, paperbacks. A man in the army doesn't need to pay for food, clothing, rent, yet he can account for only forty dollars spent on alcohol, though there is that money you don't notice drifting out of your pockets in a bar.

He brushes his teeth at the sink and admires the gold tan which masks like make-up the dark rings carved neatly into his twenty-one-year-old sockets. He will get a haircut this weekend. The easiest way to get fingered, hassled, rousted or busted is to flaunt military regulations. The easiest way to hide is to obey. He spits Crest into the sink and mops his face with Gillette Foamy for this evening's shave. Not that these women let you nuzzle their necks, cheeks, lips, but a man going to a party likes to look and feel sharp, and if the MPs pick you up, not looking like shit is a plus, if you don't know them. He knows most of the MPs. He knows their professional inadequacies and competent specialties, for his job is to process each day the reports submitted by those Military Policemen who investigate the calamities of the road.

As he returns to the barracks, he walks into that halo zone where the stink of roach-clip pinch and Glad-bag stash sweetens the night air, and he slows down to consider the pros and cons of toking, because, after all, paranoia is one of the liabilities of getting stoned. You don't want to find yourself lost in the city worried that an R&R VC might poke a rifle into your face. On the other hand, pot is an aphrodisiac, and it sometimes takes an aphrodisiac to get it up with a prostitute.

He goes to his cubicle understanding that, like a well-practiced juicer stocking up, he will purchase a Number 2 pencil sized joint from the dopers upstairs and decide afterwards whether or not to smoke it when H-hour arrives.

Sitting in front of the fan, he punches two V's into the top of a fresh Bud and quickly sucks down a third of that excruciatingly satisfying chill. He drinks it large and fast to avoid the unpleasant metallic undertaste which he supposes is a secondary brewing-stage resulting from imported crates rotting on the hot docks of Danang or whatever seaside city they arrive at. If he closes his eyes and thinks about it, he can remember what fresh beer tastes like, a difference as vast as the distance between here and home.

He turns to pluck from the thin plywood wall at his back a length of paper affixed like the unorthodox calendar it is, a folded fan of six computer pages with diminishing numbers showing how many days he has been here, and how many days he has left to go. The calendar was given to him by a thirty-year-old cousin who had used it during his own tour with Intelligence in Saigon. A gift from one soldier to another, which explains why the dates do not coincide with his actual arrival and departure dates. With a flick of his wrist he tosses the calendar full-length onto his bunk so he can look at that column of ink marked center with a little red check indicating this very day, the beginning of the second half of his tour, the downslope. He is entering the no doubt longest six months he will ever know.

He leaves an inch of beer in the old can and cracks a fresh one. Standing to punch new triangles, he can see through the screened window a man running circles around the softball field alongside the MP station. He has seen the man before, an officer he suspects, though, decked out in rumpled fatigues and with a massive handlebar mustache, he could be an enlisted man. But Palmer refuses to believe that any enlisted man would do anything as utterly meaningless as jogging in a war zone. It infuriates him to see this ambitious activity out on the softball field, even though the earth-striking arc of each booted foot is matched by the puffing of Sp/4 Gerlach down in the TV area.

But to Palmer, lifting weights, like boxing, does not seem as pretentious a form of exercise as jogging. And though he has done neither except during grab-ass barracks camaraderie, he judges weight-lifting and boxing to be the only honest sports: man measuring his personal limits against the indifference of gravity, and man measured against a venal mirror of himself.

He sits down into the breeze of his fan. There is no respite from the heat. Even the refreshing chill of the shower is gone. It will take a minor attitude adjustment to put on fresh fatigues and go back out into the heat at H-hour and face whatever he must face. Tonight's possibilities accelerate his pulse. I have been in Vietnam exactly six months, and I have exactly six months left to go. This is the most perfect truth he has ever dwelt upon drunk.

He looks at the alarm clock next to the fan. Forty-five minutes have passed since he left the enlisted men's club. The move toward his celebration will kick-off in an hour-and-a-half, and any trepidation slithering through his gut will be, by then, doused by alcohol. He drains the can, and feeling the first fuzzy-chinned numbness that signals authentic inebriation, he begins dressing and simultaneously plotting his moves. He has decided to go upstairs and find PFC Detty, his connection, his doper friend who's always got a joint to spare and who has more than once explained to Palmer that he should give up booze entirely and stick to cannabis, should wean himself off the brain-scrambling vomit-inducing factory-manufactured poison of beer, wine, and whiskey, the fuel that drives his weekends careening into the headlight glare of Sunday dawn.

The rafters rattle with the bass beat of stereos cranked to the max. He cannot smell the pot being lit upstairs, but the rumble of music and voices generates, as would a whiff, that dark scene above him: bare-chested GI's with psychedelic headbands absorbing their chemical sweat, ears plugged into the coconut rubber of headphones, and the tiniest fleck of smoldering brown-stained paper being passed from pinched fingers to pinched fingers, to lips, to pinched fingers. The one thing lacking from these gatherings, the one thing that perhaps defines the difference between the heads and the juicers, the one thing he listens for but never hears, is the rowdy howl of inane humor. Theirs is a mute muster, though punctuated frequently by slightly out-of-control, deep and incessant, but never malevolent, chuckling.

He hates to go up there. Lacing a tedious column of boot holes, he recalls his first acquaintance with the heads, and how they had seemed a fun cult. He did have an affinity for them and their music and their choice of high, but in his heart he is a juicer. Bud is his crutch, and Camel non-filters, hell, half those guys don't even smoke real cigarettes. Most of them have been busted for possession. They are all E1, E2, E3—and the E4's are just standing on the precipice awaiting their fall. They don't give a damn. They'd been hippie-types at home, but not necessarily war protesters. They will take their discharges and forget they were ever in the service.

He watches himself in the mirror as he buttons his freshly ironed and starched fatigue jacket. He clips the rank pips on his collar, and ponders whether or not to pin the battalion crests on his epaulets, then realizes that should he be picked up by the MPs, the MP Battalion crests will work in his favor. He is a former road MP, promoted to desk-jockey now, and he wouldn't have it any other way.

He puts on his wristwatch and wears his hat even though

he is going only upstairs. Don't flaunt the regulations. Trouble resides in the details. He climbs the stairs glancing around the compound cautious that a sergeant from his detachment might see him. This is an unrefined paranoia because there is no reason why he ought not climb these stairs. Not all the clerks in battalion headquarters are dopers. Just the ones at the far end of the barracks where the air is rather blue.

He pauses in the doorway buoyed not only by alcohol but by that haunting perception of the irrevocable moment entered into, stepping through a doorway to undertake the distasteful task of breaching the conversations of these dopers to inquire as to where Detty might be, for he cannot see the familiar full-head wrap of that startling crimson bandanna Detty sports after hours in feeble defiance of military dress. Palmer passes through the darkness at this end of the barracks. To him it seems that alcohol and irrevocable moments dovetail neatly into his life, moments as small as that of undertaking a distasteful but personally desirable task, or as large as the irrevocable and undefined moment that he made his first move to come to, or to accept coming to, Vietnam.

They are arranged on their bunks and footlockers as he had imagined them earlier, heads bowed toward the stereo beat and sipping on crisp roach tips. He approaches a man named Loeb, a thin zit-pocked bare-chested man with hair as long as regulation allows, for there is not one thing in an enlisted man's life enforced more rigidly than short hair-length, especially pertaining to the areas around the ears and back of the neck. Loeb's lengthy black forelock is combed forward covering one eye so that looking directly at him you might never know he'd even been drafted.

"Is Detty around?" Palmer says. He modulates his voice which he must raise above the volume of the music, and informs it with a friendly tone that, however, does not invite camaraderie. He likes to think that here, among these men whom he has never joined in the barracks to smoke pot, he is accepted by virtue of his own nonjudgmental attitude toward their lifestyle. They know he's a juicer, and he knows they know, but because he is a juicer and his mind is focused continually on more mundane thoughts than are the minds of heads, there are things he does not realize until this moment.

"He dashed," Loeb says and turns into the huddle of his friends, obviously and effectively cutting Palmer out of the scene.

Detty has slipped downtown to a whorehouse. Palmer stands a moment indecisively glancing around at the men who will not look at him. He understands that because he has never made their crimes a part of his own, he will always be peripheral, will always be only tolerated.

He wants to leave, but because his alcohol-conditioned mind has already made being stoned intrinsic to tonight's celebration, he decides to go ahead and ask for a joint. Loeb is one of the men who, along with Detty, turned him on three months earlier, gave him his first toke, stood by him out beneath the water tower until he began to feel the frozen surface of his memories cracking like an eggshell oozing a childhood forgotten.

"Can I buy a joint from you guys?" he says loud enough that Loeb is certain to hear.

Loeb giggles as his head sweeps out of the huddle with his bloodshot slightly-crossed dope-frosted eyes fixing on

Palmer. His lips split his face with what turns into a laugh of derision, unmistakable. "We don't sell joints up here, Palmer, we share joints."

It plows like a crack across the face of a china plate which instantly separates into two pieces moving inexorably away from each other: here are the heads, and there is Palmer standing with his shoulders slightly hunched from the effort of having to pretend a friendship and ask these men for pot because, out of a fear of getting caught for possession and receiving an Article 15 with a reduction in rank, he will not score and store pot in his own cubicle downstairs.

But even during the second following this blatant snub, Palmer is still wondering if there is a possibility he can procure a joint from these men in spite of the humiliation wrapping a cocoon from his feet to his head, for he is drunk, and in drink there is no pride. He could wait here until he's reduced to a babbling clown if there's even the slightest chance he will get what he wants.

This has always worked for him. In childhood, in teenage years, a year and a half in the army, when all else fails, abandon your dignity and grovel, although he has never physically groveled. His fawning blandishment has always been manifest in varying degrees of self-deprecation. If he can make himself seem not a threat but a well-meaning and slightly naïve goof, he can get his way. When sober, this tactic is employed for simple survival and is never as demeaning to his person as when he wields it drunk. And when he wields it drunk, it is usually with sheer contempt for the person he is cajoling, contempt for an intellect that cannot see through someone as obvious as himself.

But the huddle bows into its communal blue smoke and rock music, and Palmer need not be told. There is no cause for anyone to disparage his intellect's capacity to take a hint.

He turns away and walks up the aisle toward the open doorway feeling as if he has no feet. He goes down the wooden stairway unconcerned now about who might see him, for he is not carrying a joint like a length of lumber which would have imbued him with an intense paranoia prior to his having taken a single puff.

Walking into his cubicle, he feels as though some critical element has been pilfered from his night. He is not used to not getting his way when it comes to the small shit. He never expects to win the big one, whatever that might be (got drafted), but with the shit insignificant to anyone but himself (indulgent pleasure) he expects always to win. Now, expectation itself has become a kind of barracks thief.

·CHAPTER 23

Palmer removes his wristwatch and places it on his foot-locker next to the fan, as though to distance himself from its jerk-tick demolition of time. There is less than an hour to go until he must rise and go, a second time, to the main gate. He removes his wristwatch because he does not want it stolen tonight. It is the first move he makes toward the crucial preparations that he has put off until this final hour. He is a child of procrastination, habits bred out of homework scribbled prior to the bell and lessons learned in the army: if you finish your job ahead of time, they'll just put your ass to work doing something equally boring.

He meticulously peels the wrap off a small travel-size bottle of Listerine, unscrews the cap and sniffs the antiseptic blossom which dissipates rapidly under the wood-rot odors. He sets it next to the fan where he will not forget it at bedtime. He opens his wall locker and reaches behind the draped khakis and grabs the plastic stock of his M-16.

He keeps his weapon in his locker in violation of battalion regulations because he does not trust the arms clerk to open the arms room quickly during red alerts. This is the only regulation he flaunts. Twice during the previous three months he has been reprimanded by his First Sergeant for failing to properly secure his M-16 in the arms room. It is a minor infraction. He knows the First Sergeant does not care because the First Sergeant has his own machinations toward personal profit and covert pleasure during this final tour before receiving his retirement discharge. He reprimanded

Palmer only because the battalion supply clerk had performed inventory and came up with a missing rifle and passed word along to the Provost Marshal's Office. Men pull guard duty every night, rifles come and go in the arms room, there is little traffic control, the men are trusted, who is to know whether a lockered weapon is legal? He accepts the fact that he will always be reprimanded, and each time it happens he leaves his weapon in the arms room for a week, then checks it out impermanently again.

He raises the open chamber to the fluorescent light over-head and looks up the barrel. Silver rifling spirals into his eye. He picks up one of two bandoleers on the bottom of his locker and toes the tin door shut. His flak jacket and steel helmet rest on top of the locker, battle-ready, dusty. He retrieves them and shoves all this business, this costume, this ticket out of here, beneath his bunk.

Forty-five minutes to go. He finishes the warm dregs sloshing on the bottom of his latest beer and sets it quietly in the tin wastebasket beside his bed. He bows his head button-ing his fatigue jacket and looks at the seven dead soldiers, don't speak of the dead, and ponders pulling a cold draw on a fresh beer before going out to the gate for round one. But in the false sobriety borne of alcohol manifest in false logic, he decides to forego another beer. He doesn't want the gate guard to smell his breath which will, by dint of that false logic, repudiate his tendered claims.

He walks out of the barracks and past the dayroom to the main road and sees the single cone of white light which glares against the gate shack at the end of the road spotlighting that weak link on the perimeter. The main gate is shut for the night but not locked. Seated on a high stool inside the shack is an MP whose face he cannot see but whose presence is overwhelming because the man has a pistol and the power to say yes or no to any request. He will die first if the unlikely should occur, if the VC should ever drive down the road from the foothills as they did during Tet, when Palmer was getting Ds in high school.

He makes a casual show of his approach and keeps his hands out of his pockets. Unarmed, and in proper uniform, and putting one foot in front of the other with an artificial sobriety and a distaste for this necessity, though not as distasteful as that encounter with the dopers which still rankles and alters to an unaccountable degree his moves tonight, he smiles at the silhouette in the guard shack and pauses to tap a smoke from his pack and light up, letting the flare highlight his features as did the man who had taught him this ploy.

The PFC in the shack nods hello as Palmer once had nodded hello, and he sees that the PFC's uniform is as green as the green of old leaf or a cherry boy. Gate guard duty is newbie duty, and because this man is fresh in-country he looks young to Palmer, even though he could be a twenty-four-year-old college graduate who had finally lost his 2-S deferment.

"How's it going?" Palmer says.

"It's quiet."

He turns to one side so that the battalion crest on his epaulet, and the sleeve MP Brigade patch, catch the cone of light letting the guard see that this is another MP and not a supply battalion dud or a cook off-duty as did the man named Aldhoff who is long gone, three months gone, who came here that night and lit a cigarette and turned to the side so that Palmer could see his insignia, Palmer seated in the guard shack leery of being assigned a duty station blasted white by a light with an unfortunate tilt, my God, the VC could drive by and pop me with a grenade launcher, this is a crock of shit. Aldhoff came up to the shack and began talking, and it wasn't until a month later when Palmer was reassigned to the PMO detachment that he learned that Aldhoff was just a clerk, who had said to him on that night, Oh by the way, I got motor-pool guard duty at ten o'clock. And Palmer said, Is that right? And Aldhoff said, Yeah, I'll be heading down the road about ten. And at ten o'clock, Aldhoff came walking up to the guard shack wearing his steel helmet and flak jacket and carrying an M-16, and Palmer noticed that he did not have any ammo. But Palmer thought, They must keep the ammo secured down at the motor pool, even though he wasn't quite certain where the motor pool was, or who else was involved in guard duty down there.

"How long have you been here?" Palmer asks.

"Three weeks," the gate guard replies. "How about you?"

"Six months," Palmer says, and wants to tell the kid, he thinks of him now as A Kid, that he has been here exactly six months this night and is on the downslope, and that he is sneaking out of the compound tonight to find a prostitute and celebrate this perfect stasis between time endured and time which has yet to be endured.

He asks the guard if he had trained at the MP school in Ft. Gordon, Georgia, and when the man says yes Palmer knows that a totally artificial bond, almost as strong as friendship itself, has been generated that will expedite this evening's celebration. He dredges from his memory an anecdote or two about MP school, classes in writing traffic tickets, investigating traffic accidents, and rousting drunk drivers, the only memories he can attach to his current vocation, which is that of traffic clerk at the MP station.

The gate guard nods with understanding but doesn't laugh, and Palmer surmises, though he hasn't the interest to inquire, that this man came to Vietnam directly from MP school and thus takes himself seriously as an enforcer of the law. This juvenile sense of self-importance reverberates occasionally in Palmer's own memory, but only when he is drunk. When he is sober, or when there is sunlight, he refuses to think about himself in the past tense because it foments a bitterness for which he has no stamina.

"I got guard duty at ten o'clock down at the motor pool," Palmer says.

The guard doesn't nod, doesn't respond as Palmer had on that night. Palmer peers into the dark beyond the perimeter fence and dredges up a banality that he hopes will successfully cap this delicate moment. "Hope everything stays quiet."

The guard at last nods, and Palmer says, "Catch you later," and field-strips his cigarette, twiddling shreds of tobacco onto the gravel road and rolling the paper into a pebble which leaves a faint stink of smoke on his fingertips as he flicks it away.

Buoyed by not only his standard round of nightly drink but by the satisfaction of a potentially disastrous job well-done, Palmer decides to go back to the EM club and fortify himself with a scotch or two. Now that the prospect of leaving the compound stoned on pot has been voided, he wants something equally as strong if not as mentally debilitating to carry him toward ten o'clock.

But when he enters the club, the lights of last-call have already risen and drunk men are leaving in groups. A panic unreasonable, a panic programmed into Palmer by dread experience, kicks in and he goes to the bar fast and leans toward the bartender who is packing the ice cabinets below the counter with warm beer for tomorrow. He asks for a scotch-and-soda. The bartender glances at the clock on the wall. It is a quarter-to-ten, and drinks are cut off at a quarter-to-ten. As the bartender's close-cropped neck-naked lifer head is still turned reading the clock, Palmer experiences a swell of rage that he is in a place where bars by law close at ten o'clock at night, and that swell breaks into a torturous nostalgia for civilian life and the cheesy red-velvet walls of neighborhood bars and the utter luxury of drinking until two A.M.

"Drink up fast, the bar's closed," the bartender says, spilling a double-shot of Johnny Walker into a plastic cup and spritzing it with bottled soda.

Palmer's body goes into automatic, his hand picking up the drink and guiding it to his lips as his mind is dealing with amazement and gratitude. He drains the cup in one gulp, drops a twenty-cent bill on the bar and exits the club thinking, There's your difference between juicers and dopers. That right there is your big difference.

He returns to the barracks and spends his final moments drinking beer. At five minutes to ten he carries his guard paraphernalia outside and steps into the shadow of the day-room so that none of the men or sergeants in his detachment might see him and ask what he's up to.

Standing in his favorite element, darkness, armed and

armored, he can feel the delicate muscles of his neck flexing to balance the small unaccustomed weight of his steel helmet. He listens for traffic along the road beyond the cyclone fence as he drapes over his shoulder the bandoleer containing eight magazines holding eighteen brass-jacketed rounds apiece. His flak jacket binds his torso but feels good, and the thick plastic stock of his M-16 feels good in his grip. When the silence along the road complements the shadow of the day-room, he steps out and proceeds to the main gate not caring about the calamitous possibilities of what he is doing, for alcohol has put into its proper perspective the utter banality of this entire situation. The army is a dull game, its rules a joke.

He approaches the white glare of the main gate with a weary stance, just another shafted EM hauling his oppressed ass toward another shit detail. With his head bowed he watches his boot toes kicking up the white dust of the road until he comes abreast of the gate shack, and as he looks up he experiences a giddy thrill, the gambler's rush, thinking, What if a different MP is now on guard duty?

But the same man is there and nods at him, and Palmer steps through a gap in the gate wide enough only for a single man but which could be made wider easily by VC in a fast truck.

He begins thinking about VC the instant he steps outside the safety of the compound. VC are background noise. There is never a moment when the abstract image of gun-toting black-pajama'd straw-hatted men are not flitting along the walls of his most unconscious thoughts. Now that he is outside the perimeter fence and walking along the edge of the asphalt toward the motor pool a hundred yards away, he brings the cast of his fears center stage where he can look at them as he walks: strangers, angry, armed, they look like the house girls and his secretary and the office boy who is not a boy but a man of fifty.

His heart is beating fast and not from the massive influx of alcohol within the past forty-five minutes, nor from the anger that flares and wanes from his encounter with the heads, and not from walking fast, and not even from a fear of VC which he reasons is ludicrous because it has been at least three years, according to legend, since the VC came into the city at Tet. The VC are all up in the hills. His heart beats fast because now that he is out in the open, unauthorized, AWOL frankly, he is listening for the sound of a jeep, any jeep, an MP jeep, a VC jeep, a tank, a truck, a sergeant, or a fretting captain, to drive at him from behind and slow down and put him in a bind not on this evening's agenda.

He wishes he had put a beer and a church-key into a loose pocket on a thigh of his fatigues. In the barracks, for some now incomprehensible reason, it had seemed a foolish risk to smuggle beer off the compound, even though the concept of going AWOL with an unauthorized weapon and one hundred and forty-four rounds of ammunition while drunk on his ass in order to visit a whore had not struck him as unreasonable.

He crosses the asphalt road so that when he comes abreast of the guard tower at the corner of the compound he will be an obscure and murky shape in the eyes of the tower guard. When he pulls tower duty he sometimes sees men walking along the road toward the motor pool, but until Aldhoff had taught him this ploy it had never occurred to him to wonder

where those murky shapes were headed. Now he has become
one of them, drunk, confident, grateful that he did not after
all smoke a joint before coming out here, though that snub
still rankles him so that feelings of vengeance simmer impo-
tently in his mind beyond the calculated motions required to
pull off this idiotic move.

Black and indistinguishable from a distance, the rusted
fence posts and sagging cyclone fence of the motor pool gate
become distinct as he draws near. He sees huddled back
beneath the fronds of an exotic bush two women in pajamas
whispering and smoking cigarettes and watching the road for
customers.

They drop their cigarettes and step on red ash, and fold
their arms and watch him silently as he approaches. They
know why he is here.

"Ciao, dap," says one.

"How you?" says the other.

The first one comes out from beneath the camouflage
branches and Palmer recognizes her. She is a gravel-voiced
notorious madame legendary in this neck of the war who
goes by the GI-labeled moniker "Motor Pool Mary." She is
not especially pretty, the flesh of her face is puffy, ruddy, but
what she lacks in looks she compensates with a personality
so brash, so lewd, and so aggressive that she is reputed to be
the toughest and wealthiest prostitute in the city. Palmer
doesn't know. GIs talk, tell lies, foment rumors spotlighting
their own sexual prowess. All he knows about Motor Pool
Mary from first-hand indisputable experience comes from
two encounters, both of which took place while he was on
guard duty at the main gate.

He had been a cherry boy, annoyed at his assigned duty in the shack lit by that irritating floodlight. He was seated on the high stool watching the road intently when he heard a voice coming down the asphalt road, a woman barking an occasional phrase that he could not understand. With a cautious hand planted on the polished black leather of his .45 holster, he saw the stranger, a woman, coming toward the gate. She was smiling big, she was swaggering, and she passed by and hollered to the soldiers within the compound: "You want free fuck? Motor Pool Mary give it away tonight! I got VD!"

The other encounter took place when Palmer was pulling tower duty, and the circumstances were identical. Motor Pool Mary came down the road chanting: "Pussy is sweet, and so is honey, so beat your meat, and save your money."

Palmer steps close to her, and Mary reaches up and strokes his cheek with callused fingers. A smile breaks across her face. "Babysan!" she laughs aloud and her laughter is hoarse like the voice of a heavy smoker. She is enamored of his childish cheeks. This is old hat. He is "babysan" to all the Vietnamese women, to the KP women and the EM club waitresses and the house girls and the office secretaries. He is beaucoup dap, and dap-wah, and all the girls love him, but only the prostitutes prove it.

She leads him into the bushes, into a right-angled alcove of the cyclone fence hidden from the street and backed by the tarpaper-walled monolith of a motor-pool bay across the fence. Trash, pages of the Stars and Stripes, rusted pop and beer cans, and muddied, crusty clothing surround a trysting blanket. Mary gets down to business fast, efficient, she yanks her blouse over her head and her bra glows white in this shadow. He looks at it as he sets his helmet, flak jacket, weapon and ammo behind him on the ground.

"Twenty-five dollah fuck, ten dollah sucksuck," Mary says, slipping out of her pajama bottoms. She is wearing panties. They don't always. He hands her two tens and a five recalling a night when he had tried to palm off some piasters on a prostitute who got mad because she wanted military money. It's worth more on the black market. The piasters were to be used to pay his housegirl at the end of the month, a standard army farce.

Palmer pulls his pants on and retrieves his gear looking around with a head now dramatically clearer than it had been five minutes previously. The endless keening of that bell of desire, that madhouse momentum which drives all his insane plans, has ceased. He can hear vehicles accelerating a mile down the road, can hear the spattering of inexplicable and routine rifle shots near the foothills, can hear the muted squeal of rock music coming from the compound, perhaps from the dopers' room. He feels in fact sober. His only desire now is to get out of here. He looks at the pale band of white encircling his wrist and wonders why he thought a prostitute would steal his watch. There's no money in rolling Americans. They want their customers to come back.

He says Ciao to Motor Pool Mary and begins walking down the road toward the guard tower where that copy of himself sits with only the silhouette of his helmet showing above the walls. Perfect target for a sniper. Perhaps it is his imagination but he believes he hears a laughing throaty voice following him down the road and rushing past him saying with a derision borne of bad experience, "Fuck you, MP." He cranks his head to the side and glances at the MP battalion crest on his epaulet and realizes through his still alcohol-saturated brain that the drawback to this regalia is the fact that while there is no money in rolling American soldiers, there are still prostitutes with scores to settle, prostitutes who hate MPs, just as everyone else hates MPs: the infantry, the supply battalion troops, the motor pool troops, the signal troops, the engineering and airport and PX troops. It's a simmering hate that they do not seem to hold even for the Viet Cong. He remembers a story he was told about Motor Pool Mary by a G.I. She purportedly knifed another prostitute and was arrested and charged with murder, but her wealthy father had paid her way out of jail. It's a plausible story, but probably bullshit, the best kind of story.

He approaches the white light of the main gate not knowing how much time has elapsed since he left. He supposes it has been at least twenty minutes, and no guard-duty lasts twenty minutes, but it doesn't matter because he is not going to explain himself to a cherry boy. He walks through the gate and feels an almost tangible sense of false security that he is now back on American soil and surrounded by hundreds of unblooded men like himself whose firepower might conceivably stall a VC attack long enough for the helicopter gunships at the airfield to get here and plaster the enemy with rockets — possibly even long enough for the righteous Phantom jets of Phu Bai to save a bunch of born-again-grunt clerk-typists.

He passes the guard shack with his head bowed as if truly wearied by the burden of a shit detail gotten shut of, and the gate guard asks if he has a match. Palmer slaps his pockets and starts to say no, but then tells the guard he has some matches back in his hootch and will bring them out. The guard thanks him and Palmer moves down the road and into the shadow of the supply room wishing he hadn't made the offer but aware that this small favor could pay off another night. And besides, he has made the grievous error of going on guard duty without matches. In the end you don't think about the VC, you think about that unlit cigarette.

But he has a beer first.

The aisle lights are out in the barracks. He sits in the cone of a small yellow reading light nailed to the wall above his pillow and drains half a beer before scouting a pack of matches and rising feeling his cock sticky and itchy beneath his skivvies. He walks fast out to the gate stripped of incriminating evidence, feeling free and innocent, and hands the matches to the guard who thanks him. He hears the soft scratch of sulfur as he heads back to the barracks.

He finishes the beer as he steps out of his fatigues, picks up that bottle of Listerine and shaving kit and a clean pair of issue skivvies, and walks to the showers.

In the corner of the tin-walled shack, with his back to the door, he lathers his cock with this product guaranteed to kill germs by the millions. He conjectures there must have been one million germs on Motor Pool Mary's teeth alone. Then he uses soap, feels its residue enter his urethra, and the pain is the pain of those clap germs biting the dust, a pain which is immaculate and which to his drunk brain seems apart from him, as though he is observing, and to a tangible extent empathizing with, someone else whose dick is on fire.

He walks back to the barracks and goes around to the side, to the piss-tube, three upright outhouse walls surrounding a length of steel pipe jammed into the ground at a 45-degree angle, and empties his bladder, bringing that brief cleansing violence to an end.

Walking back to the barracks for a last beer to put a cap on this significant date, and to celebrate the approaching midnight stroke of the first second of his official downslope on the calendar, he tosses his old and guilt-ridden skivvies into a dumpster.

CHAPTER 24

Palmer is surprised to find, on Friday morning, that he is capable of lessening the pain of his hangover by telling himself that the downslope is now irrefutably real. He opens his eyes into the breeze of the fan, its hum muting the reveille creak of cot springs and the sounds of boots hammered upside down on the floor to evict insects. He looks through the haze of his hangover at the calendar on the wall, looks at that tiny red mark above the date which is today. He is on the downslope, and he is thus able to rise smiling and work himself into fresh fatigues laid out by his house girl and take his time lacing his boots until all of the other clerks have gone. There are only two minutes left until seven o'clock, the beginning of his military working day.

He is painfully thirsty but does not drink from his refrigerator-chilled plastic water-filled canteen. He instead seizes a Budweiser and drains it, pouring the beer in a single uninterrupted flow down his throat, an auger of icy refreshment, his breakfast, his cure for dreams of drinking incessantly from a water hose which will not cool his tongue, a hose attached to a house he lived in when he was five, a place he remembers only when dreaming or stoned on pot.

He arrives at the office smelling strongly of Listerine. The clerks are already hard at their Smith-Coronas typing into legibility the hand-scrawled reports delivered by Military Policemen who have investigated burglaries, robberies, drug deals, assaults, rapes, sodomies and other microcosmic crimes imported by this foreign power. He enters by the front door so that the Operations Sergeant will see that he is on time, is not five or ten minutes late, for which he has been reprimanded in the past.

He goes into the tiny cubicle of his office and sits at his desk only long enough to nod at his secretary, Missy Anh, who is seated at her desk typing, and to establish his presence in this place. Then he rises and goes to the rear of the PMO to get a cup of coffee. The percolator is alive, the coffee is hot and fresh. Though he is a sugar freak he takes his coffee black because it makes it a cutlass to cleave his hangover, not to kill it, not to diminish it, only to separate it into two manageable halves which nevertheless are diminished by his contented knowledge that he is going to be in Vietnam less than he already has been here. A slow, and steady, and infuriating, and granted, and guaranteed progression toward freedom, and home, and bars which stay open until two A.M.

He rolls a blank traffic accident report into his typewriter, a ruse, for he has no intention of doing any work today beyond giving his secretary a few corrected reports for her own quota of deceptive work. The beer boils in his empty belly and cold bubbles erupt into his esophagus. He stifles them with soft burps that explode in his mouth leaving a pleasant beer-flavored mist on his tongue.

To complete the ruse, he pulls a report off the top of his IN file and begins typing appropriate information into blank boxes: name, date, location. But he stops when he realizes this is a report about a fatal traffic accident, FTA. It is one-day old even though it happened in the Central Highlands at a place called the Mang Yang pass (they always rush the fatals through). A five-ton truck overturned and the driver's head was crushed. Palmer opens the report to read the hand-written statements by the witnesses, American enlisted men. He is interrupted by the Operations Sergeant, a lifer named Ancil who was a grunt in the Korean War, who walks into this hole-in-the-wall and gives him the bad news.

"Palmer, you're going up for the soldier-of-the-month board next Monday."

Palmer listens to this enraging news without expression.

"Everyone else in the office has already done it, so it's your turn," Ancil says, as if to explain why he's picking on Palmer. When Palmer doesn't respond, Sgt. Ancil turns away and goes back to his own office. He has been in the army twenty years, and probably understands without malice or interest the mindset of sullen corporals.

Palmer takes a sip of coffee which has cooled to the heat of the office, of the day, of the simmering anger which cannot find release inside him because he will not scowl, will not punch the desk with his knuckles, will not go so far as to hiss a curse. He simply lets his utter disgust with this order roll right through him because he knows that the thing he must do now is shut up. Don't complain. Don't gripe. You could have been drafted into the Infantry, you could be lying prone in a rice paddy right now watching VC approach with AKs, so turn your mind completely off for the next three days, until this cup has passed and the horseshit has ceased.

This Zen approach does not work, of course. He is infuriated by the idea of standing before a review board wearing freshly-starched fatigues and spit-shined boots and answering a slew of questions pertaining to things he doesn't care about.

After fifteen minutes he gets up and passes through the outer office. "Going to the latrine," he says to Mueller who is seated motionless at his typewriter reading an MP report. Motionless but for the miraculous blur of high-school trained digits driving his platen like a piston.

Mueller nods. Palmer walks out of the office onto the sun-blasted gravel of the MP station parking lot. A jeep pulls in hauling two newbie MPs. He does not know their names. Their fatigues are dark green, as his once was. His own fatigues have faded into a smart pale olive, shiny with ancient starch ironed into the weave, but they have not yet reached the astonishingly alkali-white hue of fatigues worn by men who have been stationed here almost a year, fatigues worn with a pride that has nothing to do with the military.

In the barracks the two house girls are squatting near the front door sorting out damp, matted, freshly-laundered fatigues, and their presence irritates Palmer because he can usually count on no one being in the barracks when he slips in for a beer. He knows their daily schedule, knows when they are out at the water tower washing fatigues or in the barracks sweeping and making beds and shining jungle boots.

He goes into the privacy of his cubicle and pulls a beer out of his icebox and snaps two holes into the top. While he does not care that they know what he is doing, since there is nothing that takes place on this compound they do not know about, his violated secrecy lessens the satisfaction he always takes out of this illicit and illegal activity. He sets the empty into the waste can and without thinking about what he is doing, opens another.

He gives himself permission to deviate from what has been a rigid adherence to his morning drinking pattern because he has been ordered to go before the soldier-of-the-month board. His anger gives him permission. His oppression gives him permission. He must now foment a balance of vengeance, even if it consists only of having a second beer in one sitting, a thing he has been determined never to do simply because it takes too much time and might cause him to be found out. So finally, it is the alcohol itself which gives him permission.

He sets the second empty into the waste can and rises feeling the sweet penetration of his hangover by the tentacles of his first morning beer enhanced by the flavor and chill and massive injection of two beers within five minutes.

On the way out, he stops to joke with his house girls before going back to the office. Missy Nu, the younger of the two, tells a story. Her accent is thick, her English is the awkward argot of the untutored genius. Palmer cannot imagine working-class Americans picking up the language of an occupying power. She tells him that a GI came into the barracks earlier and asked if she could buy him coke. She told him yes. He asked how much it would cost. She said twenty-five cents.

The other house girl, Cue, begins chuckling. She knows the punchline. Nu continues: "He say no, I not mean Coca-Cola, I mean cocaine!"

Cue squeals and Nu erupts into laughter. And as if Palmer does not understand the story, or perhaps because they love the way American idiocy rolls off their tongues, they repeat the story, both of them, contrapuntally.

"I think GI want Coca-Cola."

"He want cocaine."

"I say no-can-do."

"G.I. beaucoup dinky-dau."

"I say no-can-buy."

Palmer smiles. He envisions some hatless jerk of a dope addict wearing last week's fatigues entering the barracks and whispering his urgent plea, and that image angers him.

"Don't let GIs come in here," he says, but they know, they understand barracks security, they know what barracks thieves are. On the way back to the office he stops off at the piss-tube and holds his breath as he aims the hair of this dawn's dog down the steel hole.

Back in the office he sits poised in front of his typewriter as motionless as Mueller, his fingers only touching the silent keys. The thin rush is on and the irritation at being ordered to go up before the board has lessened. The carbonated cure-all is taking effect, and he sits this way for a few minutes enjoying his high while the typewriters in the outer office rattle and ding and men walk past his door toward the filing cabinets.

"Palmah."

He looks around at Missy Anh, whose wide eyes and somber face and mute whisper telegraph her intent. She wants something besides help with a report.

"Yes?" he says.

"You go to PX today?"

She is wearing a startling red au-dai which outlines her figure as she sits primly at her desk. Her smooth moon-shaped face is powdered white, her lips waxed scarlet. Palmer watches her from across the cubicle, a distance of four feet, with the reined lovesick desire of a teenage kid. She is untouchable.

"Why?"

"You can buy for me baito bimo?"

He doesn't understand what she is saying, and asks her to write it down. She scrawls the words "Pepto Bismol" on a scrap of paper. She sets her pen down and looks at him with an excessively thespian tilt of her eyes indicating discomfort, and touches the round firm slight bulge of her belly.

He looks down at her palm splayed gently across that anatomical catalyst, and looks away. "Can do," he says. "I go at noon."

She digs out two dollars' worth of MPC and, though he is willing to pay for it himself, he accepts the money, having learned long ago that these people prefer to pay their own way.

At noon he eschews the mess hall for the EM club at the edge of the green, sail-dotted China Sea. He sits on the back patio beneath the cooling shade of a tin umbrella shaped like a flower. For lunch he orders a hamburger, a scotch-and-soda, and a Budweiser from the Vietnamese waitress. When she goes inside, he is alone on the patio. He can hear the club filling up and knows that in a few minutes men will begin drifting out to sit at the white tin tables or the stained redwood picnic tables to shatter his serenity bestowed by a hot sun upon his fatigues and the sound of surf thinning on the sand beyond the barbed-wired perimeter fence.

When lunch comes, he tips the waitress a buck and waits until she has walked back inside before he drains the scotch in a gulp. The drink is cold and hot and sweet, it stings his throat and gives him the secure sense that he now possesses an ace in the hole, a wad of quick liquor tucked neatly in his gut as he takes his first bite of food since last evening's chow and washes it down with sips of beer.

There are sixty minutes left of the ninety-minute lunch

hour by the time he gets back to the barracks. He feels slightly drunk now, having bought another quick scotch before leaving the patio. He decides not to drive to the PX but to ask Mueller if he will drive. Mueller is his choice because he is the only man not snoring on a bunk. He is seated in the TV area sipping Coke and watching a Ralph Story episode with the sound down low.

When Palmer asks if he wants to go to the PX, Mueller nods and switches off the TV. Together they return to the Provost Marshal's Office and commandeer the maverick, a jeep without portfolio which is available to the clerks for use at all times.

Mueller drives. Palmer sits up straight on the sprung canvas shotgun-seat with his right hand gripping the canvas safety strap which serves as a door. They drive through the main gate and bounce onto the asphalt and head west toward the PX compound near the foothills.

Palmer loves being drunk and out on the road. Loves moving fast through the odorous tableau of a palm-frond culture, of old Vietnamese men hiking stiff-legged along the dirt shoulder, of serious women squatting in front of camp-fires tending rice cuisine, of girls seated behind card tables hawking contraband cigarettes and Coca-Cola. Being drunk in the daylight and moving through these sights exhilarates him. He feels safe, feels like shouting friendly hellos to these almond-eyed indifferent faces. But instead he looks over at Mueller who glances quickly at him, Mueller who is sober and thus sensitive to every motion within his field-of-vision and field-of-fire. Mueller doesn't like being outside the compound. Neither does Palmer, except when he is drunk, the invulnerable time. Back home, this is when he would enter strange and dangerous bars and strike up conversations with men whom he would, sober, cross the street to avoid.

"Got picked for the board, huh?" Mueller says, shattering Palmer's mood. Until this moment, the irritation of that chore had been shunted out of his consciousness. He had hoped he would not have to think of it until Monday morning when he would be forced to confront its dismal inevitability for a few hours. He doesn't want to talk about it, and he only nods.

"Gonna study for it?" Mueller says, forcing Palmer finally to confront the inevitability of the truth that he is not alone in this thing, that the whole barracks is going to be yammering at him about soldier-of-the-month all weekend.

"You have got to be shitting me," Palmer replies. "Why the fuck would I study for that?"

"Winner gets a three-day R&R to Danang," Mueller says with what could pass for a faraway look in his eyes.

Palmer's dislike for Mueller is immediate. He suddenly cannot bear to be seated in this jeep and forced to endure this moronic conversation. He looks up ahead toward the far white warehouse mass of the main PX in the center of a compound accessed by a single gate, hoping that Mueller will shut up without taking offense at this snub.

But Mueller does not shut up. Instead he invalidates Palmer's dislike by asking if he's going to the beach party tonight.

Palmer looks over at him with renewed interest and asks what's the occasion. Mueller tells him that an enlisted man from battalion headquarters is going home next week, and they're throwing the requisite farewell Good Conduct Medal ceremony at the Port Beach party patio, all battalion personnel welcome.

A Friday party at the beach, a wet-bar, and of course, there will be women. There will be nurse women and prostitute women. The tall blonde nurse women will dance with the junior officers and palaver with the top brass and turn their eyes askance from the little brown prostitute women in colorful pajamas being bird-dogged by the enlisted men. He will be one of those men. Bunker rendezvous, with the discreet exchange of cash. A good time will be had by all.

"What time do we leave?" he says.

"Seven," Mueller replies. Palmer is nonplused by Mueller's civilian reply. The average Sad Sack would have said nineteen-hundred. Palmer has always felt that his refusal to play the army game, to walk the army walk and talk the army talk, is his personal quirk, and this makes him like Mueller.

Seven. The work day ends at five. This gives him two hours to eat a hamburger at the club, down a few mixed drinks on the back patio, and reinforce himself with beer in the barracks before the jeep leaves for the wet-bar at Port Beach, which is across the road from the PX. He looks over at it as they pass, a small R&R compound with furnished rooms for men on leave, EM and officer clubs, and recreational facilities, boating and swimming, the sort of place where the man who wins soldier of the month will stay in Danang.

The asphalt parking lot of the main PX pleases him with its fading white angled lines. It is a massive, elephantine shell, reminds him of his favorite mercantile back home. He and Mueller agree to meet back at the jeep in fifteen minutes.

Enjoying a high enhanced by the presence of this building,
by the noise of wandering soldiers shopping, and by the sight
of jeeps lined up at the pop-shack loading wholesale cases of
soda and beer which will probably be sold illegally on the
black market downtown, he enters the building which is a
few degrees cooler inside than outside.

Except for picking up a bottle of Pepto Bismol, his shopping
habits are fixed. Five minutes at the news rack where dozens
of soldiers leaf though soft-core porn pulp magazines.
Women in black-lace underwear, third-rate photography, no
hard-core porno, no split beav, no massive plunging cocks,
just lace panties and bras and a few tits. *Playboy* is better: Hef
raising a Pepsi surrounded by lingerie-clad babes. If you buy
a lifetime subscription to the magazine, a Bunny will visit you
in the Mekong Delta or the DMZ. Hef hasn't forgotten us,
even if everybody else has.

He picks up a bottle of Pepto Bismol and goes to the beer
aisle which extends from the front of the building to the rear,
stacked solid with Budweiser, Miller, Carling Black Label,
Schlitz, Pabst Blue Ribbon. Three bucks a case, get your ration
card punched and you're in business. But he's already got his
stash. He moves over to the liquor aisle and picks up a fifth
of Johnny Walker Red and carries it to the cash register like a
loaded gun.

Four bucks for the scotch, he's in business. He walks out
with a tug of regret because he hates leaving the PX. He loves
shopping there. It's like being back home. He steps into the
hot sun and squints, and there is Mueller seated in the jeep
fiddling with the dials of another goddamn radio/cassette.

"It was on sale," Mueller says as Palmer climbs into the
jeep. Mueller has gotten a reputation in the barracks. Around

payday he will buy some ludicrous electronic gadget at the PX, and three weeks later, flat busted, he will scour the compound trying to sell it at a dime on the dollar. Mueller isn't a doper or a drunk, he just isn't good with money. Palmer finds this character flaw both charming and irritating. He doesn't want to look at the thing which Mueller is holding up for inspection because he knows it won't be in the barracks long. This shit gets old. But he does look at it.

"You got a good deal there," he says, with benevolence aforethought, just as he had spoken to the gate guard the previous night. Mueller grins with his lips clamped tight. He is pleased. He's got that I'm-never-gonna-sell-this-baby look on his pimpled mug.

"Let's run over to the Mariner's Club for a drink," Palmer says, and he adds fast, "I'm buying," and pulls from his billfold a stack of piasters he was saving for payday.

Mueller looks at his watch. "Lunch is almost over."

"We got forty minutes," Palmer assures him, settling into his seat as if settling the argument. "It's a ten-minute ride to the pier. We'll knock back a martini. Let's live a little."

Mueller has been in the detachment a little over three months and is therefore considered a cherry boy, and Palmer enjoys corrupting him, enjoys fine-tuning and adjusting his attitude so he won't take the army too seriously, won't panic at the thought of doing what he feels like doing during his free time, and lunch is free time.

Mueller acquiesces.

CHAPTER 25

They take a back road to the pier, the most direct route. The road begins as a dirt two-track across a weed field, then becomes concrete passing between the rotting husks of abandoned barracks on a former engineering compound, now a ghost town. Black doors and windows checker barracks walls. Limp perimeter wire combs newspapers and rags from a slow breeze. There is no one around to police up this dead place.

Palmer realizes he can pop the scotch top with impunity. After he tips a fast sip, he holds the bottle over to Mueller, who grins shyly. He's got the attitude of a lifer-to-be. Drinking while driving, and drinking on duty, even if this is break time, is a concept beyond the scope of his basic-training ethics.

Palmer caps the bottle and crushes the sack top closed as they come to the compound gate. Two SPs are standing in the shadow of the guard shack. Palmer isn't surprised to find men guarding these acres of military firewood, but his hand tightens on the sack as the thinnest fiber of irritation threads his heart. He suddenly remembers that neither he nor Mueller have travel-authorization papers, and it is always a pain in the ass to explain the status of the maverick to non-Military Police authorities.

A man steps out of the gate shack. His fatigues are rumpled, two or three days worn. The humidity destroys a starch-press in a day. But this is just an engineering dud or a signalman from the adjacent compound who was collared for shit-detail guard-shack work. He looks like a slob, but he has a shiny black helmet and armband, though no .45 on his hip, just an M-16 in the shack. He glances at the insignia stenciled on the bumper, then leans into the jeep on the passenger side. Palmer instinctively holds his odorous breath.

"Are you MPs?" the man says.

"Yes," Mueller replies.

The man stands erect and waves them through the gate smiling and says, "We don't even fuck with the MPs."

Out on the road Palmer and Mueller grin at each other. This kind of treatment is rare, and a kick. Palmer discreetly unpeels the bottleneck and takes a fast sip of hot scotch and sits back feeling like the king of the city as Mueller takes it slow cruising along the street. Though wide with generous dirt shoulders, it seems narrow because it is crowded with loafing Vietnamese slicky-boys, pimps on Hondas, and honest tired women carrying loads of vague work under their arms.

And then, just as they drive past the two-story stucco buildings of central downtown and roll into the shadow of the green-tiled spire of a cathedral built by the French, Palmer sees Detty. The man is alone in a jeep coming this way. He has no hat. His pale blond bristled hair and pale eyebrows and skin made pale by too much heroin glow in the sunlight. His jeep passes into the shadow of the cathedral, and Palmer waves and shouts, "Detty!"

Detty is driving too fast for this road, hunched over the steering wheel and peering through the dirty glass of a dirty jeep. But he hears his name being shouted above the tumult and looks over at Palmer startled like a man discovered in the worst possible way, his name being hollered in a place he believes himself to be anonymous. Their eyes meet as the jeeps pass. A feeble smirk shapes a corner of Detty's lips and he raises his chin in acknowledgment and recognition and what seems like relief to Palmer who, after the jeeps have passed, is struck by the quick but concrete image of Detty's eyes, the pale drained orbs of a doper, his pupils like hard black BBs.

Mueller glances over at Detty but looks back at the road, a conscientious driver, slowing for chickens and children.

Palmer settles back into his seat clutching the sacked whiskey and extrapolates upon this encounter. He decides that Detty has been out making a score, pot certainly, possibly heroin, and this makes him feel good. It is a good omen, after his inability to find Detty the previous evening during his sour encounter with the dopers. If Detty has scored heroin, it is possible Palmer can cadge a hit off him this evening. Just a pinch, a few flakes on the tip of his little finger, enough to saturate his body with a pleasure more intense than any eroticism conceivable, though heroin is not a head-trip. That's what pot is for. It was Detty who turned him on to both pot and heroin, and it is with a perverse sense of pride that Palmer has chosen not to become a regular user of heroin. He had snorted heroin four times during the past two months, and it became tangibly and thoroughly obvious to him why narcotics are illegal.

He hides the sack beneath the back seat as they approach the guard shack at the port compound. The Mariner's Club is a lounge at the edge of the bay, a clean dive which was established to service the merchant marines who man the docked cargo ships. The club accepts only piasters. Palmer tried to pay for his drinks with Military Payment Certificates the first time he was brought here by a fellow detachment clerk. It was apparently a kind of fraternity prank, his buddy yukking in the background while Palmer stood there baffled and holding out his funny-money while the cashier shook her head no. His buddy finally forked over the piasters, and Palmer had to admit that it was a pretty good joke. Embarrassment is one emotion he had not expected, consciously expected, to experience in Vietnam.

There are no other customers in the club, and Palmer and Mueller take a table by a picture window which offers a panoramic view of navy ships at anchor. Palmer orders a scotch-and-soda rather than a martini, which he has never really liked, and Mueller has a Schlitz. Mueller glances at his watch after they order. There are only twenty-five minutes left of the lunch hour.

"We'll drink up and go," Palmer assures him. "Isn't this a nice place? It's like a bar back home."

Mueller's neck swivels as he takes in the bright airy pastel decor, and nods, yes, this is a nice place, and glances again at his enemy, the wristwatch.

Palmer is bored and irritated with Mueller's worry, and wishes he had been sober enough to drive here by himself. He couldn't care less if they are a few minutes late for work. Sgt. Ancil is a bear on punctuality at dawn, but things loosen up at noon, probably, he thinks, because Ancil himself knocks back a few at lunch.

He thinks of the sack of scotch hidden beneath the back-seat of the jeep, and of the drinking he will do tonight at the party, and this serves to dispel his irritation. It is too difficult to involve other people in his drinking, and he has always known this. With an internal shrug of resignation, he sucks the last bit of scotch from his upturned glass and stands up even though Mueller has not finished half his bottle. "Let's hit the road," Palmer says, and Mueller hops up eager and relieved and leads Palmer to the Vietnamese woman behind the cash register in the foyer where Palmer pays for his drink and for that wasted beer which, even as he walks out the door into the noonday heat, calls to him.

Fifteen minutes till one, they will make it with five minutes to spare, long enough for a man to have lingered over a second scotch-and-soda.

They pass through the port gate and drive into the city to retrace their route as far as the abandoned engineering compound. From there they will head south toward Camp Quincey and the PMO. But Mueller is forced to slow by pedestrians who are crowding into the street. Faces peer into the jeep as they penetrate what now appears to be a mob. Palmer detects hostility, which he finds surprising because this has always been a peaceful and friendly city.

"It's an accident," Mueller says.

Palmer's vision is blurred by the afternoon sun shining directly into his face and by the alcohol in his brain, so that he does not see at first the jeep parked at an odd angle halfway off the shoulder of the road within a ring of shouting people.

The flashing lights of a Military Police jeep are coming from far down the opposite end of the street, and Palmer points at it. "Let's get back to the compound, they'll take care of it," and realizes as he says this that he recognizes the jeep.

It is the one Detty was driving, and he hears a wail of grief crossing the sky, and thinks at first it is a siren.

"That's Detty's jeep," Mueller says.

And though the day is hot, and his blood runs warm with alcohol, Palmer feels a chill growing beneath his breastbone, for if what he believed when he first saw Detty is true, and if that sound of a woman's grief means what it sounds like it must mean, there will be consequences so dire that the very thought sobers him a bit, but only a bit.

"Stop the jeep," he says. "I want to take a look."

"But lunchtime is almost over," Mueller says, practically whines, and Palmer frowns at him thinking Christ it's like riding with a little kid. "I'm the traffic man at the PMO," Palmer says even though this sounds a bit silly. "This is traffic business." The jeep is moving so slowly, almost at a standstill, that Palmer simply steps out of it and begins making his way through the people whom he senses rather quickly are angry.

He is concerned that the approaching MPs will find dope on Detty. If Detty has been knocked unconscious or hurt badly, Palmer intends to rifle his pockets and toss the shit only because Detty will be in enough trouble for wrecking a jeep, the man doesn't need a dope bust to boot. This idea is unarticulated. It is a feeling that he hauls through the crowd, a feeling grounded in the concept of helping out a buddy rather than that of breaking military law. It is instinctive. He peers toward the driver's seat as he breaks through a wall of grass hats and white blouses.

Most of the onlookers are women. They turn and squint up at him as he touches their shoulders, and he sees it all, reads it fast and understands as his eyes move past combinations of people frozen in appropriate tableaus, the most significant being the absence of Detty whose retreat from this crime is indicated by a series of horizontal arms and fingers extended as if dragged level in his hurried wake: that of angry men shouting and indicating the direction Detty has fled the scene of the accident.

Palmer understands, and turns away, parts the crowd again and moves toward his jeep slowly and heavily as if glutted with revulsion at the sight of a dead child lying near the blood-washed tire, at the demoralizing comprehension of Detty's worst mistake, for he will be caught. A man cannot go AWOL in this city, especially not a drugged man or a man who has killed a civilian, and expect to get away with it. He cannot hide in the city or out in the countryside or up in the mountains, and he cannot escape back to America. Detty will be caught.

As Palmer takes his place in the jeep, he sees his own crack traffic-accident investigation team, Sp/4 Saunders and PFC Lester. They park their jeep and climb out with nightsticks clenched apprehensively as the sounds of outrage flowing around the street rise in volume. They are touching their leather holsters as they make their way toward the dead child and the wailing woman and the arms of the men who are pointing in the direction that Detty has fled.

The shouting of the crowd grows louder, as though in competition with or in denial of the wail of the grieving woman who squats over the body of her dead son, and Palmer begins to feel oddly safer. As long as the violence remains vocal, neither he nor Mueller will be in danger. The jeep is nudged, rocked, as bodies becomes more compacted.

People are coming from other neighborhoods to see what the noise is all about, and the street is now completely impassable.

Mueller's fingers are shot absolutely white as he grips the steering wheel, and Palmer finds this amusing. Mueller is generating enough fear for both of them. And as on those invulnerable nights when Palmer had mingled foolishly with violent people in strange bars, he feels the peril not only lessening but in some way coming under his control, as if a riot cannot begin in earnest until he wills it.

It finally becomes clear that the anger and the shouting are directed primarily at that empty direction in which Detty ran. The men are demanding that the killer be pursued, but Lester and Saunders have not had time to investigate what has happened, to get their shit together and call the desk sergeant and ask for a backup unit on not a simple accident, or a fatal TA, but a hit-and-run, even a potential murder. Some Vietnamese take it upon themselves to run in Detty's direction, they will be sure bloodhounds, vindictive, successful, they won't wait for the U.S. army to get its shit together, and this roil, this bedlam increases in volume and madness until the sudden noisy, careening, wild approach of Vietnamese Military Police in jeeps absolutely parts the crowd.

The TC are small men, young, they look like pubescent boys, helmeted, armed, they leap from their jeeps gripping pistols and kick and scream their way toward the scene of the accident. Their heads are slung low between their shoulders like boxers poised to deliver blows. They walk slightly bow-legged, relentless, arms flicking random nightsticks herding the people aside, and the people quiet fast in the presence of these duly authorized and dangerous men.

Another American MP jeep comes down the road with a slow, almost elegant roll in comparison to the TC. The red lights are on but not the siren, and when it is parked off to the side of the road, the men get out and pause a moment to adjust the pleats and tails of their fatigue jackets bundled beneath their pistol belts. They pull their helmets low to their eyes and walk slowly into the crowd to confer with Saunders and Lester, to take control of the situation, to find out who did what to whom and what must be done about it, a scenario Palmer once found fascinating when it was his vocation but now finds dull. He wants to get back to the compound and have a few drinks. The deadline for lunch hour has passed, they are late for work, and the only compensation for this minor mess is the humor which Palmer finds in Mueller's despair at having gotten enmeshed in an incomprehensible shafu for which he must surely receive some sort of reprimand. Palmer would like to say aloud, but doesn't, "Wise up, Mueller."

"Maybe one of these units will escort us back to Camp Quincey," Mueller says.

"What are you talking about?" Palmer says. "Let's just go."

"But look at these people," Mueller says, pointing vaguely through the dusty windshield at a newly established wall of faces blocking the road. The noise of the crowd has abated, but after looking at their faces, at their number, Palmer decides that there may, after all, be danger here. The crowd is growing, and those who are arriving, after the violent advent of the TC, are becoming as enraged and loud as the first crowd had been.

This makes him instinctively reach for his sack of scotch, even though he knows he cannot unpeel and drink from it. He holds the sack ass-end up as if clutching a nightstick and sits up straight to see if any MPs are nearby because in a small part of his mind he can see himself sneaking one last quick drink to fortify himself before confronting whatever is going to take place this afternoon. His death perhaps. Like that head lying on the ground in a blossom of blood.

"Palmer! What the hell are you doing here?" Out of the crowd appears the freckled, cherub-haired head of a Hoosier named Potter, a man whose traffic accident reports are outstanding in both form and content, whose handwriting is always a pleasure to encounter, the ink pressed thickly onto the pages, his letters squared and bold, readable, with each drawing of the evolution of an accident a study in accuracy and precision.

"We were coming from the pier," Palmer replies as the MP grabs the canvas top of the jeep and leans in. "We got caught in this."

"You better get on back," Potter says with a slight drawl, a Midwestern twang, an American voice stating the ridiculous.

"Can you clear the road for us?" Palmer says, but it is a joke. The road is packed solid, from shop to shop with rubberneckers and troublemakers, the ugliness of the crowd mushrooming. Detty apparently has escaped, and the people at last have something to complain about besides the stultifying occupation by a foreign power not the Japanese or the French and not yet their obnoxious brothers from the north.

Potter smiles at Palmer. He likes being a cop. Crowd-control is just one small facet of his expertise. He once told

Palmer that when he goes home he wants to become a police officer in Los Angeles. He consults with a Vietnamese patrol, and TC nightsticks commence to waling upon the backs of a mob in retreat. The crowd parts biblically. It is as if Palmer has willed it. He most certainly has, words are magic. Mueller puts the jeep into gear and they proceed along a human corridor held at bay by the furious authority of boysans with guns.

Mueller drives too fast back to Camp Quincey. Palmer is holding onto the safety strap unable to take a desperately-needed drink and so he is irritated, once again, at Mueller. But his irritation is submerged behind a realization that penetrates his inebriated consciousness as he gazes about the street which an hour ago was crowded and alive. The streets are empty. The storefronts are closed, windows and doors shut. There is an immaculate silence on the streets which he has experienced before and which makes him uneasy because the only time the streets are ever deserted like this is at night, just before the Viet Cong launch rocket attacks on the city.

But this is noon, the VC don't set up mortars on the mountainside in full daylight. They'd be picked off by Huey gunships in a turkey-shoot.

So bafflement is the emotion that Palmer brings into the compound as Mueller wheels the jeep through a gate quickly closed behind them by two MPs in combat regalia.

Palmer asks Mueller to slow and let him off to go to the barracks, and for one sickening moment he thinks Mueller is not going to slow, that Mueller is angry for having been led astray and made late for work and is going to drive right up to the PMO where Sgt. Ancil might see Palmer gripping his sack of opened, incriminating, scotch. But Mueller only drives to the corner of the battalion headquarters building and stops at the intersection. He says nothing as Palmer climbs out, and Palmer does not look him in the eye. He hurries to the barracks to stash the evidence and retrieve the bottle of Pepto Bismol for Missy Anh.

The barracks is silent, and after swallowing a solid sip and putting the scotch into his locker and heading for the door, he realizes that the place has that prim swept and finished look it always has after the house girls have gone home for the day: everything tidy, brooms put away.

He is crossing the parking lot when Sgt. Ancil comes out the PMO door frowning. He is not wearing his hat, which means to Palmer that the sergeant has stepped outside specifically to intercept him, to instigate a showdown. Palmer looks at his wristwatch. It is past one-thirty.

"You're AWOL, GI," the sergeant says with that serrated voice that makes Palmer think that Ancil might have suffered a throat wound in Korea.

Palmer stops and nods, but then the sergeant gives up a smile that Palmer usually sees only when Ancil is dealing decks with his cronies at the EM club, or pandering to visiting officers.

"Mueller tells me you two were in the middle of the shit," Ancil says.

"I told Mueller to stop for a look because it was a traffic accident," Palmer replies, listening to his voice to determine if he sounds drunk, and listening to the content of his words to determine if it sounds lame.

"The city has been put on yellow alert," Ancil says, glancing toward the street beyond the cyclone fence. "The Vietnamese help was sent home. The roads are closed. You were lucky to get back to the compound."

"Why?" Palmer says, and realizes he has been totally oblivious to the import of everything that has taken place in the past hour.

"The fucking riot, GI. When they catch the AWOL mother-fucker who killed that kid, the shit's gonna fly."

Palmer nods but stops himself from asking the sergeant if he knows who is responsible for the hit-and-run. Surely Mueller has revealed that it was Detty. But he cannot bring himself to ask. It is instinctive. He does not want to inadvertently finger Detty.

"Have you got a good pair of fatigues for soldier of the month?" Ancil asks.

This shift in midstream takes Palmer by surprise, and he parts his lips but cannot focus his mind to reply. The alcohol drilling his thoughts has rendered him incapable of dealing effectively with anything more immediate or important than the next drink.

"Get your ass over to the supply room and pick up a new pair," Ancil continues in a friendly, conversational, and helpful tone. "I want you looking sharp for the board."

"All right, Sergeant," Palmer says, two syllables in the word sergeant, don't get chummy with the cadre, don't flaunt regulations, don't draw attention to yourself with an attitude that does not reflect proper military bearing.

He goes into the PMO, into his office, and sits at his desk with one hand gripping the slick glass of the pink bottle of stomach medicine. He didn't get back in time to give Anh this blessed relief. She has gone home.

He puts the bottle into his desk drawer thinking, hoping, that she can pick up a bottle on the black market. Then he realizes, as he begins to reread his FTA from the morning, that all the shops downtown are now closed because of the riots.

He turns his mind away from his failure to help Anh by burying himself in an hour's worth of deliberate, accumulative work. His IN file is bulging with overdue reports.

He squints at the small print describing the fatal TA on the Mang Yang pass. A five-ton truck rolled over the head of the driver who had jumped out of the cab in panic, and he stops reading.

The top of the child's head had been taken off just at the hairline. The lashes of his closed eyes were like black thistles. His pouted lips seemed to have been outlined with India-ink on smooth child flesh, a face napping, but the flesh had no color. It had drained off into a red lake shored by asphalt. The wailing woman was squatting by her boy, the edge of a single sandal touching his curled, lifeless, fingers.

Palmer sets the report aside and looks around at Anh's desk. Her work has been put neatly away, her desk is clean just as the barracks was made to look as if no one had been there to do the dirty work. Palmer gets up and tells Mueller he is going to the latrine, and he hurries to the barracks, to his locker, and to his waiting bottle.

CHAPTER 26

Though one of their own is AWOL, possibly a murderer, definitely a hunted man, battalion nevertheless holds the going-away party for Sp/4 Nolan that evening. Palmer is drunk enough now to be disappointed that the party is not being held at Port Beach but at a small concrete patio north of the Camp Quincey EM club within a grove of incongruous evergreen trees. There is a barbecue pit and picnic tables. The office houseboy, a fifty-year-old Vietnamese man called Papasan, has stayed on the compound to cook the chicken and drink American beer and laugh with a grating squeal at jokes he could not possibly understand. He is a buffoon whose furtive moves around the office, whose sudden appearances at break time and disappearances when it is time to work, whose overall surreptitiousness, reminds Palmer of himself and thus makes him feel uneasy around Papasan.

Palmer drinks beer at a table out on the sand beneath the stars with men from the detachment and battalion headquarters who come and go. He gets up long enough only to fish another icy beer out of the tub. There will be no prostitutes at this party, the city is on yellow alert, off-limits to everyone but road MPs who are still looking for Detty who, to everyone's surprise, has disappeared successfully into the surrounding slums which comprise most of the city.

Palmer moves to another table watching the brass come and go. The battalion commander, a bird colonel, shows up for the award ceremony. The battalion sergeant-major calls "Attention to orders," and everyone stands. The sand beneath

Palmer's boots shifts as he sways maintaining a practiced balance. The colonel awards Nolan an ARCOM medal, and the battalion sergeant-major hands Nolan a memorial plaque. The crowd shouts for a speech and Nolan steps into this traditional, brief, and singular military limelight to sum up his drafted career. He tells everyone how sorry he is to be leaving his good friends and the army itself, as Palmer's hearing drifts away and focuses on the heavy sound of breakers on the beach.

"When I was drafted, I thought it was the worst thing that ever happened to me," Nolan says, and this draws Palmer's attention away from the flux. "But after two years in the army, and a year in Vietnam, I think it was probably the best thing that ever happened to me."

There is an eruption of applause that overwhelms the roar of that ceaseless reach of nature. Palmer watches Nolan being surrounded by officers and enlisted men, who shake both his hands and slap him on the back.

The water in the tub, a moat embracing a glacier of block ice, is so cold that it hurts to reach in and grab a can of beer. There is no one else around the beer tub, they are all congratulating Nolan, and Palmer stabs the unpleasant chill, snatches a can and opens it with a twine-bound dangling church-key attached to a tub handle. He shakes his hand and flexes his fingers. He cannot believe water can get this cold without freezing, and while he is contemplating this satisfying and meaningless enigma, he begins to sense a distinct change in the tenor of the party. It is not the rustling and dimming of voices that indicates the celebration is coming to an end, this party has another hour of life, it is early, barely nine, but heads are turning and voices are speaking low and fast here and there, and two men in MP uniforms have walked up and spoken to the Provost Marshal, whose face turns toward the lights of the MP station across the softball field.

Alarm, like a cold wet thread dragged across Palmer's neck, stays his lifted beer. The riots of the afternoon have faded, the noisy citizenry who had marched past the compound shouting epithets of anger and frustration and revenge are all home eating rice cakes. But maybe they have come back, or worse, maybe the VC are taking advantage of this rift in public relations to send in sappers. Maybe rockets will be incoming. These concepts flow unarticulated through Palmer. They are not thoughts, words, images, they are intuitive, like the response of an arm fielding a grounder and chucking it toward home-plate solely through the memory of muscle (I'm going to die).

But, as it turns out, as always, his fears are self-indulgent. Detty has been caught and is now sitting in a detention cell in the MP station. As though anyone here below the rank of E5 gives a shit. Detty bollixed the beach party, there are no women here and no one will be getting laid tonight because that asshole doper fucked everything up. He is as close to being a buddy-fucker as a man can get without doing it on purpose.

The brass departs, for Detty's capture has ramifications which go all the way up the chain of command to USARV in Saigon. The senior NCOs leave with the brass, and there is only an E7 from battalion left, a few E6, a few E5, and a lot of drunk enlisted men who will not admit, though they know, that the lower ranks have their share of privileges too. Normally, when the brass leaves, this is the unwritten signal that women can be brought in to the parties, but the city is off-limits, the women are home watching their contraband American PX TVs, an unscheduled night off.

The men raid the beer tub, the older soldiers hit the hard liquor, and the laughter is audibly bitter. Nothing to do now but get drunk. Thank God the colonel didn't cut off the booze.

Palmer's thoughts at the picnic table drift across the softball field and beyond the perimeter fence where there would normally be women in colored pajamas walking slowly by or riding fast on the back of pimp Hondas, where there would be the sounds of the city, not the mute rumble of an American city, but distinctive sounds in the palm night, mini-bikes, shouts, farm-animal squeal and squawk, a populace barely separated from their own earth, a truly medieval land. And outside all this, the occasional punctuation of gunfire.

Then his thoughts drift back into the MP station. He imagines Detty seated in a detention cell, probably glowering. Palmer has seen the faces of AWOLs before, like the faces of pushers, rapists, thieves, cowards, a surly lot, given to whining. His connection is in jail. He wants to go see Detty, to find out what happened after he fled into the crowd. But all this information will appear on his desk in the morning, a Traffic Accident report combined with a standard Military Police report describing the crime, witness statements, they will want it processed fast and couriered by air to Saigon. Electric threads connecting this city to the south are already vibrating with information, the lights in the CID office above the MP station are ablaze, the given peace of the graveyard shift abrogated indefinitely.

Palmer leaves the battalion men to their drinking and walks across the softball field. There are no dopers at the party. Those men will be congregated upstairs, but because one of theirs has been apprehended, perhaps the conclaves will move to safer locations tonight. Dope will be smoked in small groups beneath the water tower or in certain designated sandbag bunkers along the perimeter where the heads can watch for MPs.

He crosses the road and looks at the MP station where a half-dozen jeeps are parked. The roads are unsafe tonight and the patrols will venture out only on emergencies. Nobody will be dashing. The double doors of the station are open, and uniformed MPs loiter outside smoking cigarettes and laughing, exchanging lies about their crucial role in Detty's collar.

Palmer goes back to the barracks and gets his bottle of scotch which he had originally planned to dent severely tonight. Though he is already good and drunk he knows enough to lay off. He will have to be at work at seven A.M. to process the report. He cannot stumble in badly hungover, there may be brass, possibly even the battalion commander, hanging around waiting for him to type those carbon copies. His typing will have to be impeccable, finished quickly, and just before he takes a good hit of Johnny Walker to bring this drinking session to its disappointing end, it occurs to him that Sgt. Ancil might order him to come to the station right now and stay up all night working on the report so it will be ready for a courier at dawn.

The plausibility of this bullshit angers him, and he takes two good hits and caps the bottle, puts it away and goes up to the TV area to watch the end of whatever might be on. He

sits in the Naugahyde chair, Mueller's spot, and watches the
American National Anthem and the sign-off, then switches
channels to catch the South Vietnam National Anthem, a
tinny orchestral march which seems an Asian imitation of
Sousa, and he wonders if they inherited this western dirge
from the French.

At his back, Gerlach wrestles with the iron, lying supine
on his fabricated bench, and when Palmer rises and turns off
the TV and goes to bed, Gerlach is still at it, the rhythmic clink
and gasp of his desperate bellowed lungs finally silenced by
the hum of Palmer's fan switched onto high.

CHAPTER 27

Instead of pain, the first sensation Palmer experiences upon awakening Saturday morning is the comforting raw taste of scotch on his tongue. He would prefer to dwell on this but his mind drifts to less interesting matters. Detty is in jail and there is an important report to be dealt with this morning, and he knows he cannot drag ass to the PMO, cannot forego a shower and a shave. There is formal military business to be taken care of, and this reminds him of his date with the board on Monday. Depression sets in, and he walks to the shower with his eyes closed against the risen sun, wearing only fatigue pants. When he arrives and does not hear the chatter of working women beneath the water tower, he realizes he need not have worn anything at all, for the compound is off-limits to the Vietnamese. The city is still on yellow alert.

Washing grit from his hair, he sees through the screened window Papasan burning shit in a washtub behind the latrine. Papasan must have stayed on the compound overnight. What does Papasan know about the Viet Cong? Is anybody in this country not a Viet Cong? What's all this about anyway? Palmer brushes the pleasant veneer of scotch off his tongue with Crest, and rinses it away with Listerine.

He walks across the PMO parking lot at five minutes to seven, and for all practical purposes he does not have a hangover, which is a marvelous feeling, as though he has recovered from some awful tropical fever, for he has not come to work without the baggage of booze wracking his body and brain to some degree in a long time.

The feeble shouts of Vietnamese protesters come from beyond the fence. Angry citizens are arriving to protest the killing. There are school children among them, girls in white blouses and blue skirts, boys in blue beanies, blue pants, white shirts. They are grinning, watching shyly on the shoulder of the road as their elders mill around and grouse at the gate guards, with younger men occasionally ranting some indecipherable slogan of outrage.

Palmer finds the office quiet. He has arrived ahead of the other clerks, an anomaly, possibly a mistake. Sgt. Ancil might expect him to do this every morning, might want to know why he cannot manage to do this all the time. But Ancil is up in the MP station proper, and by the time he returns to the rear of the building, the other clerks have arrived, it is ten after seven, and the only thing Palmer can think about is those five minutes he could have remained in bed, five minutes during which he could have downed at least one beer which he wants very badly.

Ancil heads directly for the traffic office, which takes Palmer by surprise. He is not typing, he has no coffee, he is doing absolutely nothing when the sergeant enters. He is sitting at his desk staring at his empty typewriter, and a panic seizes his heart.

"File this, GI," is all Ancil says. He sets a carbon copy of a finished traffic accident report on Palmer's desk. It is neatly typed, one of six carbon copies. The work which Palmer had anticipated has already been performed.

"Who did this?" Palmer says to distract Ancil. He is sure that the sergeant's awareness of his inactivity is as intense as his own awareness and guilt and feeling bordering on shame and foolishness, but Ancil merely replies, "Sergeant Tyler," and walks out oblivious to Palmer's alcoholic paranoia.

Tyler is the night desk-sergeant, a lifer in his thirties whom Palmer gets along with well. He is a friendly, well-groomed man, the sort who will go home one day and perhaps become a liquor-store clerk or a short-haul delivery driver. He will never again know the power and prestige of being a sergeant, and in these times back home he probably will have to teach himself not to expect respect from anyone ever again. Palmer is surprised at a faint sense of resentment that begins to well up within him at the thought of another man doing his work. But then he accepts it as he has always accepted evidence of his own pretentiousness.

He reads the report, the slick documentation by a professional, meticulously correct, the diagram of the fatal traffic accident carefully rendered with a plastic template showing Detty's vehicle veering off the road and striking the victim who was squatting alongside his mother tending a fire, making rice cakes to be sold at a roadside stand. There is a large X drawn with red ink at the point of impact, and a simple rectangle indicating the position of the dead boy. Sgt. Tyler went over each carbon copy and marked the impact with a red inked X, so that those up the chain of command would quickly comprehend what had happened, a thing which Palmer has yet to grasp.

He carries the copy to the filing cabinets at the front of the office, but before he places it in the correct folder, he carries it through the door into the adjoining MP station to see Detty.

Sergeant Owens is on duty at the desk, a short red-headed asshole lifer whom Palmer does not get along with at all, but he nods at the sergeant with military courtesy and looks into the detention room, at its three barred cells. An MP is sitting on a bench adjacent to cell number one, the cell occupied by Detty, who is sitting on the floor wrapped in an OD green blanket which covers his bowed head.

"I have to ask Detty something about this report," he says to Owens at the desk, who grins big and nods. Owens is a man convinced of his own popularity, a fifteen-year man whose Mickey Rooney-like hypertension drains his co-workers of energy. Palmer knows this because he was required to work the blotter one day when the MP company was short of men. Owens is a joker. "Doing a job in the army is just like taking a shit," he said over and over. "The job isn't finished until you've done the paperwork."

Palmer enters the detention room and informs the MP guard that he has to ask Detty a few questions about the accident. The MP gets up and leaves the room with an empty coffee cup in his hand.

Palmer sees now that the blanket is shaking, and he has to squat to see Detty's face. Detty looks at him through the bars seemingly without recognition. The knuckles of his right hand are shiny. His fist taps his runny nose and he looks at Palmer with a face, eyes, flesh, gone paler than that albino countenance has ever appeared to Palmer before.

"Score," Detty whispers.

Palmer shuffles closer to the bars gripping the traffic-accident report and frowns.

"What happened yesterday?" he asks.

Detty pulls the cowl away from his ears and moves closer to the bars. "Score for me, man. They took my stash." He is talking so softly that Palmer can barely hear him, but he does hear this, and he can barely believe it.

The MP comes back into the room, Palmer hears the cup tap the table top. He looks at Detty, whose addicted, blood-less, desperate eyes silently repeat his plea. The man is skeletal, he is shaking, he is going into withdrawal, and he is going there cold-turkey, and Palmer knows it, and knows with a comprehension that begets horror the meaning of the thing Detty is asking him to do.

The cure, for almost everything, but specifically for the irritation of having been drafted for a job he does not want, is booze. The cure for thinking, worrying, caring, is booze. And though it is barely nine o'clock, and though he has lived eighteen months in accordance with a vow never to drink hard-stuff at all on duty, excepting lunch hour, he stands now in the barracks uncapping the bottle of scotch and tipping the rim against his teeth and measuring a shot onto his tongue.

Even though the house girls are not squatting near the front door with their baskets of laundry, he is overly cautious about making noise because he is into the hard stuff. He never attempts to conceal the sound of a church-key penetrating the tin lid of a beer can, it could be a Coca-Cola for all anyone knows, he always tells himself, with the alcohol-logic which carries him through incalculable situations of embarrassment which he subsequently tries purposefully to forget.

The hard liquor is like thick candy to him, Firestix, it goes down with a sweet burning sensation that he chooses not to chase with canteen water or beer or Coke. He takes another drink and hears a man come into the barracks and he nearly drops the bottle capping and putting it into his wall locker. His hands are shaking, adrenaline has fused with the booze, he expects to be caught, the thing that he always expected would happen if he ever broke that vow born of lame wisdom.

He walks out of his cubicle and nearly bumps into Sp/5 Nelson who is coming up the aisle.

"Shit GI!" Nelson says surprised, grinning. "Are you fucking-off in here?"

Nelson runs the Vietnamese employee ID section at the PMO and has no authority over Palmer even though he is an E5. Palmer keeps his lips clamped tight to hide the odor of booze, and smiles and nods and plays the fool. He hurries back to the PMO and takes his seat at his desk and realizes that Missy Anh will not be in this morning, not because of the protests but because the Vietnamese secretaries who work on the compound do not work on Saturdays. He has looked forward to apologizing to Missy Anh for not bringing the Pepto Bismol back in time, has been looking forward to her absolution.

Saturday is half-day for the PMO clerks, which is part of Palmer's justification for drinking scotch at this early hour. With only two-and-a-half hours left of work, it is not that different from having drunk at noon on a weekday. But all this rationalization is rendered moot by the pleasure already welling in his brain. The two hits have given a soft edge to everything, and the irritation at being asked an outrageous favor by Detty is lessening to a tolerable level. The caress of booze makes him think about approaching one of the dopers at battalion headquarters. He might pass the word on to one of them: Detty needs H. A few more drinks, and he just might be stupid enough to do that.

He gets up and goes for a cup of hot coffee rather than Coke, but then fills it with so much sugar that it is syrupy, a sweet cleaver to cut the odor of booze, to wake him up so that, high but not yet drunk, he will be alert to his own errors in speech and action until eleven-thirty when the office closes for the weekend. He knows he will be back at the barracks at ten o'clock for a beer and probably two more hits of scotch and he doesn't care. Noon will be like evening. Nobody cares, a half-day is bullshit anyway, the war won't be won by working Saturdays.

He throws himself into his work by typing at a pace he could maintain sober for perhaps fifteen minutes, and he finishes three reports in an hour, his fingers hammering the keys with a liquid precision. When he removes the third report and separates the carbons from between the white pages, he sees that he has put the carbons in backwards. He wads the mess with a smile and trashes it and gets up and tells Mueller he is heading to the latrine, which is true.

He goes to the barracks and has a shot of scotch and walks to the latrine behind the quartermaster barracks. His head is buzzing now, partly from the exhaustion of having worked steadily for an hour, unused to that sort of menial concentration, but also from his high that increases after he has taken his seat on the twenty-holer with two other men who are seated silently and spaced evenly apart reading old copies of *Rolling Stone*.

The tin tub below his bare ass thuds as he stares at the high screened-window across from him with a kind of mindless satisfaction. He has no reading matter. He hears Papasan tugging a shit tub out of the latrine in back, hears a splash of diesel fuel being poured and patiently lit, and he smells the mechanical odor of disaster filling the air. A residue of flaming diesel-fuel-and-shit lingers in his sinuses after he pulls up his fatigue pants and steps outside to light a cigarette and look at Papasan, who is grinning like a madman.

"Beaucoup shit, huh Papasan?"

"Beaucoup shit!" Papasan squeals, laughing. The man begins to stir the fuel in order to appear to be working. Papasan can drink a beer in a long gulp in less than ten seconds. Palmer has seen him do this at parties, and he understands why he must do it. The house girls had secretly told him that Papasan steals beers from the barracks, but rather than getting angry at the poor guy, Palmer simply began locking his icebox in the daytime.

He returns to the barracks and has a sip of scotch. By the time he gets back to the office, he has lost most of his concern, his sense of obligation or responsibility, toward Detty, whom he knows is sitting in his cell waiting for Palmer to engineer some sort of transfer of heroin, perhaps a palmed vial during a conversation. But if things work out the way Palmer now hopes, he will never see Detty again. Because of the riots, Detty may be transferred to another city, possibly Saigon for court martial. And if he does not get any heroin soon, he will most likely go into total withdrawal and be sent to the evacuation hospital by the airfield for detoxification. And if he ever returns to battalion for duty, it will no longer be as clerk-typist in Headquarters Company. At best he will be put to work painting things green, the barracks, the offices, anything made of wood. This is what becomes of all the dopers who are busted down to E-nothing. By then Palmer

will have fabricated a lie which even Detty must accept, that
he was absolutely unable to score H and deliver it to the jail.
Too many people were around, security was too tight, or
some such bullshit. And maybe, by then, Detty won't even
care. He might not even remember that he had requested
heroin, might forget that just before rising to walk away
Palmer had nodded as if to reassure Detty that his heroin
would be coming soon, whereas Palmer had nodded simply
to cut the conversation short and get out of there.

He shouldn't have nodded, he knows that. But he
couldn't bring himself to shake his head no because, after all,
if he had done that, they wouldn't be friends anymore. Detty
wouldn't like him, just as the dopers upstairs don't like him,
because Palmer is not one with them, or with anyone. He is a
juicer.

CHAPTER 28

Palmer is typing as the minute-hand falls degree-by-degree toward the half-hour mark, as the muted explosion of breaking glass and torrential waters comes from beyond the door leading into the MP station. Men begin yelling.

He knows what it is without looking up. His fingers continue their rapid stroke. He is not a touch-typist but need only stare at the keyboard to guide the first two fingers of each hand toward their proper plant. He has heard it before, four times in six months. A prisoner has gotten rowdy and there has been a scuffle, and the glass-bottled potable watercooler in the MP station has been knocked over. Then, when he finishes typing and sits back smiling through his alcoholic haze, he realizes that Detty is the only prisoner in the MP station.

By the time he steps through the door to look across the shoulders of the grinning clerk/typists at the mess, Detty has already been shackled and handcuffed and placed in the rear of a jeep which will transport him to the hospital. The concrete floor of the station is wet, but already the water is evaporating in the heat leaving whorled stains sprinkled with shards of glass. Sgt. Owens puts Papasan to work on the broom, plowing the scattered glass into handy piles.

The six MPs in the room are red-faced, angry, their starch-pressed fatigues wet and wrinkled, their polished leather web-gear askew. They tug belts and gather pleats and mumble curses at the fucking doper in the jeep. Palmer stays away from the front door. He does not want Detty to see him and

does not want to see Detty, who must by now be in the throes
of withdrawal pain. Detty had been taken out of the D-cell
and had probably tried to make a break, but Palmer doesn't
want to know.

Two MPs enter the doorway, one of them wearing a bandage on his hand which was cut by glass during the wrestling
match. Palmer looks around the floor and sees a pale swath
of blood near the metal stand of the water cooler. The man
was cut, which means he has a score to settle with Detty, who
only compounded his problems by his futile struggle. He
may get punched in the face a few times on the way to the
hospital. It has happened before, except that the MP who did
it last time was almost court martialed for abusing a prisoner
and was taken off road duty for a month. Best not to beat up
on prisoners. It could just create problems when it comes time
for your discharge.

Palmer goes back to his office and clears his desk. He
looks at his watch. Eleven thirty-one. The weekend has
begun, and Detty has gone away.

Palmer walks across the softball field to the EM club,
which is crowded. It is always crowded on Saturday, and he
discovers to his amusement that because there are no waitresses and no cooks, the bar will not be serving food today.
He orders an army drink, rum-and-Coke, and takes it outside
and sits at the end of a picnic-table bench occupied by three
men from the quartermaster battalion. He sits with his back
to them and stares out at the China Sea sipping his diluted
rum. He decides to go ahead and eat at the mess hall toward
the end of the hour, when the place will be relatively deserted.
It has been a long time since he has eaten mess hall chow, a long

time since he has picked little pink spots out of white bread, those crispy baked bodies of fallen insects. Then he realizes there will be no KP women at the mess hall, and he wonders who will end up scrubbing pots and pans and silverware.

He recalls his first week in-country, on a day when all the MPC was to be turned in and exchanged for new money. No Vietnamese were allowed on the compounds, and because he was a cherry boy with six days under his belt he was drafted for KP along with a couple other newbies. In the States he had been told that one of the best things about duty in Vietnam was no KP, and there he was, pulling KP.

The breakers shake the beach as he rolls his neck and looks out at the small soft shape of a ship poised in a haze of blue-green where the sea meets the sky. Because of the tension that comes of drinking during working hours, Palmer's high is almost always experienced as a form of containment. He can never quite let go and enjoy the full effects of drinks sipped in secret in the barracks. But now that the working day, the entire work week, is over, he senses another kind of high melding with his inebriation, the sheer joy of unemployment, the absolute freedom of fucking-off without having to look over his shoulder every time he raises a cup to his lips. The sun is hot on his back, and this tactile comfort lulls him with a physical high that reminds him of the effects of heroin. Which makes him think of Detty, and irritates him.

He finishes his drink and leaves the club, walks toward the barracks and pauses to peer through the dusty screened windows of the mess hall. There are empty tables all around. Satisfied that he will not have to sit across from the masticating face of a stranger as he had done every morning throughout basic training and MP school, he goes inside and fills a tray with barbecued chicken and scalloped potatoes. He wants no vegetables, no fruit salad, no pie, and no bread for that matter. But he does have a glass of milk, imagining that the corroded walls of his stomach will be coated and thus protected from the abuse of the scotch which he knows he will be drinking over the next day and a half.

The ceaseless flow of warm air blowing across his damp chest finally becomes annoying as he sits cross-legged on his bunk in front of his fan. He shifts his body around and sits with his back to the breeze. Every few minutes he hears the rattle of sand-filled weights as Gerlach presses steel toward the rafters in the TV area. Palmer is experiencing a rare drinking moment, for the shots of scotch he has consumed, chased by two beers, have put him into a state of almost preternatural contentment, the sort of alcoholic high he has pursued desperately and without much success incalculable times since he was eighteen. The icebox is stocked with beer. There are three-quarters of a fifth of scotch in the bottle, and on top of his wall locker is a carton containing nine packs of cigarettes. All of this feels like perfection to him, and though he cannot concentrate well enough to calculate the number of free hours ahead of him, he knows it is more than thirty including tonight and all day Sunday, and Sunday night, when he plans to taper off and sober up to be in relatively good shape to face the soldier-of-the-month board on Monday.

Which is a mistake to have thought about. It lessens the intensity of the pleasure he has been experiencing for the past hour or so, and he whispers an almost inarticulate curse at the minuscule irritations which comprise the bulk of military life. How he dreams of the day when he will be a civilian, when nobody will ever be able to tell him what to do again, when he can walk off a job he hates and sleep until noon and loaf in a bar until two a.m.

He hears the zig-zag drone before he sees the slow bulk of a mosquito fighting the fan's current. He turns his head to the sound and there it is, a dark winged dot angling toward his face for a needled drink. He watches its futile progress until it comes within reach, then he grabs it out of the air. It rests beneath his curled fingers near the knife-edge of his palm, and when he opens his hand he sees translucent webbed wings protruding from a mass of body-husk and blood. He leans down and scrapes it off on the bottom edge of his bunk frame. He is bending to the side in an awkward position when he hears an explosion right outside his window. It is not the sound of a rocket or mortar landing, and as he slowly sits upright and frowns at the glow of sky-light coming through the screens, he wonders if some sort of small hand-grenade has been detonated.

He gets up off the bed and leans against the window to look outside, but he knows there is no such thing as a small hand-grenade. He looks across the stretch of dirt toward the dayroom, but there is no one around. The piss-tube shack stands silently fermenting in the sun.

He sits back down into the cooling breeze and decides it must have been a vehicle backfiring out on the road beyond the perimeter fence. He opens a fresh beer even though he has a half-finished one waiting. He puts that one in the refrigerator to cool down, no use wasting beer, you never know when the PX will run out of beer, which is not a joke. At

Christmastime he had discovered to his horror that there was
no Budweiser available, no Schlitz, no Miller, only Pabst Blue
Ribbon and Carling Black Label. He was told by a lifer that the
PX stops distributing the good beer during the holiday season
in order to force soldiers to purchase the crap beers which
no one will buy at any other time of year, the unpopular
beers rotting in warehouses from Saigon to Hue.

He had become a connoisseur of scotch during that Yule-
tide, and to toast that special season he uncaps the Johnny
Walker and measures a double onto his tongue. He has found
that the drunker he gets, the more able he is to drink scotch
straight out of the bottle without a chaser. It's a satisfying
achievement, and fortified by that accomplishment he lights
a fresh cigarette and walks unsteadily up to the TV area
clutching his beer to see what's on this afternoon besides
delayed-broadcast football games from home.

Gerlach is sitting on his bench breathing hard, his face
flushed and shining with sweat. Palmer nods at him, and
Gerlach smiles briefly, nods, and begins sliding larger plates
of sand-filled plastic onto the bar. Palmer sits in the Naugahyde
chair and views the only shows available short of indecipherable Vietnamese soap operas. He watches a Ralph Story
episode, then gallops through a rerun of *Hee-Haw* hoping that
Laugh-In will follow. He is not aware of the absence of Gerlach's
rattling and grunting until he hears footsteps trudging up the
aisle and turns to see who it is. It is Gerlach.

"A man just shot himself," Gerlach says in a mournful voice,
looking at the concrete floor as he walks back to his bench
press.

And now, with the same sort of mindless trepidation and
confusion of entering new territory which he had experienced

the moment he stepped off the plane in Bien Hoa six months previously almost to this day, Palmer gets up and moves toward the front door which glows brightly because of the afternoon sunlight, and because of the size of his pupils which have nestled in the darkness of the barracks and alcohol since one o'clock.

He hears the murmur of men outside before his pupils shrink to withstand the painful glare of the afternoon light, then sees men hatless under the sun, men wearing towels around their waists who have paused on their way to or from the showers, men holding beers in their hands, men with manila folders tucked neatly under their arms. Dust drifts slowly, gently from the overhead landing as he pushes the door open and steps out into the heat and light which engenders a tiny headache behind the bridge of his nose.

The electric wail of an emergency vehicle racing to the compound from the evacuation hospital rises in the distance. He can tell when it turns the corner a block down from the compound and comes toward the main gate, and after it enters with its white crosses blaring from the walls and hood and pulls up at the bottom of the stairs, the siren falls to a purr, a mutter, dies.

Two men hop from the cab and grab a stretcher, but as they rush up the stairs, an officer from battalion headquarters comes outside and waves them off, "Forget it, he's dead, his head is gone." His voice is filled with contempt for what he has had to look at. The medics ignore him and climb past and enter the darkness of the doorway.

Palmer eases through the crowd until he is standing in the shadow of the outdoor theater across the dirt road where he has a clear view of the landing on the second floor. "Who was it?" he says softly to a stranger at his side wearing MP battalion crests. "Detty," the man replies without looking at him.

There is no action from the second floor for at least five minutes, and a large but incomprehensible mutter of voices begins to fill the road until a medic walks out the door backwards gripping the handles of a stretcher. The only sound now is the slow apologetic thud of boots as the medics maneuver the stretcher down the stairs. A poncho has been tossed over the body, and Palmer is struck by how small the lump is that lies beneath the fabric.

When the ambulance is loaded and pulls away, the officer climbs halfway up the stairs and takes hold of the handrail and looks down at the enlisted men silently watching the vehicle depart.

When the officer speaks, it is a shout of outrage and disgust. "Why don't you all come up and gawk at the blood!"

But instead, they all turn away. The officer is a captain in charge of battalion supply. Like most officers assigned to trivial commands, he is contemptuous of enlisted men. He wears sunglasses on duty.

Palmer goes back into his cubicle and sits in front of his fan, and the words, "Detty is dead," move uninvited through his mind, again, and again, and in spite of the beers which he opens and drinks quickly and the scotch which he sips, the words break through with a clarity which invites constant disbelief. Detty is dead.

CHAPTER 29

This feeling of the loss of the acquaintance of a man who was fundamentally a stranger is as unpleasant as would be a small electric current that shoots through the nervous system at random moments. On the flight over he had expected to see a lot of death, and was braced for it in the small way that a kid can make that sort of attitude adjustment. He had expected to take a bullet himself somehow, somewhere, had expected he might die, but all of that was as vague as the prospect of death from old age.

The compound seems more quiet than it had been earlier, but perhaps he only wants more noise, the grind of deuce-and-a-half gears, the shouts of enraged players bickering on the softball field. Thanks to the alcohol, he cannot imagine how he really feels about Detty's suicide.

The bulk of a mosquito flashes near his left eye and he waves his hand automatically and uselessly at the already flown shape. The sound of the fan softens the occasional sound from outside. He cannot hear the buzz of the mosquito, and when the thing flits past again in the same left quadrant of his rather fuzzy vision, he backhands the empty air where it had dropped in a kind of dive-bomb pattern, as if it is circling the same space awaiting the opportunity to battle the rapids of fan-stirred air and attack his flesh.

When it makes another pass, he turns his attention to the bug and holds out his hand in preparation to grab it out of the air. He waits.

The shape drops directly onto his palm and he snaps his

fingers closed around the dark blur. He takes a sip of beer to toast this accomplishment and spreads his fingers wide to view the remains. But there are no glassy wings, no crushed husk. There is only a splash of bright red blood, far too much blood to be contained in the body of a mosquito. It has enough mass to pool along the bottom edge of its own stain and trickle toward his wrist.

He gazes at it. He is holding the can of beer close to his mouth and can smell the pungent alcohol odor through the punched triangles. Before his hand moves, even as his un-comprehending mind has decided to dispense with this odd mess, to reach down and wipe the blood off his hand against the bunk frame, even before his brain has sent that simple message which he has already acknowledged and will do in another moment, even as he is still staring at this wingless, huskless, spot of red trickling toward his wrist, another drop of blood splashes onto his hand. He looks up at the rafters.

A stain has formed directly overhead where Detty's blood has leaked through. The inverted pool of blood on the ceiling is generating drops which have already made a small lake on the concrete beside Palmer's bunk which he has not noticed because he has been concentrating on drinking, on the next drink, and on the drink to follow that one.

He sets the beer next to the fan and steps off the bunk out of range of the leakage. He walks outside and crosses the dirt road with his left hand balled to hide the blood. In the shower room he stands at a sink and washes the blood quickly down the drain. When he enters the barracks again he grabs a poncho liner from the unlocked wall locker which is used to store the house girls' brooms and boxes of Tide.

In his cubicle he raises the liner to the ceiling and presses hard against the rotting wood, dabs at it and then stares at the stain which is black against the pale brown roofing until he sees that the congealed blood is no longer being gathered by gravity and dispensed like clockwork.

He becomes aware of the heavy sounds of footsteps above and realizes that someone must be mopping up the blood. Because Detty had shot his head off, there must be an enormous amount of blood.

He performs these actions, from setting his beer by the fan to stuffing the bloodied poncho liner into the Dempsey dumpster outside the barracks, without a single thought. The phonics of silent language have been absent from his brain. He has moved as if by rote, his actions the product of the power and process of denial, which is the fountainhead of all his drinking.

It is only after he has trashed the poncho liner and is looking at faint streaks of blood on his hands that he sets his mind into motion, "I better wash again," and heads across the dirt road aware now of sounds on the compound, the voices of men behind dusty screened windows, the muted putter of Hondas beyond the cyclone fence, and the distant, dim, almost inaudible, ceaseless and rhythmic wet thunder of breakers on the beach.

From inside the washroom he can see two men standing outside his barracks, and because he does not want to talk to anyone, he remains at the sink with the cold spigot running full-blast thinking of where he might go instead. But he is not dressed for the EM club or the library, and he cannot get off the compound because of the yellow alert (this suicide ought to put an end to the protests) so there is really nowhere else to go except the dayroom, but he can hear the clack of socketed pool balls from the screened windows of that room in the building adjacent to the barracks, and so he decides to run the social gauntlet and hope neither of the men, whom he recognizes as battalion headquarters clerks, speaks to him.

But when he arrives at the entrance to the barracks, the proximity of these men ignites the uncontrollable force of camaraderie which is the legacy of booze. He stops and nods as they stand aside to let him pass. He shakes his head, "I can't believe Detty did that," and pays attention to the sound of his voice as he often does when he has been drinking, in order to see how bad off he sounds.

One of the men is a doper, a mechanic at the battalion motor pool. The other is a battalion clerk who has been known to toke on occasion, but is a fairly straight-arrow. Their identities though, the identities of all three men, have been replaced by a common identity, that of men dealing ineffectively with shock.

"Killing that kid sent him overboard," one of them says, but Palmer is not listening very hard to what they have to say. He is trying to decide whether or not to tell them that Detty begged him to smuggle heroin into the MP station, whether to tell them that he turned his back on Detty.

But, "How did he escape from the hospital?" is what Palmer finally says, because this is the only real mystery in this whole desolate scenario.

"A key," the doper says, lowering his voice. The man reaches into his pocket and withdraws a familiar device approximately one-inch long. Palmer has used the tool in the past to unlock shackled wrists: a handcuff key. Anyone in a Military Police battalion can procure a handcuff key if he wants one bad enough. "He was handcuffed to a bed. His guard went to take a piss and Detty split." The man places the key beneath his tongue, tucks it alongside his gum and wisdom teeth. Then he removes it and lets it drop back into his pocket.

"How did he get back to the compound?" Palmer says.

"Hitchhiked," the doper replies. "He caught a ride at the main gate. Went to the arms room and checked out his weapon."

"Didn't Willis know Detty was supposed to be at the hospital?"

"That fucker Willis. He should have known. He gave Detty an M-16 and a bandoleer."

"Stupid fucker," says the other man. "He fucked up royal. He'll probably get fired."

Willis is the arms-room clerk, a slovenly dud, a bifocaled overweight Sp/4 not very well-liked by anyone in battalion. He talks too much, he makes excuses.

"He'll probably get promoted to battalion commander," Palmer hears himself say, and the men smile. This is an army witticism. The way to get a dick job in the army is to fuck up badly. The company bartender is a former turnkey who fucked up by letting a prisoner steal the keys to the D-cells when he wasn't looking. The battalion commander demoted him from Sp/4 to PFC and took him off MP duty. He was made company bartender and has stated publicly that he is now a fulfilled and happy man.

The smiling fades, their personalities emerge, and Palmer finds he has nothing more to say to these men, though he has an urge to ask if they'd like to come into his cubicle for a shot of scotch.

"See ya," he says as he steps between them and enters the barracks, which is silent. No TV, no weights being hefted and lowered. He wonders where everyone can be, especially with the yellow alert on, although as MPs they do have the option of taking the maverick just about anywhere inside or outside the city.

He ponders the concept of simply taking the jeep himself and driving down into the city. It's a plausible foolish idea, for he has never been hassled by MPs during any of his surreptitious jaunts, mostly to the Mariner's Club by the bay. He is thinking about yesterday's trip as he enters his cubicle and looks up automatically at the dark stain on the ceiling and knows that as long as he continues to reside in this cubicle that spot will be the first thing he sees when he wakes up in the morning and the last at night. It will replace the two previous thoughts he always has, "I made it through another night without getting killed in a mortar attack," and "I made it through another day without getting killed in a mortar attack."

Though there is a dark shiny smear on the floor where he wiped away the blood, it seems to be dry, and rather than get a bucket and soap from the house girls' locker, he decides to simply move his things out of this cubicle tonight. There is an empty space down near the door which has been vacant ever since Aldhoff went away.

But he has another beer before undertaking any efforts at relocation. He had gotten out of the habit of making efforts after he had decided he would most likely be killed in a mortar attack. He has believed this ever since his arrival in this seaside city, which rendered moot all ambition. He is consciously and deliberately putting his future on hold until he knows for sure he has one, and if it ever arrives he will recognize it by its dimensions, eight-and-a-half by eleven inches, and it will look exactly like an army discharge.

After one beer, he finds he cannot drink in his womb of a cubicle because those dark stains above and below him are too oppressive. He takes his Budweiser and Johnny Walker and a fresh pack of Camels to the TV area and watches delayed football for an hour until he realizes that he is waiting for someone, anyone, to come into the barracks. Gerlach has abandoned the weights for the day, and everyone else is gone. He doesn't really know if the others even heard about Detty.

Who might, after all, still be alive if only Palmer had made the effort to slip a pinch of heroin into the cell. He might have salted the tip his finger with H and passed it through the bars to Detty, just enough to get him through the day, to get him through his detoxification at the hospital. Might even have given him enough time to delay his suicide for another six months, until Palmer went home.

The overhead fluorescents remain off as golden planks of sunlight on the bias pass through the screened windows, as rapid shadows grow like fungus on the lower walls. The dead blue light of the TV becomes the dominant wellspring of motion in the barracks. Palmer is seated in the Naugahyde chair clutching the bottle of scotch erect on his lap like a mutant glass cock. He drinks it like pop. Empty beer cans lie where they have toppled from a whimsical tower stacked with incompetence.

He lifts the bottle and eyes the slant meniscus. There is just less than half-a-fifth remaining, and he judiciously decides to put the bottle back in his cubicle and return to beer so that he will have a decent supply of scotch for the night.

During the past two hours he has heard the occasional tramp of boots entering cubicles, heard wall lockers squeaking, but a strange silence has lain over the barracks. There is no conversation or laughter. The clerks have all found some place else to use up their weekend, but the silence most notable is that from overhead. Since he came into the barracks he has not heard a single footstep above, and now, when typically and traditionally the bass beat of a doper stereo ought to be gently rattling the rafters, there is an awesome stillness. Something bad has happened to Saturday night.

He goes to his cubicle and secretes the scotch between his bunk and footlocker and removes two beers from the icebox. He opens one and puts another in a thigh pocket of his fatigues, and before he leaves he pockets a church-key. The nightly movie will be starting in a few minutes and he does not want to make too many beer runs. Two beers are good for half-an-hour.

The theater across the street is a converted vehicle-bay and therefore has a roof. The benches are already filled with men who are relatively quiet. The nightly performance normally has the brawling atmosphere of a stag party. These men do like their movies. But the silence of the barracks seems to have spilled into the theater, for the men wait patiently for the movie projectionist, a heroin addict, to finish fiddling with the tin canisters in the projection shack and get on with the show.

Palmer leans against the wall of a quartermaster barracks rather than search for a seat among those racks of body heat, and when the cone of light hits the white paint slapped against the back wall, Palmer leaves the theater because Tobruk is tonight's movie. He has learned to shunt aside his disappointment whenever a war movie comes to the theater. He doubts he will ever again know the peculiar joy he experienced when Darby O'Gill and The Little People was shown a few months back. Men had walked out in disgust, but Palmer and his bottle of scotch had stayed to watch the whole show, and when it was over, he and the projectionist were the only ones left.

A tang of damp dust hangs in the air, and though there is no breeze to herd the stale heat along, clouds hang low overhead, and he supposes it will rain later tonight, which will make for a damn nice Saturday night. The temperature might drop to eighty. He stands in the middle of the empty dirt street gripping his sweating beer and listens to the drum beat and trumpets of the movie's credits. There is no one else outside right at this moment. He is alone on the street, which is fine with him. Inside or outside, he doesn't care where he is, as long as everyone leaves him alone.

He looks at the top floor of the barracks. The screen door is standing open, and there appears to be one light on at the far end of the room where normally the dopers congregate. Detty's former area is halfway down the aisle, as is Palmer's on the ground floor.

He goes to the EM club, orders a scotch-and-soda and sits on the back patio where a steady breeze moves with the speed of waves plowing against the beach. Lights glide across the black bay, portholes of ships, red and white lights, warning lights. Palmer drinks his scotch and goes in for two more and drinks them until he can feel a fresh inebriation like a new coat of paint on the walls of an empty room bringing new thoughts to replace the shabby redundant thoughts of death which he is now beginning successfully to eradicate.

He wants to be with a woman, and he smiles thinking that Detty is responsible for just about everything wrong with this Saturday night. He ponders another dash to the motor pool, but knows that no one is going outside the compound tonight without sheets of paper signed by men older and wiser than he will ever be. Even the thought of getting in the maverick passes through his mind. Make up some excuse to tell the gate guards about an emergency run to the hospital. There are two now. The PMO always posts two guards at the gate during alerts, so that one can run for help while the other is shot dead by the Viet Cong, he thinks, as he picks up his drink and rattles lodged alcohol out of ice onto his tongue.

The thought of being with a woman is now inside him like a virus, and because in this state of mind he is rarely harangued by reality, he thinks for a moment of how he might actually connect with a woman tonight. But the only way in or out of the compound is the main gate. He knows as he rises and goes out the front door that the chances are slim, but he also knows he has accomplished things drunk and has won through degradation and stupidity and unjust luck things he would not have dreamed possible if he'd had any access to sanity.

He crosses the softball field with its pock-marks of rocket hits from an attack a month before he arrived in-country. It is legend here, was vital history when he arrived. Men told him about that night. They were sitting in the barracks drinking beer and watching TV when the first explosion erupted on the softball field. They sat up and looked at each other, which is always the first reaction. There was a moment of silence, suspension, and then they heard an odd rattling on the tin roof, like rain, and they realized it was the dirt and rocks which had been blown into the air.

He steps into a small circle of sunken earth, zit crater, a grave, and wonders if some fragment of Viet Cong artillery lies buried in a frozen molten ball beneath this ground. But the CID always perform an archaeological search for crude evidence. Palmer is glad he wasn't here then, but also wishes he was. He has no good war stories to take home.

The maverick is parked ass-end to the waist-high bunker-wall surrounding the PMO, right next to the volleyball court. He slides onto the driver's seat and grips the steering wheel, and with the feel of the wheel and the clutter of pedals at his feet, he considers for one outrageous moment the idea of actually getting the keys from the office and driving right up to the front gate and telling the guards he has somewhere important to go. And then driving downtown as though he were back home driving with that manic teenage angst that sweetened his junior and senior high-school years: get in dad's car and drive, put one buck in the tank and cruise till dawn with a handy can of beer set in your crotch. Then sneak home.

It is too easy and too awesome, so he decides to stroll over to the main gate and see who is on duty. He has not discounted the notion of driving into town and finding a woman, but he thinks overall it would be better to go outside the compound on foot if he really is going to do anything illegal tonight.

He rounds the corner of battalion headquarters and walks halfway up the block toward the main gate, then stops because he can see two men in the cone of light, and both of them are strangers. Both are newbies from the road company. His chances of talking them into letting him go outside the gate are nil and he knows it. You can fool one man most of the time, but two guards are difficult because they can draw upon each other's fear of making a wrong decision. They can say no just because there are two of them to say it.

He lights a cigarette and tosses the lit match onto the road in violation of military protocol, and heads back to the barracks.

CHAPTER 30

The idea of achievement is appealing to him now, getting something done, moving all his shit down the aisle to the empty cubicle near the front door. But after he takes a settling sip of scotch and surveys his meager furnishings, he realizes that it will be hard work to drag out the bunk and the wall locker. The thought of drafting someone to help with manual labor on a Saturday night seems ludicrous even to himself, drunk as he is. He sees that the thing he has chosen to achieve is impossible for now, and its appeal fades. He sits on his bunk wanting nothing more than another drink.

He turns the fan on and lights a cigarette and sips at the scotch in between lengthy draws of beer until the current need is sated and he begins to remember what it was he had wanted only moments earlier. A woman. He looks at his wristwatch and counts the hours he has been drinking. Nine o'clock is coming up, and he is fairly certain now that he couldn't get it up even if he had the opportunity. But that doesn't matter. He is thrilled in a small way by the idea of paying a woman to simply lie with him beneath his covers, and he is outraged in a small way because he cannot do even that. If there were no yellow alert, he could at least do that. If Detty hadn't screwed things up, this would be just another wild weekend in Vietnam.

He becomes aware of his head beginning to waver as if balanced on some sort of liquid pivot, when he begins to effect precise movements in order to achieve something as simple as capping the bottle of scotch and placing it gently on the concrete floor in order to avoid spilling or breaking it. He is always aware when he has crossed the line of ordinary drunkenness and passed into the dark neighborhood of involuntary moves. This is a drunkenness beyond the tepid high he enjoys at work, the five or six ounces consumed over four hours just to get him into ninety minutes of lunchtime drinking or sleep, the buzz that keeps him stable throughout the afternoon and lets him down gently at the cocktail hour on the back patio of the EM club.

It's the scotch, of course, which does it. In the past he has drunk beer for as much as eight or ten hours straight and ended up feeling only a heavy, groggy inebriation. But scotch is a supercharger. It takes him higher faster, until he reaches that point where a sober self is watching him act out his rages and stupidities with perfect clarity and inability to do much about it.

So he is not surprised when he decides to put on a fresh set of fatigues and the second pair of boots left unpolished from the day before and go outside and see about getting off the compound. He knows as well as anyone that the army's yellow alert hasn't changed much, that the Vietnamese are still out there. The women are sitting at home disappointed, angry probably, because there are no customers, and the pimps are probably gathered in front of bars slouching on their Hondas and cursing the fucking Americans.

He puts his pips and crests on carefully, inspecting himself in the reflective porthole of his shaving mirror. If he's going to do something risky tonight, he wants to be sure not to commit any uniform violations. A drunk soldier can talk himself out of just about any kind of trouble if he looks sharp.

Mueller is watching TV and Gerlach is seated on his bench-press reading a muscle magazine. Palmer sees the glow of lights above Coughlan's cubicle, and Phillips'. The men have returned from wherever they've been, but each is by himself. Palmer pulls his cap low to his eyes as he walks out of the barracks carrying a can of Budweiser, and watches from the promontory of his head the progress he makes toward the perimeter fence. He has concocted a juvenile notion of finding a hole in the perimeter, an exit through which he can step out into freedom and perhaps work his way toward the motor pool, or toward the conglomeration of ramshackle structures a quarter-mile away where he once had dropped off a woman who had called herself Suzie. She had come to a beach party wearing tight blue jeans and a sweater, and he later drove her home in a jeep with three other giggling businesswomen who hurried into the darkness toward suddenly opened yellow doorways.

As he prowls the perimeter, slipping silently past sand-bagged bunkers sprouting guard towers, Suzie becomes the focus of his activity. If he can get through the fence, he will walk to Suzie's. Maybe she will recognize him, and if she doesn't, she will recognize his money.

He walks along the fence behind the quartermaster barracks and studies the double rolls of concertina wire on both sides which are decorated with aluminum pop and beer cans which somehow have succumbed to rust. It becomes clear to his unclear mind that the perimeter is secure. There are no holes in the fence because it is inspected daily for breaches. He sometimes sees squads of Vietnamese women supervised by GIs laying down new concertina wire. He is not halfway to the EM club before he knows that there is no way to get out of this cage except by the main gate, and he knows that he is not capable of standing up straight enough to convince the guards that he should be allowed out by himself.

He continues on though, no longer hampered by automatic caution. Whereas up until a moment ago he was a furtive man seeking an exit, he is now just a soldier taking a stroll around the compound and lighting a cigarette. He passes the EM club and continues on past the party patio where the previous night he had first heard of Detty's capture. He walks along the cyclone fence which borders the softball field adjacent to an ARVN compound with its fragile bamboo barracks which fall down every time the ammo dump a mile away blows up. He still eyes the fence for weak spots, but without hope.

When he comes again to the PMO parking lot, when he passes the maverick again, when he has come full circle this night, he lights another cigarette off the last one and tosses the butt into the center of the volleyball court where each evening battalion clerks gather to giggle like girls and play games. He hates volleyball.

He watches the scattered red sparks die on the concrete, and sees one large red ash suddenly go black as if someone has stepped on it. But before he has time to think about that, he feels a large drop of water tap his naked forearm. He looks up to see fast-moving clouds coming off the mountains.

Then he hears a familiar voice growing loud, also coming from the west. Motor Pool Mary is out tonight, walking ahead of the storm. Palmer steps close to the perimeter fence and sees her coming along the opposite shoulder of the road.

She's chanting her filthy rhyme, pussy is sweet and so is honey, and Palmer calls to her just before the wind begins to pick up.

She looks both ways before strutting across the road. She's wearing tight white Levis and a simple blouse. She's smoking a Salem.

"Who you?" she says.

"I saw you Thursday night," he says through the wires, and he draws his head back to give her a good look at him.

"Aaaah, babysan," she says with a grin.

He nods.

"Hey, what happen today?" she says, suddenly serious.

He knows what she is asking about, but even in his drunkenness he discovers that he does not want to talk about it. Not because he is revolted by the idea of Detty's suicide, but because he is embarrassed by it. He feels ashamed to tell a Vietnamese that an American soldier shot his own head off. But Mary answers her own question. "GI cockadow self, huh?" she says. She makes a pistol out of her left hand and points it at her temple and utters a soft throaty hiss.

Palmer can only nod, but it takes an effort, which surprises him because he himself has done truly disgraceful things while drunk without giving them a second thought.

"Who did it?" Mary says, and Palmer answers easily. The name has been fixed in his thoughts since he heard it spoken by the man who had stood alongside him in the afternoon. "Detty."

Mary nods an affirmation. She knew Detty. She knows all the dopers. "Numbaaah ten," she says slowly, and it strikes Palmer that this is an odd idiom spoken by all these agrarian people. It has a coldbloodedness about it, befitting a technology-oriented culture. "On the calamity-meter, this man's death rates a number ten."

And in thinking this, he realizes what it is about Motor Pool Mary that makes her seem so different from the other Vietnamese. It is not just the total absence of shyness, not just her blustering no-bullshit persona or her fluency in English. Those characteristics are a part of it, but he realizes that Mary in fact does not seem like a Vietnamese at all. She seems like a loud-mouth street-wise smart-ass American girl who got lost in Southeast Asia, who could have been bred in the declining fringe-neighborhood of any overcrowded city in the U.S.A.

"I want to buy heroin," Palmer says.

Mary looks up and down the street, and this causes Palmer to look to his own left, toward the guard tower twenty meters away, at the shack on top twenty feet in the air. He and Mary are probably being watched.

"Twenty dollah," she says.

Palmer opens his billfold and pulls out a brightly-colored rectangle of joke dough. He passes it through the fence, and Mary grabs and stuffs it into a pocket.

"You wait ten minutes," she says. "I be back."

It's only after she has strolled down the road and hollered laughing at the two gate-guards huddled in their shack, "Fuck you, MP!" that Palmer realizes what he has done. He expected Mary to reach into a pocket and pull out a vial and pass it through the fence. The alcohol has made him think that all he has to do is mouth a desire and its satisfaction will be forthcoming.

He has never bought drugs directly from a Vietnamese dealer, and as he walks beneath the shadow of the PMO stairway which leads up to the CID offices, a bit of sanity slips in the back door of his mind, and he realizes he could be caught accepting the heroin. The man in the guard tower might even intervene. Or an officer or NCO might have seen him talking at the fence and suspected something was up.

But this is more a categorization of possibilities than a litany of potential dangers. He is going to stay here regardless and wait to see if Mary is going to return. He wants that vial of heroin.

He grows tired quickly from standing upright. The strength that once bore him literally from sunrise to sunset in basic training has been burned out of him by beer and cigarettes. He decides to sit on the tarp-covered seat of a contraband Honda shackled to the stair post. The machine was confiscated from a pimp long before Palmer came to Vietnam, CID evidence of some sort. It has no key and no gasoline, an appropriate place to rest his sorry ass.

His eyes flicker from the guard tower to the fence where he expects Mary to show up at any moment. Dust explodes at the edge of the volleyball court as heavy drops of rain begin falling, and when ten minutes pass and she still has not shown, he knows in a small and meaningless way how Detty had felt waiting for the connection that was never going to come.

He lights a cigarette to help disengage his mind. The busyness of his fingers and lips distracts him from burgeoning pathos conceived unwillingly. Surely Detty must have stared hard through those bars waiting hungrily for him to reappear. And who knows? Maybe Detty made that break in the station because he wanted to kick the shit out of Palmer for nodding, for lying, for filling his void with expectation.

A Honda passes on the street and Palmer throws his cigarette to the ground, surprised to find within him fear begetting nervousness, for he has drunk far more alcohol in far fewer hours than he ever has before. Enough to kill the skittish rationality of intellect, he would think.

He sits back and quickly fires his Zippo for a relight and snaps it closed with a mechanical click recalling the first time he bought dope, except it was not heroin, it was pot, and he bought it from Detty. Three months in Vietnam, he was charmed by the idea of owning his own stash, having gotten high for the first time a week earlier with Detty and Loeb out beneath the water tower by the shower rooms where the dopers kept a communal coffee-tin filled with dried pot. He gave Detty ten bucks. Detty was making a dope run into town for the men upstairs, and an hour later Detty handed him a plastic bag the size of a catcher's mitt filled with marijuana sticks as long as pencils. Palmer smoked a joint alone later that night, and then, overcome by paranoia, became afraid that there might be a surprise inspection at any minute. He didn't know where to hide his stash except his locker. For one day he sweated through his working hours, unable to kill his worry with beers sipped on short breaks. He finally gave up and put the pot inside a paper bag and, waiting until dark, threw the bag into the Dempsey dumpster outside the quartermaster barracks. The following Saturday night, Detty came to Palmer and quietly asked if he could borrow a couple joints because he was headed for a party. Mortified, Palmer lied and said he had already smoked the stash. Detty's eyes got as big as if he had just been told the war was over, then he smiled and shook his head with admiration and said that's cool, meaning thanks anyway, and walked out.

Maybe it wasn't admiration, Palmer thinks, rolling the Camel between his fingers and watching the gelatinous red ash wiggle. Maybe Detty knew I was full of shit and believed I was just lying to keep the pot for myself.

It makes him smile though when he thinks about the conversation. It was funny. Funny things happen to people who are full of shit and lie all the time.

The rain which began with random sweeps has now settled into a light patter. He hadn't expected Mary to arrive on a Honda, so when he hears a quick puttering deceleration and sees a woman hop off the rear of a Honda driven by a pimp, he just sits and watches as she hurries up to the perimeter, then finds himself rising and moving toward her because she has chucked a plastic vial through the fence. It falls to the rocky ground. Mary sees him come out of the shadows.

"Ciao, babysan!" she laughs as she runs back and hops onto the rear of the Honda. Palmer has only a glimpse of the pimp. He's wearing a raincoat, a sort of dull brown Swiss hat, and looks straight ahead as Mary wraps her arms around his waist and they buzz off into the night.

Palmer walks away from the fence and guard tower with the plastic vial in his cupped fist ready to drop it fast if he is approached by anyone who may have been watching this transaction. He feels stupid for getting into a situation in which he might be convicted of buying dope. His record is clean. As far as the cadre knows he's a straight-arrow, even if he drinks a little too much at company parties. He doesn't want a bad-conduct discharge. He wants to come out of the army admired by friends and especially total strangers.

Because it is raining, he decides no one except the tower guard would have bothered to watch him, but he hurries now across the road toward the barracks, still with that plastic vial at-the-ready to be tossed for the slightest reason.

Gerlach is at his weights, and a few other men are gathered around the television. Palmer goes into his cubicle and sits on the bunk and does nothing for a minute, waiting in case anyone wants to talk to him.

The vial is in his pocket, and it feels evil in there. He is doing practically the worst thing an enlisted man can do in this place in these times, short of desertion or murder. Possession of heroin is the one bust for which there is no redemption.

The sounds of individual raindrops hitting the earth outside his window merge into a dull monsoon, and the volume of this pleasing beat rises with his sense of excitement, for to possess a full vial of heroin, a week's worth of skag, makes him feel debonair, because no one else in the barracks, as far as he knows, even smokes pot. They would be flabbergasted to see him holding a vial of heroin. He removes it from his pocket and sets it on the footlocker as though it were nothing more than a can of beer. He smiles at his impunity. He imagines calling his buddies into the room and passing this horse around and saying fuck regulations, let's have a party.

He picks it up and gently works the plastic lid off and sniffs at the packed powder but can smell nothing. Cigarettes have destroyed his ability to smell any odor weaker than burning diesel-fuel-and-shit. He recalls stories, warnings, about pushers putting laundry-detergent or even battery-acid into plastic vials to screw dopers, but he doesn't put much stock in these stories. They are like razor-blades-in-the-pussy stories. Scare-tactics thought up probably by chaplains.

He caps the vial and puts it back into his pocket, opens the scotch and drinks straight from the bottle and holds the mouthful bobbing against his tongue as he punches open a new Bud. He swallows the scotch and chases it with beer, then goes down the aisle and joins his friends at the TV cubicle with the vial in his pocket like a loaded gun, a terrible secret, a helluva joke.

Even Gerlach is watching the TV between lifts because tonight The D.I. is on starring Jack Webb as a Marine Drill Instructor kicking ass on some pansy rich-boy maggot who can't endure the rigors of boot camp. There is a grin on everyone's face. Randall's and Mueller's, Coughlin's and Phillips', and even on Gerlach's with his sweating bench and brawn. They all love it. Basic training memories are bittersweet, but a soldier only really misses it when he's drunk.

The rest of them are unaware of the rising storm until the incandescence of close lightning sends the TV screen diving into black and rising into a pool of blue again. The resultant explosion of thunder seems to accelerate the rain which begins spraying through the long screened windows and puddling along the base of the wall from one end of the barracks to the other.

The velocity of freefall rain finally overwhelms the sound of the TV, so that the men begin yelling at each other, yelling at the storm, but Palmer can barely hear them. Phillips and Coughlin go down to the front door, and Palmer follows them as though the hard-core entertainment on the TV has somehow entered into the barracks itself. He stands behind them looking through the screen at a Niagara wall pile driving puddles becoming lakes and spilling into a current flowing toward the main road which becomes a river driving past the EM club and into the China Sea.

The ghostly filament of a quick bolt strikes a telephone pole and dims the compound's power, and when Coughlin howls at the top of his lungs in unison with the sudden thunder, Palmer turns his head and grins at the man's light-ning-lit twisted mouth delivering its comparatively feeble load.

The fluorescents pop briefly with flickering light which hovers above the aisle as the power dies, and in the blacken-ing barracks Palmer hears the rest of the men cursing at the TV and stumbling toward the front door where the rain is paler than the night, white where it hits, where the plunging sound of the river rides the road.

Water slops in the front door and the men walk in place unconsciously as it crawls around their boots. Palmer feels the rain spraying through the screen door onto his face, and even though the evening had been warm, this water is cold and unpleasant, irritating, and he steps back from the door and listens to the deafening monsoon.

He touches the plastic bulge in his pocket and lifts his beer and drinks, and within the short space of time it takes to do this he hears the storm falter, as though someone has turned the volume down on a television set. He hears a choking putter as frustrated quartermaster men across the street try to pull-start the gasoline-powered emergency generator. Lightning has destroyed the telephone pole which feeds the compound.

He sips at his beer and wants to go back to his cubicle for a shot of scotch, but is fascinated by the straining combustion in the dark across the flooded road, by the vocal silence of the quartermaster men as they take turns yanking the rope and bringing the pistons to life with a winter-sound of automotive despair. And then bulbs high on poles, and windows distant and small, flicker and grow bright with the rising roar of the machine's combustion.

The rain dies slowly as the generator purrs, and Palmer walks back down the aisle satisfied, goes into his cubicle and takes his first solid drink during what he now considers, as he does every Saturday night prior to the only morning he is allowed to sleep late, the night watch.

CHAPTER 31

The storm and the TV show end at ten, and as the men gaze vaguely at the GI anchorman in his jungle fatigues reading aloud the world's headlines, the conversation begins.

Palmer is aware that the others are talking, but he is not listening. He is leaning against a cubicle wall with a fresh beer in his hand gazing at the TV and feeling like a true rogue with that plastic vial in his pocket. The last four or five shots of scotch have lifted him to a less intelligent frame of mind in which he is actually considering doing a tiny hit of heroin. Earlier in the evening, a rising notion of disposing of the vial had born a significance that is now lost upon him, and he wants to reach into his pocket and pull it out, display it to his buddies.

"That fucker could have killed somebody else," a voice says, and Palmer realizes that Eckert has joined the group, sitting on a folding chair and drinking Carling Black Label. Eckert is from Iowa or Indiana or Illinois, one of the I states. He lived either on a farm or in a small town, Palmer cannot recall, but does perceive Eckert's anger which is out of character for this inarticulate plough jockey. "Did you see that blood coming through the ceiling?" Eckert looks at Palmer as he says this, and Palmer nods. The blood-stained rafters are visible to everyone from here.

"I went upstairs," Coughlin says, and the barracks grows silent. Everyone looks at him. "I went up by the back steps," he says, staring at the TV. "I saw something lying under

Detty's bed, and I thought it was a cereal bowl. It was the top of his skull."

"You know what they ought to do," Phillips says, squeezing his beer can, making it pop. He speaks slowly. "They ought to take all the dopers out and put 'em on an island and give them all the heroin they want and let them kill themselves."

"Fuckingay," Eckert says. "I'm sick of typing up reports about fucking dopers."

Palmer remains silent and keeps his hand out of his pocket and decides to stay only a few minutes longer before moving back to his cubicle. It's getting late, though ten p.m. would not be considered late anywhere else in the world, and most of the men will be hitting the sack soon. Mueller will stay up to watch both stations go off the air, the American and Vietnamese. A few men will sit up listening to their PX-sale stereos through headphones, and even one or two might read, but Palmer is planning to go where he always goes when his drinking is allowed to transpire unfettered by time or responsibility. He will be going out into the night.

He is fairly certain he is not going to attempt to leave the compound now, especially with this storm's aftermath, the mud and the cold. He listens to the men expressing their outrage a little while longer, then crushes his beer can, a standard parting signal, and moves back to his room.

The body of the small refrigerator shakes when he opens the door, and the quick slithering of a thing with less density than a shadow registers on his eyes, and he is slow to look down. But its blind random run, twisting and circling, makes it easy for Palmer to focus on it as he stands upright without taking a beer from the icebox. Though he is thoroughly drunk, fear cuts through his impediment, slices right to the core of his being, and makes him cry out with a squeal like a girl, "Goddamn!"

He exits the cubicle with a kind of spastic dance to avoid stepping on the multi-legged flight of a foot-long centipede which has been startled from its insect slumber beneath the comforting hum of the icebox.

He is in the aisle backing away and hissing with disgust when he is joined by the men of the barracks who watch him wide-eyed and grinning with wonder because Palmer is a known drunk, his party antics are familiar, but when he points at the concrete-gray snake with its fluttering legs scrambling for an exit, the men begin raging at the abomination. They form a loose circle in the narrow aisle and stamp their feet at it as Palmer backs away.

The creature doesn't cease its liquid curling run as it turns swiftly away from stomped boot heels that miss because the men are afraid to actually make contact. Nobody wants to touch the fleet ugly and perhaps poisonous indifferent scuttling bastard, so Eckert comes up with the solution as the bug is herded back-and-forth, back-and-forth, to keep it from crawling into a cubicle where it may escape into the walls of the barracks where God knows if wives and children might be hiding.

Eckert comes out of his cubicle carrying a blue-and-yellow can of lighter-fluid which he uncorks and aims at the insect. "Get back!" he shouts and shoots at the centipede, follows it with a stream which leaves a damp circular line on the floor. "Light it!" he yells, and two men produce Zippos and squat to touch the wet fuse connected to the beast.

Blue flames sputter along the butane track and, circling to find an exit, the centipede is engulfed. Eckert stands over the insect whose circular velocity increases astonishingly. He squeezes the can harder, and the arc of fluid hits the centipede squarely. Blue flames flutter across its body. The men shout with a kind of cock-fight fanaticism as the insect curls in upon itself as if to huddle against the flames. Palmer looks at the faces of his friends flushed red and snarling with a hatred so pure it is almost exhilarating.

"Mother fuck!" Coughlin shouts as the skin of the beast sizzles and pops. "Where the hell did that come from?"

"From under my icebox," Palmer says.

"Well get rid of your fucking icebox!" Coughlin barks, and the men begin laughing at each other and at the carbon husk going limp at their feet.

"I'm gonna start sleeping with a .45," Phillips says, batting at the cremation smoke rising to the rafters. "I didn't know this fucking place was inhabited."

"Police up your bug, Palmer," Coughlin says, "and fumigate your goddamn cubicle."

The men go back to their rooms chuckling, and Palmer disposes of the insect by scooping it up with a piece of cardboard scavenged from the house girls' locker. He deposits the corpse in the Dempsey dumpster outside the barracks and returns to his cubicle. He tentatively gives the icebox a shake and waits for another bug, but the one-and-only intruder has been rousted.

He has never before seen a centipede that big, and for one brief moment reason returns to his brain long enough for him to decide that this was a fluke, that the motherfucker must have come in out of the rain, and if there are any more monsters in this place, they will hopefully leave when the flood has subsided.

With that thought, he pours a slow shot of scotch into his mouth to settle a stomach tightened and made slightly nauseous by unprecedented activity and fear.

The solution to the problem of leaving his bottle of scotch in the barracks when he goes out into the night is to fill one Budweiser can half-full of Johnny Walker, and to plug two Buds into the thigh pockets of his fatigue pants so that he can stroll and sip and keep handy the reinforcing punch of a shot when necessary. He pats the upper pocket near his hip to feel the secured vial of heroin, then he moves toward the front door of the barracks.

The air is cold when he walks outside. It is the irritating tail-end cold of the monsoon season which he knows he will miss in the middle of the coming summer. He walks through puddles formed in dips in the dirt road. He breathes air raked clean of its palm and pig-shit stink, and he looks up at the sky and marvels that already stars are beginning to show through a membrane of clouds moving toward the east. He looks at the stairway leading to the second floor of the barracks.

The decision to go upstairs, the actual physical shift of his frame toward the stairway, is made quickly, almost instantaneously, because he knows that sober he will never go up those steps, and in daylight he would not walk up because there would be too many people around. So as a man would step on the clutch of a standard transmission, he disengages his thoughts, which allows the momentum of this small decision to carry him up the steps.

The sweet saturated fragrance of communal crime is missing. He notices it as soon as he steps through the doorway. The far end of the barracks is vacant beneath the single length of a flickering fluorescent. The dopers have fled. He walks down the aisle and makes the tour quickly. Detty's bunk has been stripped, the mattress rolled up at one end revealing square-linked springs. The linoleum flooring around the bunk shines. It has been scoured and disinfected and is totally bereft of that tell-tale stain which Palmer seeks fearfully. His eyes scan the floor unrewarded as he strolls casually past like a man looking for a friend or a man delivering a message from, say, battalion. Just a quick casual walk through a room in which he isn't welcome.

Thinking that perhaps the suicide bullet might have penetrated the tin roofing, he looks up. But as he does, his eyes sense a shadow out of place, something not quite right at the screened window, and he looks at it. A splash of brain-matter clogs the fine rectangles of wire mesh. A fleshy starburst three feet in diameter backed by a light affixed to a telephone pole outside.

His thoughts are disengaged altogether as he descends the staircase at the far end of the barracks and walks toward the road feeling the presence of Detty's remains above his shoulders.

The road which leads to the EM club has a slick riverbed sheen. He looks back at his own footprints as he crosses the road and steps up onto the wooden sidewalk which borders the softball field. The depressions where the Viet Cong shells once landed are mirrors. The softball diamond itself is still flooded, slowly draining, but the raised edge of the field where that man jogs each night is dry. Palmer walks onto the edge, and with a Bud can in each hand he alternates sips of scotch and beer as he circles the diamond beneath the high bright tin-shaded lights which are being kept alive by the emergency generator.

At the backstop, which is like a backstop in any ballpark in America, he stops and looks up at the wires and thinks for a moment about climbing it. This was a thing he often did at home, getting drunk and scaling handy promontories: trees, telephone poles.

But it seems an unwise thing to do, and he marvels at his ability in the depths of unconditional drunkenness to make wise decisions. He circles the softball field until he meets his own footprints, then he sets the two cans on the ground and removes the third from his thigh pocket and sets it beside them. He stands erect and begins running.

He does not have access to a car, or even to that Honda chained to the PMO. He has no way to simulate the sort of cruising that in his teenage years was a bleak and fruitless form of escape from home life and high-school except his own legs that, approximately eighteen months earlier, had possessed a strength and stamina that made him, at least among his fellow basic-trainees, a first-class runner who gave a respectable five-and-a-half minute showing in the final PT-test mile-run before graduation. A thing that he knows now and knew even then that he would never again repeat in his life.

He is amazed at how his thigh and calf muscles seem to recognize immediately the thing he is doing, how his long strides on the wet sand as he passes home plate seem effortless.

He is barely breathing. He is running at top-speed and it feels so fucking good that a vague idea with the ominous characteristics of ambition begins to take shape in his mind, that this is something he might start doing every day. But as he rounds the field and comes within sight of his beer cans, that notion fades and he begins to feel the muscles of his legs reacting to the strain that he knows he has inflicted upon them unnecessarily, and knew when he started out was a foolish mistake. But it had just seemed right, at that moment, to take off running, a thing he would never have done sober.

He feels it in his ankles as he applies the brakes, a splintering kind of pain that reaches up into his calves and down into his heels. And as though a tired ghost of himself is approaching from behind and collides with him as he is picking up his beer cans, he begins breathing hard and his heart begins picking up speed, and he experiences all the exhaustion he had reasonably expected to feel during the brief run. He pulls out a cigarette but stands with the unlit tube hanging at his side as he pants and wets his drying mouth with beer and feels knots of congestion gathering in his lungs for a good cough.

Carrying all this frantic physical aftershock, he walks across the dirt road and hikes himself up onto a four-foot high bunkerwall which surrounds a quartermaster barracks. He continues panting until he can no longer fend off the desire to light the cigarette. He torches it with his Zippo and continues to pant in between sweet drags of smoke and sips of scotch and beer. There is a numbness in his hard-pressed heels dangling down the bunkerwall, and he is amused by it, amused at how absolutely shitty his physical shape is. He remembers with resignation the immaculate health he had brought home from basic training, remembers it as though remembering the death of an interesting friend.

The sweat cooling his neck and armpits is of a different breed than he is used to, the sweat of hard labor. He feels the air cold against his neck and back and wonders if he will catch a cold. He is a passive hypochondriac, and it now occurs to him that he has never had a cold since being in Vietnam.

When he slides off the bunkerwall and stands up straight, his legs are shaking slightly, his thighs and calves are sore, and he walks unsteadily back to the barracks feeling a sort of exercise-nausea. He remembers the can of tuna in his icebox and decides that this is a good moment to put something into his stomach to carry him through the next few hours so that he won't have to experience those irritating cramps of hunger that always put a damper on his drinking.

The inside of the barracks is dark. He hears snores. His thoughts go to the TV. But all broadcasts have ceased for the night, and he experiences a sorrowful longing for American television which he misses more than he misses anyone back home.

He goes into his cubicle and sits on his bunk, switches on the fan and opens the icebox. He is down to twelve beers. He decides he should make a beer-run Sunday afternoon. He has drunk more beer this weekend than he expected, than he normally does, and he does not want to find himself dry on a Sunday night only to end up doing a little desperation drinking at the EM club when he'd rather be planted bootless in the comfort of Naugahyde watching *Laugh-In*.

He has been constantly aware of the vial of heroin in his pocket. It presses hard against his thigh and makes a bulge beneath the tight rip-stop fabric of his fatigues. He reaches into his pocket and withdraws it, pops the top and looks again at the pale powder, impressed by the power he knows is contained in each granule. He sets it uncapped on his foot-locker and removes the can of tuna from his icebox and lifts his dog tags over his head. He keeps a P-38 can-opener on his dog tag chain, a souvenir from basic training. It is a flat, inch-square, mid-hinged, knife-edged tool made by the army and provided in C-rations boxes, and is to Palmer a thing of beauty, of practical perfection, a device which actually makes him feel good whenever he uses it.

The fresh stink of dead fish fills the cubicle as Palmer plucks chunks with his fingers and nibbles them. They taste like home. He closes his eyes and feels as if he is home, living in the basement apartment he shared with his brothers before getting drafted.

He eats only half the can. His stomach is tight from all this evening's action, and he sets the remains on his footlocker, satisfied that he is now fortified to carry on with this night's drunk.

He picks up the bottle of scotch and is startled to see that it is almost empty. He becomes enraged thinking that some-one has slipped into his cubicle and robbed him. But then he remembers that he poured most of it into the Budweiser can which he had left out on the quartermaster bunkerwall.

He lights his cigarette and leans down to set it on the edge of his footlocker, planning to open his wall locker and get the ashtray which he stole from the EM club and which he likes so much, a deep-dish of black plastic with six notches for cigarettes. It is a luxury and a treasure, but as he sets his cigarette down he sees that he already has one going, burning a brown line into the green wood of his foot locker.

He grins as he knocks the expiring tuber onto the floor and brushes at the burn-stain with his finger. This is a familiar signal. He supposes now that he will not be aware of anything he does until a minute or so after he has done it. He steps on the floored butt and finds himself chuckling, and the smoke sticks in his throat and he begins coughing.

He chokes exhaling a few times, but when he inhales it is as though his lungs no longer want any part of it. They do not want smoke or even air. They want to go on exhaling until all the shit has been expunged from his body. This, too, is a familiar signal. His stomach joins his lungs in a chorus of excretion, and he knows with wide-eyed apprehension that he is going to vomit.

It was the tuna, he thinks as he stands up making high-pitched gasping sounds forcing air into his lungs. He walks down the aisle toward the door thinking that if only he had skipped the tuna this rupture in his otherwise flawless bender would never have occurred. But he also understands that this is part of the penalty for excessive drinking. Sometimes you forget what you are doing and make the unpardonable blunder of eating.

As he walks with a kind of staggering momentum around the side of the barracks toward the piss-tube, he sees the light of the softball field and thinks, It was that damn running, and he looks for the Budweiser can of scotch resting on the bunkerwall but cannot see it. He is still five feet away from the piss-tube when he begins to smell the odor of urine unleashed and amplified by the monsoon downpour. The air around the shack is vile, and when he inhales it, the stink is like a hammer swung into his chest.

He vomits as he drops to his knees. Though not quite projectile-vomiting, it nevertheless is launched with painful spasms, liquid splashes containing chunks of recently-eaten tuna.

The odor of piss and vomit become intolerable and he crawls away from that obscene halo as still his gut heaves fluids which seem to take with them fractions of pain and discomfort, for with each expulsion of the contents of his stomach he feels better and his mind goes into neutral because he knows that all he has to do is wait. There will probably be a minute or so of dry-heaving, but after that he will be okay.

With the pain and discomfort shot from his system however, so too it seems goes his strength. As he rests on his hands and knees, his arms begin shaking terribly, and his feeble thighs cannot hold him upright. He slowly collapses sideways into the wet sand and holds his head up so that his cheek does not rest in the vomit that trickles from his slack lips.

He lies in this outrageous position until his neck muscles begin to complain, then he scoots with a kind of sidewinder determination until he can lay his head in clean sand. He remains there concentrating on one goal, that of staying awake, because he does not want to pass out by the piss-tube where he would no doubt be discovered in the crucifying light of Sunday dawn.

He finds the will someplace outside himself. He literally jerks and yanks and levers and throws himself into a tenuous standing-position where he squints through wet eyelashes at the disheartening sight of his scotch and beer splattered in the sand a few feet away which he is connected to by a damp narrowing path ending at his feet. He raises his head to take a deep breath of air and looks directly at the pale dried splash of Detty's brains clogging the screened window.

He walks, refusing to allow himself a coherent thought, walks back into the barracks and into his lighted cubicle. He looks down at the sandy wet mess of his fatigues. He strips and steps out of the gritty pile and, in a state of auto-pilot, moves out of the barracks and across the road toward the shower shack.

This is how most of his Saturdays end. A practiced maneuver carries him past the sinks and into the chilly tin-walled shower room. With his eyes closed he feels for a handle and turns on the water. He lowers his head and leans into the icy stream which does not have the flow to startle him sober or even more awake.

His hands slap awkwardly at places which he imagines are smeared with vomit and sand, but because he cannot open his eyes to see if he is making any progress, he grows tired of this business and turns the handle off until the water merely drips with a hollow ringing shower room sound which pleases him as he lowers himself to the wet concrete floor and lies on his left side to rest a moment before heading back to the barracks to start drinking again.

His right ankle lies directly beneath the showerhead, the target of a rhythmic drip, so that as his mind tries to settle into oblivion it is constantly being startled awake. Though it would take only a little kick to move his foot out of the way, it seems like too much effort because he is so drunk that it is easier to endure this unpalatable irritation than to move his foot a few inches.

When he finally does get up the energy to relieve that infuriatingly chilly beat against bony flesh, it is because he is somewhat rested. He opens his eyes and is surprised to find himself lying on hard wet concrete. His right foot is numb with cold, the flesh reddened from the wet battering inflicted upon it for what Palmer calculates must have been at least five hours.

He can see daylight through the screened windows. A panic seizes his heart as he realizes that he has lost his Saturday night. His drinking is finished, even though he still has that scotch in that beer can out on the bunkerwall and all that beer left in his icebox.

He has trouble getting to a standing position, then has more trouble finding his clothes. A vague thought that a barracks-thief has pilfered his belongings passes through his fuzzy mind, but he doesn't care, he wants only to get to bed.

He staggers to the shower room door and looks out. The sun is above the horizon, which means he has no chance of getting back to the barracks without being seen.

Oh God, he thinks because it is too much effort to even say it, and he stands inside the door and looks at the distance he must travel along the wooden sidewalk and across the open dirt road to the barracks, maybe thirty yards.

Oh God, he thinks again, peering through eyes aching from sun and lashes matted with, he supposes, vomit. He stands in the doorway to see if anyone is up and about. Sundays are usually quiet. He knows that the only thing that really matters is that he make it without falling down. And he is not that certain he can do it. He could quite easily lose touch with his equilibrium and find himself skinning his knees and elbows in the dirt midway to the barracks and possibly passing out. This is not naive apprehension. He is analyzing things based on experience.

The one thing he is not sure about is whether or not to make a show of covering his dick with his hand like an idiot. At least the house girls have been banned from the compound. There are infinite ways this situation could have been worse. This could have happened to him on a weekday. There is not an atrocity conceivable that he could not have brought upon himself, provided he'd drunk enough alcohol.

When he makes his run though, it is fast and uneventful. Most of his atrocities lack melodrama. He staggers down the quartermaster sidewalk and crosses the dirt road toward his barracks deliberately refusing to look around because he does not want to know if anyone is watching him hobbling obviously hungover and totally naked in the dawn.

He enters the barracks and makes it to his cubicle, but when he enters he sees the open vial of heroin on his footlocker and he gets a cold feeling because he knows it has been sitting there for the past five hours and that anyone could have stepped into his room to see why his light was on at, say, four in the morning, and would have seen that contraband. Sgt. Ancil maybe, or one of the lesser cadre.

He shuts off the reading lamp above his bunk and sits down. The muscles, tendons, bones of his foot are cold and stiff and sore. He can feel it clearly through the general pain of a hangover which he knows is going to get much worse. He has trouble capping the vial of heroin, his shaking hands threatening to toss powder onto that dark stain at his feet. He wants desperately to lie down and go to sleep, but he knows he must dispose of this evidence. A survival instinct that overrides every emotion and protesting shattered nerve motivates him to pull from his wall locker a clean set of fatigue pants and a clean T-shirt.

He slips into his Ho sandals and walks back down the aisle with the vial cupped in his hand to hide it. He steps into the sunshine feeling that because he is no longer naked, none of his potential witnesses can connect him with that panicked phantom who had staggered from the shower room.

He walks past all the evidence of his good times of the night before and steps into the piss-tube shack. He unzips his fatigue pants, but the only thing he grips in his hand is that vial. He looks over his shoulder, looks up at the second-story screened windows above his exposed back to see if anyone is watching, then pokes the vial of heroin into the damp mouth of the steel tube and listens to it rattling down into an unimaginable swamp where it will remain unobtainable as evidence at least until the end of the war.

He is dehydrated, but his bladder is firm with one last load and he empties it, then walks back to the barracks, and it occurs to him that he ought to have wiped his fingerprints off the plastic vial. He knows he probably will be tormented by this sort of petty and unreasonable worry for a few days, and he accepts it as a part of the mental toll he has always paid for his crimes and sins and fun.

It is only after all this mess has been taken care of that he finally comprehends the magnitude of his hangover. He is used to wiping vomit from his floor with dirty fatigues and trashing them in the dumpster, and he has many times found himself waking up on the floor just a few unsuccessful steps away from his bunk, and those penalties have always seemed to him not unreasonable. But as he collapses onto his bunk and closes his eyes to the merciless light of day, he understands that he has crossed the line. The ache in his right ankle is bone-deep, as though the flesh, the blood and tendons, and marrow within those bones, have been soaked too long in water too cold until the life in that pale matter has simply been extinguished.

But it is the pain inside his head as he closes his eyes on that dark stain on the rafter above his bunk which finally promises to become unendurable. He curls into himself and grips his right ankle to warm it. He closes his eyes until he can clearly see the luminous red bubble shapes which float inside his corneal darkness, familiar haunts which he sometimes sees even with his eyes open, precursors, he supposes, to the DT's which he has always expected to experience at the end of some dismal bender down the road.

He thinks as he descends into the maelstrom of uneasy sleep that what he is doing to himself is real.

And because the terrible phrase which he has not been able to fend off, dim, damper, subjugate, or kill throughout the entire evening—Detty is dead—has stayed with him even unto the ragged edge of sleep, he supposes that this, too, may have been the very last thought Detty ever had.

CHAPTER 32

Though Palmer had plunged into the healing darkness of sleep with the alcoholic confidence that a good eight hours would cure him of his standard pain, he awakens with his fear and guilt as fully intact as the ache extending from his right ankle to his hip. Fully intact also are the usual peripheral pains, the swollen cracked lips, the dehydration soreness in the back of his throat, the joints sore from having remained in one position too long throughout his ineffective sleep, as well as inexplicable pains of scuffed skin on his left arm and leg. The flesh there is still red. It has bled a tiny bit. He lies with his eyes closed facing into the lukewarm wind of the fan trying to recall what it was he did last night to injure himself.

But it is the awful memory of letting that vial of heroin roll down the piss-tube which leads him correctly along the labyrinth of memory to where he lay twice in the night, on the sand and on the floor of the shower room, which is so embarrassing, in spite of the evidence that no one saw him in the shower or else they would have checked to see if he was dead. He pulls the light fabric of his camouflage cover over his face and groans quietly in unison with the fan's hum.

The headache and stomach nausea of his hangover are of greater magnitude than he has ever experienced before in his life, in his entire five years of drinking, from high school to Vietnam. He knows that he has never drunk so much, so intensely in so short a time, and the physical aftereffects have the characteristics of an auto collision, an image which comes immediately to mind because it is the subject of his current vocation. He is the accident man at the MP station.

He finds the strength to open his icebox and quench his bleeding thirst, and to eat five aspirin. But he must lie down immediately afterwards because he feels like vomiting again and does not want to perform the necessary mechanics or endure the probable public humiliation. It is broad daylight, and there is no place on an army compound where you can vomit in broad daylight in privacy.

The mercy of the aspirin lets him drift into a half-sleep that lasts another three or so hours, and when he finally awakens he knows he will not be going to sleep again for a few more hours. He remembers that tomorrow morning he must face the soldier-of-the-month board, and the realization generates a new layer of depression that he can feel in the quivering muscles and singed skin of his still hungover body.

It occurs to him that perhaps he has already slept his way through Monday and is actually lying here awaiting a court martial. He has absolutely no idea what time it is, and this sends him standing upright and opening his wall locker to find his wristwatch. It is four-thirty, and by the light against the screens he determines it is afternoon. He steps out of his cubicle in order to ascertain whether or not it is Sunday.

A few men are sitting in the TV area. Phillips and Coughlin are fucking around with Gerlach's bench press. Mueller is watching TV. There is a Sunday quiet and calmness within the barracks which is comforting, and which Palmer is not a part of.

The act of standing up has made his heart hammer, is making him dizzy. He is too embarrassed to ask anyone if today is Sunday. He is going to assume it is, and let the cards fall where they may. He stands a moment in the aisle to let them see him, because if they do have any bad news he knows they will not waste a moment telling him. Phillips glances at him but doesn't speak, and Palmer goes back in and lies down on his bunk and wonders if they are silent because one of them came into his cubicle last night to see why his lights were on and saw the vial and told everyone, so that now they are ostracizing him out of apprehension and disgust.

These thoughts continue for a few minutes. He is at a point in his hangover where he is capable of imagining every possible combination of embarrassing or simply awful things which he has done and for which he must be called upon to answer. Even such an innocuous event as running around the softball field at midnight has taken on the proportions of an act of evil that must be justified to somebody, to everybody.

His mind refuses to stop extrapolating until hidden beneath his camouflage cover he sticks his index fingers into each ear to muffle the terrible silence of the barracks, until it seems he can hear the rotation of warped wheels spinning inside his head, until that sound is replaced by the brief and unsuccessful hush of two or three lackluster sobs.

His cubicle contains the only darkness in the barracks when he awakens. He feels the cubic box of night surrounding him as he opens his eyes and simultaneously thinks, "Detty is dead," and looks at the dark stain on the ceiling. The moonlight glow of fluorescent lights hovers along the top edges of his plywood walls. He calculates that it must be past six, and that he has slept approximately eighteen hours altogether from midnight of the previous night, long enough to put a dent into any hangover.

When he sits up to get his canteen, he feels the slight dizziness a patient might feel when recovering from a relatively long fever, accompanied by a kind of wrung out, feeble, tissue fragile sense of well-being. Every cell in his body seems to cool down as he swallows ferocious quantities of water until his canteen is almost empty. When he leans to put the green plastic back into the icebox, he is revolted by the sight of the dozen Budweiser cans stacked like artillery shells awaiting detonation.

Though darkness has always been his medium, he wants to get out of it, get back into the light. But he does not want to turn on the reading lamp above his bed. He wants to get out of the cubicle. He pulls on clean fatigues and a T-shirt and stands up rubbing his fingers through the stale sweat in the bristles of his neatly-trimmed GI haircut. He supposes he smells of booze, but the idea of going to the shower before joining his buddies in the TV area demoralizes him. He has no desire to go back to the scene of that damp debacle, the place where by the grace of God he was not discovered and delivered unto a humiliation that would have taken weeks to live down.

The carbon scar where the centipede had bought it last night is smaller than he remembers. He recalls paths of flame encircling and engulfing the insect in a holocaust which was certain to leave a stain eternal on the concrete, but in fact is no more than a smudge.

Mueller is seated in front of the TV, and Gerlach is doing curls with a single dumbbell stacked with plastic maroon-colored weights. Palmer nods at the two men and takes a

seat on a folding chair and stares at the TV without compre-
hending its content. He is waiting for one or the other of his
buddies to say it, to say the dread thing that will sum up his
atrocities of the weekend, because even though he remembers
fairly well everything he has done since Thursday night when
he went off the compound to visit Motor Pool Mary, he
feels surrounded by cold winds of guilt, apprehension, and
condemnation for things he cannot even articulate.

He is familiar with this mental condition. He has experienced it before on smaller scales after benders, so that he
knows time will relieve him of the unpleasant feelings of
paranoia and the sense that he is forgetting something
important or is heading toward calamity. These are the
mental effects of hangovers in the way that nausea and thirst
are the physical. Time will take care of it. It takes care of
everything good and bad and worthwhile and wasted. In the
end, all of it goes into that insatiable dumpster Time.

When he returns to his cubicle for something to drink, he
opens the icebox and looks at the beers, and already in the
undertow of his ebbing hangover he feels the compulsion
coming over him again to drink and bring back that astound-
ingly sweet state of non-being. But he knows he has to stay
sober until after the soldier-of-the-month board on Monday.

He grabs his empty canteen and makes a water-run to the
mess hall where the potable water is chilled by machine. On
the walk back he looks for the can of scotch/Budweiser, but it
is gone. He cannot imagine who might have disposed of it.
There are no Vietnamese workers on the compound today.
The yellow alert will remain in effect until Monday dawn, he
knows this from experience.

It occurs to him that perhaps he did, after all, drink that can of scotch. Maybe after vomiting, or even before the episode at the piss-tube, maybe he did go back and finish it off. This theory makes sense to him because it would account for the fact that he can't remember doing it.

Back in his cubicle, the fact of drinking from his canteen and not drinking alcohol gives him a small sense of accomplishment. He is doing something that could be defined as good, and he is doing it for a reason. He cannot think offhand of anything he has done in the army, or in his entire life, that wasn't simply meaningless motion orchestrated to satisfy the whims of others.

For the next twenty or so hours he must remain sober for an actual, tangible, substantial reason, because if he goes up before the board hungover as hell, which he in fact had more-or-less expected to do when he was given this assignment, he would no longer merely look like a fool, he would actually be a fool. He would be a disgrace.

The horror of this pathetic truth sends a wave of nausea through him so that he remains in his cubicle rather than getting up to join his buddies which he wants to do. His paranoia has manifested itself in the idea that his buddies know exactly what he is thinking. They are dwelling upon him. They know what an asshole he thinks he is. He is the focus of their entire universe.

After a few minutes, this standard and predictable feeling fades, and he puts his canteen away and steps out of his cubicle to join the living. He decides that the best thing to do is go and sit on the folding chair again and watch TV alongside Mueller and not say a word. Silence can be as much a part of healing as time. If he sits long enough without saying a word, things will gradually mend.

Gerlach's rhythmic puffing as he raises the weight bar overhead attracts Palmer's attention in a way it never has before. Palmer does not hold any scorn for weight-lifting because it is so simple, so basic. You cannot rationalize a failure or blame anyone else. You either can lift the weight or you cannot, and while you can be weaker than you are, you cannot be stronger than you are.

He walks over to the bench and asks Gerlach if he can lie down and give the bar a heft. Gerlach seems pleased with this request. The man has not mingled with or spoken to anyone in the barracks for the past three weeks except on duty, and except to say that Detty had shot himself, but the aura of antagonism that surrounded him when he first quit talking to his buddies is no longer there. It is as though Gerlach has deliberately and effectively altered himself and his relationship with the world. He is now simply a guy who doesn't talk much and probably won't for a long time. Prior to this he had been a good drinking buddy, and somewhat of a loudmouth when he drank, though he also seemed abnormally worried that the compound might get hit or overrun by VC. All of that had been replaced with anger, and now the anger has settled into a seemingly hard but not dangerous silence.

Gerlach arranges sand-filled weights until the bar weighs seventy-five pounds. Palmer lies on his back on the wooden bench which is warm and damp with Gerlach's sweat. When he grips the iron bar, he feels strong. He takes deep breaths preparing himself, then lowers the bar once to his chest and is astonished at how difficult it is to raise his fists, to lock his

elbows and place the bar back into the grooves. He doesn't
think he can do two reps even though it's only seventy-five
pounds. A girl could do two reps of seventy-five pounds, he
thinks as he sits up grinning with embarrassment at Gerlach
who seems disappointed when Palmer confesses that this is
all the bench-pressing he is up for tonight.

He goes back to the folding chair and sits rubbing his
triceps that feel strained. He cannot believe how weak he is.
He could not have done another rep if he had wanted to, which
he did. A girl dying of polio could do two reps of seventy-five
pounds, he thinks as a general sense of gloom settles over
him. He knows now exactly how strong he is, which is also
exactly how weak he is, and on a normal Sunday night this
sense of worthlessness would have sent him to the icebox for
a beer, and he knows it, and this depresses him even more.

He doesn't want to drink. He is enjoying this absence of
panic-obsession for the next can of beer. He has six months
to go in Vietnam, and all the drinking he can do won't speed
up his discharge. He could stay sober and the discharge date
would still take six months to get here. If only he had something besides drinking to help him ignore this infuriating
creep of time. He wants to go home so badly, but it only gets
to him when he is sober.

It is almost eight o'clock and he has been sober, in the
sense that he hasn't been drinking, for twenty hours. Nor has
he had a cigarette. He cannot tolerate cigarettes when he has
a severe hangover. Inhaled smoke seems to magnify a
headache, nausea, diarrhea, the shaking of the hands. His
hands can be nearly rock-steady during a hangover, but if he
lights up, his nerves go to hell and he has to hold a can of

Coke or a canteen with both hands in order to drink, and he does this only in his cubicle, out of sight of anyone who might see him.

These twenty hours of sobriety seem to him the nearest thing to an accomplishment that he has achieved since he was sworn in. He feels like a man who has crawled out of some hellish storm and is just waiting, knowing all along he will eventually go back into that storm which never ends because it is in his nature. But the calm he feels, the absence of those petty furies (drink up, light up), this contentment bordering on joy compares well with the pleasure he gets from drinking, and he recalls his run around the softball field last night, the thoughts he had as he completed that first and only lap. He rarely has any trouble remembering the things he has done when drinking. He knows what blackouts are supposed to be like, but he is blessed with the curse of an excellent memory, and thus has trained his mind through necessity not to dwell upon things which are simply too unendurable to live with. He remembers the brief elation he felt when rounding the softball field, the familiar sense of wanting to shape up, to stop drinking, to give up smoking, to get in shape. But of course, it never goes beyond this because after all, he has been in good shape before. He once did not drink or smoke, and it didn't get him anywhere except Vietnam, which he could just as easily have done as a physical wreck, so that in the end none of this adds up to much of anything at all.

The men of the detachment begin drifting in from wherever it is they hide out at night, the EM club, the outdoor theater, other compounds, so that by the time Sergeant Ancil walks in, everyone except Phillips is present.

It's odd having a sergeant in the barracks. Cadre rarely come in here. He stands with his hands on his hips looking the place over. He looks at Detty's stain on the ceiling, and though his face lacks emotion, the creases on his forehead and cheeks seem to harden just a bit.

"Where's Phillips?" he says.

No one knows. Ancil nods as though he had expected a few men would be absent. He walks up into the TV area and looks at the bench press, looks at the TV, at the men seated around him, and continues to nod as though affirming a conversation he has been carrying around inside his head for quite a while.

"You men all know what happened yesterday, and you know why it happened."

Ancil looks each man in the eye as he speaks. When he looks at Palmer seated on the folding chair, it takes all of Palmer's will-power not to look away because he instantly knows that Sergeant Ancil went into his cubicle last night and saw the vial of heroin on the footlocker.

As he speaks to the men, Ancil keeps looking from one to the other, but it seems to Palmer that Ancil is looking at him more than the others.

"We've got a good detachment here," Ancil says in that serrated voice which cannot hide the disgust he feels for what Detty had done. "I know none of you men use that shit," and he looks right at Palmer, who finally cannot look his operations sergeant in the eye any longer. He nods in order to cover up the shaking that is beginning to envelop his entire body. He stares at the floor as though to say tsk, what a terrible thing, what a world.

"Pass this along to Phillips when he gets back," Ancil says, and Palmer looks up at him. "You're all good men. The Old Man wants you to know he's pleased with your performance at the PMO. I just came in here to tell you that you're all doing an outstanding job. We've been given our mission, and we're getting it done." He stops talking then and looks squarely at Palmer. "That's all I wanted to say."

But it isn't, because Ancil's eyes stay on Palmer, pick him out of the silent shyly embarrassed group of men waiting for their operations sergeant to go away and take with him the emotions overt and implied in his statements of affection. Ancil's dark eyes zero in on Palmer, fix him where he sits unable to turn his eyes away. The one thing Palmer has feared most in his life is now unfolding before him.

Ancil points at him and says, "Come on outside, GI. I want to talk to you."

The tendrils of a growing poisonous knot stab Palmer's gut, and he feels his face redden, feels something like armor at last peeling away from his body exposing raw flesh as he falls in step behind this twenty-year lifer whose hunched shoulders bespeak two decades of dealing with dud privates, whose weary gait seems braced to deal out one more dressing-down and revelation of punishments assembling in a military queue.

Palmer supposes there will be a humiliating meeting with the Provost Marshal tomorrow morning. The Major's large physique is intimidating, but he is a kindly, collegiate fellow, and as Palmer follows Ancil outside, he can think only of how disappointed the Major will be when he has to administer the Article 15 and the reduction in Palmer's rank.

It is only twenty or so paces to the screen door, but in that brief time Palmer calls upon resources honed by a frantic lifestyle that allows him to accept the sheer shittiness of what is happening to him, to prepare himself for the absolute worst, because this is familiar territory, this is home ground, he's lived in this sorry neighborhood all his life.

When they get out on the porch, Ancil turns and looks Palmer up and down in the pale white light of the streetlamp at the end of the block.

"You look like shit, GI," Ancil says.

Palmer stands not quite at attention with his lips tight. He doesn't bother to nod. He knows what he looks like. If it wasn't for his golden tan, he would look like dead shit.

"You got drunk this weekend, didn't you?" Ancil says.

Palmer smiles. This is fair ground. He can say, Yes sergeant, I got drunk this weekend, can admit to this without looking or feeling anything more than stupid.

"You're in bad shape," Ancil says. "I don't want you to drink anymore tonight."

Palmer feels an anxious sense of irritation at this remark because he has already made a decision to not drink. He wants to tell this to Ancil, to confess it, but he remains silent.

"I want you to hit the sack right now and get a good night's sleep," Ancil says. "I want you to be in good shape for the board tomorrow." And then Sgt. Ancil reaches into a fatigue pocket and glances around as if to make certain no one of importance might be watching. He pulls out a folded sheet of paper and hands it to Palmer, and lowers his voice. "These are the answers to the soldier-of-the-month quiz."

Palmer holds out his hand and accepts the piece of paper.

"I want you wearing a brand-new set of fatigues tomorrow," Ancil says. "First thing in the morning, you go get a haircut. Is your name printed on your web belt?"

Palmer nods.

"All right. Get this memorized. Then hit the sack, GI."

Ancil turns and walks off into the darkness. Palmer remains standing on the concrete porch until he can no longer hear his sergeant's fading footsteps. He feels drying sweat tightening the skin of his flushed face. The paper rattles in his hand.

He stands on the porch until his system settles down a bit from the adrenaline that has been coursing through his body, then he goes back into the barracks and says nothing to the men who are seated silently around the TV.

He steps into his cubicle and sits down on his bunk, unfolds the sheet of paper and looks at the answers to thirty questions about the muzzle-velocities of weapons he has never fired, about map-reading that he vaguely remembers being lectured upon during one single day in basic training a year-and-a-half earlier while inhaling the hot red dust of a Kentucky classroom, about the nomenclature of military vehicles which he has never seen on Vietnam highways much less Stateside roads, obscure questions pertaining to military protocols, tactics, and logistics which ring only the faintest bells in the stillborn experiences of his drafted, expedited, and futile training memories.

He stares at the typed words until he knows that he cannot memorize them. Knows that even if he wanted to, his brain could not retain any of this jumble, this forged ticket to a three-day R&R in Danang.

He puts the paper down and sits in the breeze of his fan

staring at nothing, thinking about nothing, until he hears the men going into their cubicles and turning off their reading lamps. Someone shuts off the overhead fluorescents, and Palmer waits in the yellow cube of his own lamplight until a silence has settled over the barracks.

He will not drink tonight. He will go to bed now, and in the morning will get a haircut, and in the afternoon, wearing fatigues smelling of packing crates, wearing buckle-brass shined to a mirror-gloss, wearing boots with toes glowing like polished black glass, he will go across the street to battalion headquarters and wait in line with all the other soldier-of-the-month candidates who will be coming from across the Central Highlands to participate in this competition: eager, clean-shaven, STRAC troops who will have their shit together. And when the time comes, he will go into the room and stand before the board, and with every question they put to him, he will do a thing he cannot recall having done in a long time — without resorting to fraud, or subterfuge, or ingratiating self-deprecation, he will look each one of them in the eye and answer the questions honestly by saying simply: I don't know. I don't know. I don't know. I don't know. I don't know.

PART THREE

CHAPTER 33

The monsoons have come and gone, have been replaced by a wet heat that has slowly dried with the arrival of summer. The scorching heat that Palmer remembers from his first day in Vietnam is returning but will never quite make the mercury rise in Qui Nhon as it does in Long Binh. It never had really gotten cold during the monsoon season, not Denver cold, but tropical cold, so that sometimes at night Palmer would be forced to reach up into the darkness and switch off his fan. The silk-like fabric of his poncho liner did not keep his body heat in, and was not designed to do so. He would awaken shivering in the fan breeze, and would smile because he could not recall shivering since MP school, on a day that it had snowed for the first time in that part of Georgia in more than a decade. Two months ago he woke up to find himself with 99 days left in Vietnam. Palmer is a two-digit midget.

The descent toward his DEROS and his ETS and his discharge had begun five months ago, during a weekend that he tries not to think about, the weekend that Detty killed himself. The next major mark on the calendar of his descent occurred when he had 65 days left in Vietnam, which meant he had been here for 300 days, the bulk of his tour as he thinks of it, had thought of the remaining 65 days like a LEM module breaking away from the bulk of a rocket ship, leaving the dull brainless monstrosity behind, that he might circle the moon and return to earth in little more than his own skin, baked bronze by the sun, chilled by monsoons, and splashing down just east of the Pacific in Ft. Lewis, Washington, where his brother Phil had once trained to come over here and maybe die like the 44,000 men before him.

They don't print a running tally of Vietnam dead in *The Pacific Stars and Stripes*. An average of ten Americans die every day, though not all of them in combat. There is the occasional suicide, or fatal traffic accident, or drug overdose. Palmer has to glean these stats from other sources. *Rolling Stone, Grunt, Time, Newsweek,* information that the army, the Pentagon, the government, doesn't want to burden their GIs with. Sixty thousand Americans died in auto accidents last year in the U.S. according to an article in *Newsweek*. Ever since he became the traffic man at the PMO Palmer has acquired a passive interest in auto accidents and traffic statistics. Traffic jams are intriguing, their causes, their inexplicable cures — one minute you're stopped on QL-1 behind a hundred jeeps and trucks, and the next minute the road is clear and everybody is breaking the 25 MPH speed limit. Speeding is the number one cause of traffic accidents according to the running tally he keeps in the official traffic-section book of records. Improper passing and following too close are next in line. An average of 164 Americans die every day in auto accidents back home. Statistically speaking, his fear of dying in Vietnam is ludicrous, but he still can't quite get it out of his mind, the sensation that something lethal might thump the back of his head at any moment.

Last December a 707 carrying troops to Vietnam crashed on takeoff in Anchorage, Alaska, killing 400 men. Newbies. Cherry boys. Probably a few lifers going back for their second or third tour. Palmer read the story at the same table where he is seated now, in the airfield cafeteria, fucking off before going back to work. When he read the story he recalled his own takeoff from Anchorage. Thrust like a bullet into a blizzard. He had expected to die, either in Anchorage or on the flight down the wall of the world to Southeast Asia. Flying is a crock of shit, but he hadn't died. Had expected to die sometime during the past 335 days, but hadn't, and still expects to die before his DEROS arrives because he is entering new territory, though not particularly unfamiliar, which GIs refer to as the "short-timer shakes." If I can just get through this last month, everything will be okay. He doesn't look forward to his flight home; fifteen hours in that false blue medium. If he makes it back to America alive he will never leave the United States again as long as he lives.

They're crushing slot machines with army tanks in Saigon. Palmer studies a black-and-white photograph in the newspaper, a mountain of slots being trampled by the treads of a tank with a grinning GI sticking his head up out of the hatch. Someone has decided that playing slot machines is an inappropriate form of recreation for American soldiers. Probably a general's wife. Maybe a group of chaplains. Do chaplains pass the collection plate at services? He doesn't know; he's never been inside an army church.

He stubs out his cigarette in the stamped tin-foil ashtray on the table heated by morning sunlight streaming through the picture-window. There are not as many people in the terminal today as there had been all year, had been on the day he arrived in Qui Nhon. Not as many people in Qui Nhon itself as eleven months ago. America is withdrawing from Vietnam, and this has manifested itself in ghost towns that have sprouted all over the city, American compounds

abandoned one by one until there are only a few units left—
engineering, hospital, and of course the MPs because MPs are
always the last to leave a war zone. Palmer was told this in
MP school but he didn't really believe it. He thought the last
to leave a war zone would be infantrymen walking backwards with rifles blazing, but he had thought an awful lot of
things that bore no relationship to reality before he came to
Vietnam. The last to leave a war zone are cops looking for
looters, AWOLs, deserters, tying things up neatly and leaving
the devastated landscape behind for whoever owns it, or will
inherit it. He rises and walks to the doorway of the terminal,
pushes it open and steps out into a morning air that retains
some of its nighttime coolness and will never really grow
unbearably hot, though maybe he has gotten used to it. His
fatigues stopped turning black in the underarms and back a
long time ago, he never even noticed when it ceased. He has
become acclimated. His fatigues have paled to the color of
silverfish, the only pair of fatigues that have survived his tour
without ripping out at the knees, the collar not quite frayed
enough to receive a chewing out by a sergeant. He wears
these fatigues in lieu of his newer greener fatigues because
he is a two-digit midget and wants everybody to know it. He
had never played sports when he was in school, neither grade
school nor high school, never won a trophy or wore a letter
jacket, and that is what this cloak of pale rip-stop is. Palmer's
letter jacket that he will wear every work day for the next
month until it is time to go home. Wear it among the newbies
and the cherry boys whom he passes outside the terminal
wandering around in the same daze that had a hold on him
when he was a cherry, when he looked at every face in the

crowd as if searching for the face of death, for death to do it now, to get it over with as soon as possible. But he no longer wants to get that over with, or get his wound, he wants to go home.

He is one of the oldest men in the MP battalion, in terms of time in service. There are a dozen or so who have been here longer than him and who will remain in Vietnam long after he has gone for reasons of their own, sometimes having to do with dope that can be had so easily in this virtually lawless country. You can have anything you want in Vietnam.

The maverick is parked at the curb right outside the door of the terminal. It is his private jeep for all practical purposes, but only because his job is to drive to the 109th motor pool and get daily travel authorization papers for the jeep from the motor pool sergeant, an affable E7 named Turner who is in his late thirties and whom Palmer gets along with, one of the few sergeants that Palmer has ever gotten along with. He has never understood why some sergeants seem to take an immediate liking to him and other sergeants seem to loathe him on sight. He has tried to analyze it, to find the thing inside himself that generates such dislike, but maybe it's just the way he looks, the set of his jaw, the color of his eyes, but he had given up trying to understand that a long time ago. His discharge will render moot these mysteries.

He backs out of the parking slot and drives across the road, heads down the curving length of the airfield, past the mummy Hueys which were there on the day he arrived and are still there. He expects them to disappear any day now. The airfield is slowly being transferred to the command of the South Vietnamese Army. Almost all of the American units that had functioned within the airfield perimeter have left the country, including the USO, a barracks building that he is just now driving past. He had been inside there a few times, it was an okay place, had pool tables and ping-pong and American women serving pop and Kool-Aid, but it could be depressing and he went there only to look for paperback books on the long shelves on the second floor. The women were older than thirty and seemed driven to somehow try and help the men who had been drafted into this country, comfort them like the Beav's mom or Donna Reed, always smiling and offering plates of cookies to young men half of whom had probably gotten drunk last night with hookers.

The paperback selection in the USO was incredible, he found books published during WWII with blurbs that said, "Send a book to a boy overseas" or a tiny paragraph on the endpaper explaining that this edition was produced in full compliance with the government's regulations for conserving paper and other essential materials during wartime. Yellowed pages, crisp, brittle, first edition paperbacks by Damon Runyon or Ring Lardner. He wished he could have loaded the entire USO paperback library onto an airplane and shipped it back to Denver. He supposes that when the USO had shut down for good the books were simply tossed into dumpsters, or maybe shipped to USOs in other locations, Danang, Hue, Nha Trang, but probably not.

He guides the jeep around the end of the airfield where fewer American planes land each day. The TMP is still there, though no vehicles are parked at the pumps right now. Maybe fuel-depot personnel are the next-to-last to leave a war zone, topping off MP vehicles before bugging out. Palmer has always thought that the TMP shack would be one of the worst places to have to sit out the war, surrounded by gasoline and diesel fuel, the sparse naked pumps tempting targets for the Viet Cong.

He continues on up the road in the direction of the 109th. There is only one other unit still functioning on this side of the airfield, a signal corps company a few blocks away from the MP compound, tucked in between the abandoned barracks of other American units that Palmer had never learned the purpose of, one-story green barracks buildings, their doors and windows gone, stripped either by the Americans before they left or Vietnamese thieves, like the ones that cut through the fence near the PX on his first day of MP duty last year. Thieves got into the U.S. Army Post Office over by the airfield around Christmas but they were caught by MPs who came into the PMO enraged, carrying packages and envelopes addressed to men of the 109th as evidence along with all the other mail that had almost been stolen. The thieves were eventually turned over to the South Vietnamese military police, and Palmer imagines that they were beaten or tortured, maybe killed, who knows? Maybe they were given medals and promoted to dick jobs. The ARVN are worthless. South Vietnam doesn't stand a chance after the Americans leave and everyone knows it.

He drives up the dirt road to the 109th, passes the company area and pulls into the fenced-off battalion motor pool compound where shirtless GIs are tinkering with jeeps in the big wooden bay like a barn with one side missing. He parks the jeep backwards outside the office and goes inside to get his travel papers.

The maverick has never had any papers at all. It was stolen by an AWOL years ago who was captured. The jeep subsequently had been used by the PMO without any actual authorization or paperwork. Nobody really knows when it had appeared at the PMO or even who the Provost Marshal was in those days — a handful of PMs have come and gone since Palmer first went to work there. And then one day the 109th motor-pool sergeant found out that the PMO was using a jeep that had no paperwork, and he demanded that it be brought in every morning to be given travel authorization papers. The sergeant's fiefdom was being threatened. Palmer was given the job of driving it to the motor pool every morning by his new operations sergeant, a tall, lean, black E7 named Ebbets. Sgt. Ancil went home two months ago.

Palmer doesn't really know the men who work in the motor pool office. He sees them every morning but doesn't get chummy with them, doesn't crack jokes. Most are newbies in comparison to him, their fatigues a darker green. They had been suspicious as hell when he first drove in with the jeep weeks ago and explained that it had no papers and they would have to create new ones. Almost everyone who had been in the 109th when Palmer first arrived has gone home, including Captain Metzler. The new CO is another young captain named Swales. Palmer has met him only once, on the day that Palmer was promoted, after twenty months in the army, to the rank of Specialist Fourth-Class. There was a small ceremony.

"That vehicle needs a new paint job," a sergeant E6 tells Palmer. He's a short man, red-haired, seated at a desk. Palmer has never seen him before. This has become a big thing at the motor pool, all the battalion jeeps are being repainted olive-drab, new numbers being stenciled on with bright white paint, everything being tidied up before the last Americans go home, Palmer supposes. He couldn't give less of a shit about the maverick's paint job. "I'll tell my operations sergeant," he says.

"Make sure he gets the word," the sergeant says, adding this bit of emphasis that sergeants who have no direct power over a particular EM are reduced to giving. He doesn't know that Palmer is still a part of the 109th, is merely detached.

Palmer nods and walks out of the office. He has no intention of telling Sgt. Ebbets that the E6 wants to take the maverick off line for a few days to make the piece of shit look new. If the maverick disappears for a few days, the clerks of the PMO won't have a vehicle to make PX runs whenever they feel like it. It would be like being a teenager without wheels back home. He tosses his travel authorization papers onto the floor of the shotgun seat, starts the maverick and drives out of the motor pool before the E6 can think up some other meaningless bullshit to harass him with.

The sun is higher now than it was when he had entered the airfield terminal to eat breakfast with the golden light streaming through the picture window illuminating his edition of the *The Pacific Stars and Stripes* that he reads each morning at his leisure. When Sgt. Ebbets had first given him the job of taking the jeep to the motor pool every morning Palmer had been irritated, but only because everything about the army irritates him. Sgt. Ebbets knows that he has very little work to do, what with Missy Anh doing most of the typing. Everybody in the PMO knows this, has always known it, but the traffic section needs an individual in charge of the paperwork, a dick job that a lot of men would kill for. Then Palmer discovered what a great deal this small assignment was. Every morning after he arrives at the PMO he gets into the jeep and drives to the airfield cafeteria for a leisurely breakfast. He stretches this twenty-minute job out to more than an hour before he returns to the PMO.

When Dobnik and Hillis had first learned that he was put in charge of the traffic section, they were pissed off, he could tell every time they came in and had to ask him for some blank 19-68s or new books of traffic tickets to take out on the road with them. The fucking newbie got the best job in battalion. Palmer had wondered if either Dobnik or Hillis had been hoping to get the job after working so hard and doing their best to be good MPs. They acted like it. He has called MPs into his office at different times and told them that their written descriptions of accidents were illegible, and that the paragraphs would have to be rewritten. He likes the small bit of power that the army has doled out to him. It makes him feel pissant and chickenshit, and he likes it.

On his way back around the airfield he sees three GI's walking along the shoulder of the road. Probably hiking from the signal unit. They glance back when they hear him coming, wave for a ride, the day is already hot. Palmer slows. Giving rides to GIs on foot is customary, like picking up hippie hitchhikers on the roads of America.

He pulls up next to them and stops. "Need a ride?"

One of them leans down and looks into the jeep, looks at the battalion crest pinned to Palmer's breast pocket, and says, "Are you an MP?"

Palmer nods.

The GI, a PFC wearing rumpled and slovenly fatigues, stands erect and waves him on saying, "No thanks. We don't *even* ride with MPs."

Palmer puts the jeep into gear and pulls away, stifling his irritation. The emphasis on the word *even* is part of the jargon that he first encountered in the army and which he hates with its hip intonation: I don't *even* want to do that; We don't *even* go there; Everybody doesn't *even* do anything. You try to help your buddy, Christ, fuck all these fucking GIs with their hatred of MPs. Basic training is dead.

CHAPTER 34

Palmer enters the MP station by the back door, passes through the office that leads to the Provost Marshal's private refrigerated office where the newest PM, Captain Costan, sits doing whatever he does and will continue to do until his DEROS comes up as has the date of rotation of so many PMs during the past year. Major Wilhelm was here for only a few months, leaving just after Christmas, and was replaced by a cocky young captain who bragged that there was a price on his head down in Saigon—the Viet Cong supposedly wanted him dead, which was why he was transferred to Qui Nhon.

He was here for a few months before he was replaced by a pudgy lifer who had risen from the enlisted ranks, had been a sergeant: Captain Woodward. He wore wire-rimmed glasses and had the air of an affable Protestant minister who wanted to be friends with the young folks. That was back in the days when Palmer smoked pot and drank alcohol.

He had smoked a joint one evening after work and was sitting on his bunk when a PFC named Welch knocked on his cubicle. Welch was the new head-clerk in the PMO and was wrestling with the monthly report that took a week to fill out, describing the MP activities that had taken place in all of Military Region II during the previous four weeks. He needed to know something about the traffic section records. Palmer was stoned at that point and so was not irritated at being asked to come over to the MP station to check his records. There was still light in the sky, and as he escorted the newbie over to the office he felt as if his head was floating, the dirt road seeming like a moving conveyor belt that his feet were negotiating with consummate skill. He had never been stoned inside the PMO but he wasn't worried because it was after hours. As he dug out his records and explained the monthly rate of traffic accidents and tickets to Welch, he felt as if he was talking with big rubber balls inside his mouth. He didn't know if Welch could tell if he was stoned or not, and didn't care. He didn't care about anything back in those days. Welch was a newbie and Palmer didn't give a shit what newbies thought. Then Cpt. Woodward walked into the room.

Paranoia welled up inside Palmer, who nevertheless was able to maintain his composure because the pot also made him feel as if he was standing outside himself objectively viewing his panic even as he was experiencing it. He knew it was just pot paranoia, and so he stood at semi-attention along with Welch as Cpt. Woodward struck up a conversation, told them that he would be leaving the PMO soon and going home, and was sorry that he hadn't had the opportunity to get to know the men of the detachment a little better, but he wanted them to know that he appreciated the hard work they were doing to help him fulfill his mission as Provost Marshal. Palmer kept his lips pressed tightly together and tried to keep from busting out laughing. He hoped he didn't reek of pot, or that at least this lifer officer wouldn't recognize the odor. Palmer was saved by the nature of the conversation itself, his lips free to warp into a grin that felt massive and idiotic as he acknowledged the captain's heartfelt sentiment, his hilarity transformed into continuous and tiny breathy chuckles.

Missy Anh isn't in the office when Palmer enters. Probably went to the latrine with the other Vietnamese secretaries who work in other sections of the PMO or the Vietnamese ID office. All the secretaries get together to go to the female-personnel latrine over by the water tower each morning, strolling like a group of little nuns in colorful habits, all seeming to talk simultaneously like high school girls clutching books to their breasts between classes. The orphanage across the street from the main gate of Camp Quincey is run by Catholic nuns. Palmer sees them sometimes in their white habits herding the children around the grounds behind the high brick wall accessed by a barred gate. Must be a lot of orphans in Vietnam. What will become of the nuns when the communists take over? The mechanics at the battalion motor-pool once told Palmer that they worry about what will become of the boy who helps them out, a ten-year-old Vietnamese kid who wears an olive-drab GI cap like Dondi and washes jeeps and brings them Cokes and cleans their tools. What will become of Missy Anh? What will become of all the South Vietnamese who have jobs with the American army? Will they be tried as traitors by the NVA? Will Ho Chi Minh's troops be like carpetbaggers descending on Atlanta? But he tries not to dwell upon these things over which he has no control. Maybe the South Vietnamese will greet the northern invaders the way the French welcomed the Americans who liberated Paris, standing along the sides of QL-1 waving the appropriate flag of the day and applauding.

He goes to the small refrigerator and buys a Coke, puts ten cents into the cigar box, and ponders the necessity of making a PX run for more Coke and Pepsi and 7-Up. Sooner or later that E6 will get his hands on the maverick. Probably should stock up so the PMO doesn't run short, although they could always take the paddy wagon, or else ask an MP unit to make a quick run to the PX. MPs buy their pop here too. Everybody's kidneys are getting a hard workout in Vietnam.

Palmer is sitting at his desk doing nothing, staring at a blank traffic accident report form rolled through the platen of his Smith-Corona, when Missy Anh comes in looking wide-eyed and breathless with news, Palmer recognizes the expression. Her big beautiful eyes always get bigger when she's hauling the burden of some lowdown. The Vietnamese know everything that goes on in Camp Quincey, in all of Qui Nhon, maybe all of Vietnam. She comes up to his desk and leans toward him and says quietly, "You hear what they say? We move."

"What?" Palmer says. He hates the pidgin-English that both the Vietnamese and the Americans use to communicate with each other, like GIs in WWII movies talking to brown or yellow people, like cavalry talking to Indians, as if everybody in the world is a drooling idiot.

"Missy Tuong tell me MP battalion move to Camp Redstone next week," Anh whispers.

The hair on the back of Palmer's neck almost rises, an ominous tingle sprouting at the base of his neck. "How does she know?" he says.

"Firs Sajen, she hear him say."

Missy Tuong is the First Sergeant's private secretary. This is how news is passed along the grapevine, a latrine-run among colorful nuns where every secret known to Mankind is parsed and disseminated. The military Police battalion will be packing up next week and moving a mile away to Camp Redstone, the large American compound which includes the PX at its southernmost perimeter.

"Oh Jesus," Palmer mutters to himself as Anh goes to her desk and sits down to begin pretending to work. There have been rumors for weeks that the MP battalion might make the move to Camp Redstone, a move that almost all the other American units still remaining in the city have made. The Camp Quincey quartermaster battalion is already making preparations to leave. The army is consolidating compounds, bringing everyone together in one location where, as far as Palmer is concerned, one grenade will get them all. Camp Redstone has been hit many times by the Viet Cong on the mountain, but it isn't the prospect of getting hit that fills him with dread, it's the idea of loading every fucking piece of equipment in the PMO onto deuce-and-a-halfs and hauling all of it over to Camp Redstone. Up to now he was hoping like hell that by the time the move came down he would already be in Denver. He knows exactly who's going to be doing all the lifting.

He stands up and steps to the doorway of the traffic office and looks out at the clerk/typists seated erect at their desks. All of the clerks who had been here when he first arrived have gone home, Aldhoff, Canfield, Schafer, Evans and the others who had been members of the detachment on the day that Detty killed himself. The presence of these new men who know nothing about that terrible weekend makes Palmer feel safe in an odd way. It is as if he has run away to some place where nobody knows him, and has done so without moving—everybody that he never really wanted to face again, including Sgt. Ancil, ran away for him. He wants to ask one of these new clerks if they know anything about this most recent rumor that the PMO will be moving to Camp Redstone next week, wants confirmation from an American, not that he doesn't believe Anh or Tuong, but he wants the news made official; one of them might know some of the details. But he decides not to ask. He goes back and sits down at his desk. One thing he has learned during the past eleven months is that knowing things does not change anything. No matter how much you know, learn, experience, you will still be here exactly as many days as you have left to be here. Best to sit tight and wait for unavoidable shit storms to roll over you like Christmas monsoons.

At noon he crosses the softball field and goes to the enlisted men's club where he orders a chicken dinner and takes it out to the vacant back patio. He had eaten lunch here almost every noon since Christmas after he had finally quit going to the Camp Quincey mess hall tired of eating his meals across from the chomping jaws of slobs like himself, tired of picking little pink spots of dead bugs out of the white bread that is cooked in some filthy fucking kitchen somewhere in Vietnam, he has no idea where. He sips at a can of Coca-Cola and gazes out at the South China Sea which glimmers green as it had glimmered for the past eleven months, the past eleven hundred years. The Dutch were the first to invade Vietnam from Europe. After Palmer quit drinking he began going to the air-conditioned library on the compound at night, a room on the second floor of a quartermaster building where he began reading, among other things, histories and contemporary books on the Vietnam War. He wants to know where he really has been all these months, not in space, but in time.

The library is run by a young woman like Anh, a pretty Vietnamese woman who sits all day in the cold room wearing a sweater and shivering. During the monsoon season Anh had worn a heavy sweater to work every day and Palmer had teased her, "A sweater in Vietnam for god sake!" in the flirtatious way he has always related to her, his virginal secretary, his partner in crime. She had taught him the finer points of pretending to work.

Palmer had been the traffic man at the PMO for three weeks before he realized that, while Anh seemed to type reports continuously, she in fact turned out only three per week. In the beginning Palmer had approached this job with absolute seriousness, coming to the office each morning and working on reports, typing up 19-68s and filing traffic tickets, motivated by a not unreasonable fear of blowing it and being sent back to the 109th for incompetence, of losing this dick job due to forces that he might not be able to understand, office politics, army politics. But Sp/4 Shappler had been right. There was nothing to the job. Anh had taught him to leave a half-finished report rolled through the platen of his Smith-Corona, and to begin typing if anybody above the rank of corporal passed by the doorway. The secretary had taught the boss how to turn out three reports per week while seeming to type continuously.

Two months ago Anh had told him that her father had arranged for her to meet a young man from another family, with the possible prospect of marriage. At first Palmer didn't grasp what she was talking about. Her English is excellent, she studied it in high school, yet because Americans talk like drooling idiots she has succumbed to the pidgin-English that she believes it takes to communicate with Westerners. She explained that whenever she got married, it would be arranged by her family, that Vietnam girls do not fall in love with just any nitwit they encounter on the street as girls do in America. Palmer was appalled. This was something out of a 19th-century European novel.

"But my mother didn't like him," Anh said, supplying the denouement to her wistful story.

Palmer asked how she felt about the idea of marrying a man whom she had never met before and wouldn't even get to know until after the wedding.

"I hope he will be nice," was all she said.

Anh had once told him that there is no such word as Vietnamese, "That is what Americans call us," she said. "But we are not Vietnamese, we are Vietnam." Palmer was fascinated by this linguistic squaring of the deck, and understood intuitively how outraged Americans would feel if the rest of the world talked about the Americanese People in newspapers and TV broadcasts. Irishese. Germanese. Italianese. Mexicanese. Chinese—that's where it must have come from. But why bother to ask these little bronze people what they call themselves? They're just dinks, slopes, slants, zips, gooks. What will become of Anh when the communists finally take over? He doesn't like to think about it.

He returns to the PMO feeling more refreshed from his hour-long noon nap than he used to feel when its purpose served solely to diminish the pain of a hangover. As soon as he arrives, the First Sergeant, a lifer named Gorman, calls all the clerks into the back office near the PM's door to make the big announcement.

"The Provost Marshal's Office is going to be moving to Camp Redstone next week. On Monday morning we're going to begin transferring files to the new MP station."

All of the Vietnamese secretaries—Palmer will never get into the habit of calling them by their correct name, Vietnam, the GIs would think he was a drooling idiot—are gathered around to hear this small change in their fates. Will they get to keep their jobs after the move? But this won't compare to their fates after the Americans go home for good. They listen silently, clustered like colorful nuns as Gorman explains the procedure. "The PMO will be transferred to the new building first, hopefully in one day so there will be as little interruption in work as possible. After the PMO is up and running, you troops will transfer your bunks and lockers to a new barracks that's already been picked out. The 109th MP Company will be moving to Camp Redstone too. The whole MP battalion will be located in one area."

Palmer listens to this announcement with a mounting sense of disgust. Why couldn't they have waited another month until he was discharged? It's the Presidio all over again, those double-wide fuckers that they spent weeks it had seemed, hauling and bolting together from oh-seven-hundred hours until closing time at the bowling alley.

It's been a long time since Palmer has been in a position to dodge a major shit detail, but that old feeling of entrapment combined with the urge to goldbrick wells up inside him. It's instinctive. Maybe he could take an R&R next week and hide out in Bangkok or Sydney. But you have to put in for an R&R weeks in advance. He never took an R&R during the past year because he didn't want to leave Vietnam only to return a week later. When he leaves this country it will be for good. His expertise tells him that there is no way out of this massive detail. All the exits have been blocked. There is nowhere you can run to in Vietnam, unless your name is Omar.

First Sergeant Gorman dismisses the clerks and they go back to their desks silently mulling over this latest news. Palmer almost makes it to the doorway of the traffic section when Sgt. Ebbets intercepts him. "Specialist Palmer, I need to speak with you for a moment."

The operations sergeant has a precise, clipped way of speaking, something almost British in his enunciation but for the southern accent. He's probably in his forties, might have served in the Korean War but Palmer doesn't know. His hair has gone a bit gray but is clipped short, eschewing the modified Afro look that a lot of black EM try to slip past their cadre.

"Are you caught up in your work?" Sgt. Ebbets says. He has a way of frowning, his lips stretching back from his teeth whenever he asks Palmer a question. Palmer senses that he would never have been able to get away with drinking on duty if Ebbets had been the operations sergeant instead of Ancil.

"We're right on schedule, Sergeant."

Sgt. Ebbets' question has sent up red flags in Palmer's mind. He doesn't like telling anyone where the traffic section stands in terms of output. It can only lead to trouble, which this does.

Sgt. Ebbets nods and touches his chin, frowns again and says, "That's good, that's good, because I've got a job for you. We need a man to paint the interior of the new MP station at Camp Redstone. You're going to have to start in on it right away because the Provost Marshal wants the building painted and cleaned up and ready for the move on Monday."

Palmer feels something inside him starting to turn, an unpleasant emotion seeking an exit as he takes in this information. He stands perfectly still, speechless, as he had stood when Sgt. Wesser had told him that he was going to have to pull KP last year.

"Yes, Sergeant," he finally says.

Ebbets nods, frowns deeper, continues to tap his chin. "I want you to give your secretary plenty of work to do. I don't know how long you'll be out of the office and I do not want the traffic section to get behind in its reports."

"That shouldn't be a problem, Sergeant," Palmer says, telling a truth. "We're pretty much caught up right now."

"Good, good, that's good to hear," Sgt. Ebbets says. "This afternoon I want you to take the jeep over to the new MP station. There's a group of engineers finishing up the carpentry work. I want you to look the place over and see how much paint you will need to requisition from supply."

Palmer has been getting peculiar vibes from this black E7 ever since the man had replaced Sgt. Ancil, senses that Ebbets can see right through him, knows that he is a fraud who never has any work to do. Palmer has deliberately avoided giving the man any sort of static because he has the funny feeling that Sgt. Ebbets would like to replace him with someone else and send him back to the 109th. It's like pot paranoia without the pot. Palmer never did get along very well with Sgt. Ancil, so maybe Ancil had spilled the beans and told Ebbets what a dud the traffic man is.

After Ebbets goes back to his desk, Palmer steps into the traffic office and sits down on his chair, wheels it over next to Missy Anh and quietly explains the situation to her, tells her that she will have to keep the reports coming along steadily so that Sgt. Ebbets doesn't get dinky-dao as they say. Missy Anh nods. She knows. She had taught Palmer everything he knows.

CHAPTER 35

The engineers working on the MP station, five young EM and a sergeant E6 overseeing them, are a friendly group who seem to Palmer like a crew of AWOLs on a punishment detail. They're not very military, though Palmer has come to notice this about a lot of non-MP personnel, but beyond that they are like high school kids, even the sergeant has a kind of adult immaturity to him, not quite irresponsible but not especially hung up on regulations either. They drink beer while they work, they laugh a lot, and find it funny that they are building an MP station.

Palmer learns this when he drives over to Camp Redstone and scouts the burgeoning PMO which is tucked among a maze of old barracks buildings that had belonged to some other unit that had left Vietnam long ago, had furled its colors and held a stand-down party and departed like all the other American units that seemed to have simply evaporated while Palmer was sleeping. He hates the way the American presence has diminished over the past three months. What if the VC decide it's time for another Tet Offensive now that the odds have turned in their favor? He imagines Camp Redstone becoming another Khe Sahn while the trapped troops wait for the Phantom jets of Phu Cat to show up and blast the hell out of everything beyond the perimeter. At least Phu Cat is still active. Thank God the VC don't have an air force.

While driving over he had expected the engineering squad to be surly, maybe dope smokers, resentful of having to help build the very jail that might one day hold one of their own in a D-cell, but the carpenters putting the finishing touches on the PMO and the MP station turn out to be sort of silly guys who sip at their beers in between hammering away at the plywood walls, and seem amused to find an MP roaming around the building trying to figure out how much paint he will need to cover everything. They find it especially funny when he tells them that he has been ordered to paint the interior of the building by himself. They are like civilians to him, all of them bare-chested and tanned but for the E6 as they go about their work, some wearing sunglasses. Doubtless younger than him. Palmer had turned twenty-two a couple months back, and felt sort of bad that he had given up drinking—birthdays had always been one of the best excuses for getting blasted out of his skull.

"What do you guys think?" Palmer says. "How many gallons of paint will I need?"

One of the men approaches him with a toothy grin, scratches at his breastbone where a tiny peace-sign dangles on his dog tag chain, and says, "Here's what you do, man. Requisition ten gallons of paint, and whatever you don't use you sell on the black market."

Everyone within earshot, the entire squad, busts out laughing. They probably know their business. Palmer wonders what he himself is doing in the MPs. He feels an affinity for these guys, feels he should always have been working alongside them. Before he leaves to go back to the PMO, the E6 asks him to drive over to the Camp Redstone NCO club to pick up a case of beer. "Tell the bartender that Sergeant Mulroy sent you."

On Wednesday morning Palmer puts on a pair of new
fatigues rather than his letter jacket and pants. He doesn't
want to splatter any green paint on his silverfish threads. He
plans to take them home, a souvenir like the embroidered silk
pillows and ivory knickknacks that so many GIs buy at the
PX before going home, cheap junk memories of their time in
service. He knows that some day he will look at his old army
uniforms with a nostalgia that he does not presently own, or
particularly believe in. But throughout his childhood he had
examined the brown uniform coat that his father had worn
in WWII with its intriguing and unidentifiable campaign
ribbons pinned above the left breast pocket, and had wondered
how his father had endured three and a half years in the
South Pacific, same latitudes as Vietnam, same heat, same
slow march of time, the Philippines, the Solomon Islands,
New Guinea. As much as Palmer hates Vietnam, he knows
that he will one day examine his old uniforms and wonder
the same thing, will probably keep his uniforms hidden in a
closet, as does his father.

He goes to the battalion supply room and requisitions five
gallons of green paint and stows them in the rear of his
jeep, then heads for the 109th to get the maverick's travel
authorization papers, wondering if anyone will try to steal
the paint from the rear of the jeep while he is inside the
airfield cafeteria. Should he linger for forty minutes in the
cafeteria as usual, or just eat a quick breakfast and get on with
this detail? Having an actual job to do makes him feel guilty
about fucking off, something he has never felt before.

But when he drives up to the terminal and parks the
jeep he is stunned to see that there are no tables beyond

the picture window where he has eaten every morning since he first began making this run. He gets out of the jeep and goes inside the terminal and looks around. No cafeteria, but people are still working behind the counter where a Spec Four had made a phone call for him last year to have a jeep take him to the MP battalion. He goes up to a sergeant E6 and asks about the cafeteria.

"Finny," the sergeant says with a grin.

Palmer is too depressed by the news to be disgusted by the pidgin English that he hopes he will never have to endure again in his lifetime. But that single word *finny* says it all. Now that the airfield is being turned over to the ARVN, the civilized amenities of America are evaporating. *Finished.*

He leaves the terminal bummed out and hungry, and realizes it's too late to go to either the Camp Quincey mess hall or the 109th mess hall where he is still a member, detached to the PMO but authorized to eat their chow.

This is all it takes to relieve him of his guilt over fucking off. After he gets the travel authorization papers from the motor pool he drives to the main PX, passing Camp Quincey and looking over at it thinking how strange it is that he will be leaving that place a month before he actually goes home. Almost his entire tour in Vietnam spent there, he rarely went outside the compound for anything except PX runs and a few shit details that he couldn't avoid, like setting up speed traps on QL-1 or posting four-foot tall speed-limits signs that the Vietnamese stole as soon as he drove away. A sergeant told him that they use the signs for walls in their houses. Funny how the army has gotten everybody used to using the word *tour* for this shit. Did his father refer to his three and a half years in the South Pacific as a *tour!* Maybe the genius who designed the M-16 helped devise some of the army jargon that Palmer hates. Words are bullshit. But then, he has spent his whole life trying to reshape his world with words, deluding himself constantly. If you say something, that makes it true.

The main PX has a small snack-bar that sells oven-warmed hamburgers, and Palmer buys two of these for breakfast and sits in the maverick in the parking lot eating them and drinking a can of Coke, the kind of breakfast he used to eat when he was always hungover, even when he was a civilian, scarfing down canned spaghetti for breakfast before staggering off to one of the shit jobs that kept him in beer money when he was eighteen, nineteen, before he got drafted. This is the only drawback to getting discharged from the army, he will have to get a job. Specialist Fifth-Class Saunders, who ran the Vietnamese ID section before he went home, once told Palmer that he ought to go to college after he gets out of the army. "Drink a little wine, chase a little pussy. The GI Bill pays you three hundred bucks a month." Palmer hadn't responded to the suggestion, bristling mildly, he hates school, but he was struck by the financial coincidence: he earns that much right now, combined with sixty dollars a month combat pay. He was surprised when he first learned he would be earning combat pay in Vietnam, two dollars a day extra for serving in a war zone. The men out in the bush getting shot at by Charlie receive the same two bucks. This breaks down to a little more than fourteen bucks a week, eight cents an hour for a twenty-four hour day. His mother had earned forty dollars a week working in a jewelry shop in Omaha in 1940.

When he arrives at the new MP station there are no engineers working on the walls. The interior of the building is finished, the workers have packed their tools and gone. Wasn't much of a job to begin with, mostly partitioning the building into small rooms, and erecting the high platform for the desk sergeant. As Palmer wanders around the new PMO looking at everything that he will spend the next few days painting, he has the feeling that he is walking around a movie set. And not even a movie set but a model of a movie set, the wood unpainted, no details, no color, no characters performing their roles as cops or prisoners. Sort of like a false front in a cowboy movie, the cattle drovers striding through the swinging doors into emptiness because the interior of Miss Kitty's saloon is over on Stage 9. This hollow, unfinished, unpainted set won't become real until he slaps on the proper olive-drab. And even then they will have to bring in the props that will give the setting verisimilitude, all the desks and filing cabinets, shit, he gets pissed off just thinking about it. They couldn't have waited another fucking month.

But as he sets about painting the MP station, using a roller and dripping olive-drab onto copies of the *The Pacific Stars and Stripes* spread around the concrete floor, he begins to realize that this job is not so bad at all. For one thing it doesn't take much time to paint a wall with a roller, this detail may not take as long as he had thought it would. But also, he is alone, doesn't have to pretend to be working, doesn't have to listen for the heavy sounds of boots approaching the doorway so he can start hustling. Alone like on tower-guard duty, but actually doing something, not just sitting on a stool and staring, and wondering if any VC will bother to come racing down the road in a truck and break the monotony. As the hours roll by he realizes this shit detail is putting momentum into time, he is concentrating so much on making everything look good, getting the paint right up into the corners with a brush, that he doesn't even glance at his wristwatch. He had finally gotten around to buying a Timex last Christmas. He had come to realize that he was annoying the clerks by always asking them what time it was, especially after Aldhoff had said, "Jesus Christ, Palmer, why don't you go to the PX and buy yourself a goddamn watch?"

It's because I'm too cheap, he ought to have replied. It's because I use all my money to buy beer.

Rolling long green overlapping arcs onto the wall of what will be the First Sergeant's office, Palmer recalls the way he used to try to cover up the odor of alcohol when he drank on duty. Every morning he went to the showers and scrubbed himself with Dial soap, shaved with Gillette Foamy, gargled endlessly with Listerine, then chewed on Clorets to kill any more alcohol odor, combined with the Rolaids that he popped to stifle his perpetual heartburn. He would put on fatigues washed in Tide and freshly spray-starched, thank God for Missy Cue and Missy Nu, then walk over to the MP station still a bit high from the booze he had drunk the night before, though sometimes it was hard to tell if he was high or just mildly hungover, since he saw everything through an unnatural filter inside his brain, behind his eyes. With all the camouflage he used to cover his crimes, Dial, Foamy, Listerine, Tide, Clorets, Rolaids, Christ, he must have smelled like a drugstore.

He never really knew if any of the clerks were aware that he was always buzzed, was slipping out for drinks during the day, covering it with chalky tablets and cigarette smoke. Nobody ever said anything. Sgt. Ancil never seemed to know, but shit, looking back on it now he can't believe he got away with it for one second. He probably didn't, but nobody ever said anything. Maybe they had their own secret scams going that had nothing to do with alcohol. Women, black market deals, funny business with money, greenbacks, who knows? Maybe they were just trying to help their buddy by remaining mum. Enlisted men do tend to stick together, until one of them gets fucked over. He knows a little bit about that. He still wonders if there is some way he can avoid helping to move all the desks and filing cabinets. If he can keep it up for another month, he will have spent his entire army career trying to think up ways to avoid shit details. A perfect record. He will come out of this clean.

On Thursday morning he walks over to the Camp Quincey PMO in his paint-stained fatigues, the olive-drab splatters of the office lighter than the olive-drab fabric of these recently requisitioned fatigues. One afternoon around Christmas when he was wearing a pair of fatigues ripped out at the knees he was accosted by the battalion sergeant-major, an E8 who resembles Frank Nitti. Still believing that he was going to die in a mortar attack, and filled with a disgust that would eventually lead to his drinking on duty but had not yet, Palmer had stopped caring about his appearance, did not even wear the battalion crest or attach his rank to his collars when he trudged off to work each morning. He continued to wear the torn fatigue pants because he was disgusted that the army issued clothing so fragile that the knees ripped out the first time you squatted to sort your equipment in your footlocker. Fuck the army, he told himself, fuck their cheap shit uniforms, he told himself, if they issue me garbage I'll wear garbage, he told himself, then as he walked out of the PMO he heard a gravelly voice call his name. "Palmer! Come here!" It was Sergeant Benedetti who looked like a Mafioso but was in fact an affable man in his late forties, big, round-shouldered, but who didn't brook any bullshit. He was standing at the bottom of the stairs leading up to battalion headquarters. "Where's your rank, Palmer? Where's your battalion crest?" Palmer had no answer. Being a rebel without a cause was easy when you lived inside your own safe little world. "Look at your pants, the knees are torn out." If Palmer hadn't liked Sgt. Benedetti he would have bristled, putting another notch in his disgust with all things military, but instead he just explained that he had gotten these fatigues a week earlier and the knees already had ripped out.

"I want you to go over to supply and requisition a new set of fatigues," Sgt. Benedetti growled. "And make sure you have your rank on your collars and your unit patch sewn on your sleeve, and if you don't have a battalion crest go get one from the supply officer. I don't ever want to see you looking like that again."

A nice affable chewing out. Sgt. Benedetti was talking tough, but his eyes were smiling. Palmer was just another kid draftee that the lifers had to endure. Palmer never let Sgt. Benedetti see him looking like that again, but his disgust and surliness returned like a slow tide, which manifested itself in a few sips of scotch now and again, and again, and again.

Anh is seated at her desk typing when Palmer enters the traffic section. She smiles at him and says good morning. Palmer smiles and asks her how the reports are coming along.

She nods, shows him two reports that she had typed up yesterday while he was at the new PMO. A small neat stack, should Sgt. Ebbets come in to check on her. She could turn out eight reports a day if there was any reason in the world to do so, which there isn't.

Palmer brings his transistor radio with him today, as he does when he pulls guard duty. He buys four cold Cokes from the PMO icebox even though he knows they will grow warm in less than an hour. After he arrives at the new PMO he switches on AFVN and sets the radio on the ledge below the long screened window where the clerks will be typing, an unobstructed line of sight to the AFVN transmitting station on top of the mountain to the south. The AFVN compound perimeter fence glows like a crown of lights at night. If there is any movement on the mountain, if any VC are sneaking around, the guards fire .50 caliber bullets vertically down the slope, spraying red streamers like red waterfalls raining on the hillsides. Yet the VC continue to lob their mortars from the mountainside every two months.

He listens to rock music as he paints. He no longer hates acid rock. After he started smoking pot last Christmas his attitude changed. On New Year's eve when he was upstairs in the barracks smoking dope with the heads, the battalion clerk named Loeb handed him a set of headphones and told him to listen to "Whole Lotta Love" by Led Zeppelin and then side two of "Abbey Road," neither of which Palmer had ever heard before. He had never even worn headphones before. Stereo was as new and interesting to him as a pot high. It made things move back and forth inside his skull. He had never really liked much of the music that the Beatles had put out since 1965. He thought their "Rubber Soul" album stank except for "Nowhere Man." He likes Bob Dylan's lyrics now. Things have changed. He first met the dopers, the heads, one week before Christmas. On that night he was in the dayroom drunk on beer and playing pool. Two heads were playing ping-pong, as high as kites, hitting nothing, laughing. And because Palmer will talk to anyone when he is drunk, he struck up a conversation with them, and they eventually inquired as to whether he got high. And because Palmer will do anything when he is drunk, he followed them out to the showers where the heads kept, and still keep, a coffee can filled with pot secreted on an overhead plank of wood beneath the water tower. One of the men, a battalion clerk who introduced himself as PFC Dorset, rolled a joint and the three of them smoked it. Palmer didn't get high that night, but he did remark upon the fact that the odor of pot was the same odor that he used to smell at the Underground Cinema 12 at the Vogue Theater back in Denver. He rarely toked with the heads again, afraid he would get busted, and he wanted to come out of this clean even if he wasn't clean. He would slip over to the water tower at night and pilfer pot and twiddle the tobacco out of a Camel cigarette and load the hollow tube with marijuana and smoke it quickly and then go back to his cubicle to sit on his bunk and wait to see what happened. The heads had told him that it would take a while for the pot to build up in his system. He was beginning to believe that it was bullshit, that the pot smokers were just pretending to get high in the way that grade school boys pretended to inhale cigarette smoke just to look cool. And then one night he started having peculiar thoughts.

The PMO is half-painted before he realizes that he had better slow down. He likes doing this job, alone with no one around to harass him with meaningless questions. He might conceivably finish the job today, and he wants to drag it out until Friday evening. If he finishes the job today he will have to go back to the PMO tomorrow, and he would just as soon never go back there again. It will be another two weeks before they find a replacement for him to train the way Sp/4 Shappler had trained him to be the traffic man last year. How many traffic men have there been? How many will there be? When he was eighteen he had thought the Paris peace talks might bring the war to an end before he got drafted. He can't imagine how much longer the war will go on, and doesn't care, because in less than four weeks he will no longer be a part of it.

On Friday evening around four he is just putting the finishing touches on the interior of a detention cell when Captain Costan and Sgt. Ebbets show up to see how things are coming along. Palmer stands at semi-attention while the PM wanders around the station smiling at everything and telling him that he has done an outstanding job, as if he had something to do with the construction of the place. The only thing he had to do with it was its appearance, and appearances mean everything in the army. Even Sgt. Ebbets seems pleased, and it occurs to Palmer that he wouldn't mind after all getting booted back to the 109th at this point. Finish out his last few weeks in Vietnam as a road MP. This might relieve him of the small burden of having to train a new traffic man. One last shit detail avoided before he receives his discharge. But it's only a passing thought. Now that the American presence in Qui Nhon is diminishing, the road MPs are becoming the first line of defense should the VC decide to instigate another Tet. MPs are always the last to leave a war zone, and Palmer doesn't want to start messing around with his fate and end up being the last MP in Qui Nhon.

CHAPTER 36

There is a small wooden shack at one end of the street that has a two-foot hole in its tin roof. The shack used to house a MARS radio station where anybody who wanted could make a phone call to America for free. The call had seemed complicated to Palmer when he first heard about it months ago because it apparently involved a simultaneous telephone and radio hookup in order to connect with the relatives back home. You were supposed to say "Over" when you finished each sentence, Palmer wasn't too clear on the procedure, but he could not imagine putting his parents through the hassle of saying "Over" at the end of their own baffled, uncertain sentences broadcast out of Nebraska. Why would their son call home from Vietnam?

And then one night seven weeks ago the MARS shack took a direct hit from the VC on the mountain. According to the story Palmer got, that was the only mortar which landed on Camp Redstone on that particular night. It completely destroyed the interior of the shack, pulverized the radio equipment but left the walls intact, did not balloon them, so that, but for the two-foot diameter hole in the roof, you wouldn't even know it had been hit. The former MARS shack is approximately thirty yards up the road from the barracks where the PMO Detachment will be living as soon as they get all their bunks and wall lockers and footlockers transferred from Camp Quincey. According to GIs who know something about mortar armory, "the PMO Detachment is just one click away," meaning that if the Viet Cong make an altitude adjustment on their mortar tube by rotating a small knob one click, the detachment barracks will come within range of a rocket like the one that put a hole in the MARS shack.

The entire MP battalion is moving into a small compound within Camp Redstone, and the MARS shack is at the southernmost edge of the perimeter which is demarcated by a fence topped by barbed-wire and barricaded on both sides with rolls of concertina wire laced with Coke and Budweiser cans, draped there by members of the engineering battalion that had formerly resided here, the battalion that had helped to build Camp Redstone at the beginning of the war, not quite ten years ago, when most Americans didn't even know there was a war. The buildings look old now. But for the green complexion they remind Palmer of the crappy WWII barracks he had bunked in during basic and MP school, almost tenements, yet the buildings are less than a decade old. Everything grows old so fast here. Warps, rots, flakes away in the heat, the humidity, the monsoons. The Vietnamese are reduced to stealing speed-limit signs to shore up the walls of their spongy rotting homes.

The quartermaster battalion at Camp Quincey has already moved out. The last quartermaster truck left on Sunday evening, and the barracks that stand in uniform rank-and- file extending to the fence that borders the South China Sea are empty shells. On Saturday evening they held their stand-down party. The battalion furled its colors. The colors will be going back to America, but Palmer doesn't know if the men themselves will be going back home or if they will be dispersed to other units in Vietnam. He never asked any of the quartermaster men because the quartermaster men hated the MPs and never spoke to the clerks of the PMO. Palmer assumes they mostly hated MPs because the gate guards would never let them sneak off the compound to visit prostitutes. During the stand-down party Filipino strippers were brought in and, according to the story that Palmer got from the PMO clerks who attended the show, the Philippine women "took it all off" but Palmer didn't go to the party. What's the point of going to a party if you don't drink alcohol? On the Monday morning that the PMO Detachment begins its move to Camp Redstone, Palmer has twenty-two days left in Vietnam.

The detachment barracks is in the middle of a single long block that runs the length of the new compound. The barracks is rotting, as Palmer discovers the first time he enters the hollow shell of his new quarters which were abandoned by the engineers and is now his home. The Redstone buildings seem twice as old as Quincey's and might be. Even the concrete floor seems to be rotting, the smooth surface rubbed away here and there revealing the pebbled rocky interior of the poured cement. The floor is damp in spots. The entire compound reeks of oldness, yet is barely half as old as Palmer.

The compound road comes to a dead-end at a perimeter fence but it's obvious that the road had once extended out onto the civilian road that leads to the airfield. Fenced off. A fabricated dead-end probably created for security reasons, maybe during Tet of '68 when the Viet Cong were running all over the cities of Vietnam trying to drive the Americans out or whatever they thought they were going to accomplish. The library where Palmer has spent so many nights trying to get a fix on the Vietnam War has closed down for good. The last event he read about was the battle of Dien Bien Phu where the French made their last stand and lost. There was an accompanying photograph, the French army crossing a bridge near Haiphong, retreating forever, the Viet Minh troops standing around wearing their gray uniforms and those fakey-looking pith helmets, holding their rifles at port-arms and watching their former overlords straggle back to France. Palmer knows there won't be anything like that when the Americans leave forever. It's already started, and the abandonment of Camp Quincey is a part of it. The American presence will simply evaporate, as it already is doing, as Palmer is helping it do with his lifting of desks and placing them on the long flatbed of a five-ton truck that has been brought in for the job.

After all of the desks are loaded onto the flatbed, four detachment clerks climb into the maverick and follow the five-ton on its short trip to Camp Redstone, to the dirt parking lot of the new PMO. Palmer is among them, and when they arrive he shows his buddies around, points out the PM's new office, the First Sergeant's office, the traffic section.

One of the clerks has to go back to Camp Quincey to retrieve more clerks, since only four men can ride in a jeep at one time, a military regulation that will not be flaunted even during this mildly chaotic movement of men and equipment. Palmer volunteers for the job, the closest he will come to dodging shit details this week. He climbs into the jeep and heads back to Camp Quincey leaving the cherry boys to start unloading the desks and filing cabinets. It is his status and only his status that allows him to get away with this cheap trick. He is the oldest clerk in the PMO. It feels good to be this old.

After all of the detachment clerks have been chauffeured to the new PMO, Palmer goes inside to help move things around, and sees that the troops have made a lot of progress, having lifted half the desks off the five-ton and carried them inside. Desks aren't really that heavy when you remove the drawers cluttered with folders, pens, office supplies, and with all the clerks gathered around like tenderfeet eager to unload double-wide fuckers, Palmer gets away with helping carry only one desk into the building.

None of this takes very long, which bothers Palmer slightly because his distaste for shit details is always balanced by his distaste for going to back to his real job. He simply doesn't want to be doing anything at all, and he daydreams of home while he works, as he had daydreamed of home ever since he was sworn in. He looks forward to going back to the basement apartment in Denver where Mike still lives, of sleeping until noon, of drinking real beer and watching American TV and not the bizarre edited stilted censored shows of AFVN where they broadcast either good news or indifferent news but never bad news, never any body counts. Appearances mean everything.

After the desks and chairs are arranged in the new PMO, after the five-ton heads back to Camp Quincey, Palmer chauffeurs three of the men back to the old place, then returns for more, doing things the army way, slow and complicated. The biggest job left is the loading of filing cabinets, an entire wall of them, tall fuckers that are as heavy as hell. The procedure is obvious to Palmer: remove the drawers that contain the records of all the crimes and traffic accidents that have taken place in Military Region II during the past year, and load them separately onto the five-ton. Then load the empty shells of the cabinets themselves, made so light that a single man might be able to pick one up and slide it onto the waiting flatbed.

But one of the clerks disagrees with him, a newbie named Rudduck, a stocky dark-eyed kid from somewhere on the east coast of the United States and whom Palmer has never particularly liked. PFC Rudduck has been a clerk/typist for six weeks, is younger than Palmer, is noisy, and always looks you in the eye when he talks, as if the eye-contact alone will convince you of the rightness of his ideas.

"Let's just load the cabinets onto the truck now and forget about removing the drawers," Rudduck says. "That'll save us time."

The discussion takes place in the office where Sgt. Ebbets had his desk, where Sgt. Ancil used to sit, the room now empty of everything except filing cabinets. The clerks stand around waiting while Palmer and Rudduck hash this out, the newest man and the oldest man in the detachment.

Palmer makes his case based on acquired logic. He had delivered sofa beds when he was a civilian and knows from experience that you do not lift as much weight as humanly possible in order to do something as pointless as save time. Save your back, is Palmer's philosophy. But Rudduck disagrees, and insists that if six men take hold of a single filing cabinet together, they will be able to hoist it onto the flatbed of the five-ton. Palmer cannot believe what he is hearing, and finds himself doing something he hasn't done in so long he can't even remember, which is get mad at an enlisted man in his own unit.

"These things weigh a *ton* with the drawers in them," he says. "Let's take the drawers *out*. It'll be easier."

It makes him crazy to be having this conversation. Does Rudduck think the army will let him go home from Vietnam sooner if he works harder, if he busts his ass, if he saves time, if he gets a hernia?

Logic never has gotten Palmer anywhere in the army, so he is surprised when another clerk takes his side, a thin draftee named Tachwitz. He is from Chicago, has a college degree, and once told Palmer that he had taken a class in fencing using rubber-tipped rapiers.

"I think we should remove the drawers like Palmer says."

Having someone agree with him makes Palmer suspicious, even wary, he is so unused to it. But then the other clerks side with him, and they start removing the drawers from the filing cabinets and carrying them outside.

Rudduck is utterly disgusted by this vote against him, and demonstrates it by slamming drawers around on the flatbed. But Palmer understands. It's a terrible feeling to have people vote against your idea, to lose an argument, to have the mob turn on you, to be refused a promotion because you're a total fuckup, to have your arm broken because you finally went too far.

He goes about his work silently, camouflaging the heady feeling of victory with a bland expression and without once meeting Rudduck's eyes. He is glad that he will be going home in less than three weeks. Rudduck is the kind of person that he has spent the past two years trying to avoid, an energetic and ambitious GI who takes manual labor seriously.

Every piece of furnishing and equipment in the Camp Quincey PMO is transferred to the Camp Redstone PMO before five p.m. and quitting time on Monday. The army is a Spartan thing, there really hasn't been much to move. None of the Vietnamese secretaries came to work Monday morning, had been told to stay home because there would be no work for them to do and they would only get in the way. On Tuesday morning the detachment clerks begin transferring their bunks and lockers to their new barracks. The secretaries show up at Camp Quincey so they can be chauffeured to Camp Redstone and shown their new bailiwick and get back to pretending to work.

When Anh arrives, she climbs into the maverick shotgun and Palmer drives her out of Camp Quincey for the last time, forever, she will be working at Camp Redstone until the last MP leaves Qui Nhon, and after that Palmer doesn't know what she will do. She makes good money working for the Americans, as do Missy Cue and Missy Nu. Thousands of house girls will be out of work when America goes home, a depletion of the economy that is too complex for Palmer to grasp. Somebody used to be making money off this war. As they ride down the road, Anh looks over at him and says, "Palmah?" in that soft musical voice with a lilt on the end which warns him that a favor is about to be asked, like a sister, she rarely calls him by his name unless she wants something from him. Anh is a year older than he.

Palmer looks over at her seated primly in a burgundy ao dai, wearing a light blue sweater that she almost always wears to work, but not like the thick monster she wore during the monsoons. "What?"

"Maybe when you go home, you sell icebox to me?" A close-lipped smile, her eyebrows are raised, she watches his face for his reply.

"Sure," he says, but even as he says this he starts contemplating the logistics involved in the act of illegally selling his refrigerator to Anh. It is a violation of military regulations to sell anything to Vietnamese civilians, especially items purchased from the PX, the stereos, the fans, the electronic gadgets that all Vietnamese have in their homes because nobody except maybe a few lifer officers obeys this rule.

"My mother wants very much to have an icebox," Anh says, as though going ahead and springing the biggest argument in her favor which she might have rehearsed the night before, perhaps after a conversation with her mother. Anh lives with her parents and brothers and sisters in downtown Qui Nhon. Palmer has been there one time. He delivered soda pop and beer to her home last New Year's Eve. On the first day of work after the new year, after GIs in all the compounds had fired M-16s at the sky in celebration and in violation of weapon safety, Anh had told Palmer that she thought maybe the VC were attacking the city.

"I will sell you my icebox," Palmer says.

Anh continues to watch his face, her eyes searching his, which makes him uncomfortable until she says, "How much?"

Palmer grins. He had in fact purchased the icebox from Sp/4 Aldhoff before the man went home. Fifty bucks, a bargain, they cost twice as much at the PX.

"How much do you want to pay?" he says, only teasing her. He contemplates simply giving it to her, except that giving women expensive gifts can be misinterpreted in this Victorian society.

"How much do you want?" she says.

He doesn't want anything. He wants Anh to be happy all her life. He wants Ho Chi Minh to go fuck himself.

"I don't know," he says. "How much do you think it's worth?" Anh's face falls. She is exasperated, and it occurs to Palmer that he is not playing the game by the rules, the Vietnam game, the barter game. Vietnamese are used to haggling over prices at roadside stands, it's a part of their culture, it's not like America where a thirty-cent can of spaghetti costs a non-negotiable sixty cents at 7/11.

Anh purses her lips. She will have to teach this American how to haggle. "Forty dollah?" she says, and Palmer senses that she is lowballing it. Probably expects him to come back with an outrageously high counter-demand, like ninety bucks.

"Okay, forty dollars," he says.

Anh's jaw drops. She frowns at him, and says, "You will sell your icebox to me for forty?"

Palmer nods.

Anh's shoulders slump, and Palmer wonders if she's thinking she should have started out with a thirty-dollar lowball. "Choi oi," she says, which Palmer knows is a Vietnamese idiom that can be loosely translated as "Good grief" or "Holy shit" or "Are you kidding me?" This American doesn't know how to swindle anybody. He is obviously a rube.

The deal is sealed just before they arrive at the new PMO. Anh digs into her purse and pulls out forty dollars' worth of MPC and stuffs it into his extended hand before he can renege. "You can bring to my house?" she says.

"Maybe next weekend," Palmer says, uneasy about the prospect of transporting a refrigerator to downtown Qui

Nhon in violation of regulations, but knowing that he probably will be able to pull it off because MPs can travel anywhere in the city without being hassled by other MPs. His last shit detail. He wouldn't do it for anybody but his mentor.

CHAPTER 37

The PMO Detachment is the last unit to leave Camp Quincey. The clerks spend most of Tuesday loading bunks and wall lockers and footlockers onto the five-ton, and then unloading everything at Camp Redstone and setting it up in the new barracks. There are no cubicles in the Camp Redstone barracks and never will be. Sgt. Ebbets has already told the clerks that the barracks will remain an open bay.

After dropping off the last clerks at the new barracks, Palmer tells them that he is going back to Camp Quincey to check the old barracks and make sure they didn't leave anything behind. This is true, but is also a kind of lie, and has that feel to it as he says it, because he is not going back just to search for stray equipment, he is going back to look one last time at the place where he has spent most of his tour in Vietnam. The compound will be turned over to the ARVN tomorrow.

The main gate is still open. There are no MPs in the guard shack. There is nothing left to guard now. He guides the jeep down the dirt road, then turns left into the dead-end where his old barracks stands a hollow shell. He brakes and cuts the engine. Who would have thought that Vietnam could be such a silent country? The compound itself has never been so quiet. There had always been the sounds of MP jeeps going in and out the main gate, the sounds of Vietnamese workers mending the perimeter fence under the supervision of a quartermaster sergeant, the sounds of men in the showers at odd times of the day, occasional laughter from the latrines where men sat reading scattered copies of *Rolling Stone* or

Grunt. Always some ambient noise that he was never aware of until now, now that there are no sounds at all except the soft distant sifting of waves breaking on the beach beyond the abandoned enlisted men's club. It is late afternoon, but the sun is still high.

He gets out of the jeep and goes into the barracks where the cubicles stand empty like cow stalls. No plastic streamers hanging in the doorways, no lockers or bunks visible in the two foot space between the floor and the plywood sections nailed to the four-by-four uprights. Who constructed these cubicles, and how long ago? Which of the Provost Marshals had begrudged his troops this bit of privacy? What is the small history of this building that is less than a decade old? The clerks have left behind a lot of trash, newspapers, a few magazines, old uniforms scattered around the floor, the disarray unmilitary and nobody cares.

He walks to the end of the room which a former clerk/typist had once referred to as "the cave." He doesn't remember the name of the man who had called it that, and nobody had ever called it that after the man left. He had been a short-timer who was leaving a few days before Sp/4 Shappler, which was why he was off-duty that day. He was involved in out-processing. Two weeks from now, after Palmer has trained his replacement, he too will begin out-processing.

The bench press built by Sp/4 Gerlach still stands in the empty space at the end of the room, topped by a bar weighing one hundred and twenty-five pounds with its maroon-colored sand-filled plastic disks. After Gerlach had gone home nobody used the bench. It sat there gathering dust until Palmer quit drinking and decided to start lifting weights, since there was nothing much else to do on this compound at night except go to the library and try to locate himself in time. During the past four months he had progressed from hefting a fifty pound barbell ten times, to one hundred and twenty-five pounds, his personal best since last week, and will never get any better. This morning he had decided not to move the equipment to Camp Redstone, and nobody else was interested in it. With less than three weeks to go, it hadn't seemed worth the effort to move it. When he first began using the weights, he could not lift a seventy-five pound barbell ten times, the weight that he had tried to lift exactly once when Gerlach was here, the weight that had made him feel weaker than a girl with polio. He was forced to start at the bottom like a freshman in high school. After he stopped drinking, his appetite returned, was robust, he ate steak and chicken every day at the EM club and got stronger. Every afternoon he drank two milkshakes from the snack truck that had traveled from compound to compound like the snack truck that used to appear outside a warehouse where he had worked a shit job in Denver before he'd gotten drafted.

After the other American units began pulling out of the city, he used to take the maverick and explore the compounds, looking for barbell weights and anything else of interest that the departed GIs might have left behind. He found a dozen ten-pound weights here and there, some half buried in the sand outside empty barracks, or strangely lying in ditches. He took them back to his barracks feeling like a successful gold-miner. He had entered basic training weighing one hundred and sixty pounds, and now weighs one eighty-five. His father had gone to the South Pacific weighing two hundred pounds and returned weighing one thirty-five.

Walking back down the aisle, he steps into his old cubicle. Seems a lot bigger with no furniture. The one memory of this empty space that stands out most vividly is the sight of a vial of heroin resting open-lidded on his footlocker that terrible weekend five months ago. If a sergeant or an officer had seen it, Palmer would have been busted. But even at that, he probably still would be leaving Vietnam in less than three weeks. Doubtless not as a Specialist Fourth-Class, and possibly not as the traffic man. He might have ended up in the PBR unit.

He looks up at the stain on the ceiling, Detty's blood still visible though not as dark as it had been on the day it was made. There is nothing left of the stain that had formed on the floor by his bunk. He had scrubbed it all away the day after the soldier-of-the-month board. The screen splattered with Detty's brain-matter was eventually replaced by a detail of Vietnamese workers.

He leaves his cubicle, goes back down the aisle and steps outside the barracks, walks around to the side of the building where the piss tube stands drying in the sun. Somewhere down at the bottom of that steel tube, beneath a hideous murk, lies the vial full of heroin. Fingerprint evidence. Even a week after that terrible night he had still felt edgy knowing it was there.

He gets back into the jeep but instead of returning to Camp Redstone he drives slowly down the dirt road past the softball field where the indentations of the only mortars to hit the compound in the past year have disappeared entirely. Wind, rain, monsoons. He pulls up in front of the enlisted men's club, gets out and climbs the step and tries to open the door, but it is locked. He had thought perhaps he might find some interesting souvenir to loot in there. A bar spigot. A forgotten beer. When he gets back to America, the first thing he intends to do, after he receives his discharge and is turned loose from Fort Lewis, is get a room at a Holiday Inn in Seattle and buy a six-pack of Budweiser. He cannot remember what real beer tastes like, remembers only that it tastes good.

He turns and stands for a moment on the top step of the EM club and looks out at the landscape of this relatively small compound. To his far left, the barbecue patio like a grotto in the pines where the battalion had held a Christmas party last year, and where he was drinking ice-cold beer the night Detty was captured and jailed. The softball field lies in front of him where he had run at top speed one night, circling the perimeter with a belly full of scotch. On the far side of the softball field, the MP station, the volleyball court, the guard tower, the fence where he had purchased that vial of heroin from Motor Pool Mary. What will become of all the prostitutes when the communists arrive? To the right, across the main road, he can see the start of the dead-end road that leads to his old barracks and the movie theater, his only form of entertainment on the compound before he discovered the library because he never played softball or volleyball. The library building is hidden in the midst of the quartermaster barracks set up in their neat rows extending to the South China Sea. The entire compound is deserted but for himself, and after he drives out, he is the last MP to leave Camp Quincey forever.

When he gets back to the MP station he hears a bit of news from Tachwitz that would have annoyed the hell out of him if he was going to be here more than a month. Because the MP compound at Camp Redstone is so crowded, clerk-typists from battalion headquarters and from the 109th will be

bunking in the PMO Detachment barracks. Palmer shrugs off
the news that is bad only for the other PMO clerks. You don't
like to have strangers bunking in your quarters, there have
always been barracks thieves. It seems like half the reports
the MPs hand in involve barracks thieves, with GIs coming
back to their quarters and finding the padlocks jimmied from
their footlockers or wall lockers. Enlisted men rush into the
MP station in a panic proclaiming that they have been
robbed, and the desk sergeant has to calmly explain that the
MPs are only a reporting agency, they do not go out and track
down criminals like Sherlock Holmes. The victims are always
surprised when they hear this, surprised when they realize
the MPs are not going to help them recover their valuables,
and Palmer is certain that this serves only to make them hate
the MPs all the more. What good are MPs? They hand out
speeding tickets left and right, but when you come to them for
help they say you're on your own. And if the MPs do happen
to step into your barracks for a look-see at the crime scene and
discover that the stolen stereo had been sitting in plain view
beside your bunk, they will tell you that you ought to have kept
the stereo inside a locker when you weren't present, that you
can make no claim whatsoever against anybody because you
were responsible for seeing that your equipment was secured.
A terrible lesson, to be told that you are responsible for your
own life. Who wants that responsibility?

At quitting time the PMO clerks walk back to the battalion
compound which is a few hundred yards away from the
PMO, although their new barracks is no more than fifty yards
as the crow flies but there are two cyclone fences between
the PMO and the barracks. They have to walk up and

around a maze of empty buildings, then cross a road to the MP compound where a guard is seated in a new gate shack. The compound is a noisy, crowded place now. The 109th MPs live across the street though farther up toward the main gate. The battalion motor pool has been set up near the old MARS shack, and vehicles are coming and going. The enlisted men's club is directly across the street from the PMO barracks, and Palmer notes the irony of this, how paradisiacal it would have been to have a bar right outside his doorway back in the days when he drank, before the terrible weekend that had scared the shit out of him. Laughter comes from the EM club. Farther down the street, beyond the PMO barracks, stands the mess hall with men drifting toward it from all directions. This is where Palmer will be eating until his time comes to leave. No more steaks and chicken dinners, no more sitting on a redwood patio and staring across ripples of glistening green thinking that he could get into a boat and row right back to America. Time to start picking dead bugs out of his bread.

The PMO clerks have congregated at the far end of the new barracks, and strangers already have set up bunks near the front door, though the place is still only half filled. There is a faint swampy odor to the air in this place where the floor is damp in spots. It has the feel of a transient barracks, like the ones in Long Binh, a feel of impermanence, but maybe only because Palmer will not be here very long. He goes to the far end of the barracks and steps out the back door. This place has two exits, and he realizes now that he doesn't like having a building with so many exits. Easy for barracks thieves to slip in and out. The cave had a feel of security to it, like a real cave that might be defended by a man with plenty of food and ammunition, like an ocean at your back. The perimeter fence is barely five feet away from the back door. Beyond the fence is the main road that extends all the way to the PX compound across a landscape of abandoned buildings as well as an area where Hueys are lined up in rows. He can hear the soft putter of slapped wind coming from that direction, choppers lifting off or landing. He once had a conversation with a helicopter mechanic who told him that the theory behind a vertical landing is that you want your velocity and your altitude to equal zero at the same time. If one or the other is off, you might be in trouble. This made Palmer laugh, the concept reduced to such a simple formula: when everything equals zero, you are safe.

The MPs once utilized choppers to catch speeders out on QL-1, a program that was so chickenshit that Palmer hated to be a part of it. Four months ago he was ordered to drive out to QL-1 and paint big white stripes across the road so the MPs riding in the chopper could use them as reference points to calculate the speed of American vehicles breaking the law. It didn't matter how fast the Vietnamese were driving, or the Koreans, or the Australians, but if an American went faster than twenty-five miles an hour on the road that stretches all the way to Hanoi, he would get a speeding ticket. Didn't they need choppers out in the boonies to rescue wounded Infantrymen? The program came to an end after two months. Who knows why? Who understands anything about the army?

He looks around at the muddy weeded ground outside the back door and suddenly sees something that stuns him.

It is a marijuana plant, at least three feet in length but lying on its side as if trampled by the men who had formerly lived here. He looks around feeling a bit guilty, then steps over to it and squats down, careful not to rip out the knees of his fatigues, and picks up the plant to examine the familiar long thin leaves spread like flat fingers waving at passersby to step over and have a toke. It isn't rooted to the muddy ground, so he can't tell if it was grown right outside the door or was just tossed here during the mildly chaotic movement of men and equipment, some engineering head forced to leave his stash behind, throwing it out the back door where it can't be pinned on anybody because it is unsecured. Or it might have been tossed over the fence from the road. Who knows where all the weird things of Vietnam come from?

He drops the plant and stands upright and brushes off his hands wondering how long it will take a sergeant to find it and start a bullshit investigation that will lead to nothing. Maybe the CID will get involved. The CID are the only American soldiers who wear civilian clothing, which is supposed to fool everybody, but it's nonsensical. Whenever Palmer sees a middle-aged white man or a slick young dude in shades walking around downtown Qui Nhon wearing an aloha shirt and khaki chinos, he knows it's a CID man trying to crack a case.

CHAPTER 38

The PMO clerks fall into the old routine quickly because it is a small and effortless routine. On Wednesday, the first full day of work, there is a shuffling of desks, with Sgt. Ebbets moving things around to suit his own vision of a PMO, possibly based on the decor of some former duty station. Seven months ago a sergeant E5 who had served in Germany had worked briefly at the PMO before moving on in the way that so many Provost Marshals have come and gone without having served a full tour of duty. Palmer doesn't know what's going on there, what scams or secret deals or asses kissed or noses browned that allows so many men to serve only a few months before disappearing. The sergeant had been stationed in an MP unit in Germany, and talked endlessly about how they did everything back at his old unit, the procedures, the methods, the techniques of traffic investigation, as though hinting around that the PMO ought to change its policies to match his, which Palmer had interpreted as "the right way" of doing things, like someone correcting your grammar.

Anh comes in to work, but Palmer waits until all the clerks are typing away on their reports and Sgt. Ebbets is seated at his desk up front before he rolls his chair over to Anh and quietly tells her that he will try to bring the icebox this Sunday. Her eyes light up with eagerness when he says this, she smiles and says, "I told my mother you are going to sell it to me. She said to tell you thank you."

Palmer smiles, nods, and rolls back to his desk, but that small statement of gratitude depresses him a bit. What a terrible country this is, the people sneaking around and pulling cheap scams just to get refrigerators. Why can't they buy things from the PX? Westinghouse would make a fortune.

Around ten o'clock Sgt. Turner, the battalion motor-pool sergeant, strolls into the traffic office and grins at Palmer and drawls, "Hey buddy, how ya doing?" He has a Texas accent reminiscent of Beaudry's. Turner is a lean lifer who keeps himself in good physical condition, unlike so many of the lifers that Palmer has ever known. But maybe it just comes from working all day at the motor-pool. Palmer has seen him perched on the front bumpers of deuce-and-a-halfs, leaning under the hoods and wrestling with engines. How do all the overweight lifers manage to pass the annual PT test back in the states? Palmer has never been involved in a PT test in Vietnam — maybe the Pentagon figures the war is enough PT. He has never run anywhere since he arrived here, barring the night he ran around the softball field.

"What can I do for you, Sergeant?"

Turner glances, around at the new office, then looks at Palmer. "I need some information, Specialist, and I guess you're the man I have to talk to."

Red flags sprout in Palmer's mind.

"Battalion wants me to tape a half-hour TV show up at AFVN about vehicle maintenance as it pertains to traffic safety," Turner says. "So I need some statistics about traffic accidents and speeding tickets, especially anything involving improper maintenance of vehicles."

"I've got all the records in my books," Palmer says. "How many statistics do you need?"

"I was thinking of a monthly average."

Palmer nods. "I could get the stats for last month pretty quick. But we don't get many violations having to do with improper maintenance." Then adds, "Your people do a pretty good job of taking care of the vehicles." Is this ass kissing? But it's true.

Turner grins. "Whatever you got, buddy. I also gotta give a little talk about maintaining control of vehicles in all types of weather and road conditions."

"We get a lot of TAs involving driving too fast for road conditions," Palmer says. "Back in the rainy season GIs were always sliding off the roads."

"That's what I'm talking about. Can you give me stats on that?"

"How soon do you need them?"

"As soon as you can put 'em together. We tape the show next Friday afternoon."

"When's it going to be broadcast?"

"Who knows? They'll probably use it as filler for the next ten years."

Like all the dull filler that AFVN presents in between *Hee-Haw* and taped football games from the States or Ralph Story episodes or programs about getting your GED or going to college on the GI Bill or buying a house with VA benefits. "I can have it by this afternoon, sergeant."

Turner taps his knuckles on the rubbery material on the top of Palmer's desk and says, "Good enough, bud. Battalion's gonna have charts made up for the show based on your stats."

After he leaves, Palmer wonders who is going to be drawing those charts. Sgt. Ancil once ordered Palmer to create a chart covered with acetate to be hung on the wall showing the number of weekly traffic accidents scribbled in red grease-pencil, but Palmer had seen to it that the chart hadn't survived the big move. So far Sgt. Ebbets hasn't seemed to notice. Palmer is pleased with this small detail. It will give him something meaningless to do for the rest of the morning, digging through his records and writing down stats.

Just before noon, two black GIs walk into the PMO and ask where the traffic office is. Tachwitz directs them to Palmer's office where he's sitting at his desk not even pretending to type, having already finished collecting the information for Sgt. Turner. He's clutching a cold can of Coke and wondering how soon his replacement will be sent over from the 109th. Anh is out goldbricking at the latrine. The two men fill the doorway, one walking ahead of the other, two infantrymen, judging by the reddish color of their boots rising to dusty fatigues tucked into the tops of the tinted boots. Their fatigues are faded though not as faded as Palmer's, and as he looks up at the bulk of these two big men he is reminded of the two black Infantrymen whom he had met on his first day in Qui Nhon, the GIs who had broken out laughing when they found out he was going to have it dicked.

"You the man in charge of traffic tickets?" the lead GI says. He's carrying an M-16 but Palmer notes that it has been cleared, does not have a magazine poking from the underside. Could be a bullet in the chamber though. Palmer nods, says yes, then says, "What can I do for you?"

The man glances back at his buddy crowding into the small office behind him. A look passes between them, and the second man smiles briefly. He's a bit taller than the other, whose name tag says "Rusher." Rusher looks at Palmer and says, "The thing of it is, man, we were given a traffic ticket that we don't feel we deserve." They are Infantrymen, Christ knows what their lives have been like since they arrived in country, but there is a shyness, a hesitance in Rusher's voice as he explains the reason for his visit. Palmer sets his Coke on the desk and intertwines his fingers. He knows what's coming.

"When did you get the ticket?" he says.

"About an hour ago," Rusher says, and his buddy says, "Yeh," nodding, a witness offering his support, his version, his evidence.

Boonie hats hang down their backs from straps around their necks. Boonie hats are coming under attack from the brass in Saigon, and it looks like MPs will have to start handing out citations to anyone caught wearing the floppy ring-shaped headgear within the city limits of Qui Nhon. That's the latest rumor. Like slot machines, it's something that somebody with power doesn't like. But it's the MPs who will have to go around telling the grunts they are out of uniform. Palmer is glad he's not a road MP anymore.

"Why don't you feel you deserve the ticket?" Palmer says. "Were you speeding?"

Rusher glances quickly at his buddy, and they both grin, each giving out a single breath of a laugh before Rusher looks back at Palmer and says, "Naw, man, we wasn't speeding. They said they *clocked* us. But we wasn't speeding."

The other man edges farther into the room, now that the story is being laid out before this Spec Four of a judge. Palmer sees that his name is Washington. The man continues to nod as Rusher describes the events that had unfolded out on the road.

"This MP that wrote us up, he had a radio, and we heard him clocking other GIs."

A speed trap. Every time some member of the top brass gets a wild hair up his ass about moving violations out on QL-1, Palmer has to go out with an MP unit and set up a trap involving mirror-boxes, a cheesy form of radar that surprisingly gives an accurate mile-per-hour calculation of the velocity of a moving vehicle. It involves a chart, a stopwatch, and numbers — Palmer's worst subject in school. He always lets the other MPs do the calculations while he stands by the side of the road with a stopwatch clocking vehicles as they pass the mirror-boxes, and calling in the seconds over a walkie-talkie.

"But this other MP didn't know what he was doing, man. You could hear him talking, and he was getting it all wrong. He'd be saying wait a minute, um, wait a minute, um, just a minute. He kept giving wrong speeds, ya know? We could hear him."

"Yeh," Washington says.

The men look completely out of place in the PMO. The bandoleers crisscrossing their bodies are filled with magazines of bullets. Their uniforms are slovenly, dirty. Their heavy bodies crowd the room, fill it with their shyness and umbrage. Palmer figures they had talked each other into coming here to complain. He imagines them privately cursing the MP who had written them up, building it into a major outrage — then they arrive at the PMO and their anger recedes into a kind of giddiness that now makes both of them give up soft laughs in between sentences, unsure of themselves and what they are doing. It is their word against the MPs, a hopeless cause under any circumstance.

"So you don't think you were speeding?" Palmer says, his voice a little bit quieter than before.

Rusher frowns, sure of himself now. "Naw man, we was doing the posted speed limit, twenty-five. That MP didn't know what he was talking about."

The men seem to believe what they are saying, and Palmer has no idea whether the MPs might have made a mistake out on the road—those mirror-boxes are amazingly accurate—but it doesn't matter. "Do you have your ticket with you?"

"Yeh," Washington says, reaching into a fatigue pocket and pulling out the copy of his citation. He hands over the white slip of paper which is as thin as onionskin. Palmer looks it over, 29 in a 25 MPH zone. All the zones outside the city limits are 25. Americans have to drive 15 inside the city. Strange laws, Palmer has always felt. Army laws.

He nods, then looks up at them and speaks quietly. "All right. I'll tell you what I'll do. When the MP who wrote this hands in the copies of his tickets for the day, I'll pull yours." He has done this before. Any time anybody comes in with a complaint, he pulls the ticket, just like his own first ticket written at Ft. Chronkhite was pulled more than a year ago. He doesn't care whether a ticket is justified or not. He has his own personal policy here in the traffic section. He will pull the ticket of any enlisted man who has the nerve to come into the MP station and complain. A very small kind of courage is the only qualification for redemption.

"You keep this copy, but don't tell your First Sergeant you got written up," Palmer says, handing the white copy back to

Washington. "When the pink copy comes in, I'll trash it. That way your CO will never get his copy in the mail. I'll have to keep the yellow copy in my files in case anybody comes around asking about it. That's to cover my ass. But it won't happen if your CO doesn't know about it."

The two GIs have been watching Palmer silently, listening closely to his explanation, simple and to the point, like the landing of a helicopter. Palmer sees on their faces the realization of what he is doing for them. The shy smiles and quick frowns have evaporated, have been replaced by sober expressions. In fact, their faces are expressionless. Who in this world ever expects a complaint to be listened to?

Rusher starts nodding, a grin starts forming, showing a single gold-capped tooth with a hollow half-moon exposing white enamel. "Thanks, man," he says, and he reaches out to shake hands. Palmer stands up and sees that he is taller than either of these men. "You a good dude, man," Rusher says, a subtle chortle entering his voice. His hand is gray with dirt, seems twice as large as Palmer's clean and nail-clipped grasping fist. Rusher takes hold of the fist with his other hand, shakes with both arms and says, "You all right," his smile stretching his cheeks, his head lolling to one side as he speaks.

"Yeh, thanks man," Washington says, reaching out and giving Palmer's hand a quick shake.

Palmer smiles and nods. He stands because he wants to ease both of these Infantrymen out of the PMO before Sgt. Ebbets comes around and starts asking questions. This is the first ticket he has pulled under Sgt. Ebbets' command, and these guys are getting a bit too effusive in their thanks.

He leads them outside to their jeep which is parked next to the maverick. He stands with his back to the door feeling like a barricade between the GIs and Sgt. Ebbets somewhere back there in the PMO. He watches as they climb into their jeep, their grins clenched tightly. Victory is a heady thing. After the jeep rolls safely out of sight, after all evidence of his latest crime has evaporated, Palmer goes back inside and sits down at his desk thinking that, right at this moment, those two men might be the only GIs in the army who don't hate MPs.

When Anh comes into the office she looks at him with wide questioning eyes. "Missy Tuong say you talk to two black men."

The secretaries know everything. Palmer nods.

"What they want?" Anh says.

"Nothing," Palmer says with a light lilt in his voice.

He waits for her to say, "You pull ticket huh?" She has seen him do this before. But she doesn't say anything, just gives him a knowing look and goes to her desk. She sits down primly and types a few lines on an accident report that she has been pretending to work on since eight o'clock this morning.

CHAPTER 39

At noon there is nowhere to go except the mess hall for lunch. The 109th MPs as well as the battalion clerks eat there, so the place is packed from the moment the door opens until the last GI hands his tray to one of the Vietnamese KPs and walks out the door. There is a kind of basic training feel to the place, but Palmer doesn't know if this is because there are so many noisy strangers eating here, or if it is the newness of this old one-story building. A move to a new compound has a new-beginning feel to it, as did his move to Camp Quincey last year, as did every year of grade school and high school which settled into the dull routine of incomprehensible arithmetic and angry nuns. This feeling of newness, of a new beginning, is undeniable and makes Palmer feel foolish, a slave to sentiment. But it doesn't matter. Things are beginning to matter less and less as he feels himself withdrawing from the army in a way that is different from that which he has always felt. He had never felt a part of the army after he had gotten over his small disappointment that the army wasn't like it is in the movies. He had thought it would be different, more real than it is, something that he could take seriously, but the sergeants had turned out to be like the foremen of the all shit jobs he had held before getting drafted, and the officers were like rich kids or throwbacks to feudal lords, like how you never saw them wearing wrinkled fatigues.

Because there is no library on this compound, and no theater set up yet, and because Palmer doesn't drink anymore, there is little to do between the end of the work day and lights out in the barracks, though there is no official lights out, just bored men turning off the overhead fluorescents around ten P.M. leaving the less bored to stare at *Hee-Haw* or *Laugh-In*.

Just before lights out that night Palmer is seated on his bunk thinking about the logistics of transporting his icebox to Missy Anh's house, an onerous burden, in that anything anybody asks of him seems onerous, but at the same time has a feel to it of a puzzle, a brain-teaser that he does not dislike. In size alone it is different from most of the surreptitious shit he has pulled off during his time in service, like slipping out for a swallow of scotch. The only way to do it right is with the Black Maria, the paddy wagon that the PMO uses to transport prisoners, a three-quarter ton truck with a big box on the rear and a metal door that can be padlocked. The truck is painted black all over, the only black vehicle he has ever seen in the army. It would be too risky to be seen driving out of Camp Redstone with a refrigerator in the rear of the maverick. Prima facie business there. One of the newbie MPs theoretically could stop him out on the road. He barely knows any of the 109th men. The newbies come to his office for ticket books or blank accident forms, but he hasn't made friends with any of them, and knows only a few of the older men, like Sp/4 Siever, his best traffic accident investigator. Siever is from Tennessee, a tall lean GI whose reports are always legible. Palmer hates having to decipher the scribbles handed in by MPs who write like little kids. Sp/4 Shappler had been right. Some of these men are illiterate.

The thing to do is find out if Siever is working on Sunday, and ask for an escort. He can tell Siever he's selling his icebox to Missy Anh, the man won't care. Palmer gets along well with Siever, whose overt friendliness had put him off when he first met him, the man coming into his office to talk about MP business but then turning the conversation toward talk about his hometown football team or his plans to earn a degree in police science after he gets out of the service. He has a heavy southern accent, is always smiling, seems happy in his work, and whenever he describes some horseshit situation that he had gotten involved in out on the road, it never comes off as a GI complaint but more of a tall tale that Palmer is expected to laugh at and always does. He had been put off by Siever's friendliness in the beginning, didn't understand it but then decided that Siever would have gone out of his way to make friends with whoever was in charge of the traffic section. A political thing, like befriending cooks or supply clerks. Position yourself, carve out a niche, find the angle. Palmer can appreciate that.

The thing to do is get up early Sunday morning, say around seven, when the rest of the compound is sleeping it off, and simply go get the keys to the Black Maria and drive the thing over here without authorization and load up the refrigerator, then meet up with Siever and drive downtown with an escort. That'll keep the newbie MPs off his back. And hope that Sgt. Ebbets or some other sergeant or even an officer doesn't question why he is using the vehicle. But he has used it before. Whenever the maverick is off line for repairs, the PMO clerks pile into the paddy wagon for a trip to the PX.

He ponders these tactics as he sits staring vaguely at the front door of the barracks and listening to the rowdy sounds of the MPs in the enlisted men's club across the street. He can see the lights of the bar through the screened door. He misses it.

He unbuttons his fatigue jacket, and as he reaches up to yank it from his shoulders, the color of the night sky draws his eyes to the screened window above his bunk. The sky is as red as the ambient glow of a forest fire. The angled roof of the barracks next door stands out in distinct silhouette like a paper cutout pasted against that odd crimson glow. His fingers slide slowly down the fabric of his jacket until one thumb touches a button and the other rests against the stitched hole opposite. His lips move, seemingly involuntarily, forming a querulous O.

"What...?" he says softly but the impact of the explosion generating the red light answers his unfinished question. He sees a curtain of dust jarred from the front wall of the barracks and hauled like vertical flotsam, a pale curtain carried on a wave of sound that touches his face and passes by, feels it in the floor, the mattress, it tips wall lockers that begin falling, unhooks hanging mirrors one by one making glassy explosions in the wake of the wave which rolls out the back door. Palmer is under his bunk only a moment before his wall locker falls, his helmet and flak jacket sliding off the top, the tin box bouncing against the bed frame and rolling against the mattress and lying still. His flak jacket slaps the floor in front of his eyes where he lies curled in a ball peering toward the front door, his helmet landing beside the jacket then grabbed and tugged onto his head, all this dive and desperate reaching completed before the rumble of the explosion has faded beyond the fence where the pot plant lies rotting in the mud.

Every two months since he has been in Qui Nhon the Viet Cong have hit the ammo dump beyond the mountain to the west of the city, and as he lies curled and motionless waiting for another explosion he realizes this must have been an ammo dump strike, the red light lingering in the sky as if waiting for the sound and impact to catch up. But never an explosion so large. And never had there been any damage to American barracks like the ARVN barracks that always fall down. Things continue to collapse, pictures slipping off nails, coffee cups, beer cans. Cokes plunging from sills and rolling on the concrete floor. Palmer crawls from beneath his bunk, grabs his flak jacket and puts it on as he stands up wishing he had his M-16, but during the move to Camp Redstone all of the weapons were accounted for by the arms clerk. Palmer had to turn his rifle in, reluctantly, because he always kept it without authorization in his wall locker for nights such as this.

The lights outside flicker. The compound goes black. He stands still wondering if he ought to get back under his bunk. Maybe a mortar hit a power line. But no, it's just the cheesy security system going into effect — turn off all the lights and nobody can see you. His eyes adjust to the darkness quickly, his senses seeming to speed up as they did every time the VC hit the dump and Camp Quincey went on red alert and his entire world dwindled to only himself and his rifle, his fears vanishing, the waiting was over, the other shoe had dropped, something was happening at last and he could do something about it, even if it meant only crouching in a bunker and listening to the slow stroll of mortars approaching one by one, or finally having to lock and load and take part in a firefight which has never happened, but something, anything other than the waiting that ate at him day and night, like a man in a prison cell being threatened constantly by faceless voices down the hall.

He begins making his way toward the door, stepping over fallen lockers, his fears not only vanished but replaced by a familiar sense of exhilaration. The loudness of the bomb, he'd never heard anything so loud in his life, and the carnage, Jesus, the barracks is a mess. It makes him smile as he picks his way across the rubble, it fills him with a heady and irrational sensation of glee that he lets wash over him because this is the most exciting thing he's ever experienced in his life.

He steps out of the barracks into the strange silence that always follows a hit. Stillness. Preamble. Then the night air is filled with tiny and distant shouts as the interrupted nighttime activities of all the troops begin turning toward this one thing, coming together to get their weapons from the arms room and go to their assigned positions. At first there is no one on the street, but as Palmer stands looking off toward the lone mountain where a pale light in the clouds separates the peak from the glow of smaller bombs popping, men begin coming out of barracks, out of the EM club, black shapes, all the same, indistinguishable, emerging from doorways and hurrying out to the street, some stopping and looking toward the mountains to the south where the VC who have tossed the mortar might already have disassembled their armory and are scrambling to safety before the AFVN compound can open up on them.

The shouts grow louder, come closer, sergeants now beginning to bark orders. Clerks are coming from the doorway behind Palmer, those who had gone to bed before the explosion, or men who had dived under the TV table. One moment Palmer is alone and the next moment the dark street is almost as crowded as the day Detty ran over that child.

"Get your weapons and go to your positions," sergeants are saying, Palmer hears it coming from both ends of the street. He joins the crowd moving toward the arms room, watching the mountain and wondering if the VC will toss a rocket this way. A single click on the tube. One minute from now I could be a mangled mess, my ghost floating away. He slows as he approaches the arms room. Until he gets his hands on his rifle he will feel naked though not afraid. It's always like this. Whenever a bomb goes off his fears disappear and he feels exhilaration filling him like inhaled air filling his chest cavity. Will the VC try to overrun the compound? But they never do, they just hide in the hills and harass the Americans. They never blow up the PX, but maybe because that's where the VC get their contraband Coke and beer and fans and TVs and cameras and stereos. If a rocket lands where I am standing I will find out what death is like.

He shuffles into the arms room behind other men and feels uneasy trapped inside this small place, he wants sky over his head, wants to be able to see everything around him. He takes his rifle and a bandoleer of ammunition from the clerk and hurries back outside where his uneasiness disappears because he can see the mountains and the sky and the stars and the street where some men are gathered in groups and others are going to their positions along the bunkerwalls that encircle the barracks. The VC couldn't have waited another month. When was the last time they hit the ammo dump? He can't remember and doesn't try, he is concerned only with everything around him now in time because now is the only place you can get hurt. You're safe yesterday and tomorrow but now you're vulnerable, the now of each tick of the clock, the next now, and the next. He watches the sky for the spark trail of tossed rockets but doesn't see any. Now. He positions himself behind the bunkerwall that encircles his barracks and looks up at the mountains to the south as if his watching is the only thing that anchors his life to the earth. Now. I will know what Thorpe already knows, and Detty. Now.

The muted mutter of engines turning over, the slap of paddled air, Hueys begin rising from the airfield. From the top of the mountain to the west the single beam of light shoots across the sky and slaps the mountainside. He hears the sounds of the choppers behind him, beyond his barracks, following the road that passes Camp Quincey where the ARVN already have begun to move in. He stays behind the protective bunkerwall with its fifty-five gallon oil drums filled with sand and listens for the thin whistle of mortar rounds overhead, but the thudding of the distant Hueys drowns out that possibility.

"Jeez, what was that?" a voice near him says.

Palmer looks over and sees PFC Rudduck standing beside him pipping an M-16 and looking him right in the eye.

"What was what?" Palmer says.

"What kind of *bomb* went off?"

Palmer is wondering the same thing. He has no idea except that the VC must have lucked out and hit something really big. He's heard of five-hundred pound bombs but doesn't know much about them. Isn't that what they drop on the jungle to create an instant LZ? Flatten trees and anything else for hundreds of yards. Then it occurs to him that Rudduck is asking him because he is the oldest man in the PMO, has been here the longest and is expected to know things that a newbie who has been here barely seven weeks doesn't know. Rudduck who had hassled him about file drawers is now looking him right in the eye expecting him to have answers. "I don't know, some kind of big bomb," is all Palmer has to offer.

"Does this happen very often?" Rudduck says.

Palmer remembers himself wanting to ask questions of men who had been here a long time when he himself was a newbie. You want answers that have no meaning. You want reassurance that has no meaning. "Ever since I've been here the VC have hit the ammo dump every two months," Palmer replies, "but I've never heard a bomb that big go off." A meaningless answer that contains no reassurance, and is possibly ominous. Now that the Americans are pulling out, the explosions are getting bigger. There's nothing you can do about anything, he wants to tell Rudduck who will be here for ten more months. Christ only knows what this city will be like by then. All you can do is keep your head down and keep a tight grip on your weapon. It's too late for answers, he wants to tell Rudduck.

The Hueys begin blasting the mountainside, and this brings the conversation to an end. Men are beginning to emerge from bunkerwalls and drifting out into the street to watch the light show. Palmer remains behind the wall. In two weeks he ought to be on a 707 headed home.

Officers begin appearing on the street with the camouflage covers of their helmets marked with their rank in felt-tip on the front, one stripe for lieutenants, two stripes for captains. The supply officer is a captain, he starts yelling at the men to get back to their positions. Half the men here have seen hits before, and know from experience that once the Hueys start raking the hillsides with rockets and bullets the VC stop lobbing mortar rounds. The men reluctantly return to their positions along the bunkerwalls. Officers have to be obeyed. The brass showing up after the enlisted men have already gotten their shit together, lieutenants and captains and majors barking commands as if they're restoring order to chaos: things are going to be okay now that we have arrived. Palmer taps his breast pocket to find a cigarette, but his Camels are back in the barracks. Then he realizes that his fatigue jacket is unbuttoned. He thinks about buttoning it but no. He'll wait to see if some major walks by and chews him out. He's never been chewed out by a major.

The explosions on the mountain have ceased. He can hear the Hueys roving back and forth, some of them following the disk of light that he can now see clearly on a hillside looming above the MARS shack at the far end of the street. Already this hit has the feel of winding down. It's always like this. It's harassment by the VC, maybe a team of two on the mountain with a mortar tube, lob a few rounds, put the Americans on alert, then slip away, probably back down into the city. They could be any of the slicky-boys or pimps riding Hondas up and down the streets with hookers seated behind them. They want us out of here.

Palmer stands watching everything as the alert winds down, waiting for a sergeant to come along and tell them the red alert has been reduced to yellow or gray, and that the troops can go back to bed. He wonders who makes that decision. Someone has to say I guess everybody can put their guns away and turn in. Palmer wouldn't want to have to make that decision, but hopes someone else makes it as soon as possible. And when it's over, he knows his uneasiness will begin creeping back as it always does. He once had a conversation with a liaison from the 101st Airborne who was stationed at Camp Quincey, a sergeant E5 who said he hated living in the city. "I don't feel safe here." He told Palmer he felt safest out in the boonies, which Palmer found hard to believe, but had to anyway. A grunt's point of view.

Half an hour later, after the lights flash on inside buildings across the street and high on telephone poles, Palmer knows that the all clear is coming soon, and carries his rifle back into his barracks. His wall locker is lying at an angle on his bed. He lifts it upright, unlocks and opens it. Fatigues and khakis fallen from hangers, he drags the mess out and stows his rifle inside, then quickly hangs up the uniforms and closes the door. What with the chaos of the move to Camp Redstone, plus the hit on the ammo dump tonight, he calculates that his rifle just might be the last piece of equipment he will turn in before he leaves Qui Nhon.

CHAPTER 40

Detritus. Gnarled, twisted like taffy, no larger than a Lionel train engine clutched on Christmas morning, Siever holds it out grinning, his eyebrows raised, his tongue poking a cheek as Palmer reaches for it, takes it, hefts its weight in his right hand. Not quite an inch thick, a plate of metal folded in upon itself. Maybe part of the shell of a bomb.

"It was sitting in the middle of the road out near the T-intersection. There's shrapnel a mile away from the ammo dump."

Palmer reads the story of the violence that had warped this fragment, written like a map in its impossible fold and shredded taffy edges. Something brought back from a place that no one has ever come back from: epicenter.

"I'm gonna take this home as a souvenir," Siever says as Palmer places it back into his hand. Heavy, it feels like it ought to be hot, ought to still be smoking.

"I want to ask a favor," Palmer says.

Siever listens silently as Palmer explains about the icebox. Anh is out of the office right now, had left a few minutes ago with the other secretaries. Siever says he is working on Sunday. Palmer remembers, when he was a road MP there was no such thing as a Sunday or a Saturday, the concept of a week itself was obliterated by rotating schedules, day shift, night shifts—swing shifts back at the Presidio. Road MPs pull twelve hour shifts here. Calendars meant nothing, and when each shift ended Palmer couldn't wait for the next shift to begin, was bored when he wasn't out on the road listening to the radio dispatcher or eyeballing jeeps going down the road not quite fast enough to ticket. He gave only warnings to violators E4 and below. He always ticketed sergeants and officers. Time flew by on road duty. Maybe it had been a mistake to accept the job as traffic man, where time has always been tar.

"When you're ready to go, just ask the desk sergeant to call my unit in to the station," Siever says.

"It'll probably be around nine o'clock in the morning."

"Oh nine-hundred," Siever says softly, like scribbling a note on the pad that all MPs carry in their breast pockets.

Palmer nods. The instructor at Ft. Gordon told them to take clear and concise notes, and don't jot anything down that doesn't have anything to do with police investigations. "I once wrote a hooker's name and address in my MP notebook and they threw my notes out of a court martial because of it," he said, which made the MP trainees laugh but was probably bullshit, like the last-man-to-do-that stories that Palmer heard throughout basic training. A good method of teaching though, he supposes. You learn best by fucking up, so maybe it'll stick if you learn the details of someone else's fuckup.

After Siever leaves the office lugging the steel garbage he had scooped off the road out near the T-intersection that links Qui Nhon to QL-1, Palmer sits silently on his chair feeling the delicate sensation that always comes over him whenever he has started engineering some surreptitious scam. He felt it a lot back in the days when he would slip out of the office about this time of the morning to swallow a Bud. Like a balancing act. Make sure Sgt. Ancil is distracted at his desk, tell Mueller you're going to the latrine, hurry past the house girls, grab a beer, and if there's time, gargle fast with Listerine, then go to the latrine or at least the piss tube. Then hurry back to the office while pretending you're not hurrying at all. A delicate moment, entering the PMO, like landing a helicopter. Jesus what a lot of effort that took. This icebox scam has the same feel to it, except he will be sober which will make it that much less pleasant. That's one thing about being drunk all the time, you get pretty fucking fearless. Then you get careless and leave a bucket of heroin on your footlocker for all the world to see.

"You talk to Sievah?" Anh whispers, walking into the office big-eyed and flush with impending lowdown.

Palmer nods. "Can do."

She grins, raises her eyebrows that are plucked narrow, tinted black, and says, "Sunday?"

Palmer nods. "In the morning," he says, lowering his voice.

Anh goes to her desk, sits down and begins typing, and Palmer wonders if Sp/4 Shappler had bought her anything before he went home last year. Maybe this is how the Vietnamese always do it, Anh waiting a year for each traffic man to go home before hitting him up for a stove or a stereo or a TV. Acquiring things slowly, like Mexico, mañana, no reason to hurry. But the communists will eventually take it all away, split it up among the poor, jail the rich, square the deck, turn this whole smelly country into a workers' paradise.

Sgt. Ebbets enters the office and Palmer feels caught, sitting and staring at nothing. Starting to lose his edge with his DEROS so close at hand. Give a fuck. It's too late to send him to the PBRs.

"Specialist Palmer, there's something I want to talk to you about," Ebbets says, putting his palms on his hips and peeling his lips back from his teeth.

"Yes Sergeant?" Palmer says. He feels he ought to stand up, as if Ebbets were an officer. Ebbets has that air about him, authority, not like most of the lifer sergeants Palmer has ever encountered. But he remains seated, looking up at his operations sergeant and trying to quell the sense of guilt and foolishness growing inside him at having been caught fucking off.

"A couple things," Sgt. Ebbets says, reaching up and stroking his chin with a single finger. "I spoke with the operations sergeant at the 109th earlier today, and he told me that your replacement will be coming in next Monday, a PFC named Dugan."

It's like a small tick of something, of the clock, of the knob on a mortar tube, hearing Sgt. Ebbets say this. The machinery is being set in motion, the green machinery, time has been given momentum. It is becoming official. Palmer's ETS. He is no longer moving toward it, it is pulling him toward itself.

"You are scheduled to leave next week," Sgt. Ebbets continues, maybe unaware of the effect that these words are starting to have on Palmer. Ebbets has been in the army since the Fifties, has himself departed dozens of duty stations, has sent so many young men home that the romance of this procedure might have been dulled by repetition. "The Provost Marshal wants to hold a going-away ceremony for you at Port Beach this coming Saturday night, but unfortunately your name was not put in for an Army Commendation Medal in time to have your orders cut for the party. I know that this might be somewhat of a disappointment to you, Specialist Palmer. The Provost Marshal will be awarding you only a plaque this coming Saturday night."

This is one of the longest conversations that Sgt. Ebbets has ever held with Palmer, who listens politely, nods at key statements, but shows no particular disappointment at the news that he will not be receiving the ARCOM medal which all the other PMO clerks had received during their going-away parties, one per month during the past year, the ARCOM like the red-and-yellow striped KP ribbon that everyone is awarded at the end of basic for service during time of war. Every soldier needs a medal. No bronze stars or silver stars are ever garnered around here, but a soldier needs a medal to put on his uniform after a year in a war zone, so they give you an ARCOM, a green-and-white striped ribbon to show the folks back home. Thanks for your time in service. Palmer wonders if he might finagle a Good Conduct Medal out of the army. As far as he knows he's never been caught.

"That's all right, Sergeant," he says, sensing that Ebbets needs to hear this — some men might resent being denied a medal, Ebbets probably knows from experience. "I'm just looking forward to going home," then wonders if he ought to have added this. You always end up tip-toeing around authority. I'm just looking forward to getting out of this shit hole it might have sounded like he was saying.

Ebbets nods. It seems to Palmer that it takes an effort for Ebbets to even speak to him, the man seems to be reaching down inside himself just to communicate, as if he knows Palmer is not worth communicating with. It's like he's holding his breath, waiting for Palmer to evaporate. Palmer senses some mild form of disapproval emanating from Sgt. Ebbets, but it's probably just his own inherent guilt, always fleeing from the light. He doesn't envy the clerks who will serve under Sgt. Ebbets for the next year. The man is obviously a disciplinarian.

"Next Tuesday will be your last official day of work," Ebbets says, still touching his chin. "You can begin your out-processing on Wednesday morning. However when you are not involved in out-processing I would like you to make yourself available to answer any of the new man's questions before you depart for Cam Ranh Bay."

Palmer finds himself smiling uncontrollably with his lips clamped tight as though Ebbets is taking his time leading up to the punchline of a hilarious joke. Like watching Laurel and Hardy carrying a couch down an icy street, the punchline doesn't matter.

But after Sgt. Ebbets goes back to his desk Palmer starts thinking about the ARCOM medal and wonders why he wasn't put in for it on time. Who's in charge of doing that anyway? Maybe one of the battalion dopers. The only thing he has ever cared about since arriving in Vietnam, since getting drafted, is going home, but he finds himself getting irritated thinking about the fact that he, of all the clerks, won't be getting a medal at his going-away party. Always a party when one of the other clerks left. A sergeant would bark "Attention to orders!" and all the drunks would set their beers down and stand weaving at attention, and the Provost Marshal would read a brief citation and pin a medal on the clerk's fatigue jacket above the left breast pocket. Even as Palmer feels slighted he realizes that his reaction is foolish. A slave to sentiment. Then it occurs to him that if he doesn't get awarded a medal at the party, everyone in attendance will think the army has refused him a medal because he's a dud. Two years of dodging shit details and fucking up and breaking laws left and right, and now everybody will know it, but for the wrong reason.

He tries to put this crock out of his mind by getting to work on a traffic accident report. Today is Thursday. There is only Friday and Monday and Tuesday work left, and his two years in the army will be over for all practical purposes because every effort he will make after Tuesday will be directed toward getting home. Three and a half days to go, and the weekend doesn't count. Too bad he doesn't drink. Missing out on a medal would have been a great excuse for getting blasted out of his skull. A rare opportunity lost. Comes along once in a lifetime, although he is amazed at how many excuses there are in this world to get drunk. They stand arrayed like shiny packages in a department-store window at Christmas. The variety is astounding, and the supply seemingly limitless.

CHAPTER 41

When Palmer arrives at the PMO on Friday morning it occurs to him that this is, in fact, his last real day of work. He sits down at his desk and gazes at his typewriter which, after today, he will never be using again because on Monday morning the new man will be coming from the 109th to replace him.

One of the clerks has already made coffee in the machine that everyone including the MPs up front use. Palmer goes for a cup of coffee. When he gets back to his office and sits down and takes a sip, he thinks again about the fact that this is his last day of work, and the thought suddenly makes him grin because he realizes he is doing what he has always done, which is reshaping his world with words. He did this even before he got drafted, has done it all his life, attempting to alter reality through language, using a kind of verbal logic which is completely false but which makes him feel good. If he works at it hard enough, he can convince himself that at five o'clock this evening he will be stepping off a plane in Denver.

This is not your last day of work, he tells himself, his lips silently moving over the rim of his cup. His upper lip grows damp from steam as he gazes at the wall above his typewriter. Your last day of work will be the day someone hands you a discharge.

Anh comes into the office. Palmer sets the cup down wondering if she might have heard him muttering aloud to himself. The short-timer shakes. If I can make it through the next ten days and wake-up, someone will hand me a discharge.

Anh is grinning big. Friday is here, the weekend, and her icebox should be arriving on Sunday. She is as excited about her kitchen appliance as Palmer is about going home. Her excitement makes him feel wistful. It's a cheesy world. Last night he had felt a little closer to death than he had ever felt before, but still didn't want to leave this cheesy vale. "I'm going to the motor pool," he tells her. He tries to use proper English syntax when he talks to Anh, but falls so easily into the drooling argot, especially when talking to the house girls. It takes too much effort to be grammatical when you subconsciously feel your listeners won't understand anyway.

The trip to the motor pool takes less than a minute, but it is still his job, now just a shit detail. He will try to see that PFC Dugan takes over this minor job on Monday, part of his training. The training won't take more than ten minutes, but Palmer will do it the army way, slow and complicated, the way Shappler did it. Examining traffic accident reports, making corrections, proofing, filing the reports up front in PFC Tachwitz's fiefdom, filing traffic tickets in a desk drawer, writing down information in the record books. A nothing job. He will put Dugan to work typing reports right away, as Shappler had done with him on that first day last year. Shappler was in and out of the office all day, disappearing for long stretches then returning. Nobody cared. A man approaching his end time in service is like a fading ghost. How do they do it out in the bush? Do infantrymen get taken off jungle patrol a few days early? Do grunts dive onto choppers in the middle of a firefight and say take me home? He doesn't know. He knows nothing about the infantry.

Sgt. Turner isn't at the motor pool. One of the clerks tells him that the sarge is already up at the AFVN compound getting ready to tape his TV show. Filler for who knows how long. It seems strange to Palmer that the war will keep right on going after he leaves. Seems like his leaving ought to mark the end of it all, that time should come to a stop forever. Right at this moment somewhere in America a teenage boy is opening a draft notice.

Palmer drives slowly on his return to the PMO. Down the block, through the unguarded gate, past the abandoned barracks that may never be filled again. Camp Redstone is vast, and there may never be enough GI's to fill all the barracks that stand hollow under the sun, the pale paint fading paler and peeling away, red dust gathering like minuscule dunes along the bases of bunkerwalls. He parks the jeep in front of the PMO and gets out hoping that this has been his last trip, alone anyway, to the motor-pool for travel authorization papers. A nice gig which ultimately had disintegrated as all sweet deals do. At least it had gotten him out of the office for a while, a peaceful breakfast in the airfield cafeteria, the morning paper, coffee, a chunk stolen from the slow march of time. He steps inside the office and sees Sgt. Ebbets seated at his desk, talking to a road MP decked out in web gear and pistol belt. Sgt. Ebbets looks around and points at Palmer. "There he is."

Irksome to be pointed out like that. Red flags spring erect. Palmer wants to get into his office fast, but the MP looks over at him, a young kid with black army-issue glasses that make him look like every GI with glasses, a newbie whom Palmer has never seen before, his fatigues a dark and untailored green. He grins at Palmer, toothy white smile, probably not a smoker. The MP stoops a bit and picks something up, sheets of cardboard leaning against Ebbets' desk, and starts walking toward Palmer saying, "You're the traffic man, huh?"

Palmer doesn't want to reply. To finger himself. It's ten steps to the door of the traffic section where the click of Anh's typewriter keys suddenly starts up, soft pecking at the sound of passing boots. Palmer nods.

The man looks down at the sheets, arranges them in front of himself, two-foot by three-foot posters with colorful numbers and bars-graphs drawn by someone who is good at what he does. "You're supposed to courier these charts up to the AFVN compound. Sgt. Turner needs them for a TV show he's doing."

Red flags are exploding in Palmer's brain, staking out virgin folds of gray matter, questions unfurling like stop-motion flowers blossoming in a Disney short. AFVN compound? What the hell? Why me? Why didn't Sgt. Turner take...?

"They just finished drawing the charts and I was supposed to courier them up to Sgt. Turner on the mountain," the man says. His name tags reads *Grieg*. He continues to grin as he speaks, poking the center of his glasses with a single finger. "But the desk sergeant doesn't want to use my unit to go up there, so he asked Sgt. Ebbets if he could spare a man." Grieg stops speaking and gazes at Palmer, waiting for a response to this circuitous excuse for placing a burden on the traffic man's shoulders. "Which I guess is you," Grieg finishes, a newly-cautious look in his eyes seeming to ask that he not be blamed for this bullshit.

Up the mountain? Palmer looks at Sgt. Ebbets who is busy with paperwork at his desk, paying no attention. Palmer's mind is making a rapid search for a way to avoid this detail.

An exit. The mountain is where the VC fire mortar rounds. But whose shoulders can he slough this off onto? All the other clerks are seated erect and typing industriously as though they know exactly what he is thinking. It has been sloughed off onto him by this newbie, though not on purpose. Palmer knows he cannot pass this along to anybody else, something a true buddyfucker would go to extreme lengths to do.

"Specialist Palmer," Sgt. Ebbets says, rising from his desk. "You will need to requisition your weapon and a bandoleer from the arms room before you drive up to AFVN. And you had better go to the TMP and fill the gas tank on the jeep." He never says *maverick*. "You do not want to run out of gas on the mountain." Palmer's racing thoughts are instantly replaced by static resignation. Well, he's never refused an assignment yet, if he doesn't count all the desperate dodges he has gotten away with, like Oakland KP which fate had rescinded. In the final tally, you never get away with anything.

He nods and reaches out, takes the charts and raises them for a closer examination. Traffic tickets and accidents. Sketchy ruled pencil lines outline the bright bars, the monthly rate of accidents in December of last year. Speeding in general. Excessive speed for road conditions in particular. More of these than in the dry months. Percentages of overall accidents broken down into following too close, improper passing, careless driving, and Palmer's favorite traffic charge: inattention. A few fatal traffic accidents. Sgt. Turner ought to have no problem turning these alarming stats into a dull half-hour that nobody will ever watch.

Palmer goes into the office and tells Anh that he will be gone for at least an hour, maybe longer, then he carries the charts out to the jeep and stands them on the metal flooring in the rear, lays them tilted against the low seat. The drive to his barracks takes only a little longer than the drive to the motor-pool. He goes inside and retrieves his M-16 and bandolier from his locker. These he sets on the shotgun seat where he will be able to get at them easily.

He drives out of the MP compound and down the road to the main gate of Camp Redstone where an SP is manning the gate. The man doesn't ask for his travel authorization papers, just waves him on through as SPs have done so many times in the past, as they did on the day that he and Mueller went to the Mariner's Club, the day Detty killed that child. Mueller went home seven weeks ago, got an early out in order to go to college. Palmer hadn't understood how he was able to swing a sweet deal like that, but didn't ask. That was when he realized that he himself wanted to pull his entire tour, three hundred and sixty-five days, without finagling an early out, even a legitimate one. He realized he really did want to come out of this clean, wanted to serve his entire two years and not weasel out of it at the last moment which would almost be like dodging the draft in his mind. This is unlike him and he knows it, and doesn't understand it except that it had always made him sick of himself whenever he backed down in the clutch. See this one thing through to the end and you will be clean all your life.

An American SP and a Vietnamese MP are manning the main gate to the airfield. The ARVN will be taking over the compound one of these days. The SP, who is two feet taller than the TC, does ask for his travel papers, but Palmer doesn't mind. He's fascinated by the latest changes in the main gate, the rolls of concertina wire stacked all over the place, burying the cyclone-fence, piled high to keep out the VC that everybody knows are coming. It's pathetic, all these rolls stacked like Slinkys and about as effective. A desperation move. The SP hands his papers back and waves him on through, and Palmer drives into the airfield compound which looks absolutely deserted right at this moment, though the evacuation hospital and the air terminal are still operational. But there aren't any people outside, not like that first day a year ago when it was like a carnival, with military personnel and civilians milling around and vehicles traveling back and forth and airplanes taxiing and helicopters hovering above pads. This place is dead.

He drives past the hospital, looks over and sees a few ambulances but no people. He follows the road past the air terminal and glances through the picture window but cannot see anyone manning the counter. He looks across the parallel landing strips and sees the empty barracks of the former 109th compound small in the distance. Weeds are beginning to grow long at the edges of the runways. Last year the steady landing of C-130s took a while to get used to, roaring to a stop less than a hundred yards from his bunk, the propellers reversed for braking generating incredible artificial thunder that rolled right across the MP compound. In fact, he never did get used to it, another reason he was glad to make the move to Camp Quincey.

There are no other vehicles at the IMP, which has always had a bleak and lonely look to it, like a giant colorless gas station, all concrete with pumps spaced far apart. He pulls up to a pump and gases up the jeep while staring at the peak of the AFVN mountain blue in the hazy distance. He's never been up there before but knows there is only one road that leads all the way to the top. He has passed the road many times, a dirt road that splits off from the apex of a hairpin turn. Just looking at the mountain gives him the same distasteful feeling he got when he received his draft notice, the same feeling as riding the bus into Fort Campbell on his first day of basic training, the same feeling as seeing his name posted on the Vietnam roster at the Presidio. The unknown, all mapped out for you by someone else. He tops off the tank, then steps into the shack where a young kid in new green fatigues sits on the stool and smiles at him. Probably a newbie who hasn't been in the army long enough to develop a hatred for MPs. Palmer smiles back and signs the roster as Tom Terrific. Who reads these fucking sheets of paper any way, some oil company exec?

When he gets back out to his jeep he decides to go ahead and slip a magazine of ammo into the M-16, though he won't lock and load. He doesn't want to waste precious seconds digging through a bandoleer for bullets after the VC start shooting at him. He doesn't actually think any VC will be roaming around the mountainsides in broad daylight, but he had long ago lost faith in anything he thinks.

He drives back around the airfield road, passes through the main gate bulging with its useless moat of razor wire, but turns left rather than right toward Camp Redstone. Down the street he had ridden on his first day in Qui Nhon, the same route as on the day of Detty's riot, then turning right and heading up toward Camp Quincey which the ARVN have taken over.

They are tearing down Quincey. Palmer slows as he rolls past, and gazes at the piles of lumber. The building which had housed the dayroom is gone. Palmer's old barracks stands waiting to be torn down. Out on the softball field stands a row of ARVN barracks, low and bamboo and straw, did they fall over when the big bomb exploded? He wonders why the ARVN don't use the American barracks, move right in, why bust your ass to build new structures? Strange to see it all disappearing. How many soldiers have ever gotten to see the dismantling of their compounds? This will be his memory of Camp Quincey and not all those tedious days and nights of wading through the tar of time, the nights of drinking, and later the chilled nights of library research. The history books hadn't helped him understand much of anything, had only made the baffling tapestry longer and wider. Why would Ho Chi Minh waste the lives of millions of his own people just so he could be a communist? What's the attraction? Palmer will never know.

He passes beyond Camp Quincey, passes the main PX which is still operational but with fewer customers. He can see the white jeeps of the ROKs, the Republic of Korea soldiers lined up at the pop shack loading up on cases of Coke and beer that they will sell on the black market and probably send the profits home to their families in South Korea. In his letters that have finally stopped coming, Gilchrest says South Korea is one giant pig-sty. Palmer might stop in and see Gilchrest after he gets his discharge, since the man lives in Seattle. Army reunion two days after getting out of the army.

He slows as he approaches the hairpin turn, peers at the dirt road which cuts to the left and rises like a crooked paper snake on the first gentle foothill slope and disappears around a fold in the mountain. He cuts across the asphalt road and drives onto the dirt road, the land rising immediately though gently, rutted, he has to go slowly. He shifts into second gear. Up this close the land really does resemble the foothills of the Rockies, the road up Lookout Mountain beyond Golden, weeded dry earth with evergreen trees sparse at the base but thickening as he negotiates the rise. Where did these evergreens come from? Maybe the Dutch brought them. He leans to peer out the windshield, looks up and to his right, scans the hillside topped by the AFVN compound maybe a mile up the winding road, maybe not that far, but far enough. He feels completely vulnerable inside the open jeep, no protective doors, just a canvas roof. He looks over at his M-16, reaches out and adjusts its angle on the shotgun seat so he can easily grab the pistol grip. Another handy innovation, like the briefcase handle. Maybe the designer was an infantryman.

The jeep at a steeper angle now, he can see the top of the mountain to his left, with its eastern cliff dropping straight down into the water. He makes a curve that takes Qui Nhon out of sight behind him, he twists around to look, the city is gone, he is in the mountains now, like the road from Golden to Central City, earth looming above him, rocks. He feels claustrophobic even though he is skirting the edge of a road that falls sharply into emptiness on his left, with erosion at the road's edge like notches on a pistol butt. The sky is clear, cloudless, blue, like a roof waiting for him to reach the top and touch it. Do the VC hide out in caves, tunnels, waiting for the right moment to emerge? Spider holes. In basic training the instructor popped out of the ground wearing weeds in his helmet and fired blanks. "You're dead." Palmer expected to be sent to infantry school but his orders read Military Police School, Fort Gordon, Georgia. "Are there MPs in Vietnam?" he said, and the drill sergeant replied, "*Youuuuu* better believe it, trainee."

He drives around another fold and sees flush up against the side of the mountain to his left, across a shallow valley, the silver body of a jet airplane lying belly-down among the trees. He slows the jeep and stares at the plane. The bright body scorched here and there, the cockpit canopy gone, the tip of the nose gone, but the wings intact, not a Phantom jet but like something out of the Korean War, like a toy jet, a movie jet, the wings perpendicular to the body. Shot down? Crash landed? But not broken into pieces, whole but for those few missing parts that could have been vandalized. When did this happen? Did the pilot bail? How could it have remained in one piece? Might have been guided down, sliding along the tips of evergreens, but is facing up the mountainside, nose to the sky. Spun around? He keeps driving but gazes at the wreckage, a chunk of mute history, and when his jeep makes another right turn along the road he looks at the jet in his side mirror until the horizon of his own mountain rides across it like a closing curtain.

The road goes on, rising, following the curves of the mountainside, he has no idea how much farther he has to go, cannot tell so close to the mountain where the top is. Did army engineers plow this path? It is so badly eroded in one place that he has to drive close to the mountainside, hugging it as he eases the jeep past a runneled pit that spreads in a deep fanned funnel ending at the edge of the cliff. How do trucks get past here? Then coming around another turn he sees smoke like a low cloud hanging in the air up ahead where the road begins to level off. He shifts back into third gear. The source of the smoke appears to be some sort of plateau down off to the left of the road, and as he draws nearer he sees low cone shaped stacks burning on that flat area, an acre maybe, where a lone man is poking at the rubble with a long pike. Some sort of dump maybe. Where else would the men of AFVN toss their garbage? A short steep road leads down to the dump near the point where a hairpin turn is coming up. He slows the jeep and looks off to his right where the road climbs at an incredible angle, seemingly forty-five degrees. As he pulls around the turn he sees, halfway up the hill, a guard shack.

It is a nonsensical road, must rise two hundred feet or more, as though the engineers had thrown in the towel and decided to stop shaping a gentle circular ribbon and just plow at an angle up the mountainside. He comes to a stop and studies the path, then shifts into low and releases the clutch and begins climbing. Halfway to the shack he can feel the engine straining, he gives it the gas, the wheels spin and he has to slow even though he wants to speed. Aren't jeeps supposed to be able to negotiate any kind of terrain? Isn't that the strength of jeeps? Isn't that the magic legend? He is barely twenty feet from the shack when the engine stalls. He puts in the clutch and hits the brakes. An SP comes out of the shack.

"I'm making a delivery from the PMO," Palmer says as the man saunters down the steep road with a smile on his face. The man leans to look into the backseat, sees the charts, sees the M-16 lying on the shotgun seat with a magazine plugged into it. "I'm dropping these off for a sergeant named Turner," Palmer continues, pointing at the charts with his thumb. "He's doing a TV show."

"All right, Specialist," the SP says. "Go on up." He stands back and waves Palmer through.

Palmer puts the jeep into low and starts forward, but barely makes ten feet before the wheels begin spinning. The magic piece of shit will go no farther.

The SP climbs the road behind him, comes up next to him grinning—he has probably done this many times—and says, "Roll back down to the bottom of the hill and make a running start."

Cripes. He can't drive in reverse, and can't use the brakes —Colorado mountain driving has taught him the magic of fading brakes—so he keeps the jeep in low and eases all the way back down the hill until he comes to the level hairpin and stops and looks up the hill. Then he looks to his left and sees a Claymore mine aimed right at him. Planted in the earth with long nails, its convex face level with his own, he stares at it with a kind of disbelief and feels the ball-bearing power packed within its plastic shell. Field of fire. He quickly puts the jeep into reverse and backs up ten more feet.

He races the engine a few times, releases the clutch, comes at the rise with the pedal to the floor and races up the hill and this time makes it past the shack and halfway to the top before the engine begins to stall, the wheels to spin, no traction, he brakes and sits sweating wondering what in the *hell*? What kind of fucking road is this? He hears laughter at his back, turns and sees two SPs standing in the middle of the road watching him. One of them waves him back down.

He plays with the clutch and low gear again. It's like a road in a dream bordering on a nightmare, like being chased by dogs and your legs won't move. He backs down to the shack and the other SP tells him to drive down to the dump and try to get a running start from there. Palmer takes it to the bottom, turns down the steep dump road, glides among smoking stacks of refuse where that man, an elderly Vietnamese, stands with his pike at his side, grinning at him. Must watch this show every day. Palmer crosses to the far side of the plateau, coasts between burning hillocks, chokes on the smoke and tries to make a plan. Get up a good head of steam and really charge that fucker.

He puts the jeep into second gear and releases the clutch, races around the edge of the plateau and aims at the smaller road, glides up it with everything bouncing and hangs a quick right up the long road, pedal floored, senses the moment he must shift into low, leans to make the jeep go, races past the shack and hears the cheers of the SPs, sees the horizon of the road that breaks off into blue sky, makes the last thirty feet feeling the jeep losing power and experiencing the sensation of floating up onto the level landscape of the AFVN compound with his velocity and altitude simultaneously reaching zero.

The top of the mountain has been plowed flat like the plateau below, although wind and rain have eroded the work of bulldozers over the years, the ground rutted, lumpy, weeded, and covered with one-story buildings that look even older than the Camp Redstone buildings. The edge of the mountain is part of the perimeter, below which lurk VC on those nights when they lob mortars. Guard towers are evenly spaced along the perimeter. He can't see any fifty-caliber machine guns but knows they are there, poised, waiting, generally effective.

He asks directions from men wandering around the plateau, then drives to a building where the TV shows are produced. He parks backwards near the building, gets out and picks up his weapon, clears the magazine, slings the rifle over his shoulder and gathers up the charts. He imagines walking into some sort of studio, wires and cables strung across the floor, cameras on rolling tripods, a set with a desk where reporters feed the approved news to all of Southeast Asia. But he is allowed no farther into the studio than the front office where a Spec Four relieves him of the charts and tells him that he will see to it that Sgt. Turner gets them, that the sergeant has been expecting them. Palmer looks at a doorway leading into the studio. The door is open and he cranes his neck to see further inward, but sees only a hallway. This is as close to show biz as he's ever gotten.

His mission is over, the assignment completed, and except for that crap out on the hill it hadn't taken much time at all. Time to go. But because it's in his nature to fuck off he does not go back right away. Rather he gets into the jeep and pulls out and begins driving around the AFVN compound, looking it over, a small compound, a terrible place to be stationed, he thinks, vulnerable to mortars, although what place in Vietnam isn't? Danger lurking in the evergreen skirts, but maybe the VC aren't interested in blowing up the TV station. Anh came into the office one Monday morning and asked about a show she had seen on AFVN over the weekend: Was that really a monkey riding a bicycle on the *Ed Sullivan Show*, or just a man in a costume? It was a real monkey, he told her. Maybe the VC like American television.

He guides the jeep along the perimeter looking for the lights that glow at night but can't see them, just the cyclone fencing and beer cans that decorate all American perimeters. He comes to the northern edge of the compound and sees the panorama of Qui Nhon below. He stops the jeep, shuts off the engine, and sits looking at the triangular land mass jutting into the ocean, the curve of the earth shaped by the shimmering water. He gets out of the jeep, walks up to the rolls of concertina wire strung out at the base of the fence, and looks beyond them down the mountainside, follows with squinted eyes the thread of the road that passes the PX, the guidon that leads choppers here each time the VC hit the ammo dump. The army airfield is a massive scar congruent with a longitude. And there, just south along the coast, pale beside the tin-roofed buildings, the softball field of Camp Quincey, a square speck which was lit up every night as long as he had lived there.

He looks for the Mariner's Club where he and Mueller had gone that day. He never went back again. Can't make it out, doesn't really know where it is in relation to anything else, knows only how to drive there. He looks for the green spires of the French cathedral downtown but cannot see them. They stand out against everything when you're up close. Even at this altitude the lone west mountain looks about the same as it does from Camp Redstone. He's farther away from it now than on those nights when the spotlight flies across the valley.

He looks to the northeast of Camp Quincey and sees the clustered jumble of Camp Redstone buildings but is not familiar enough with the layout to recognize anything in particular except the PX compound, and that only because it lies at this end of a long stretch of barren fields with sparse buildings where Hueys land for repairs. His own barracks lies at the opposite end, just beyond the MARS shack that he cannot make out.

The entire city is laid out below like a map with people as tiny as molecules, he can barely detect the movement of vehicles, like paramecium motes floating on the surface of his eyes when he looks at an empty sky. This is what the Viet Cong see when they hike up the mountain and set up their mortar tubes and queue up their rockets. Pick your target. Kill as many people as you can. They're only Americans, invaders, imperialists, capitalists, round-eyes.

He looks to his right and sees a wooden guard tower, not very tall, with a man seated inside, his head and shoulders showing. A guard who actually shoots at things on occasion. Palmer had pulled guard twice a month at Camp Quincey and never touched his rifle. He smoked cigarettes and read paperbacks. He looks to his left and sees another tower. Do these men fire the fifty-caliber machine guns that rake the hills with red rain at night, or are the fifties somewhere else, maybe brought up on mobile dollies? He doesn't know. He's never seen a fifty-caliber in person. He fired the sixty-caliber as an MP trainee. It was cool. He always wanted to fire a machine gun again, but knows he never will.

He looks down at the landscape of Qui Nhon reaching into the sea. It's as pretty as any part of Vietnam he has ever seen. But for the paved roads, the mini-buses, the occasional French architecture, it probably looks the same now as it did when the Dutch bypassed it on their way to Danang. Unblemished, peaceful, serene from this perspective. It will look the same after the Americans leave, will look the same when the NVA finally make it down this far. Palmer turns away from the fence and walks back to his jeep. Time to go.

CHAPTER 42

The last party that Palmer will ever attend in Vietnam will be his own going-away party which is scheduled to be held on Saturday night at the Port Beach party patio where he has attended many parties during the past year, watching with a kind of melancholy envy the men who were going home. He had been drunk at all the parties prior to the weekend when Detty committed suicide, and after that he stayed sober at parties, drinking Cokes and smoking entire packs of Camels, surprised to discover how boring parties are without alcohol. But even sober he found that the experience of seeing a man making a shy and amateurish speech of farewell to his buddies and cadre had the same effect on him as when he was drunk. The man giving the speech seemed to be standing in an inaccessible place that Palmer would never reach. The slow march through the tar of time had made it seem like little more than a hopeless dream, his journey consisting solely of standing still and waiting. But now it is his turn.

All of the other clerks in the PMO detachment had arrived in Vietnam after he did, and he has never gotten to know them as well as he had known the men who had been here when he arrived. He sometimes thought it was because he had quit drinking and subsequently found that without the stimulant of alcohol he was not particularly interested in learning anything about their lives. But then it occurred to him that he was not interested in getting to know them better because they did not have anything to offer him as the veterans had. The newbies did not have the answers to any of his questions. He had begun going to the library at night seeking some sort of answers, but had found none. He never went to parties unless it was a going-away party where he felt obligated to say goodbye to the older men, some of whom were younger than he. He went to the outdoor theater by himself, read books in his cubicle, and gazed at the dates on the computer calendar that had been mailed to him by his cousin, subtracting the days and looking forward to the momentous date when he would at last become a one-digit midget: nine days left in Vietnam.

On Friday evening, just before Anh steps out the door to go home, she turns and looks at Palmer with her eyebrows raised and with a tight-lipped grin on her face, and says, "You come Sunday huh?"

Palmer nods at her. "Sunday morning"

Then Anh says something that both surprises and depresses him. "You no drink beaucoup beer at party huh? You be too hungover to bring icebox."

Surprises him because he had supposed that everybody knew he had stopped drinking long ago, and depresses him because Anh knows him as well as he knows himself. He has pondered the idea of drinking beer on Saturday night since it will be his own going-away party, though he has been waiting for his discharge before doing any drinking again, starting, he presumes, at a Holiday Inn in Seattle.

"I no drink," he says, falling into the slovenly argot that he despises. "I come Sunday morning."

She nods, adjusts her sweater and the woven grass purse that she is carrying, and hurries out of the office eager to get to Sunday morning.

After she is gone Palmer looks around the office trying to find the feeling he believed he would experience knowing that this would be his last real day of work as the traffic man. Dugan is due to show up on Monday. Palmer will no longer be doing *any* official typing, only supervising the incoming PFC as a kind of an acting sergeant. Specialist Fourth-Class is the highest rank he will ever achieve in his life, akin to corporal, and he still doesn't know what the Specialist rank actually signifies. What's his specialty? On the day that he had driven over to the 109th to be promoted to Spec Four by Captain Swales, he had experienced the same small exhilaration that he had felt each time he was promoted, a minor dazzle at receiving at last whatever stripe the army had finally gotten around to tossing his way: the single blazing yellow stripe awarded at the end of MP school; the PFC stripe-and-rocker he was awarded last year before being transferred out of the 109th; and finally the Sp/4 badge with its dark shade of green, it struck a chord inside him that he did not believe even existed, gave him wild thoughts about reenlisting and moving on up to sergeant because it felt so good to get a promotion. He returned to the PMO and for the first time ever gave Anh some static about a report that she had been working on for, he felt, too many days. She dropped her hands to her lap and gave him a dour look, then hissed quietly so that no one outside the traffic office could hear her: "You think you big-shot because you get promotion." That pretty much cut him off at the knees. He didn't say anything more about the report, just sat down at his desk feeling like an idiot, and quietly got back to fucking off.

The rest of the clerks have already left for the day, but Palmer stays a few more minutes searching for that feeling until he realizes that this is not the right office. The Camp Quincey office where he had worked for ten months is where he might have felt the thing he is looking for, and that place already has been torn down by the ARVN. And anyway he will be back here on Monday. He knows he is only trying to put momentum into time by reshaping his world with unarticulated words, which had never worked. When he does finally stand up from his desk and walk out of the office, he feels absolutely nothing beyond the feeling he had always gotten at the end of each day, which was also nothing.

On Saturday evening at seven o'clock six men pile into the Black Maria for a short trip to Port Beach for Palmer's party. Palmer rides in the rear with Rudduck, Tachwitz, and Hoerner, whose jobs consist solely of typing reports brought in by MPs. The truck is being driven by Spec/4 Harris, who works directly under the Provost Marshal along with PFC Scheumer, who is riding shotgun, both men typists and whose jobs include business having to do with the Vietnamese ID section. Sp/5 Saunders, who had once almost caught Palmer drinking in the barracks, used to run the ID section, but after he went home his duties were absorbed by Scheumer.

The three clerks seated with Palmer have already started drinking, each one climbing into the jail wagon with a beer hidden in the thigh pocket of his fatigue pants. They pass around a church-key. This is something Palmer himself used to do before he quit drinking, pre-party priming for the wet-bar at the beach, and for the women who would be brought in after the brass had left for the evening. At the last party Palmer went to where he drank, he found an inflated inner-tube stacked against the wall where they keep the sailboats which can be rented. He carried it down to the beach, stripped to his skivvies, and climbed onto the inner-tube and floated thirty yards along the shore before two men came running down the beach and dragged him out, admonishing him that he would ruin it for everybody pulling a stunt like that. They might have been sergeants but they were wearing civilian clothes. The next day it occurred to Palmer that there might have been jellyfish or sharks in the water, or he might have floated so far out that he could have ended up drowning, the sort of thoughts that never occurred to him when he was drunk.

A gate guard is standing in a small shack at the entrance to Port Beach, an MP whom Palmer recognizes though doesn't know his name. A newbie. Who isn't a newbie? The fact that the guard is a 109th MP means the other men will have no trouble bringing prostitutes in later on. Palmer won't be fooling around with any prostitutes at this party. One of the many rumors that he has heard during the past year is that any departing GI found to have the clap will not be allowed to go home, will be kept beyond his DEROS date until he is cured. Another rumor he heard is that if a man is found to have heroin in his system he will be kept in some sort of detention compound down in Cam Ranh Bay until his system is cleaned out, and he will then be given a dishonorable discharge. Who knows if these rumors are true? He hopes that during the past six months the heroin that he snorted prior to the terrible week-end has been flushed from his system. He can't conceive of any calamity greater than being kept in Vietnam beyond his DEROS date.

The paddy wagon rolls across the sand to the patio, a large slab of concrete roofed over like a carport. It holds picnic tables and a massive barbecue pit where Papasan is already flipping fried chicken on a grill with tongs. Papasan will drink beers in one gulp as the night wears on, Palmer knows, has seen him do this many times. The man is wearing a large white hat like the tacky monstrosity Barney Fife wears on a date. Palmer can't remember ever seeing Papasan without his hat. The man keeps a grin fixed on his face as he cooks, pouring beer onto the meat for flavoring, and laughing maniacally at lame jokes made by the officers and sergeants standing around watching him. There is something pathetic about Papasan, and seeing him through a veil of sobriety Palmer perceives that the little man is a buffoon just trying to hold on. What will become of this clown after the communists take over? Palmer used to wonder if Papasan was a VC, and will never really believe he couldn't be. Who couldn't be a VC in this country?

A lot of people have shown up for the party, including brass and top sergeants from battalion. Command Sergeant-Major Benedetti is over in one corner of the patio clutching a Bud and talking with a major wearing wire-rimmed glasses. Anyone who is off-duty will show up at any kind of party, they have not really come to see Palmer off, this he knows, but he will still have to make a speech in front of all these people later. He thinks about having a few drinks to brace himself for that embarrassing moment in the spotlight. He already knows what he is going to say. He is going to lie to them. He is going to say what they want to hear, because he could never bring himself to say what he really feels.

He goes to the beer tub at the far edge of the patio which faces the beach. The sun has gone below the horizon and the sky will turn black slowly, will not even be noticed as the party wears on within the cube of light created by low-watt bulbs in the rafters. This has been his experience at other Port Beach parties, but in those days he was too drunk to notice anything outside the realm of his reeling brain. A full moon is hanging above the horizon, casting its thin light on a bank of clouds hovering along the Pacific horizon like the skyline of a far mountain range, like the Rockies. The beer tub is eight feet long and four feet wide, is filled with water and a six foot log of ice. Someone must have driven to the ice-plant on the road to Phu Tai to requisition it and haul it back for the party, probably an enlisted man. That's one shit detail Palmer has never pulled, but would have willingly back in the days when it meant the difference between cold and warm beer at a party. The can of Coke that he yanks out of the water is painful against his fingertips. That was the best thing about the tub in the old days, he had never drunk such frigid beer, not even back home, it hurt to hold a fresh can, he had to take his sips quickly and set the can on a picnic table. The chill killed the sour taste, the unreal bouquet of rancid Bud. He looks forward to getting a hotel room in Seattle.

A battalion sergeant is mixing drinks at the wet-bar which has been set up at one edge of the patio where it's backed by a two-story building that has rooms used by men on R&R. This is where Palmer first got drunk on hard liquor. He had always been a beer man, but then at a party one night a battalion clerk named Walthers, who went home seven months ago, talked him into doing shots. Palmer didn't believe it was possible to swallow an entire ounce of Johnny Walker Red without imme-diately vomiting, another theory that buttressed his erroneous view of the world. "Just pour it into your mouth and swallow it in one hair-raising gulp," the man said. Palmer was truly surprised when he didn't vomit, was pleased, and tried it again, and again, and again.

The hiss of a needle dropped onto a turntable comes from speakers in two corners of the rafters. Rock 'n' roll will serve as the background music to this party as it always does. Palmer wonders if the lifers would rather hear music from their own generation at these parties, early 50s music, Perry Como, Johnny Ray. The record collection of his parents ends with the end of World War II. Thick 78 RPM records by Glenn Miller and the Dorsey brothers, big band music that he had listened to as a kid, intrigued by the poor acoustics of the platters that had been played thousands of times. Bing Crosby, The Mills Brothers, The Andrews Sisters, music not from just another time but another world. His father's war. His parents' youth.

He steps out onto the sand and walks down to the shore carrying his warming can of Coke. A fish smell hangs in the air. Funny how he has gotten used to the stink of Vietnam and never notices it unless he is standing on a spot where the humidity can really churn up the mixture of animal and vegetable odors, of shit and dead fish and garbage. He had stopped sweating long ago, but then Qui Nhon never has been as hot as Bien Hoa. It got down to the seventies, even dipped briefly into the sixties, during the monsoon season. Mostly in the nineties now in the daytime and he doesn't notice it although he has spent most of his days sitting in front of a fan in the office. How do the infantry stand the heat in the Mekong Delta? He has never eaten a salt tablet in his life.

An hour or so after the party has begun, Palmer is told to step on up to the patio. His moment in the spotlight is coming. The brass will be leaving early as usual, but only after this semi-official bit of business has been taken care of. The sky is black. The cubic light of the patio is packed with bodies, most of them high but not drunk, since the party will not really crank up until the brass and top sergeants have gone away and prostitutes can be brought in and the hard drinks at the wet-bar will no longer be measured in jiggers from a shot glass but poured freely from a bottle until the customer says stop.

There will be no medal handed out. Palmer cannot remember any going-away party where a medal was not pinned above the left breast pocket of some leaving man. A sergeant from battalion hollers, "Attention!" which quiets everyone down, the murmurs fading beneath the soft sound of the sea at Palmer's back. The Provost Marshal, Captain Costan, is standing next to him with a grin on his face. The captain takes it upon himself to explain to everyone about the late orders on the ARCOM medal, which surprises Palmer, for he cannot recall any time in his life when someone had made an excuse for him, had clarified any of the potential misinterpretations of facts that have dogged him throughout his life, along with all the embarrassing truths. The orders for his medal will be forwarded to him in Denver.

"But we do have something to give you, Specialist Palmer," the PM says.

Sgt. Ebbets is holding a flat box emblazoned with gaudy red and yellow flowers on the lid which Palmer recognizes, recognizes the contents when the sergeant removes the lid and pulls out a wooden plaque in the shape of a badge, curved to a point at the bottom, flared a bit left and right at the top. He has seen the same plaque at other parties, and it always reminds him of the tacky souvenirs that he has seen in every duty station from Georgia to Vietnam.

Captain Costan takes the plaque from Sgt. Ebbets and holds it up for everyone to see, then hands it to Palmer and tells him that the men of the PMO Detachment have contributed to the purchase of this plaque which he is awarding as a symbol of appreciation and gratitude not only from the Provost Marshal's Office and the Military Police Battalion but the United States Army for his service in Vietnam.

Palmer takes the award and looks down at it. The plaque was manufactured in a small shop in downtown Qui Nhon, the same shop where MPs have their helmets painted and polished black with the appropriate decals added on. The plaque is made of dark varnished wood. In the center is a metal map of Vietnam glued to the surface. Small flat metal devices are arrayed around the map, the 18th MP Brigade crest on the left, the battalion crest on the right. There's the yellow-and-red striped flag of South Vietnam, and the red, white, and blue flag of the United States. At the bottom is a silver rectangle with his name engraved, and below his name are the words "Outstanding Service."

The patio is filled with mild applause until someone at the back hollers, "Speech!" as someone always does. The knot that had grown in Palmer's gut each time he had to give a speech in front of a high school class blossoms, he hasn't felt it in years but is familiar with the foolish sensation that flows from it. He looks up at all the faces grinning at him. They want something from him, and now that the moment has come, he doesn't know if he can articulate his lie, the only thing he could think of to get him through this awful moment which so many enlisted men have passed through before him. "On the day I got drafted," he says, and the words suddenly seem to come from someone else, someone he is standing next to who is speaking in his voice, the words unnaturally resonant and concise, "I thought it was the worst thing that ever happened to me." Now that he has forced himself to articulate this truth, he feels compelled to hurry his statement to its end, to say the thing he believes they will want to hear: the lie. "But after two years in the army, and a year in Vietnam, I think it was probably the best thing that ever happened to me." He starts to say something else, but then—as if coming out of a daydream—he realizes that everyone is applauding, men are laughing, hooting, and he has to wait until their voices have quieted down before he can finish, and when he does finish, he later can barely remember what he said, something sentimental about having worked alongside all the other clerks at the PMO whom he will never forget, the kind of thing that might have been said by Captain Woodward, the Provost Marshal who looked like a protestant minister and who almost caught him smoking pot.

When he finishes speaking, he is immediately surrounded by GIs who begin shaking his hand, even Command Sergeant-Major Benedetti and Lieutenant Colonel Weldon, the new battalion commander. Everybody is grinning at him, their eyes sparkling, their hands pumping his, and it is only after the brass and top sergeants have gone away that he realizes every one of them had acted this way because they were relieved. He comes to this understanding after PFC Tachwitz tells him that when he said he thought getting drafted was the worst thing that ever happened to him, the Provost Marshal's jaw dropped a mile. "I thought you'd lost your fucking mind," Tachwitz tells him, laughing, sipping from a beer and watching the Black Maria roll through the main gate with a load of prostitutes who have been gathered off the streets of Qui Nhon for this festive occasion.

When the truck parks near the patio, the rear door opens and a dozen women spill out laughing, wearing colorful blouses and black silk pants, and immediately make for the cube of light where the free beer and chicken are. The enlisted men make a practiced head count of the number of women . brought in, and the men who are interested move toward them, pair off with a subtle polite quickness, each man touching a woman on the shoulder and leading her to the table where the food is laid out on mess hall tin, or to the beer tub for the women who drink. Not all of them drink at the parties, just as not all enlisted men pair off with women. Palmer remembers a married man named Salzman, a PMO clerk who went home eight months ago, and who could never be coerced into coming to a party. "I don't drink, and I'm not going to mess with any prostitutes, so I don't have any reason to go to a party," he explained. Palmer had found this attitude unfathomable, and was always the last man to give up trying to persuade him to come along as the jeeps and Black Maria loaded up for the jaunt to Port Beach. Now he stands looking at the women as they sidle up to a man here and a man there, the available girls diminishing until there is only one left coming from the truck, a pretty girl wearing blue jeans and a silky red jacket. They were picked up along the side streets of downtown Qui Nhon in a ritual at least a decade old. "Want to go to a party?" the driver would have said. Palmer has been on these runs himself. The prostitutes have a grapevine. Word is passed along quickly, they emerge from shadows, from alleys, from nearby houses, and climb laughing into the truck.

The woman in blue jeans strolls across the sandy ground and steps up onto the concrete patio, walks right up to Palmer and says quietly, "You want to make luf with me?"

Palmer smiles at her. "What your name?" he says.

"Suzy."

"You are very pretty, Suzy."

"You beaucoup dap," she says, and reaches up and pinches a folded sleeve of his fatigue jacket, tugs at it.

"I'm sorry Suzy, no can do," Palmer says. "I go home next week."

"Aaaah," she says. "You haf girlfriend back home huh?"

Palmer lies with a nod.

"This party for you?" she says.

"Aum," he says, then almost regrets saying it, as if he is mocking her. Aum means yes, but coming from his mouth it sounds like the slang he despises.

But Suzy smiles wide. "Okay," she says, it comes out almost as a single syllable, and she walks further into the crowd to find another customer. Where is Motor Pool Mary tonight? Palmer hasn't seen her in six months.

Near ten o'clock, the curfew of parties and enlisted men's clubs in this city, Sp/4 Palmer, the only sober enlisted man left on the patio, chauffeurs the women back to an intersection in downtown Qui Nhon. He parks the Black Maria along a dirt road, and the women get out laughing, cluster giggling in their colorful blouses and black silk pants and begin hurrying toward the lit doorway of a house in the middle of a lightless block of houses. But then Suzy comes up to the driver's door of the cab, steps onto the running board and reaches in with one hand, touches Palmer on the shoulder and smiles at him and says, "I hope you go home very happy."

She hops off the running board and hurries to catch up with her sisters dashing toward the vertical yellow rectangle of light set against a row of buildings so dark, so black, that the roofs are indistinguishable from the sky.

CHAPTER 43

There is an oddness to waking up after a party and not having the hangover that Palmer used to feel every Sunday morning following a going-away party, a feeling that something is missing and ought to be there. A contented feeling of incompleteness engulfs him as he sits up on his bunk and gazes at his alarm clock. Seven forty-five. He has slept in, though not as late as he once had, when the feeling of completeness consisted of hangover pain. Snores rise from hungover bodies in the open bay. Palmer rises and quietly puts on a clean pair of fatigues feeling as if he is moving around inside a morgue. The small mission that he has dreaded, in that he dreads any sort of responsibility, has arrived. He has to make an attempt to deliver his icebox to Missy Anh's house. He knows how to get there, was there one time last New Year's. Her house is a few blocks from the traffic circle in downtown Qui Nhon, not far from a building that everyone refers to as the Korean Hotel although he doesn't know why. Was it built by Koreans?

When he steps outside the barracks and tugs his cap on, the silence of Sunday morning is like the silence he had experienced at Camp Quincey on the afternoon he drove over to take one last look. He supposes there are a lot of lifers hungover in the NCO barracks. There are absolutely no sounds whatsoever, not even coming from beyond the perimeter fence where pimps on Hondas race by at night. No traffic. No voices. It is as if the world is holding its breath as he sets out on foot for the PMO where, he hopes, the Black

Maria is still standing where he had parked it last night. He already has the keys in his pocket. He had kept them after returning to the PMO, knowing that during the mild chaos of a going-away party and its aftermath, the disappearance of a set of keys would not be considered unusual or incomprehensible by a sergeant searching for them. Right up to the very last week of his time in service Palmer is still prepared to utilize one of the oldest survival cons of his army career, of his teens, of his life: playing dumb. Oh. Here, sergeant. I forgot to put the keys back in the box last night. I'm sorry. I've got to keep my shit together next time.

He walks out of the small compound where a newbie MP in the shack only looks at him as he passes by. Palmer crosses the road and disappears into the maze of the abandoned barracks that lead toward the PMO. Butterflies are beginning to stir in his gut because until he sees the Black Maria he will not be certain that he can pull this off. But even after he sees it parked in front of the PMO he still is not certain he can succeed. He would prefer not to be doing this at all, wishes that Anh already had an icebox, hates having to *do* things and always has. The moment he opens the driver's side door, that is the moment he begins breaking one of the lesser laws he has broken since he has been in the army, but the sensation of guilt, which seems dovetailed always and inextricably with knowledge, replaces the butterflies inside him. He knows he's taking a chance, and thus feels himself descend into a kind of robotic state of mind as he starts the engine without authorization, because he intends to see this through to the end, and not thinking at all is his only hope. Just act like you're supposed to be doing what you're doing, and nobody will question you. He first heard that in basic training.

He drives out of the PMO parking lot, bouncing in ruts made by vehicles that disappeared with the engineering troops. He follows a route to the MP battalion compound different from the shortcut that he has walked every morning since the move. He drives through the gate where the MP still stands, drives right into the risky moment of this process, the transfer of his icebox to the Black Maria. The street is quiet, no one outside. Only ten minutes since he woke up, but every second is stretching itself out a bit because he wants this to be over with soon, the desire that slows time and always has throughout the past year. Basic training too. He has spent two years wishing time would accelerate, wanting to leave wherever he was and be somewhere else. Except the Presidio. Felt like he was driving with the brakes on at the Presidio, with Vietnam in front of him, as well as, he had assumed, death.

He parks the truck in front of the barracks door, gets out not too quickly and walks around the truck, enters the door and feels safe momentarily. No sergeant would know why the truck is there, and until the icebox is stored inside, there has been no real violation of regulations.

His icebox stands against the wall next to his bunk. It is not plugged in, not running. He had cleaned it out last night, his beer warehouse, and after the terrible weekend, his Coke machine. He is actually able to lift the thing, it comes only to his waist, but it is going to be a struggle to lug it halfway through the barracks and now he wants to hurry. PFC Tachwitz is awake, seated on his bunk in his skivvies. Palmer crosses the room and speaks quietly to him.

"Tachwitz, can you give me a hand with my refrigerator? I want to carry it outside and put it in the paddy wagon."

Tachwitz raises his head, his face wrinkled still with sleep and alcohol. It's early for favors, and a Sunday, but he nods, puts on his fatigue pants and follows Palmer to the icebox. The two of them tip it over and pick it up and carry it silently down the aisle past the sleeping hungover clerks.

Palmer had moved sofa beds as a civilian, knows as much as a mover can know about the minutiae of loading heavy things, squeezing awkward objects through tight doorways and around corners. He directs Tachwitz with breathy commands, "Stand still and I'll swing this end around," having never thought that any civilian shit job would come in handy, but this one has a few times since he's been in the army. He sets a corner of the icebox on the ledge, hops into the jail wagon and lifts the refrigerator. They ease it far enough back so the door can be closed, the contraband shut away. Hidden. Invisible. Safe.

"Thanks man," Palmer says, and Tachwitz just nods. He must know what's going on. Palmer is up to something, probably selling his refrigerator on the black market, obvious as hell, but Tachwitz doesn't say a word, just watches as Palmer gets in and starts the engine, guides the truck in a tight U and rolls up the street at the five mile an hour compound speed-limit. Palmer is impressed by Tachwitz's absolute silence. Not a question asked. An apparent good man whom he will never get to know any better. PFC Rudduck would have been a disaster.

He drives to the PMO, swings the truck around in the parking lot, backs up near the front door, and shuts off the engine. This part of Camp Redstone is silent too. A Sunday silence. No MP vehicles parked outside the station right now

with radios hissing and clicking. The entrance to the part of
the building with the D-cells has only a single door unlike the
double-doors of the old station at Camp Quincey. He gets out
of the truck and walks over to the door, opens it and steps
inside where the desk sergeant is seated high against one
wall, the radio operator seated beside him with headphones
dangling around his neck.

"Good morning, Sergeant," Palmer says with a smile,
walking up to the desk.

"Hey, it's the short-timer," the sergeant says. His name is
Willis, a lifer in his thirties, an affable man, but most of the
desk sergeants over the past year seemed to have been affable
men. The desk is a tense job. Maybe the 109th looks for
mellow men who can finesse the bullshit of emergencies, of
violent prisoners, of endless streams of robbed or injured GIs
coming and going.

"Could you do me a favor and call Sp/4 Siever in? I need
to talk to him."

"Sure thing, GI," Willis says, turning to his radio man.

"I'll be in the back room," Palmer says, just to get away
from the vicinity of this passive conspiracy. He walks through
the doorway into the PMO, goes into the traffic office and sits
down at his desk, softly gritting his teeth. He has never liked
involving other people in his surreptitious schemes, not since
the first day of basic, although his schemes have almost always
involved avoiding simple shit details. Now it feels like he has
half the army in on it. Anh couldn't have asked for something
small, like a toaster or a tape-deck.

Siever and his partner, a new man whom Palmer has
never seen before, arrive ten minutes later. Palmer goes outside

and walks up to Siever nodding. "Thanks for doing this," he says, and Siever grins, says no problem, what's the plan?

"Just follow me downtown," Palmer says.

He gets into the truck, starts the engine, drives out of the parking lot and heads for the Camp Redstone main gate where two SPs are on duty, and who wave him through. Driving out onto the civilian road relieves Palmer of an enormous sense of burden. The job feels almost over only because the delicate machinations he has gone through to get the contraband off the base have succeeded, are already a part of the past. His MP escort feels like a protective shield, but then maybe the convoys that cross the Central Highlands feel the same way about MP escorts in their V-100s, until rocket-propelled grenades start flying out of the bush.

The route to Anh's house takes him on the two-lane asphalt road that traces the triangular shape of the landscape that extends into the ocean, around the tip and back toward downtown. Both sides of the road are crowded with one-story buildings, houses and shops with small palm trees growing in between. It's noisy here, people are outside walking along the shoulder of the road, or squatting in front of their houses cooking things over open flames. Children everywhere. The scene that Palmer had driven through every day when he was a road MP, faces glancing at him impassively, the locals who are not a part of the war, like himself. Is a Sunday the same thing to the Vietnamese as it is to Americans? He hasn't been to church since Thorpe's funeral. Missy Nu once told him she's a Catholic. She made the sign of the cross, then touched her palms as if in prayer, and held out her tongue in imitation of taking the Eucharist. Missy Cue is a Buddhist.

Palmer guides Siever down into the heart of Qui Nhon where the trees are thick and tall, where Anh lives in a kind of walled-off dirt courtyard. The low stone wall surrounds a dozen or so two-story houses, there is an entrance gate, and within the courtyard children are playing, screaming, chasing, but they stop and stare when the black truck enters followed by an MP jeep. Everybody knows Palmer is coming, he can see that in the way adults appear in doorways and watch curiously with arms folded as he guides the truck slowly toward Anh's house. He parks near two trees close enough together to hang a hammock. Anh appears in the doorway, she is dressed like a house girl, wearing a simple white blouse and black silk pants, and looks strange without a colorful clinging ao dai, like seeing your school teacher in a Safeway when you're a kid. Her face is all grins, eyes wide with pleasure, satisfaction, Palmah did not get beaucoup drunk at his DEROS party, has come through for her. He climbs down out of the truck feeling an electric thread of hurry pass through him, got to get this thing unloaded and get the hell out of here even if he does have an escort. He dislikes being outside the safety of a vehicle and surrounded by Vietnamese, a minor, instinctive, and irrational feeling that displeases him and over which he has no control. This is Anh's home, yet he feels a niggling sense of threat as her friends and neighbors stroll out of their houses to see the new appliance. Mostly women. More children, Anh steps off her porch and approaches Palmer with her eyebrows raised.

"You haf icebox huh?" she says, though she must know he does, why else would he be here?

"It's in the truck," he says, and finds himself doing the

exact things he used to do when he was an assistant furniture-mover, it all comes back, fits like a glove. "Show me where you want the icebox in your house, okay?" he says.

Anh turns and leads Palmer through the doorway into her home where an elderly woman stands with her arms folded, waiting, her face both tight and wrinkled, her hair white. "This is my mother," Anh says, and Palmer nods, then reaches out to shake hands only after the woman reaches toward him with a close-lipped smile. Old enough to have lived through the Japanese occupation, the French, now the American. What do these people think of the foreigners trampling all over their country? Anh points at an empty space against a wall that obviously has been cleared away for the delivery. Palmer glances around at the sparsely-furnished room. A wood-framed couch covered with a thin cotton sheet of colorful fabric. Pictures on the walls. A small shrine to Buddha in one corner with unlit candles. Colorful rugs on the floor. A doorway leading to another part of the house, a staircase to the floor above.

"All right," Palmer says feeling as if he is being pushed from behind, but only by his own guilt and sense of hurry. "We'll bring it in."

As Palmer walks out the door he is suddenly surrounded by a dozen children, two of whom throw their arms around his calves and cling to him laughing, looking up at him with mouths wide, baby-teeth gone from their gums, eyes squinting with wild pleasure as they hug this tall American, the tops of their heads barely reaching his knees. Palmer is a bit freaked out by this, and finds himself walking with two tiny kids attached to his shins, the rest of the children running in noisy circles around him as he trudges toward the truck. Anh steps outside and hollers something, and the kids let go of Palmer's calves and back away screaming with laughter.

He opens the rear of the paddy wagon, then asks Siever for help hauling the icebox out. Again it is like the furniture job he had hated but had been stuck with before getting drafted. Ease the heavy thing out, set it on the edge, hop down and take the weight as the man on the other end pivots. Feels odd to take pride in knowing how to do something you once hated and will never do again on purpose. Some of those furniture drivers had been in their fifties.

The two men make the brief stoop-backed trip up to the doorway and into the house with Palmer grunting whispered instructions, over here, set your end down first, turn it this way, no like this. The icebox resting at an angle on the floor. Palmer eases it vertical, then quickly untapes the length of electric cord that he had carefully taped into a loop last night, and holds the plug up for Anh to see. "After you plug it in, you turn it on here," he says, pointing at a knob, large like a dial on a safe with numbers tracing its circumference. OFF to COLDEST, one through ten. Anh turns the dial back and forth.

"Okay, I have to leave now," Palmer says. "I will see you tomorrow at work."

Anh glances at her mother, then says to Palmer, "Would you like something to drink?"

He sees it instantly, she is being cordial, offering her guest a refreshment, sit down and rest your dogs and stay awhile, which alarms Palmer because he wants to get out of here and has wanted it since he woke up this morning.

"No thank you," he says, feeling a bit discourteous, reject-ing the kindness that may have been suggested by Anh's mother. They want to show him their gratitude and he doesn't want to see it. "I really have to get back to Camp Redstone."

"Aum," Anh says softly, nodding and smiling at him. In truth, he could spend the whole day in this house, if he was willing to let go of the paranoia that has hounded him all his life. He feels like he's spent twenty-two years prepared to get caught.

"I will see you tomorrow, okay?" he says, trying not to edge toward the door even though Siever has already loped out and is standing by his jeep talking to his partner.

"Thank you very much for the icebox," Anh says. The word very comes out as veddy, as had Suzy's last night. Anh's mother is smiling. Funny how eyes really do sparkle. Maybe this is the first refrigerator that has ever been in this house. Middle-class Vietnamese are like poverty-stricken Americans.

"You're welcome," Palmer says, making a slight movement at last toward the door, casual, exiting, then hurrying to the paddy wagon. He climbs in and starts the engine, and because the dirt courtyard is filled with children and a few adults, he backs the truck up between the two trees and tries to foment a safe U-turn, but within half a minute he finds himself some-how wedged between the trunks, with not enough distance between the front bumper and rear bumper to wriggle his way out. He shifts back and forth from first gear to reverse as with a vehicle stuck in snow, all the Vietnamese watching curiously, the American shifting gears and frantically twist-ing the steering wheel. Palmer cannot believe he has gotten himself into this position, like something on a TV show, Gilligan in his bamboo pedal-car lodged between two palms while the Skipper fumes. This sprung trap has a comic element that infuriates Palmer as the front bumper bangs against the tree blocking his path until Siever strolls up and lifts the brim of his helmet an inch and says, "Say there, Palmer, how about lettin' me give 'er a try? I think I might be able to do it."

Was a time when Palmer would never have given up the driver's seat, not even in such a disgusting situation, back when he was younger, back when he was a civilian and any offer of aid was an affront to his imagined manhood. He yanks the door open and clambers out. "Be my guest."

Siever is from the South, maybe has an affinity for hotrods, stock-cars, he climbs into the driver's seat and with a few slick maneuvers has the nose of the paddy wagon aimed toward the exit gate. Palmer can't help but smile at his own ineptitude, says thanks as Siever climbs out smiling too. Puzzles are fun. "You don't have to come back to Redstone with me," Palmer says, no longer burdened by worry and the contraband accompanying it. This form of relief is familiar too.

Siever gives Palmer a low-handed wave and climbs into his jeep, heads out the exit, back to MP duty. He has a long time to go before his DEROS. Palmer climbs into the paddy wagon and eases his way out of the courtyard and onto the road, and heads back along the route he had come, feeling none of the caginess he so often felt after successfully pulling off some scam, dodge, or the finesse of a sergeant who hadn't known him well enough to know what he was up against. The feeling of slyness that so often filled his heart is not present, there is only a kind of melancholy relief at having done this thing that he didn't want to do, this favor that was a burden and not at all to his advantage, the last under-handed plot he will ever hatch in uniform.

It occurs to him only now that when he woke up this morning he was a one-digit midget.

CHAPTER 44

Again, when Palmer awakens on Monday morning, he tells himself that this is his last official day of work. His last official day of work will come sometime next week, but he doesn't mind reshaping his world with words. Going home breeds giddiness. The unreality of leaving this country far exceeds the unreality of arrival. He has waited so long for it that its near approach almost cannot be grasped. He has seven days and a wake-up left, thinking this as he leaves the MP compound and makes the short hike over to the PMO. Out-processing starts tomorrow, just as the Presidio would have been if he hadn't gotten his arm broken: visiting all the offices, hospital, finance, RE-UP, supply, battalion.

After Palmer arrives at the PMO Sgt. Ebbets steps into the traffic office and informs him that the 109th is sending his replacement over this morning for training.

Palmer grins big at Sgt. Ebbets, something he cannot recall ever having done. There are certain sergeants you don't grin at, an intuitive thing, no rules, but Palmer doesn't care that his grin is saying thank God I'm getting out of this office, this army, this country, this war.

"I want you to start Dugan right typing traffic accident reports," Sgt. Ebbets says. "Make certain he has a complete understanding of the process."

Palmer feels like saying Will do, Sarge, but says only, "Yes, sergeant." He has never gotten chummy with any cadre, not even the few sergeants he gets along with well.

When Missy Anh enters the office she has a look of disappointment on her face that slightly alarms Palmer who is instantly certain that the icebox broke down and cannot be repaired. Two previous owners so far, and the only used product he ever found reliable was a '54 Plymouth he owned just before he got drafted. The thing was indestructible and is, he hopes, still running, used by his brother Mike to get to work.

"How's the icebox?" he says.

Anh steps over to him with a resigned look on her face. "It not work yet. We have two-twenty, and icebox one-ten."

He doesn't understand what she's talking about until she explains that a man will have to come to her house and "change the electricity." Only now does Palmer learn that her house—all Vietnam houses—are wired for 220 volts and the icebox is wired for 110 and won't begin cooling her food until the electrician arrives.

"When will he come?" Palmer says, disappointed that his favor has fallen flat.

"This afternoon."

There's always a catch, you can't do anything, you have to do twelve other things first. Palmer has known this all his life. When he was a kid, if he wanted to nail two boards together he had to ride his bike to the hardware store to buy nails, but before that he had to ask his mother for money to buy the nails, but before that he had to fill the tires on his bike with air because they'd leaked flat, but before that he had to go next door and borrow the neighbor's bicycle pump except the neighbor had already loaned it to a kid down the block. By the time Palmer was ten years old he was shorn of ambition.

PFC Dugan arrives at the office at ten o'clock, and this event possesses even more significance than the going-away party last Saturday—one notch closer to going home, time has been given momentum. Palmer stands up as Dugan walks into the office holding his cap in his hand and looking around at his new bailiwick. His fatigues are dark green. He is a newbie at the 109th. He is the same height as Palmer, thinner, just as Palmer had come thin to Vietnam. He is wearing thick black-framed army-issue glasses and looks young to Palmer, grinning shyly with his cheeks puffing out a bit so that he looks like a kid, innocent, eager to learn a new job.

"Hey, my replacement," Palmer says, grinning and shaking Dugan's hand, and in that moment feels as if he has traveled through time, has made a full circuit of the sun, yet feels as if he in fact has backtracked an entire year and is himself Shappler shaking hands with Private Palmer, his young, thin, leery replacement. He had thought this moment would never come, and is now engulfed by a pleasant vertigo that is wrought by each longed-for reality that, up until it happens, has possessed the quality of a dream. Is my tour really coming to an end? Yet strangely none of it has as much drama as expected. It is as ordinary as his own first day on the job had been.

"Private Dugan, this is Missy Anh, your secretary. She types up traffic accident reports."

Anh reaches out and shakes Dugan's hand, Dugan looking as awkward as Palmer had felt the first time he shook Anh's hand. How many traffic men has Anh worked for? It has never occurred to Palmer to ask, and he never will.

"This is your desk," Palmer says, then stands back. "You might as well sit down. You're the new traffic man now."

Dugan sits on the gray office chair with its squeaking wheels and sets his cap on the desk. Like that Palmer ceases to be the traffic man. Another notch. He pulls open a desk drawer and shows Dugan the traffic tickets that he will have to process, shows him the accident forms, and the record books, and later that morning takes him over to the detachment barracks which is across the street and down the block from Dugan's 109th barracks, and tells him to pick out a bunk. This is where he will be living until next year, unless President Nixon pulls everyone out of Vietnam first.

At noon Palmer accompanies Dugan to the mess hall where Dugan eats every day anyway. They sit at the same table. Palmer in his silverfish threads and Dugan in his leaf-dark green among all these others, GIs in fatigues of varying hues, their jackets fading in direct proportion to their own slow march of time. Palmer knows an MP who has a handcuff key attached to the collar of his jacket and which has never been removed since he first went on road patrol nine months ago. Some sort of good luck charm, Palmer supposes. None of the MPs in the mess hall have been here as long as himself. Dobnik and Hillis went home sometime during the past year, he wasn't even aware of their departure, they just weren't there anymore. Linc and Supertroop. Dobnik is probably a rookie cop on the LAPD. He had seemed like the sort of MP who would join a civilian police force. Small town sheriff. Hillbilly fiefdom.

As they eat their fried chicken, Dugan looks across the table at Palmer and says, "Where are you from?"

"Kansas, where you from?'

"Rhode Island."

Palmer starts to say he had known a basic trainee from Rhode Island, but the guy had been a jerk who went on sick call twice a week and everyone in the training company thought he was a dud. Palmer doesn't feel like talking about him. He suddenly wonders where Krouse is, and Tigler and Willerton and Brenner. They ought to be out-processing from their own units by now. Where did they end up? Are any of them dead?

"Did you go through Fort Gordon?" Dugan says.

Palmer comes out of his brief and unexpected reverie, his quick memory of Oakland and Long Binh where he had encountered the men from basic training, and looks at Dugan. Dugan's skin is pale, as was Palmer's last year. Palmer's skin is a golden brown from lying out on the roof of a bunker at Camp Quincey on his days off, usually drying out from a bender. His friends back home might think he'd been in a war or something.

"I went to Fort Gordon out of basic," Palmer says. "I was surprised when I got orders for MP school. I thought I would end up in the infantry."

This evokes a wide grin from Dugan. "Me too."

"Where did you take basic?" Palmer says.

"Fort Knox."

Knox. Palmer knows nothing about Knox, or Polk, or Hood, or Leonard Wood, or any of the other places where men he has known took basic. But basic is basic. Drill sergeants. It's all the same. He nods. This conversation is beginning to feel excruciating. He can't remember the last time he'd had a conversation like this with a newbie. After he had been here a few months he had stopped asking the clerks at the PMO about their history, their military training. It was all the same.

"How did you get that scar?" Dugan says, and Palmer looks down at the scribble of sewn flesh that is no longer as stark as it had been a year earlier. Buried under a tan, it seems to have continued with its healing process so that people rarely mention it or even seem to notice it.

"I had an accident in a judo class when I was stationed at the Presidio last year," Palmer says. "I was in the hospital for a while." It's been almost a year since he had described the accident to anyone in detail, since an evening in the Oakland enlisted men's club when he had drunk with three strangers, newbies like himself going to Vietnam. He tells Dugan about the accident but doesn't describe the things that led up to it. The reason for it. The man who broke his arm and who was once a friend. Palmer has never seen him since. Was it an accident? He will never know. He doesn't tell Dugan about the woman who was caught in the middle of that lovesick high-school crap. After the accident he never heard from her, and knows he'll never see her again. The biggest regret of his life. He misses them both.

After they step out of the mess hall Palmer tells Dugan he can sack out for an hour. "That's what I'm going to do. The PMO clerks get an hour and a half for lunch. You have to be back at the office by thirteen hundred," then wonders why he didn't say one o'clock. Afraid Dugan wouldn't comprehend it? Palmer never articulates military time if he can help it.

And then, as he is walking down the street toward his barracks, he sees something that pulls him up short. He stops walking and stands and stares at a man in fatigues as faded as his own coming out of the 109th headquarters office and walking down the far side of the street in the direction of the enlisted men's club. It is a man he recognizes, though he doesn't know his name. A man who had served at the Presidio last year.

Shorter than Palmer, round-shouldered, his hair is jet black and his nose and lips have an outthrust, mole-like quality as familiar as a snapshot from a photo album. A guy who had been a newbie during the month before Palmer had left, and who had looked so young he had seemed a kid too young even to be in the army, and there he is walking down the street with a querulous look on his face. Palmer is staggered by this coincidence, more so than he had been last year when Krouse and the others had reentered his life.

The man slows, gazes at the dark screened entrance to the EM club, and Palmer has the urge to call out to him, to say something to him, but what would he say? He doesn't even know the name of this man who had been in the third platoon, had bunked upstairs in the same wing where Thorpe had bunked before he committed suicide. The man removes his faded cap, habit among men who have been in the army a long time, men entering buildings, and the memory of this GI grows even stronger with the revealed shape of his scalp, his round-shouldered posture, the gait of this soldier whom Palmer had never once spoken to at the Presidio but had trained with, practiced riot-control, and watched dull class-room movies. It excites him to see someone out of his past, as though he had until now believed the past dead and buried. He never thought he would ever see anyone from the Presidio again. But he just stands there and watches as the man disappears through the doorway. What would he say to him? Too late to forge a new friendship. The man is likely here for out-processing at battalion. Maybe he had been stationed in Anh Khe or Pleiku, and is passing through Qui Nhon alone just as Palmer will soon be traveling alone through Phu Cat and Cam Ranh Bay and Fort Lewis.

He goes on to his barracks and sits on his bunk, removes his boots, lies down and switches on his fan, and wonders if he ought to have said something. But what would he have said? The conversation would probably have grown excruciating. It's too late to forge new friendships, too late for that or anything else. Let the past stay dead and buried even if it won't stay dead and buried. He never wants to talk about the Presidio again.

CHAPTER 45

Though he no longer has a job to go to, Palmer awakens on Tuesday morning at ten to seven but doesn't open his eyes. He hears all around him the muted groaning and sighing of men rising and dressing and walking out of the barracks to go to their jobs, the PMO clerks as well as the scattering of battalion clerks who have moved in and who sleep near the front of the barracks. All of the PMO clerks claimed bunks near the back door early on as though emulating the cave that they had lived in during their time at Camp Quincey.

He keeps his eyes closed and tries to drift back to sleep but it's not in him. Springs squeak. Boots thump concrete. He senses men trudging past the end of his bunk, hears the soft sound of the screen door opening but not banging closed, the rusted spring so old and slack that it serves no real purpose. Even though he is as wide awake as he ever is at this time of day, he remains in his bunk another fifteen minutes, relaxing under the breeze of his fan that he will be selling to a newbie soon. The translucent blue plastic blades of the fan are covered with dusty scum raked from the humid air, collected like moss since the last time he cleaned it. He will clean it again before selling it. A last little job to be taken care of before moving on, like the out-processing that will begin today, the thought of which motivates him finally to throw his poncho liner off his sweating body and sit up. Time to go.

Missy Cue and Missy Nu enter the barracks just as he is heading for the door, and they squeal with laughter seeing him here instead of at work. "You beaucoup lazy huh?" Missy Nu says. She has a pretty face, a body like a scarecrow, walks bowlegged as so many Vietnamese women do, house girls anyway. Missy Cue is heavy. Palmer has been told that obesity in Vietnam is a sign of wealth.

"I leave Qui Nhon two days," Palmer says.

"Choi oi," they say in unison. How many GIs have these two hardworking little women said goodbye to in their lives? Missy Cue earned ten dollars a month from him during the past year, about a hundred dollars. He will give her an extra ten before he leaves. He wishes he could give her more, like a plane ticket to America. When the communists finally come, she will still be working hard but doing who knows what.

The street is silent when he steps outside, but for a bit of noise up near the 109th motor pool at the end of the block where jeeps are coming and going. He eats at a table by himself in the mess hall where a few lingering GIs sit over cups of coffee while the KPs in their colorful flowered blouses carry trays to the kitchen for washing. Almost made it through Vietnam without pulling KP, then he wonders if GIs pull KP down in Cam Ranh Bay. It takes him a moment to recall—when he was in Long Binh the KPs were Vietnamese women too. He had only raked gravel, mopped latrines, burned shit. A general's idea, no doubt, keep the men busy to take their minds off their situation. Only a general would think something like that. What the hell would he expect idle GIs to do, stage riots out of boredom? They knew the situation when they came here, and anyway all the rioters stayed home. This makes him think of the riot-control training he had undergone at the Presidio. He drinks off the last of his coffee and gets up from the table. Time to go.

Out-processing involves a bit of traveling around, so he
has to ask Sgt. Ebbets if he can have the keys to the maverick
to take care of business. The PMO clerks have to ask now, it
wasn't like that when Sgt. Ancil was here. The keys had hung
in an open box on a wall above Ancil's desk and the men
could take them whenever they wanted, but now they have
to go through the operations sergeant. Change of command.
There's always new bullshit rules. He feels like a teenager
asking his dad for the keys to the car, feels foolish with his
excuse at the ready in the back of his mind: But dad, I have
to *out-process.*

Sgt. Ebbets gives up the keys but tells Palmer he would
like the jeep back in the parking lot before noon. If Palmer
still has out-processing to go through, he can come back for
the jeep after lunch. Palmer nods. Six days and a wake-up and
he will be in Fort Lewis. Phil spent four months there, is still
in Hawaii. The last letter from him described a two-week-
long bivouac on "the big island" as Phil called it, camped on
the steep side of a mountain. It rained a lot. Rivulets trickled
down the hillsides into the tents. The troops were miserable.
Palmer rarely writes to his brother. He doesn't know what to
say to someone who finds Hawaii a miserable place to live.

He drives over to battalion headquarters, walks inside
and tells a clerk that he is supposed to begin out-processing
today.

"Go see Specialist Archer."

Sp/5 Archer is seated at a desk in a corner of the big room.
The same Spec Five who had welcomed him to Vietnam a
year ago and is still here, and Palmer thinks he knows why,
although he doesn't know for sure and will never ask. Sp/5
Archer is a head. Palmer found this out at Christmas last year

when he was smoking pot with Loeb and the others upstairs, Archer drifted in and sat with them, toking a joint and listening to records on the headphones. Palmer believes that Archer is a man who will stay in Vietnam as long as he can because of the dope. It's a doper's paradise.

"Hi, Archer," he says, and the specialist looks up at him and grins. His face looks as tired and drawn now as it had a year ago, and Palmer attributes this to dope, maybe booze, maybe heroin. Archer is in his mid-thirties and maybe knows enough not to get hooked on heroin, maybe knows that he will never find another paradise like Vietnam.

"Greetings, short-timer," Archer says in that odd but somehow not pretentious disk-jockey tone of voice. "Out-processing?"

Palmer nods. He feels a little bit embarrassed talking to Archer, since he hasn't spoken to him in months and never smoked dope with him after that Christmas night. It occurs to him that Archer might be one of the reasons he had quit hanging out with the heads last year. He hadn't mistrusted the guy, but felt weird knowing a lifer doper.

Archer tells him to have a seat on a folding chair, then begins gathering together the paperwork that will have to be signed by the various agencies that Palmer will be visiting today. Archer keeps a tight-lipped grin on his face as he fills in the blanks with his typewriter. This is one lifer who knows things about Palmer that Palmer has never wanted any lifer to know.

"When you're finished, just bring the paperwork back to me. I'll have your orders cut and ready for your flight out of Phu Cat."

"Thanks, specialist," Palmer says, rising from his chair and grinning with the obsequiousness he always hides behind when talking to people he does not really want to talk to. Unarticulated secrets here. They both have something on each other, but there had always seemed to be a kind of trust among heads that Palmer had never noticed among juicers.

He exits battalion headquarters thinking of the soldier-of-the-month board that he had participated in at Camp Quincey, in a small room upstairs in the old battalion head-quarters building. Young troops like himself had come from all over the Central Highlands for the occasion. Still in a mild state of physical and mental shock from the terrible weekend, Palmer had felt absolutely dead inside as he stood among the eager STRAC troops waiting to get inside and compete for that three-day R&R in Danang. A kid from An Khe sidled up to him and quietly informed him that his own First Sergeant had given him the answers to the questions that they would be asked by the board. He grinned as he said this, and asked if Palmer had been given the answers too. Palmer was appalled, but wasn't sure by what. The whole scene was a joke. He lied and told the kid that he hadn't been given the answers, afraid the kid might view his response as an invitation to an excruciating conversation. When it came time for Palmer to stand before the board, all those sergeants and officers tossing polite questions at him, he must have said "I don't know" twenty times. Strangely he got three of the answers correct and hadn't even memorized them from the slip of paper that Sgt. Ancil had given him. The kid from Anh Khe won.

As he guides the maverick out of the main gate and along the civilian road toward the evacuation hospital, he is reminded of the process he had gone through at the Presidio before flying to Wichita to bury Thorpe. Running around the army base in the CQ jeep, fucking off as long as possible, and purchasing the same small black plastic briefcase that rests beside him on the shotgun seat, the best money he ever spent in the army, a handy holder for his significant paperwork. That's one Spartan aspect of the military that still appeals to him. The littlest things can make you so goddamn happy.

An SP and a TC are standing in the airfield gate shack, and they wave him through. He wonders when the hospital will pack up and move out of Qui Nhon. The war is winding down, not as many Americans dying every week as there had been a year ago when he first arrived and this was a bustling compound. It looks absolutely dead, the irony residing in things growing all over the place, weeds, vines, organic clutter that used to be trimmed by squads of Vietnamese overseen by a GI. The ARVN troops don't care that the jungle is creeping back. Palmer is damn glad he's not a newbie. Qui Nhon is a different city now than it was when he arrived.

There is no one in the outpatient clinic when he walks in. Used to be a bustling place too, with GIs seated on benches waiting to get their clap cured or whatever else might ail them. Before going to the operations office to pick up his medical records, he steps onto a massive scale in the hallway where he has been weighing himself ever since he had begun eating like a human being and lifting barbells. 188. He calculates that, with his boots and fatigues, lightweight as the rip-stop fabric is, he probably weighs in at 186 tops. The final weighing. He has put on twenty-six pounds since the day he got that letter from President Nixon, although most of it is beer fat.

A nurse, a female captain, hands him his medical records through a window in a wall, and as Palmer walks out of the evacuation hospital for the last time he feels a headiness generated by the folder in his hand, the first bit of paperwork in his out-processing. He climbs into the jeep and slips the manila folder into the briefcase feeling as if he is gathering pieces of a jigsaw puzzle with a portrait of his discharge on it. If he were still drinking, tonight, and tomorrow, and every night until he gets on the plane to Fort Lewis, he would be drunk, maybe as drunk as on that terrible weekend when he still had as long to go as he had already been here, six months, when it seemed as if he had been here a year.

He makes the circuit past the old Camp Quincey site on the asphalt road that isn't traveled much anymore by Americans. Anyone traveling to Port Beach for an R&R can enter or leave Camp Redstone by the PX gate farther toward the mountains, and there isn't much of anywhere else to go in this city. He slows as he drives past his old compound. The MP station is gone, the battalion headquarters building, the dayroom, his old barracks, all gone. The structures have been replaced by small narrow one-story ARVN barracks. Half of the old quartermaster buildings are gone, and the rest are in the process of being torn down. He wonders if they will tear down that beautiful high-ceilinged tiled flag-stoned enlisted men's club and replace it with a bamboo hut. What's with these ARVN anyway? The compound looks as fragile and vulnerable as it is. Someday the communists will be living there. Maybe the ARVN just want to get rid of the evidence of collaboration, knocking down all the big green American buildings. Will the South Vietnamese who cooperated with the U.S. Army get in trouble? Anh punished maybe for typing accidents for the capitalist imperialists. But then everybody down here is living off the American army in one way or another and Hanoi can't help but know it. He rolls past his old compound and heads on down the road toward the PX, accelerating now. Strange to see his old compound gone, flattened, cleared of his former presence. He feels a tug of ludicrous nostalgia, as though he has been robbed of something he did not value, and in fact hated. But then the thing he had really hated was the slow march of time. Camp Quincey would have been an okay place to live if there weren't any VC in the mountains.

He enters Camp Redstone through the PX gate but doesn't stop at the PX as he would have at any other time, even if there was nothing he needed or wanted to buy. He always stopped by the magazine rack and checked out the same weird skin magazines that he had seen in the PX shops of basic and AIT, black-and-white pictures of women in garter lingerie. His father's pinup girls. Then looked for a paperback to read. The dayroom at Camp Quincey had been full of used paperbacks, like the old USO. He had never had any problem finding a good book to read, but he hardly ever read a contemporary novel unless it was something famous, like *Rosemary's Baby*. He always waited until the passage of time and the opinion of the critics had weeded out the new novels that weren't worth reading. He'd finally read *Catch-22* in MP school and it was pretty old by then. The stamp of approval of time. Gilchrest had loaned him a copy and said quit reading those Doc Savage novels and try this.

He drives past the PX and out onto a dirt-two-track that curves across a weed field, the same route he had taken on the day Detty killed that child. Mueller already gone. Palmer had felt robbed when Mueller left Vietnam early to go to college, since Mueller had been a newbie. People coming and going, Provost Marshals, operations sergeants, with Palmer stuck like a rock at the bottom of a slow-moving stream. But he nevertheless wants to stay until the 365th day, like policing up the very last cigarette butt on a parade ground. Clean.

He drives to the finance center to pick up his records, and as he stands at a counter waiting for a Spec Four to haul them out he thinks of the day he went to the finance office at the Presidio to get money for his flight to Wichita, to accompany the body of Sp/4 Thorpe home for burial. The clerk had told him to remember to keep all of his receipts so he could be reimbursed for his travel expenses. He had done that, had made a small collection of receipts, but then never took them to the finance office for reimbursement. He threw them all away.

The RE-UP office is in a small building next to battalion headquarters on the MP compound, down at the end of the block where the fence cuts the road off from the civilian road, the concertina wire cluttered with papers and rags that have collected during the past few weeks and that no one has tried to spruce up. He never sees any squads of Vietnamese workers attending to the perimeter of Camp Redstone. He parks the jeep and goes inside where a captain is seated alone in an impeccably appointed office. Everything neat and tidy and in its place. There are drawn curtains on the windows. The captain's fiefdom. He's a small man. Palmer had seen him around the battalion area at Camp Quincey, one of those officers who seem to go to extreme lengths to look extra sharp, almost dapper. Boots polished to an obsidian gleam.

Razor creases in his fatigues. His haircut is immaculate, squared off at the back of the neck, but longish and not a bristle-cut lifer crop. He is sitting absolutely erect, looking at papers on his desk when Palmer enters with his cap in his hand.

"Good afternoon, sir," Palmer says, approaching the desk. "I'm out-processing today and I was told to come here to get some paperwork signed."

The captain looks up at him and doesn't say anything for a moment. Then he nods once and says, "I don't suppose you want to reenlist."

Palmer almost laughs out loud. What a salesman. "No, sir, I don't," smiling obsequiously.

The man nods twice and asks for his out-processing papers. They have to be signed just to show that Palmer has been here. Who would come here if he didn't have to? The captain signs it briskly, as if he is irritated at having to perform this small chore endlessly as the battalion RE-UP officer. He has a slight resemblance to Franklin Pangborn, especially in the way he quickly hands the paperwork back to Palmer, jabs it at him, holds it stiff-armed in the air until Palmer takes it saying thank you sir. Palmer turns and walks outside. What a job for a captain. Missy Anh could do that job.

He climbs into the jeep, tucks the briefcase beneath the shotgun seat, and starts the engine. There are only a few small jobs left, and he is going to stretch them out until eleven-thirty, and it is not yet ten o'clock. He has to go to the barracks and collect everything to be shipped home, paperbacks mostly, some clothing, photo albums, and radio/cassette, take it all to a place where it will be packed in a crate and shipped home on a separate flight. He'll be sending the crate to his parents' home in Nebraska. He doesn't trust Mike to be home if a delivery truck shows up at the basement apartment. Then over to the Chase Manhattan bank where he has two thousand bucks saved up. Earned almost thirty-six hundred while he was over here. Where did the other sixteen hundred go? Did he spend it on beer? He quit drinking six months ago, but if he hadn't he would be lucky to be taking home five hundred, apparently. He owns almost nothing. Where does money go?

He drives on up the street toward his barracks, thinking how out-processing is so different from all the other forms of processing he has experienced in the army, usually in the company of other GI's, sometimes hundreds of them as in basic, with everyone going through physicals or collecting their uniforms and equipment. He is alone in this, just as he was alone when he came to Vietnam, would have been alone throughout that entire trip had it not been for his encounter with Krouse and the others. Funny about Krouse. Pleaded poverty, then spent five borrowed bucks on a massage and admitted it without even being asked. Shit-eating grin on his face. A total lack of self-awareness that had flabbergasted Palmer, but at the same time there was something in it that Palmer recognized. Cadging five bucks for a massage was something he himself might have done, but you keep it a secret from the guy who loaned you the fin. Annoying amateurishness. There was something childish about the guy's confession at his brush with sexuality, the need to brag at the risk of looking like an idiot. Krouse was not one with Beetle Bailey.

CHAPTER 46

The morning cough and clearing of throats, the slither of boots laced and the click of belt buckles, the sensation of bodies moving past his bunk and out the front door, Palmer comes to consciousness, opens his eyes to see a single clerk moving past his bunk and heading out the door. The barracks goes silent. His last day in Qui Nhon. An occasion for a hangover at one time in his life. He might have sat up until midnight drinking Budweiser and keeping everybody awake at one time in his life. Would probably have started shouting, "Short!" as so many men do when their date of expected return from overseas draws near. An obnoxious declaration that everybody tolerates because they all know it will one day be their turn to holler, "Short!" accompanied by sparse laughter. It is an old joke that begs a response, and if nobody likes the man hollering it, there will be only a polite silence. Palmer has never hollered it. He has never felt especially liked by the newbies, and would feel like an idiot bathed in polite silence. He hasn't gone out of his way to get to know anyone closely in six months. Sobriety has taught him just how little interest he has in the lives of other people, a revelation, since he had previously thought of himself as extremely interested in other people and their experiences, ambitions, dreams. But he knows now it was all pretense. You do what you have to do to make friends in this world. Ask them questions about themselves, get them talking, like hitting on a woman. Vietnam has taught him that the only thing he wants is to go home alive, has stripped him of most of his self-delusions.

He sits up in the silence and throws his camouflage cover off his body. Time to go. He switches off his fan which he was paid ten dollars for last night by a newbie clerk at battalion who bunks near the front door. He takes a sip of water from the canteen that he keeps on the window ledge that runs the length of the barracks, now that he no longer has an icebox. The water is warm. He caps it and sets it back on the ledge where it will stay after he has gone. He has taken almost everything back to the supply room. He hasn't had a mosquito net in a long time. The fan has worked adequately to keep the mosquitoes away. He had even returned his M-16 and ammunition to the arms room last night, on the off-chance that the VC would not overrun the city during his last night in Qui Nhon.

He goes to the shower room and brushes his teeth, shaves, showers, and when he gets back he stows his shaving kit in his duffel bag, locks it away, checks his briefcase for his travel orders. He has everything he needs. Money in his billfold, orders, his khakis packed away for the trip out of Cam Ranh Bay. All he has to do is go to the PMO and tell Sgt. Ebbets that he is ready to leave. Tachwitz has volunteered to drive him up to Phu Cat to catch his flight south. Palmer sits down on his bunk and looks around, but feels no nostalgia for this new though ancient barracks. Camp Quincey was his home throughout the year. This place still feels like a transient barracks, which is only appropriate since he has been in-transit since the day he was sworn in. That's the army. Kentucky. Georgia. San Francisco. Anchorage. Yokota. Long Binh. Qui Nhon. You're never anywhere but headed somewhere else. He has been halfway around the world, farther west than his father ever got. But now that it's time to go he feels an odd sense of stasis, like a drunk suddenly in no hurry to sip his first poured shot of the evening. It's right there waiting for him. What was all the rush about? He remembered walking up to the quad at the Presidio one day and thinking that he had fourteen months left to go in the army and it seemed like it would never arrive. And now his ETS is moving slowly toward him like a ship cruising into dock but in fact will not dock, will keep drifting at that slow and endless cruising speed. Someday he will look back on this. The years will pass, but he cannot imagine any of them passing so slowly.

He gets up and steps to the back door and looks out one last time. The marijuana plant is still lying in the mud, trampled and boot printed. He's surprised that none of the heads have absconded with it, dried it out, crumbled it up, smoked it. Maybe there's something wrong with it. Too green. He looks through the cyclone fence in the direction of the PMO across the road beyond a far fence. Time to go.

He makes the short walk to the PMO, will come back for his duffel bag, but carries his briefcase with him, his orders both precious and safe tucked under his arm. For all his lightheaded giddy stifled joy at parting from his unit, a small part of his mind is concerned about the potential snafus. Losing his orders. Ambush on the way to Phu Cat. He has been to Phu Cat once, hauling two suspect VC women and a CID man. They drove past the base, got lost and had to ask a wandering South Korean soldier directions. He didn't speak English. "Phu Cat?" Palmer said over, and over, "Phu Cat?" until the man wearing the ROK uniform nodded and pointed back down the road.

Everyone is busy at his typewriter when Palmer walks in, just another day at the Provost Marshal's Office. Palmer again feels that peculiar sense of stasis, the strange desire not to leave, now that he can. A childish feeling, something oddly greedy about it. This leaving is mine and I want to hold onto it forever. He walks into the traffic section where PFC Dugan is studiously tapping away at the Smith-Corona with two fingers. Anh is seated at her desk with all ten digits splayed about her typewriter, looking at a hand-written traffic accident form. She doesn't see him enter. He looks at her for a moment, at her long black neatly combed hair flowing down to her waist as she leans to examine a word probably scribbled by an illiterate. Blue ao dai. Fingernails painted red. Working hard, or at least appearing to. It will take a couple weeks, he supposes, to train Dugan. Who knows but that Dugan might be the last traffic man in Qui Nhon before the communists come.

"Ciao, Anh," Palmer says, and Anh looks up at him, her face breaking into a smile.

"Ciao, Palmah."

"I've come to say goodbye to you," he says.

Anh sits back in her chair and brushes her hair back with a thumb. "You go home huh?"

"I go home."

"Choi oi," she says, and scoots her chair back and stands up and approaches him. She extends her hand, and says, "Icebox work numbah one."

Palmer takes her hand, shakes it. It has been almost a year since he last held her hand. Maybe she'll end up marrying a communist.

"You change electricity, huh?" Palmer says, still holding onto her hand.

"Aum," Anh says. "My mother is very happy."

Palmer nods, finally gives her hand an extra squeeze, probably demonstrating to this young Victorian lady that he is ill bred. He lets go and glances at the new traffic man.

"Good luck, PFC Dugan," he says, holding out his hand for a shake.

Dugan grins at him with a shy resignation. Palmer expects him to shrug his shoulders. Kind of embarrassing to be stuck in a place like this, stuck in time, like a jail sentence, waiting for his own circuit of the sun to be completed. Well—that's that.

He goes through the office shaking hands and saying goodbye to the clerks, a few of whom he has known for almost six months, then goes to Sgt. Ebbets and tells him that he is ready for Tachwitz to drive him to Phu Cat.

Sgt. Ebbets stands up from his desk, a smile stretching his cheeks, revealing his teeth. It seems only to be the younger black GIs who wear those engraved gold-caps. Palmer has never seen a cap on the tooth of a man older than himself, but then he has never been around that many black people, that many black lifers.

"You have yourself a good trip home, Specialist Palmer," Sgt. Ebbets says, giving Palmer a solid lifer handshake. Palmer feels that he is getting out just in time, has always felt that he and Ebbets were destined for a collision, but only because he has collided with so many sergeants. Sherman. Ancil. Benedetti. Authority figures have always grated on his nerves.

"Thank you, Sergeant," Palmer says, and has the fleeting desire to apologize to Sgt. Ebbets for the things he might have done. Sort of wishes he could apologize to Sgt. Ancil too, and to Sgt. Sherman for having been such a total fuckup, now that's it's all over. What was all this about anyway? Sidetracked for two years, wearing a green costume and following orders barked by strangers. He recalls taking it all so seriously at some point back at the beginning. Maybe only the infantry can take it seriously.

Tachwitz drives him over to the barracks, then drives alone to the arms room to get his M-16 for the trip. Palmer goes into the barracks to get his duffel bag. Missy Cue and Missy Nu are squatting by the front door ironing fatigues as he walks in.

"Ciao Cue, ciao Nu," he says, stopping to look down at them.

"Choi oi, Palmah, you go home now?" Nu says.

"Aum, go home."

"You go home kiss your girlfriend huh?" Cue says.

"Aum, beaucoup kisses," Palmer says, and the two house girls scream with laughter like all the women of the world.

"Cue, come over here a minute, okay?" Palmer says. "I want to tell you something."

Cue sets her Westinghouse iron upright and rises, follows Palmer down to the area where his bunk has been stripped, the mattress rolled to the head of the bed. His steel helmet and flak jacket rest on the bare springs. He reaches into his fatigue jacket pocket and pulls out ten dollars' worth of MPC and hands it to her.

"I souvenir you, Cue, okay? You number one house girl."

Cue drops her eyes but does not hesitate to take the ten dollar gift. She has children at home. Her husband is somewhere in Kontum, fighting the communists. "Cam on, Palmah," she says. Thank you. When Palmer had first arrived in Vietnam he had thought about getting hold of a book on how to speak Vietnamese, but the notion faded along with all the other ambitions of his life. He figured he would die here anyway. He had managed to shoot only two reels of movie film, and now wishes he had shot more. But he hadn't expected to ever view the footage.

He shakes hands with Cue, puts on his flak jacket and steel pot, then hoists his duffel bag over his shoulder. He walks to the end of the barracks where Nu stands up suddenly giggling and reaches out and takes his hand and shakes it with an exaggeration that almost has the appearance of mockery, her right elbow flying up and down as though she is imitating an American. Maybe the Vietnamese never shook hands until Westerners arrived on their shores. "Ciao Nu," he says, then turns and looks back down the aisle. But he has no feeling for this ancient rotting damp-floored building. He had left all that back at Camp Quincey which is gone forever. He pushes open the screen door, steps outside, and tosses his duffel bag into the rear of the jeep.

CHAPTER 47

Palmer could have taken the wheel if he wanted to, but he lets Tachwitz chauffeur him to Phu Cat. Rolling out of the MP compound, Tachwitz starts to make a right turn to head for the PX gate, but Palmer asks him to turn left. "Let's go out the main gate," he says. "I want to drive by Camp Quincey."

Tachwitz turns left, follows the road down to the gate where the SP waves them through. Out and onto the road. Palmer looks at the Vietnamese wandering the street, at a child running along with a tiny kite that won't fly. He lets Tachwitz drive because it's hard to see things when you're driving and he wants to see these last things. They pass the airfield with all its hopeless barbed-wired, pass the TMP where he once had visited Motor Pool Mary. That place has been shut down. Prostitution in the city has taken a hit. Tachwitz turns right onto the road that passes Camp Quincey. Even with the ARVN barracks the landscape beyond the fence seems flat without those two-story green buildings. Everything has been torn down except the enlisted men's club out there at the edge of the sea. Tachwitz slows as they pass the gate where two TC stand inside a small shack, different from the shack where Palmer had marked time last year. Aldhoff lied about going on guard duty, went down to the TMP to visit Madame K. Everything's gone. Palmer twists around to look back as they pass by, then turns around and looks up ahead toward the Port Beach gate. Port Beach is still active though he supposes it will be shut down soon. Who would come to

this city for an R&R now? Sgt. Ancil once said that Port Beach
ought to be open only to Infantry for R&R. He'd been a grunt
in the Korean War.

They pass by and Palmer looks off to his right where the
white elephantine shell of the PX stands glaring in the morning sunlight, his favorite mercantile. Going inside had been
like going home though all he ever seemed to buy was beer.
Didn't go as often after he'd quit drinking, but he still made
the Coke runs for the PMO. It was like the time he'd quit
drinking at the Presidio, when he had to think up things to
do at night.

They pass by and head down the road to the hairpin turn
where the dirt road breaks away and winds to the top of
the AFVN mountain. Tachwitz guides the jeep around the
asphalt hairpin, slowing for traffic, Vietnamese on Hondas or
in minibuses, the rattle of deuce-and-a-halfs bouncing by with
their ARVN drivers who have no respect for or even sense of
traffic rules, or so it seems to Palmer. The most peculiar statistic
that he had derived from the eight hundred or so traffic
accidents that he had processed during the past year was that
in most cases the Americans were at fault, which struck him
as inexplicable, since he knows first-hand what wild drivers
the Vietnamese are.

They follow the road out into the countryside which will
take them to QL-1 and the twenty mile trip north to Phu Cat
which he doesn't hate now as much as he had hated it in the
past when he was forced to go out to QL-1 to set up speed
traps, or that time he drove the POWs. He hates being out on
the road, hates riding along QL-1 where practically everybody
he sees is wearing black pajamas, young men on Hondas

racing by, men and women strolling along the shoulders of the road. Even the Vietnamese soldiers in their jeeps seem suspect to him. An ARVN uniform would be a good disguise for a VC. Tachwitz's M-16 is resting on the floor of the jeep within arm's reach. Palmer tries not to think about the weapon. Four days and a wake-up, that's what he tries to think about.

The landscape at the edge of the city is familiar from the time he had been a road MP, and the landscape beyond the city, out toward QL-1, is familiar from the times he had been sent out to nail up speed-limit signs, or set up speed traps, or drive to the Phu Tai MP station for one reason or another. The army base at Phu Tai has a terrible PX, a little wooden building with practically nothing in it, like in a movie about the Great Depression. Soap, shaving cream, Kleenex. But he could never resist going in just to check things out. A PX is America to him.

Then they are out on QL-1 where the traffic is medium and constant. They pass the spot on the road where he had painted lines for the speed trap, a Huey clocking GIs. Pop-stands dot the road all the way to Phu Tai, Vietnamese selling warm Cokes or orange soda, cigarettes, Salem, Winston, PX contraband that never gets confiscated by the Vietnamese police the way criminals get busted in America for selling illegal shit, dope, pot, skag. Probably all the cops here are on the take, all the politicians, maybe even the president. Who is the President of South Vietnam? Palmer doesn't know.

The road eventually winds through a landscape of trash, both sides of the road stacked with acres of low hills of garbage where Vietnamese poke through the rubbish all day long searching for the kinds of things that Palmer himself searched for when he was a kid exploring the alleys of Denver. Cool junk. Toys. Small fires flicker on the hills, and the Vietnamese wear white scarves across their mouths like bandits. Sometimes the smoke gets so thick that drivers can't see the road, Palmer has had this happen to him, like ground fog on a Denver highway and the next day you read in the paper about a fifty car crackup on Interstate-25. He hasn't seen a civilian newspaper in a year. All those stories that he will never know he missed. Riots. New rock bands. Is Paul really dead? What are Nancy and Sluggo up to? Beetle Bailey gets top billing in the *The Pacific Stars and Stripes*.

After they pass the road leading into Phu Tai and head on up north, Palmer gets that clammy feeling that comes from being out in the wilderness where the war once was. Signs are planted all along the road written strictly for Americans saying Don't Worry This Area Has Been Cleared by such-and-such an Infantry battalion meaning the communists have all been routed and GIs don't have to worry about getting ambushed by VC along this road, which Palmer assumes is a crock. Words are shit, are meaningless noise. The AFVN compound shoots at VC every two months.

Heavy trees and bushes crowd the asphalt road along one stretch. In some places he can see the roof of a hut forty or fifty feet off in the foliage, the real Vietnam as he thinks of it, people living like they did when the Dutch showed up. The Vietnam of the war. Women stand by the road and stare without expression as the jeep passes by. How much contact do these people have with Americans? They don't live in a city like Missy Anh, but then the war isn't really in this part

of the country. The faces have no expressions, which Palmer
interprets as dislike. It pissed him off to see that Americans
Go Home banner during the protests after Detty killed that
child. Well, I'm going home. We're all going home. It's all
yours.

The Air Force compound at Phu Cat is an interesting
place, as un-Vietnam looking as any place Palmer has seen
over here. It has a great PX. On the day that he brought the
two female POWs he was exhilarated to find the Phu Cat PX
more well-stocked than the Qui Nhon PX. The ceiling was
lower, the aisles brighter and longer.

On the asphalt streets the enlisted men walk around with
the cuffs of their fatigue pants unbloused, the pant legs
covering the ankles of their jungle boots. They look like slobs
to Palmer's MP eye, like they don't take the military seriously,
although he doesn't know why this attitude should bother
him.

There are lawns in Phu Cat, acres of mown grass with
two-story buildings on the tops of rises, barracks that look
exactly like college dormitories off in the distance, as unmilitary a base in a war zone as Palmer could imagine, and he
loves it, wishes he had been stationed here with all the Air
Force doggies so his illusion of not being in Vietnam at all,
underscored by his ludicrous job at the PMO, would have
been enhanced even more so. But for the hammer of heat that
plagues the entire country, it would have been like serving
on a campus in Southern California. The streets have curbs.

Tachwitz drives to the air terminal, parks outside a big
hollow building bustling with the traffic of GIs and even
Vietnamese waiting for flights. It's like the Qui Nhon of last

year, a noisy crowded carnival. Palmer climbs out of the jeep and removes his steel pot for the last time, sets it on the floor of the backseat. He pulls his cap from his back pocket and slaps it onto his head, then shrugs his flak jacket off his shoulders for the last time and sets it on the floor next to the steel pot. Tachwitz grabs Palmer's duffel bag out of the rear and says, "I'll walk you inside."

A foolish feeling to have another man carry his duffel bag, but Palmer walks along with him and opens his briefcase to make sure he's got his travel orders, the very last thing a GI in-transit needs. After they get inside the high-ceilinged crowded terminal, Tachwitz sets the duffel bag on the floor. He sticks out his right hand and says, "Well, I guess this is it. Have a good flight, Palmer."

Palmer shakes his hand. Parting is strange. Seems like there ought to be more to it, but he doesn't know what else there could be except saying goodbye, knowing he'll never again see any of the men he has said goodbye to today. What do you say to your buddies anyway? Kind of embarrassing to leave them as fucked over as you were all year.

"Thanks," Palmer says, then pauses a moment not knowing what else to say. Good luck? Hope you don't die before your tour is up. "You ought to stop in at the PX," he says. "I've been in there. It's great."

"I'm going to do that," Tachwitz says with a grin, and they leave off shaking. That's that.

"So long, Palmer."

Palmer raises his hand, slices the air briefly, lets it drop. Tachwitz walks away. Seems like there ought to be more.

He turns and looks around the big hollow room. A lot of big hollow rooms when you're in-transit. He starts looking for signs that will tell him where to go. That's one of the few nice things about the military, there's always gigantic signs posted all over the place telling baffled travelers where to go.

He reaches down and hoists his duffel bag over his shoulder and begins making his way through the crowd toward an information desk where two Spec Fours are answering questions, pointing fingers, shrugging shoulders at GIs standing in line. The clammy feeling that he always gets in his gut when he has to fly begins growing. He'd been able to ignore it on the trip up to Phu Cat but now that he's in the terminal there's nothing to take his mind off it. He hates flying. The thought fills him with more dread even than seeing his name on that roster at the Presidio had last year. Orders for Vietnam, but the shock wore off after a week. There was always the possibility that he wouldn't die over here, but an airplane, Christ, you're trapped inside a tin can going five hundred miles an hour. Then he sees Sp/5 Saunders striding across the room.

Palmer stops walking and stares at the man, Saunders had gone home four months ago.

"Saunders!" he says, and the specialist turns his head as he weaves his way between moving bodies. A grin breaks out on his tanned cheeks and he changes directions, marches right up to Palmer and says, "Palmer! What are you doing here?"

"I'm going home."

"Jee-Zus, Palmer, you put on weight."

"I gained a couple pounds. What are you doing here? Did you reenlist?" Then notices that, while Saunders is wearing jungle fatigues, there is no insignia on his uniform.

"Naw hell, I ain't in the army no more," Saunders says. "I sell automobiles over there in the corner," He points, and Palmer turns and looks across the room toward a booth set up, with flyers and pamphlets tacked to the wall and spread across the countertop, Fords, Chevys, Chryslers. "If you want to a buy a car before you go home, I can get you a hell of a discount."

Palmer looks back at Saunders and doesn't know how to respond to this. He's heard of these car deals, you can get a forty percent discount through the PX or some damn thing, or maybe just no sales tax, he doesn't remember, but why the hell would a man come back to Vietnam?

"How did you end up doing that?" Palmer says, hoping his question doesn't come out wrong—why the fuck are you engaged in such idiocy, Saunders?

"There ain't no jobs back home," Saunders says. "So I decided to come back here and sell cars."

No jobs? What the hell is this guy talking about? And who wants a job anyway? Isn't this the man who said you ought to go to college on the GI Bill? But Palmer doesn't say any of these things. Mostly he's just pleased to see a familiar face. In-transit is a lonely status. "So how's the car business?" he says, and Saunders pokes a thumb at the ceiling and whistles.

"That's great," Palmer says. "Well hell, it's good to see you again, Saunders. I'd like to stick around and shoot the shit but I gotta go check on my flight," pointing at the information desk. "I'm headed down to Cam Ranh Bay."

"All right, buddy, you have a good trip home, huh?" Saunders says, holding out his hand. They shake, and Palmer wonders if it's illegal for Saunders to be wearing jungle fatigues when he isn't even in the army. But it's only a passing thought. It'll probably take a while before he stops thinking of life in terms of regulations.

Saunders gives him a kind of half-baked salute before he strides off across the room toward the booth where enlisted men are fingering flyers. Palmer gets in line at the information desk and shows the Spec Four his papers. The man tells him that his flight will be leaving for Cam Ranh Bay in two hours.

CHAPTER 48

His duffel bag tagged and tossed on a table at the baggage counter, Palmer wanders out of the terminal and looks across the mown landscape of Phu Cat and decides to go to the PX. He walks down a street with rounded curbs of asphalt lining the grassy lawns. It's like bits of America drifting toward him, now that he is on his way home, just as the inside of the PX is like a K Mart when he steps inside and feels the air-conditioning cooling the sweat on his face. Two hours to kill. He wanders up and down the aisles looking at all the things he has always looked at in PXs and never bought. Massive stereo systems. Lawn chairs. Over in one corner of the building stand tall shelves with boxed TV sets stacked one on top of another. He walks over just to stand in the midst of all this Americana. It's like a warehouse here, like a warehouse he once worked in where chairs and couches were stacked for deliveries. Sofa beds. He had gotten stronger carrying those fuckers into Denver houses than he ever got from lifting barbells as a teen.

He hears a muted booming sound behind him, and when he turns around he sees Command-Sergeant Major Benedetti leaning against a cardboard box that he had just slapped with his forearm. "Specialist Palmer!"

Palmer is shocked to see the man standing here in the PX, and feels a tad leery.

"Hello, Sergeant," Palmer says, walking toward the man who stands erect, his Mafioso torso leaning away from the box. "What are you doing here? Tracked me down? "

"I'm headed home, Specialist."

Nonplused, Palmer gazes at the man for a moment, then says, "I didn't know your DEROS was coming up, Sergeant."

"Oh yeah," the sergeant says, rubbing his belly. "I'll be leaving tomorrow. How about yourself?"

"I've got a flight down to Cam Ranh in a couple hours."

"Gonna buy a TV?"

Palmer chuckles. "No Sergeant, just looking around."

"Me too. Where's home, Palmer?"

Palmer hesitates a fraction of a second, then says, "Colorado."

Benedetti nods. "My home is New Jersey. Are you married, Palmer?"

"No, Sergeant. I'm single."

"Got a girlfriend waiting at home?"

"Oh yeah," he lies.

"That's good. I got a wife and four kids waiting for me." Palmer nods. He doesn't know what the hell to say.

"Won't be long," Benedetti says. "Looking forward to seeing your family I'll bet, huh?"

"Yes, Sergeant."

"Got any brothers or sisters?"

"Three brothers and four sisters."

Sgt. Benedetti laughs out loud. "That's great. Sometimes I meet men who don't have any brothers or sisters and I think, you know, I think it would be terrible to grow up as an only child. Nobody to compete with, nobody to fight with," and laughs again. "I got four brothers and a sister back home."

Palmer laughs along with him. Two obvious Catholics laughing about their big families.

"Well, you take it easy, Palmer," Sgt. Benedetti says, giving the cardboard another slap. "Have a good flight home."

"You too, Sergeant," Palmer says, and Sgt. Benedetti turns away and begins browsing the stereos.

Palmer casually walks away from the corner of the PX, thinking that this was one of the weirdest encounters he's ever had. Almost like being hounded by a salesman with all those personal questions. Why he didn't he know Sgt. Benedetti was leaving battalion? The cadre live in a different world. Like officers, the powers that be come and go. Then it occurs to him that he should have told Benedetti that he had run into Saunders. He turns and looks back, but Sgt. Benedetti has disappeared. Strange deal. He decides to go to the magazine stand and leaf through a few skin rags, and maybe look for a paperback to take with him on the plane. He hopes, he doesn't run into Sgt. Benedetti again. It's almost as hard to talk to high-ranking sergeants as officers.

A crowd of GIs are leafing through the magazines, some of them wearing dark green fatigues, a lesser number wearing fatigues as pale as Palmer's own. Rather than elbowing his way through the crowd toward the latest issue of *Slammer* he goes to a rotating paperback rack standing alone and unattended. He begins scanning the titles, looking for something that might be easy to read on the excruciating flight across the Pacific. He had never been able to lose himself in a book very well on a flight, raising his head at the end of every paragraph to listen to the odd thumps and hissing noises coming from beyond the molded plastic shell of coach. But reading was better than staring out a window and succumbing to images of disaster that arose as unbeckoned from his brain as peculiar thoughts did when he smoked pot. No control over it. A novel was his best defense.

Love Story. He'd heard of that one. A bestseller that's been made into a movie. *Everything You Always Wanted to Know About Sex.* A doper back at Camp Quincey had a copy. Palmer flipped through it one evening while high on pot. The author said men lose consciousness momentarily during orgasm, but Palmer couldn't relate to that. Women get a rash on their chests when they come. Was the author making that up or what? *The Godfather.* An MP at the Presidio had read it and said he liked it, an E5, a Vietnam veteran whom Palmer had patrolled with on a graveyard shift. The man's wife planned to become a hospital administrator after she got her college degree. Who would even think to get a job like that? Palmer has no interest in the mafia but a recommended book is better than taking a chance on an unknown science fiction novel, which he's been thinking about picking up, but bad sci-fi is the worst. He wouldn't mind reading some Heinlein, but doesn't see any on the rack, and anyway he's read most of Heinlein. He decides to buy *The Godfather*, plucks it from the rack but continues to examine the books hoping that something more promising might come along, like flipping to the next page of a skin magazine. *Love Story* again with its red, white, and blue cover, and this makes him think of his home movies. He had hardly taken any movies at all over here, and now it's too late. His Bell-and-Howell is packed away in his duffel bag. Ought to have at least kept it for a record of his passage through Phu Cat and Cam Ranh Bay even if they would have been boring shots of army buildings, bunkers, barbed-wire. He had planned to make a film record of every place he went to in the army but had hardly taken any movies anywhere. A few in basic, MP school, the Presidio. A couple rolls at Camp Quincey, but every time he thought about digging his camera out of the Styrofoam case he became filled with ennui. Why bother? I'm going to die over here anyway. His father had kept two journals during World War II, had filled two blank books which had gold-embossed titles. *My Stretch in the Service.* He wonders now if the army gave those out to GIs for free or if his dad had bought them in a PX. Three and a half years of life in the South Pacific, captured in black cursive. New Guinea. The Solomon Islands. Now Palmer feels stupid, and walks away from the paperback rack knowing he will regret it someday. He had been the movie man in high school, making films of football games and parties and class picnics, but then when he finally arrives in some place actually worth capturing on film, he caves in to lethargy.

He decides to go to the electronics department and buy himself a snapshot camera. Get a few still-photos anyway—but wasn't that the problem with most of his army footage? Movies of things not moving. Barracks buildings. Lines of men. Parked jeeps. Authentic home movies, the kind that drive trapped party-guests insane, though The Lieutenant Pervert Show probably still holds up. He goes to the camera department and buys a Kodak Instamatic feeling like an idiot. His final week in Vietnam and he's gearing up for a photo-shoot at last.

He walks back to the air terminal unpackaging the box, dragging the camera out and examining his new toy. He sits on a folding chair in the terminal and reads the brief instruction manual, a good time-killer, then goes back outside and takes a few pictures of airplanes racing along the runway beyond a fence, still-photos of large objects moving fast. He'll never get his act together.

He goes back to the terminal and finds another empty chair and sits down and pulls out his copy of *The Godfather* and tries to read amid the noise of bodies passing in every direction within the terminal but finds it difficult, lifting his eyes at the end of paragraphs and looking at the fatigue-clad GIs and the Vietnamese crisscrossing the floor which glares, polished so long by rubber boots. Ten years? When was the American presence finally established, like the last town built in America before the westward expansion ended and the suburbs began spreading? All these bodies. Where are they going? Home, but for the Vietnamese. They're already home. He bows his head into the book determined to stick with it, to find out what all the excitement was about when it first appeared on the bestseller lists. He's leery of bestsellers. In high school everybody was reading *The Catcher in the Rye*, and he put off reading it for two months for that reason alone.

When his flight finally is called, he tucks the book into a fatigue pocket that was built to hold magazines of M-16 ammo, another pocket stuffed with his Instamatic. He stands up and tries to fight off the cruddy feeling of impending doom by simply going where he is told to go, putting his mind on a kind of hold. He joins a crowd of GIs walking out onto the tarmac and steps up into the rear of a C-130 and finds a seat along the side, just like the C-130 he'd ridden in to Qui Nhon last year, bucket of bolts that seems as old as WWII. When the rear door rises and is locked into place the shell of the plane is cast into a darkness that does not displease him. It's like sleep. He would just as soon be unconscious all the way to Fort Lewis. Same kind of flight crew fiddling around checking the straps on cargo stacked up down the center aisle. Cool as cucumbers. He tries to take reassurance from these casual men with microphones attached to their heads. A milk run for them. They fly all over Vietnam all year long. Why would God pick this plane? He hates the fact that he hates flying. He's never heard of a C-130 going down, then remembers the plane that crashed in Alaska last year. No use trying to outguess God. When the plane begins taxiing down the runway, he closes his eyes and leans back and resigns himself to his fate. What else can a warm body do? If I relax, the plane will go down. If I make it back to America alive I'll never fly again. Take a bus from Seattle to Denver.

When the C-130 lands at the airfield in Cam Ranh Bay, Palmer opens his eyes, all the energy that went into his apprehension made a mockery of by this milk run. Every time he steps off an airplane he feels an inexplicable sense of disappointment.

The air is hotter here in Cam Ranh, but this is as far south as he will be going. From here on the direction will be east. He follows the crowd into the terminal and starts looking around for a sign that will lead him to the transient center where he will begin waiting to hear his name called one last time, just like Long Binh, just like Oakland. A few days of shit details, a fifteen-hour flight, and then home. It all has the feel of a scam, the same mounting exhilaration that comes from getting away with something he never thought he would get away with.

CHAPTER 49

The bus pulls up adjacent to a small compound topped with barbed-wire. The gate is wide enough for only one man to pass at a time, and as Palmer steps down off the bus he sees sergeants in dark green fatigues standing around watching the men in pale fatigues filing through the gate. This is how he enters the 50th Compound. Through a narrow gate that leads to a building where each GI is handed a small plastic cup and is told to fill it with piss.

The building is arranged like a simpleminded maze, in that there are no doorways off to the left or right that a man might wander through in order to avoid the process. Palmer has heard about it, and wondered vaguely but not with too much worry whether he ought to be concerned about it. The piss test. Everybody leaving Vietnam has to take the piss test, although he isn't sure if it applies to officers or even high-ranking sergeants. Possibly not. The heroin epidemic is the scourge of the enlisted ranks. He takes his plastic cup from a Spec Four and walks into the latrine where dozens of GIs are standing before long troughs peeing into cups. The entire room is lined with troughs. A partition divides the room, probably so more troughs could be added. How many EM leave Vietnam every day? Thousands he supposes. The partition is three feet thick and does not rise all the way to the tin ceiling. There are two chairs on top of the partition, one at each end, and seated on each chair is an enlisted man in dark green fatigues, his head barely grazing the slant ceiling, watching the men pissing, making certain that there is no funny business with switched cups, traded urine. Newbies involved in an especially degrading shit detail, eyeballing cocks held with thumb and forefinger, plastic cups topped off golden. Palmer stands before a urinal, unzips and cranes his neck back to look up at a newbie who appears as uncomfortable and embarrassed as any human being he has ever seen. Thank God the man is wearing dark green fatigues. Thank God the shit detail is not handed out to veterans.

He fills his cup, zips up, carries his urine around the partition, following the maze, the tips of his finger and thumb growing warm against the flexible plastic wall. He sets the cup down on a counter where Spec Fours are overseeing this crucial end of the operation, making sure everyone's quota of piss is properly labeled. Palmer heard from an MP back at Camp Redstone that there's a barracks here at the 50th where GIs who are found to have heroin in their urine are held under guard, it's been more than six months since Palmer last snorted heroin, a fleck no larger than a match head, so he supposes his system has been purified, is clean, but he doesn't have much faith in his system, his body, his luck. Who knows? One tiny atom of opiate might make the difference, bobbing within the golden folds of that cup.

He takes a small slip of paper from a Spec Four and walks toward the exit which is the entrance to the 50th in the way that a turreted fairy-tale castle is the entrance to Disneyland. The Spec Fours inform everyone that they won't be hearing whether their urine is clean, only whether it's dirty. MPs will come looking for them with handcuffs. Their tour in Vietnam will be extended a few weeks. The best system the army has come up with for the drug problem in the war,

Palmer supposes. The Generals don't want any addicts stepping off planes in America and subsequently collapsing into withdrawal convulsions in their family living rooms. Eyes watering, pupils pinpoints, noses running. Skinny as skeletons. Maybe that happened a lot in the early years of the war. He wouldn't want to be in charge of trying to control access to the heroin that can be bought on any street corner or jungle hut. All he had to do was ask Motor Pool Mary, and she poked a vial through the cyclone fence. Twenty bucks. The only heroin he ever bought. He'd always borrowed a hit of skag from the heads at Camp Quincey, until they cut him out of their scene. Had never thought he would ever do a drug like heroin, or even pot, until he came here and figured he might as well see what it's all about. You never really know who you are until you think you're going to die. Then you don't die and you're stuck with yourself.

The troops file into a long wooden building, an auditorium, where they sit at long tables and are given a talk by a captain. The atmosphere in the place is jovial. Palmer can feel it. Not out of Vietnam yet but as close as they've ever been, the troops listen up while the captain tells them a little bit about the changes that have taken place in America, which doesn't interest Palmer. "One out of every five people on the streets of America today is a Jesus freak," the captain says, which sounds like such a fucking lie that Palmer starts tuning him out, starts thinking about going to the enlisted men's club and having a beer even though up to now he hadn't wanted to touch another rancid beer; wanted to wait until he got back to the United States where the beer is real and stays cold longer than it takes to drink it.

When Palmer tunes back in, the captain is explaining the procedures of the compound which aren't much different than those of Long Binh or Oakland. Keep the men busy with meaningless shit details, as if they couldn't hire Vietnamese to scrub the latrines like they used to at Camp Quincey. What's going to become of Papasan? Always suspected him of being a VC. The captain tells them that at the front of the room along the counter is a magazine that they can take with them called *Tour 365*, and asks that they take only one magazine apiece. When he finally lets them go, Palmer wanders up to the front of the room and looks at the magazine, decides to take one. Last souvenir. The captain told them that they will have to turn their MPC in at the finance office in exchange for greenbacks and coins, but they will be allowed to keep a few pieces of MPC for souvenirs.

After Palmer has exchanged his money, he walks out of the finance building flipping through his magazine. Artsy colorful painted cover with a grunt hunched holding an M-16. Medics in the background. A GI working with a welding torch. Inside he finds page after page of all the brigades that have served in Vietnam, with the unit patches in full color along the sides of the pages. He looks up the 18th MP Brigade and is surprised when he finds it, figuring the graphic artists who put this magazine together would have conveniently left the MPs out, since everybody hates the MPs. He flips a page and examines the 101st Airborne Screaming Eagle. 14,000 jumped into France on D-Day, according to the blurb. Here's the 25th Infantry Division, Phil's unit back in Hawaii, Tropic Lightning. Phil is scheduled to be discharged at the end of the year. He continues to flip through the magazine as he

walks across a broad stretch of naked earth where formations
are held three times a day, moving toward a building where
duffel bags and luggage have been brought in from the airfield.
The pages in his hands are like the summing up of his year.
Seems like there ought to be more. Then he sees Sergeant
Lattimore seated on a folding chair at a corner of a warehouse
building, watching the troops pass by.

Palmer slows his walk, is bypassed by other GIs. Lattimore
is smoking a cigarette, sitting with a leg crossed, looking at the
troops. The chair is right at the edge of the building, at the
edge of the flow of bodies, is masked by a bit of shade from
the eaves overhead. As Palmer steps closer, Lattimore's
features come into greater focus, that smidgen of a mustache,
the prominence of his slightly buck teeth, that Warren Oates
shape to his head, cheekbones, nose. Another person out of
his past. Palmer begins to feel a small bubble of laughter
rising in his esophagus. He had always known the army was
a small world, but where do these people keep coming from?

"Sgt. Lattimore," he says, and Lattimore raises his chin,
squints up at Palmer, his upper lip rising revealing more of
those long crooked teeth. The man doesn't recognize him.

"I met you last year at Camp Quincey up in Qui Nhon
when we were both new in-country," Palmer says. "I processed
in with you and a couple other guys. We ate lunch at the
enlisted men's club."

Palmer can almost see the gears going to work behind
Lattimore's dark eyes, memories being plucked from this
past year. What kind of memories does he have? He said he
was going to drive a V-100.

"Why shit yeah, I remember you, Palmer," and Sgt. Lattimore stands up from his chair grinning that ragged-lipped

Warren Oates grin and holding out his hand. "What are you doing here?"

"I'm going home, Sarge. I just got in today."

"Well hell, that's great."

"Why are you sitting here, sergeant?"

Lattimore shakes his head with disgust, looks around and sits back down on the chair and crosses his legs. "Aw, this is just a shit detail I got stuck on. I'm supposed to watch out for uniform violations among the enlisted men."

"Really?" Palmer says, the bubble bursting in his throat. He chuckles once, and hopes that Sgt. Lattimore isn't offended.

"Yeaaaah, I gotta sit here for an hour doing this bullshit," Lattimore says, taking a puff on his cigarette, then examining it for length. He flicks the ash off and begins field-stripping it.

"Did you drive V-l00s in An Khe?" Palmer says, moving around the chair, out of the flow of foot traffic.

"You better believe it," Lattimore says, grinning up at him. "Convoy escort."

Convoy duty: As close to combat as an MP can get, Palmer supposes, not counting cities being overrun. What was the name of that man at the Presidio who was stationed at the American embassy? He can't remember. "How long have you been here at the 50th?"

"I got in yesterday," Lattimore says, looking off toward the approaching men. Palmer wonders if Lattimore would really gig a man for a uniform violation. He doesn't seem like the type. But you never know about sergeants. "How long until you go home?" Palmer says, and Lattimore glances up at him like he isn't used to being around someone full of questions. Palmer has always been full of questions, and knows that they bother some people, but he doesn't care.

"Couple days," Lattimore says, "but I ain't going home. The army fucked up my orders. They're trying to send me to Fort Polk. But I'm supposed to be going to Germany. I'm so goddamn pissed about it that I'm gonna go to the fucking Pentagon to get my orders changed if I have to."

And suddenly the conversation grows dull to Palmer. Lattimore is no longer a personage out of his past but an ordinary GI filled with the pissant squawks of all soldiers. Like someone threatening to go to the Inspector General. Everybody thinks they have power. The army can do anything it wants to anybody. But then, he himself did get Phil's orders changed to Hawaii. The army doesn't really care what happens to anybody. It's all Spec Fours shuffling paperwork.

"Where's the baggage depot, Sarge?" Palmer says. He wants to get away from Lattimore but doesn't want to appear rude. Appearances are everything.

Lattimore leans forward and points around the side of the building with a thumb. "You go three buildings down and turn left," then leans back and looks up at Palmer.

"All right, thanks," Palmer says, looking off toward the parade of men. "I gotta go get my duffel bag. It was nice seeing you again, Sgt. Lattimore," and he holds out his hand. Lattimore grins at him, squints and raises his hand, they shake, and Palmer says have a good flight home. That's what Sgt. Benedetti had said. A handy phrase.

"You too, buddy," Lattimore says. "It was good to see ya," then leans back in his chair and starts digging around in his pocket for another smoke.

Palmer enters the parade and walks toward the baggage depot thinking of the men he has run into since he left Qui Nhon. And there was that guy from the Presidio he had seen at Camp Redstone but hadn't spoken to. Now he wishes he had. He might have asked if anybody else from the Presidio had come over here. Where's Vinton? Where's Mallory? Where are all his buddies from San Francisco? Beaudry has probably left Korea, might even be headed for Germany, re-enlisted for a three-year hitch. Did Tichener ever make it over here, him and his 1049 that he kept putting in for? The army really is a small world, but so far Palmer hasn't seen anybody that he especially wanted to see.

CHAPTER 50

The enlisted men's club is a bleak watering hole, the decor no different than a barracks. No beer signs, no jukebox, just tables on a tile floor, four by four uprights painted white, the bar itself just a counter along one wall. It's not a very big place, small like a cafe, but at least it's air-conditioned. Palmer walks farther inside and looks around. There are a lot of empty tables. He had eaten chow quickly in a mess hall where Vietnamese women pull KP, got out of there quickly and came here with his copy of *The Godfather* in his pocket, deciding to go ahead and have a beer and read his book in as much peace and quiet as he can find in a place where the men are generally ecstatic about having made it through a year without dying. He can feel it in the air wherever he walks on this vast and dusty compound. There is none of the gloom that had permeated Oakland, Long Binh, where everyone, Palmer assumes, thought he was going to die except the men who have no imaginations, the kind of men who lope through life burdened by optimism. He goes to the bar, but at the last moment orders a can of Coke, picks through his new coinage and pays with a real dime. Back to civilian life. He carries the can to a table and sits down, opens his paperback and reads a paragraph. For some reason he is not as put off by this story of violence as he had been by James Bond novels. Never did finish that Bond book he was trying to read at the Presidio, doesn't even know what became of it after the judo accident. The Coke is ice-cold, tastes good. That's one thing about the soft drinks, the flavor is the same as it is back home. He lights a cigarette and waits for the small rush of nicotine to enhance the ambience of the bar. The room has already filled up. Laughing men are hurrying in from the mess hall.

"Are those seats taken?" a voice says.

Palmer looks up at three men in faded fatigues. Young, tan, lean, they look down at him with inquisitive grins. Their boots are dusted red. "No," he says.

"Do you mind if we sit here?" one of them says. "All the other tables are taken."

"I don't mind," Palmer says, closing his paperback.

The men hurry to sit down, grabbing the last three empty seats in the house. One of the men places a pitcher of beer in the middle of the table. "Thanks a lot, man," he says. "Help yourself to the beer."

"Thanks, I'm drinking Coke," Palmer says. He looks at the camouflage patches on their sleeves but does not recognize the insignia, does not know what sort of units they are from. The men are giddy. They drink their beer quickly and start talking about their former unit which, as it turns out, is an infantry unit. Two of the men are Spec Fours and the third is a PFC. Coming home from Vietnam a PFC, which was what Palmer had started to think he would do along about his nineteenth month in service. Maybe the man had been busted in rank, but he isn't going to ask.

"Where were you guys stationed?" Palmer says, and they tell him An Loc.

"Where were you stationed?"

"Qui Nhon."

"That's up north, yeah. How was it up there?"

"Not much going on," Palmer says.

The men laugh. "What's your MOS?" one of them says, and Palmer says, "I'm an MP," and feels the tenor of their giddiness change but only slightly. Everyone hates the MPs, but this one just gave them the last three empty chairs in the house.

"An MP? Really?" another man says. "Did you like doing that?"

"Yeah, I did," Palmer says, then says, "but I ended up working in an office processing traffic accident reports."

The men nod. They don't know what to say, he can tell. Then one man smiles at Palmer and says, "Well, everybody had his job to do," and Palmer knows exactly why he has said this. These men have been hassled by MPs. Pot busts maybe, maybe uniform violations when they left the boonies to make trips with their buddies to a PX in a safe city like Qui Nhon, their boots unpolished, their boonie hats unauthorized, their weapons locked and loaded, maybe not even set on safety. The man who says this is a Specialist Fourth-Class, and seems to be the oldest of the three kids. He has opted for maturity. Who wants to drink with a fucking MP?

They ask a few polite questions about his job, actually curious, Palmer senses, about what the hell MPs are like anyway. He tells them he got orders to go to MP school out of Fort Campbell and trained in Fort Gordon. He doesn't tell them that he had expected to be sent into the infantry. The three of them also are draftees. They trained at Fort Polk. They came over here right out of advanced infantry training. They were sent to An Loc. They went out on patrols. Their conversation evolves into stories about the funny things that

had happened to them during the past year, or cracking jokes
about sergeants and officers they didn't like, or reminiscing
about crazy men they had known. "Remember Hewett?" and
this question immediately evokes laughter. The older Spec
Four tells Palmer that after their compound had been shelled
by VC, Hewett used to go out and pick up fragments as
souvenirs, even unexploded rockets, which was not according
to standard operating procedure. "He was an insane fucker.
We'd all be standing a hundred yards away and he'd be out
there roaming around turning over bomb fragments and
picking things up which you're not supposed to do because
Charlie might have booby-trapped something." The other
two men keep laughing. Crazy Hewett. Went home two
months ago without even getting wounded.

Palmer wants to ask them questions about what it was like
to be in the infantry. Did you see very many men die? Did
you ever get wounded? Were there a lot of land mines? Did
you see any VC? Did you kill any VC? How did you stand the
days and nights of muggy heat in this smelly oven of a country?
But it's too late for answers. If he had wanted answers so badly
he should have joined the infantry. Or he could have just let
Phil come over here and bring the answers home.

"Nice talking to you men," he says. "I'm gonna go find a
bunk and crash," standing up from the table and pocketing
his paperback. He knows these grunts want to be alone with
their memories and reminiscences and private experiences
that Palmer can never be a part of and is intruding upon by
his accidental presence. "Thanks for the offer of beer."

The men grin up at him, and all three reach out to shake
his hand. Everyone at this table the same age and drafted.

Could have been buddies if they'd been in the same unit. Maybe if they didn't hate MPs he would have drunk some beer with them, gotten drunk with them even. They seem happy as hell that he's leaving, but then maybe they're just happy because they're leaving Vietnam.

It had been light outside when he entered the enlisted men's club, but now it is dark, more humid than it had been in Qui Nhon, but the darkness does not evoke the thread of uneasiness that he had always felt at night back at his permanent duty station. Maybe because the American presence in Cam Ranh Bay is so vast, or maybe because he is close to getting on an airplane and going home, but he feels none of the sense of danger that used to arrive with the coming of darkness. No mountains around here. The VC don't need a mountain to lob mortars into a compound, but the lack of mountains lessens his uneasiness, underscoring the illogic of his fear. Too bad he didn't know how things were going to turn out at the start of this tour. Might have relaxed a little more. He wanders into a transient barracks and climbs onto a sandy bunk and falls asleep with his camera in one pocket and his paperback in another, his black briefcase clutched under one arm.

At dawn formation he is culled from the pack to mop a latrine under the supervision of an E5 who is going home too. It's like a mirror image of Bien Hoa, even in terms of mood, because nobody is gloomy about pulling these shit details. Four days and a wake-up, three days and a wake-up, two days and a wake-up, everybody is going home soon and everybody is the same, who cares if a GI saw his buddy blow up in a fountain of blood on a trail near the DMZ or watched the light fade in the eyes of a legless man in a foxhole in the Mekong Delta? Hand him a mop and tell him to wag it and shag it.

At noon Palmer goes to a snack bar rather than the mess hall or the enlisted men's club. He enters a small white building where men are standing around eating at waist-high tables the way they used to eat on the basic training ranges. Was that roughing it or what? Standing up while eating noon chow, will our mothers ever believe it? Dipping mess kits into boiling water. Thanking God they didn't have to eat twenty-year-old canned C-rations. A man once spit on the ground while standing in a chow line and a cook screamed at him and said he ought to make the trainee pick up that wad of spit and stuff it in his pocket.

He picks out a prepackaged hamburger, potato chips in a bag, and fills a cup with Coke, then gets into line to pay the cashier. There is a quiet calmness in the snack bar, like a Sunday without a hangover, a feeling of contentment, everybody waiting their turn with military courtesy. As the line shuffles forward, something about the man standing in front of him catches his attention. He's a big man, almost a head taller, and the short-trimmed reddish curly hair on the back of his neck looks familiar. Palmer has seen this man somewhere before.

He leans to his left to get a look at the man's profile, and recognizes him. It's the PFC he had met at Oakland last year, now a Spec Four. Same boyish face, though tanned. What was his name? Palmer can't remember. He feels the hairs on the back of his own trimmed neck begin to prickle. He eases back behind the man and looks up at that short Brillo pad of a GI cut, stands there for a moment wondering if he ought to say something. What if it's not him? But he knows it's him. The kind of guy who would be nicknamed Moose by his football buddies.

Palmer steps to his left and taps the man on the shoulder. "Excuse me, Specialist. You look familiar. Didn't I meet you last year when we were in Oakland?"

The man turns to look at Palmer with his eyebrows raised, same boyish querulous expression, eyes rounded without recognition, without guile.

"We both bunked in Building 629 on our last night there," Palmer says, then sees the subtle change that comes over a face when recognition kicks in.

"You're an MP," the man says, pointing at him with his left hand holding a Coke, his right filled with snacks.

Palmer grins and glances at the man's nametag. *Carlson.* "That's right. You're an engineer."

"Yeah, I remember you," Carlson says, his voice rising, a grin breaking out, color seeming to come into his pale eyes.

The two men stand there grinning at each other for a moment. Neither of them knows what to say; parting a year earlier, they both went off to a country filled with hundreds of thousands of GIs and now here they are, standing in a snack bar in Cam Ranh Bay, clutching hamburgers and Cokes.

"Well shit," Palmer says, laughter punctuating his statement. "What are you doing here? Are you going home?"

Carlson's grin fades. "Naw man, I decided to extend my tour three months to get an early out," and there's a kind of mock mournfulness in his voice as he makes this confession, mock because he is getting what some men would view as a pretty good deal. Knock six months off your enlistment by staying in Vietnam another three months, something Palmer wouldn't do if the army threw a million dollars into the deal.

They put their conversation on hold for the time it takes to pay the cashier, then walk over to a tall table near the door and set their food down. Now they can shake hands. Palmer notes that Carlson is wearing a small peace sign on a leather thong around his neck. Maybe Carlson, too, has become a doper, Carlson, who had looked so clean-cut last year like a serious football player, married Carlson, who bore the burden of an unhappy wife.

"Where've you been stationed all this time?" Palmer says.

"Right here in Cam Ranh Bay. I'm with an engineering unit. How about yourself?"

"I was up in Qui Nhon," Palmer says. "I was a clerk in an MP station." He remembers that Carlson's wife had suggested he go to Canada. Nobody knows what it's like in Vietnam. Palmer never did until he got here. Carlson's wife, too, probably thought GIs climbed off airplanes and dove into foxholes and started shooting. Carlson must have convinced her that things weren't that way. Palmer wants to ask, but doesn't. Maybe the man never did convince her. Maybe things haven't turned out so well for his marriage.

"Well hell, this is something isn't it?" Palmer says. He wants to tell Carlson about the other men he has run across, but it would take too long and anyway words are shit and could never convey his awestruck giddiness at these random crossings of paths. The army is one small world.

"How long have you been here?" Carlson says.

"I got in yesterday. Pulled a couple shit details. I guess I'll be here a few more days." It's always been hard for Palmer to make small talk, but somehow this conversation is not excruciating. He is fascinated by the coincidence rather than disgusted. He feels no sense of wanting to hurry away, feels none of the guilt he usually feels when he meets someone he never expected to see again, as though an injured party has caught up with him at last. He wants to ask Carlson about his wife. Did she approve of his decision to remain here? Is she still even his wife? Things that are none of his business but feel like it only because Carlson had shared his problems last year at Oakland. But Palmer doesn't ask. He just stands there grinning until Carlson says he has to head on back to work, that he's only on break.

"All right...well...," Palmer wants to say sorry to hear that you're staying here three more months, but doesn't, switches his train of thought to, "...it's good to see you again, man. Good luck huh?"

"You too, Palmer," Carlson says, reaching out to shake one last time.

Palmer feels like telling the Mandatory Buddy Lie. I'll keep in touch. I'll write from wherever. This is the shortest friendship he's ever had in his life, but it doesn't seem so very odd, not in the army where everybody is on temporary duty yonder at all times, always headed somewhere else.

Carlson picks up his Coke and hamburger and steps out of the snack bar, walks across a patch of hard earth where other men are walking. He disappears into the crowd.

Palmer stands alone at the table eating his hamburger and sipping at his Coke and grinning, feeling a sensation not unlike that which he always felt during a red-alert, when the possibility of a mortar round landing nearby filled him with exhilaration like inhaled air filling his chest cavity. He remembers the first time he ran across another GI he had known from another duty station, Plamenski, who had been sitting in the cafeteria at the Presidio, the kid from New Jersey who talked like a hood and whom Palmer had not approached because the guy was an obnoxious asshole. It's all odd, like seeing Anh dressed like a house girl, seeing things you don't expect. But then there wasn't much of anything about the army that Palmer had expected. Most of his expectations had come from the movies. Basic training was too easy. MP school was a joke. The Presidio was a shock. He had expected to get sent to Vietnam but it was still a shock when he saw his name on that roster. Reality throwing him for endless loops. Hardly anything ever turns out the way he expects, and when it does he is thunder-struck. He never expected to be waiting for a plane home, yet here he is. He still hates the idea of spending fifteen hours in the air. Completely takes the edge off his joy, as he always knew it would. Maybe he'll cut loose with joy when his feet are planted on the wet earth of Fort Lewis. Phil told him that it rains all the time in Washington.

CHAPTER 51

GIs emerge from the latrine with mops in their hands, squinting in the harsh morning light and making quiet jokes. Strangers, they had briefly become friends as they dipped mops into soapy buckets of water and wiped the concrete floor with rag strings. Finished, they wander over to a small shack where the NCO in charge watches as they put the equipment away, free now of the shit detail they had been chosen for at the end of morning formation after the names had been called for the next flight home from Vietnam.

Palmer sets his broom inside the wooden shack, then walks away pulling a pack of Camels from his jacket pocket. He pauses to light a cigarette, standing on the barren earth not far from the warehouse where he had seen Sgt. Lattimore on the first day but has not seen him since. He snaps the lid closed on his Zippo, pockets it, and steps out toward a barracks where a long line of men wearing khaki uniforms are waiting to enter the customs shack where their suitcases and duffel bags will be checked for contraband. Drugs, army equipment, any item that they are not authorized to take with them back to the United States.

He had come by here last night and watched the men waiting to go into customs where he will be going if the sergeant in the tower ever gets around to calling his name. He is trying to put momentum into time by strolling past this line of men, many of whom have cameras strapped over their shoulders, most of whom are holding manila envelopes that doubtless hold their travel orders. They're a quiet group, like a silent, motionless parade. No victory parade waiting for them back home. Palmer wonders if his father had taken part in any parades when he got back from the South Pacific. Marching down Market Street in San Francisco, crowds cheering, ticker-tape falling. He had never thought to ask his father about it, about anything.

Some men are standing hatless in the sun, some with their soft flat garrison caps stuffed under epaulets on their shoulders. They don't look at all like the veterans whom Palmer had seen at Oakland a year ago, returning from their tours wearing the same grubby fatigues they had been wearing when they were called out of the field to go home. Probably a change of policy at the Pentagon. Bring the GIs home looking as if they had never been near a war, as if every one of them had been clerk/typists.

He walks slowly across the sandy ground adjacent to the sidewalk where the khaki soldiers are talking quietly, smoking, moving one GI at a time toward the fenced-off area like a sally-port into a stockade, the customs shack like a roofed carport. The gate is narrow, only one GI can edge through with his luggage. He stops to look into the fenced area where Spec Fours in jungle fatigues are poking through suitcases open on a countertop. Just like a customs station in the movies, but for the military uniforms. Nobody appears to have any drugs, contraband, and the searches through the luggage appear rather desultory. The Spec Fours close the suitcases, smile, say things to the GIs who secure their luggage and then move off to an area where the luggage is tagged.

There is another area beyond the customs shack, like a large cage, where GIs sit around on benches waiting for the buses to arrive. Public address system speakers overhead give off quiet and bizarre music. The backup orchestration is of professional quality but the words are obscene. A deep voiced male crooner is singing, "A spermy night in Georgia...." Palmer had stood here for fifteen minutes yesterday marveling at the crass lyrics being piped over the heads of the men going home, erotic parodies of pop songs, as though the GIs had to be reminded that they had wives and lovers waiting for them back home. The army and its lame wit. Like Alice's Restaurant.

Long gray buses begin pulling up along the asphalt road far beyond the perimeter fence. A voice comes over the PA telling everyone to prepare to move out. The GIs stand up and gather their luggage and manila envelopes and begin lining up at a gate that will let them outside the perimeter of the 50th to make a short walk to the buses where officers are standing around overseeing the loading, just as officers had stood around the buses at Oakland last year. Do they think anyone is going to flee into the boonies? Race away and buy some drugs and race back?

He watches the loading longingly. Time has slowed down ever since he arrived at the 50th. This is his fourth day, and he is beginning to feel as if he cannot breathe, and it is not just the heat. The stasis itself is stifling. GIs begin passing through the gate, the first ones outside walking quickly along a sidewalk of sandy metal sheets toward the first bus, the ones in the rear having to wait to make their exit as the line finally comes to a halt with the slow loading of the buses. Tomorrow for sure, Palmer tells himself as he field-strips his cigarette and starts to turn away. Then he sees a familiar figure, a man inside the cage bent at the waist and gathering up his duffel bag. It's Krause.

The glasses, the hangdog face, the lips thick and pursed as if he is about to ask a question, it all comes into focus in an instant. Krause wrestling with his duffel bag and standing upright, easing the strap over his shoulder. Palmer stares at the man who is oblivious to him, Krause taking a few steps toward the end of the line where the last men are queuing up, that funny walk like his feet are reaching out to grab the ground. Borrowed five bucks from me and promised to pay me back and I never saw him again, Palmer thinks, even if it was worth five bucks to get out of those shit details. The guy could slip that five through the fence, but then maybe the officers standing around here would take a dim view of men slipping things through a customs fence. Like Motor Pool Mary with her vial of heroin. But still, he can call out to Krouse, say hi, where were you stationed? The line is moving slowly through the gate, Krouse shuffling along, there's still time, and then Palmer sees them. Bright yellow rooftops stacked on Krause's right sleeve. The sonofabitch is a *sergeant*. A *buck* sergeant E5. Palmer's jaw, which has been slowly opening in preparation for calling out, slowly closes. He stands at the fence watching Krouse, who approaches the opening in the fence with his head hung and his eyes wide behind his army issue glasses and his three yellow stripes glowing on the khaki fabric of his right arm. *Krouse* made *sergeant!*

Krause walks through the gate and out onto the metal sidewalk raising his right shoulder and adjusting the strap. Palmer follows along behind the perimeter fence, watches as

Krause reaches the cracked and sunbaked pale asphalt road and climbs onto the last bus in line.

Krause made sergeant.

Palmer turns away and walks across the sand past the barracks with its sidewalk empty now of khaki-clad GIs. The sun is almost directly overhead and the light flashes off the sand into his face. How many grunts wear sunglasses for a real reason in the bush? He moves toward the warehouse where he had seen Sgt. Lattimore, continues to walk aimlessly, thinking that if a dud like Krause can make it all the way to buck sergeant, what does that say for himself?

Not once, not even back at the Presidio, not in basic training, not once did Palmer feel that he deserved all those denials of promotion. The sergeants just never noticed him in basic, although he barely made sharpshooter with the M-14 which was probably a big part of it, but still, he did everything he was told and did it right, and at the Presidio, Sgt. Sherman was just a lifer out for petty revenge, and then he never got promoted at the PMO because he was never really a part of the PMO but was detached from the 109th which meant he was behind all the other road MPs up for promotion ahead of him although it took more than six months but were there really all that many PFCs ahead of him? He had never thought to ask. Sergeant Wesser said promotions came faster to clerks but newbie clerks who were part of the PMO got promotions ahead of him and he never complained because he believed Sgt. Wesser, though if he had gone over to the 109th and bitched about it something might have been done because it's the kiss-asses that get the rank like the brown-noses in basic sucking up to the drill sergeants, but he didn't want to suck up to anyone at the 109th, wanted to wait until his proper turn came because he had his fiefdom and didn't want to make waves and come off like a griper and put his job in jeopardy, so it took nineteen months to go from PFC to corporal and shit, is it possible? Could it be that I really am a total fuckup?

The paperback and the camera drag at his pockets as he wades out of the sandy area and begins walking across the hard-packed earth in the direction of the snack-bar where he had seen Carlson. He still feels hungry and thinks about going in and buying another Coke and something to eat. Back in Qui Nhon he had a can of Coca-Cola on his desk all day long, an endless parade of soft drinks, the occasional Seven-Up, his kidneys are probably wondering why they aren't being hosed down anymore. Used to be beer. After he quit drinking he noticed that he always seemed to have more money than he had when his days were spent in a stupor. It had stopped disappearing mysteriously. He comes abreast of the enlisted men's club where he had sat with those infantrymen. Noon chow is still hours away. Maybe he'll buy a hamburger and a beer right now. Sit down at a table in the club beneath an overhead light and read his paperback and drink beer and try not to think about the fact that after two years in the army he has learned only what everybody else has always known. There was a time, five months ago, when he had begun to take a kind of perverse pride in the fact that the chipped and tarnished PFC pips, with brass showing through where the paint had flaked away, still decorated the collars of his paling fatigue jacket. He will never make Spec Four. He will come out of the army a private, and when people politely inquired as to why he never made corporal he would tell them proudly that he was a total fuckup. Then the army took that away from him, and he was glad. When he was eleven years old he couldn't figure out why he had been in the Boy Scouts for two years and was still a Tenderfoot.

He steps into the enlisted men's club which is black to his sun-shot eyes. As his irises unwind he sees that there are only a few other men in the bar, a pleasing sight, like walking into a movie theater at noon in Denver and seeing three other people in the seats, no talkers, just surly film buffs like himself seeking silence. He goes up to the counter and starts to order a Budweiser, then feels as if he is letting himself down as he has always let himself and everybody else in the world down. Don't let Krause fuck you again. Come out of this clean. Like Wichita. Wait until Seattle. He orders a Coke, pays with a coin, then carries the can to a table in a corner where the dim bar light is brightest.

He removes the bulky Instamatic from his pocket and sets it on the table, pulls out his copy of *The Godfather* and sits down. He lifts the Coke to his lips. Can't wait to get to Seattle where the beer is real, to a Holiday Inn, to a private room with a lock on the door and a bathroom that doesn't have seven other GIs sitting on commodes leafing through copies of *Rolling Stone* and ripping toilet paper off broomsticks. He takes a sip of soda, opens up his paperback, and picks up where he had left off.

CHAPTER 52

The feeling is like that of a plan in which everything has to go exactly right or the whole thing will collapse, like all the plans of his life. It's like waking up that Sunday morning knowing he would have to go through a certain number of motions in order to deliver Anh's refrigerator and at any moment one of the many small steps might go awry. Waking up in the transient barracks at the 50th has this feeling on the day that Palmer knows his name will be called.

He has spent the past four days wandering around the sandy landscape taking Instamatic pictures of things not moving, had run off the last few feet of a fifty foot reel of 8mm film in his Bell-and-Howell that he had retrieved from his duffel bag, the film so old that he doubts it will even develop properly, though who knows, Kodak is a good company, the best, but the heat of Vietnam can destroy the best American beer. He has been ticking off the days as he had done in basic and MP school though not so much at the Presidio but every single day and hour since he had arrived in Vietnam, ticking off the very seconds, sitting on the back patio of the Camp Quincey EM club and gazing at the second hand of his watch, the thin needle demolishing time one small jerk after another and every one gone into his account and could never be taken away but there were millions it had seemed. How many seconds are there in a year? In four days? On this fifth day he wakes up when a Spec Four wanders through the barracks politely telling everyone formation is in half an hour. A permanent party Spec Four, this is his job in Vietnam, waking up men going home, men who surprisingly have been able to sleep all night in spite of it.

Palmer sits up on his sandy bunk and plants his booted feet on the floor. Other men are rising, coughing, moaning, but not in a pained way, just the moans of men awakening, men going home. The atmosphere in the barracks seethes with quiet anticipation. It doesn't matter who they are or what their rank or where they served, they're all in the same shit like in basic, except they're going home.

He eats chow in the mess hall then wanders out to the parade ground which is a block away from the warehouse where he had seen Lattimore but hasn't seen him since and never will again, he knows. He will never see anyone again. Men slowly swarm the parade ground but it's not like Long Binh where the inherent enlisted fear of shit details had caused men to attempt amateurish maneuvers to avoid being in a line destined to mop latrines or burn shit or, at Oakland, pull KP. Even now the memory of that small victory makes him feel good as he field-strips his last cigarette before the sergeant climbs into the tower to begin reading names. This is his job in Vietnam, reading the names of men going home.

Palmer listens up as the alphabetical list is recited in the sergeant's electric drone coming from PA speakers planted on poles nearby, and he feels himself leaning as he had leaned that day at the Presidio during the mass promotion, leaned until the P's ended and the Q's had begun and he knew that Sgt. Sherman had fucked him good. "Palmer!" The single word comes as a small shock, but it always had in his army career. Ominous. When had his shouted name ever portended anything good? He raises his head as if to question the sergeant in the tower, then steps out of line, the air seeming thin where he is walking, emerging from the formation like all the other men ahead of him, each hurrying toward a transient barracks where they will claim their duffel bags, shuck their jungle fatigues, don their khakis and take their place in the line that Palmer had studied wondering when it was going to be his turn. A feeling of urgency rises unbeckoned, a foolish feeling like the foolish fears of basic when he was scared he was going to miss an order and some Drill Sergeant was going to threaten to recycle him. But it's there, a ludicrous worry of being late for his flight out of Cam Ranh Bay. Anything could fuck this up. What he has to do, he tells himself as he walks in quick-time toward his barracks, is become a perfect cog in the machine of this day and do everything exactly right so that he will not become the fuckup. GIs who don't even know he exists are depending on him not to screw them over, all of his buddies in jungle green hurrying toward this barracks or that doubtless also filled with the same lightheaded sense of urgency: I'm going home.

He enters the barracks where his duffel bag rests padlocked to the metal frame of the bunk he had slept on last night. Already there is a small stack of jungle fatigues lying in the center of the floor where they have been tossed by men whose alphabetically high names were called before him and who have already walked outside wearing their khakis. Tossed unmilitarily, they lie flat and sprawled with dark camouflage unit patches facing the ceiling, the same unit patches he had sorted through in Oakland when he had been put on the inexplicable detail. But he will be keeping his own pale letter jacket and the last of the pants that had never ripped out at the knees.

He opens his duffel bag and withdraws the khakis that he
had folded neatly last night and stacked on top. Removes the
polished low-quarters that he had put a sheen on. Never did
master the spit-shine, they look only black but not shiny. He
takes off his jungle fatigues for the last time, lays them on his
bunk and puts on his khakis that he had worn only a few
times before, in basic for fitting, trying them on back at Camp
Redstone after having his unit patches sewn on by a seamstress. Missy Cue had laundered and ironed them. He puts
on the single white T-shirt that he had brought from America
a year ago, a pair of white boxer shorts, how he hates those
things with their floppy open flies, but he'd been too cheap to
buy the briefs he had worn as a civilian. Caught the tip of his
dick in the zipper of his fatigue pants one hungover morning
when he was dressing too quickly. That woke him up. He
removes his flat garrison cap from the duffel bag. The Drill
Sergeants call it a cunt cap. He parts the soft fabric and places
it squarely on his head to get the feel. He had worn his only
a few times in basic for inspections, had worn his saucer-cap
to the Presidio and everywhere else.

There's no hurry. It will probably be two hours before he
climbs onto one of the buses that will take everyone to the
airfield. He packs his fatigues and boots and locks his duffel
bag and goes outside, steps into the sunshine in his fresh
khakis and walks over to a washroom where other GIs are
giving themselves the same private inspection that he will be
giving himself as soon as he can get up to one of the foot-wide
mirrors. Everyone is grinning, buddies cracking jokes. Some
men have no unit patches on their khakis. Maybe infantry, he
thinks, men who did not have time to seek out a seamstress

during their year over here, who have only brass on the collars, no insignia beyond the significance of the khaki itself: going-home.

He looks at himself in a mirror. Got his last haircut three weeks ago and none of his cadre had said anything. How long is his hair really? It seems long to him but doesn't even touch his ears. Hair is relative. America is full of hippies. Before graduation from basic practically everyone ran to the barbershop afraid they wouldn't be allowed to graduate if their necks weren't naked. Palmer hadn't gone for a haircut. Didn't want to walk the streets of Denver on furlough looking like a kid from the Fabulous Fifties. He examines the battalion crests on his epaulets, makes sure they're pinned properly, squares the cap on his head, adjusts the lie of the white fabric of the T-shirt revealed in the V of his khaki collar. Well. That's that. He looks like a soldier.

The stack of uniforms has grown in the barracks. Three feet deep, and there are GIs just now removing their jungle fatigues and tossing them onto the pile. He opens his duffel bag and pulls out his briefcase with his orders tucked inside. He checks his billfold for money. Everything a soldier in-transit needs, travel orders and money, everything else will take care of itself. He pulls out his copy of *The Godfather*. Barely made it a quarter of the way through the book but plans to focus on it for fifteen hours straight if he has to on the trip across the Pacific. That still impinges on the joy of this moment. How he hates flying.

The line leading to the customs building is long, follows the right-angle of a sidewalk and stretches past another building. He comes to the end of the line and sets his duffel bag down and stands erect and squints off toward the customs building where men are entering one at a time. It will take a while. The best line he's ever stood in, though probably not the last. There's a good feeling here. Conversations are muted, some men hatless, which strikes Palmer as foolish. All they need is a captain storming around telling everyone to shape up. Like the battalion supply officer. Come up and gawk at the blood.

He stands and reads his paperback as the line moves forward, lifting and dragging his duffel bag one step at a time, making the right turn and closing in on the customs shack. No word about the piss test. Must have passed it. He finds he can read only a paragraph at a time before looking up to see how the line is moving. Just like on an airplane but for a different reason: fear versus impatience. When he is among the men closest to the gate he closes his book and stuffs it into a pants pocket and clutches the strap of his duffel bag, trying to put momentum into time with these static moves. Beyond the gate, within the cage, men are sitting on benches listening to the obscene lyrics. Behind him the line of GIs stretches around that right-angle. It will still be awhile before the buses arrive, even after he makes it through customs. No hurry. Time is moving exactly as slowly as it has moved all year.

It gives him a funny feeling when he becomes the first man in line, standing at the narrow width of the gate waiting for his turn to enter and step up to the counter, like waiting for a dentist appointment. He mentally inventories the contents of his duffel bag. He's heard that if a customs man finds any item with the word "military" printed on it, the item will be considered contraband and confiscated. MPs at the 109th cook up all sorts of scams to ship their painted black helmet-liners home, so he's heard. The helmet liners belong to the army but the MPs want them as souvenirs, their names delicately painted in small cursive on the back near the bottom by talented Vietnamese in the shop in downtown Qui Nhon, the black domes decorated with the green and yellow twin-axe brigade decal, the big white non-ambiguous letters "MP" on the front. Palmer hadn't been a road MP long enough to have gotten nostalgic about his own helmet, which he had turned in to supply before he left.

"Next man!"

Palmer hauls his duffel bag up to the counter where a sullen Spec Four has been examining luggage, suitcases, hand-carries. Must be tedious work. And there's always the possibility of finding drugs, and God knows what kind of scene ensues after that. MPs, fights, tears. Palmer opens the canvas flaps and the man peers inside, digs around. There isn't much to see, jungle fatigues, paperbacks, underwear, the patent-leather MP holster and web gear that Palmer had paid for with his own money at the PX in Qui Nhon and is allowed to take home. The man snoops around listlessly, then tells Palmer he can go. Palmer takes advantage of this moment to place his Instamatic inside the bag, doesn't want to lose it on the flight home.

He walks beyond the customs table to the cage where smiling men are sitting around shooting the shit or reading magazines or just smoking and staring out beyond the fence where the buses will be coming. All the men who have made it. Ten a day average this year didn't make it, mostly Infantry.

Had any of these men expected to die this year? He will never know because death was the one subject he had never heard spoken of during the entire time he was in Qui Nhon, except after Detty's suicide, and even then it was as if the men were reluctant to talk about it. Superstitious maybe, who knows, but even Palmer never had the urge to ask any of his buddies how they felt about the prospect of dying. Something you just didn't talk about. And fear, nobody ever talked about that either. Too late to talk about those things.

He finds a space on a wooden bench not far from the very spot where Krause had hoisted his duffel bag. Jesus. *Sergeant.* He shakes his head and pulls out his paperback and tries to read, but can't. The anticipation inherent in this day is too overwhelming to concentrate on ink. As the cage fills, it becomes noisy to the point where it is almost impossible to make out the pornographic lyrics of the Muzak coming from the speakers. You would think the crooners would bust out laughing at the filthy words they're warbling in perfect vocal tones. The army must think enlisted men are idiots. All you dogfaces are going home to make it with your chicks, how about that? Cool huh? What was her name, weaving a tapestry and undoing it at night? Aaah high school English, you've let me down. His mother used to quote a poem about her by Dorothy Parker, always going around quoting Dorothy Parker when he was a kid. If your heart ever gets broken, take refuge in Dorothy Parker, mom said. "They will call *him* brave." His mother lived in Omaha for three and a half years, waiting for his father to come home from WWII. Penelope. That's it. He notes that there aren't any officers standing around in the cage. Probably waiting in some curtained, carpeted, air-conditioned building, sipping mixed drinks and telling each other how important they are.

A small man, a sergeant E5 with a voice pitched like Popeye, is standing in the middle of the cage telling nearby men about the things he's going to do when he gets home, the women he's going to see. He's making everybody laugh. He's a character, puffing on a short butt and dancing in place, his whole body bouncing up and down with the obvious excitement of going home, the excitement everyone feels but only he shows, looking left and right and nodding and puffing and cackling and rubbing his khaki-clad chest and talking about nooky. He has a face that's both young and old at the same time, like *My Favorite Martian*, what's-his-name, and is probably a lifer. Maybe he's been here before and always likes this part of being in the war, the going-home part. Some men pull two or three tours of duty. Some men like being in Vietnam.

CHAPTER 53

The announcement comes over the PA at the same time the buses begin pulling up on the road, the obscene lyrics suddenly clipped short for a voice telling everyone to form up at the gate for boarding. Palmer rises and stuffs his paperback into his pocket and hoists his duffel bag and heads toward the gate, and can feel the lack of competition he had felt in so many places during the past two years, mostly in chow lines but anywhere that men had to queue up to get something they needed or wanted. There is no rushing here, everyone drifting into a line because rushing will have no effect on the things that will take place throughout this day. They are on the conveyor belt that will take them back to America just as it had brought them from Oakland or whatever military base they had departed from last year. Palmer sets his bag down in line and watches as a captain unlocks the padlock on the gate and opens it and lets the first man through. There are officers standing all over the place, just like at Oakland. The gate and the padlock and the cage and the piss test and the guards, it's like being let out of prison, a phenomenon Palmer tries not to think about, he knows the army has to maintain security and had never expected his departure from Vietnam to be anything but mundane, but the presence of all the officers guarding everyone is annoying and takes a further edge off the joy of going home, like the prospect of fifteen hours in the air, but thoughts like these are only passing. He hoists his duffel bag onto his shoulder and steps out of the gate, looks around as he walks along the metal sidewalk, the

narrow sheets engraved with holes, what do they call these...
skids? Don't they build airfields out of these in the boonies?
He looks around at the dry brown landscape of Cam Ranh
Bay, at the dirt roads which look recently plowed by tractors,
low hills of red earth stacked at the shoulders drying beneath
a hot sun in a clear sky. He glances back beyond the cage to
the compound where new men still in pale jungle fatigues
who have recently arrived are wandering around waiting
their turn to make this walk.

He climbs onto the first bus, edging down the familiar
aisle with his duffel bag cocked in front of him and takes a
seat by a window. He sits down fast and settles the bag on
the floor and looks out through the screen at the men still
filing out of the cage, and realizes he should have kept his
Instamatic to take pictures of this, ought to have kept his
Bell-and-Howell to film a scene like this that can never be
filmed again in his lifetime, men striding out of the cage and
heading toward the buses with grins on their faces, the last
reel of the movie scrapbook that he had wanted to make of
his stretch in the service but had lost heart for doing because
he had expected to go home in a body bag. Now that he's
made it this far he feels sort of depressed. Never even took a
landscape shot of Camp Redstone with his movie camera, has
no visual record of that place at all.

Officers are running back and forth with clipboards
tucked under their arms, checking the buses, locking things
down. Their job in Vietnam. An officer job. It's hot inside the
bus. The engine idles. Trucks always idle in the army, they
never get shut off. As soon as the last man has climbed onto
the last bus the drivers engage the gears and the convoy takes

off. There is sparse cheering from the seats. Leaving this place. Heading for the airfield. Palmer leans close to the screen and looks at the 50th as it recedes, looks at the brown earth and weeds and the green of what must be rice paddies in the distance, looks at everything as the conveyor hauls him across the Cam Ranh landscape as he had been hauled across Northern California one year ago this week.

He finally stops looking out the window and settles back with the duffel bag locked between his knees, looks ahead at the flat landscape with the ribbon of asphalt winding into the distance toward a waiting airplane.

A voice comes from the back of the bus, a man saying something loudly, and GIs start glancing around, looking toward the back of the bus where a black GI is stumbling up the aisle. He passes Palmer's seat, staggering, grabbing the backs of seats, holding himself erect and saying, "Stop the bus, I want off," his voice slurred, his body swaying side to side either from the swaying of the bus or something else, "Stop the bus." Men sit up straight to get a look at him, his garrison cap askew, his body lurching toward the driver who quickly glances around to see him shuffling forward saying stop the bus. Something cold clutches Palmer's heart, a snafu rising, the thing he has been leery about like the flight home. Something weird is happening.

The GI grabs the chrome-plated poles above the driver's seat and says, "Stop the bus, I want to get off," and the driver again looks quickly around and says, "What?" Barely intelligible, the man mumbles stop the bus. GIs rise from their seats to see better. "What are you talking about?" the driver says, taking his foot off the accelerator. The bus lurches with this loss of power and Palmer feels himself thrust forward, everyone bracing themselves as the black man clutches the pole holding himself upright and saying stop the bus.

"What?" the driver says, looking up at the man. "What?"

And then some passenger hollers, "Let the sonofabitch off if he wants off!"

The driver guides the bus to the shoulder of the road, brings it to a halt and works the lever to open the door. The GI stumbles down the steps and staggers onto the ground and begins trudging back along the shoulder toward the 50th.

The bus is silent, everyone leaning toward the windows to see the man, with Palmer thinking he's probably fucked up on heroin. Then a captain comes sprinting up the road and leaps into the bus and yells, "Why'd you stop! Why'd you stop?"

The driver shrugs and points out the door. "Some guy wanted to get off the bus, so I let him off."

"What? What do you mean, what guy?"

"A black guy. He got off the bus and went back down that way," pointing toward the 50th. Palmer closes his eyes and groans silently, inwardly. This is going to fuck everything up for everybody. They will have to go back to the 50th and will miss their flight and Christ knows when they'll get home.

The captain looks down the road, then looks up the road in the direction of the airfield and says, "All right. Get this bus moving now!" and hops out the door and runs back to the bus he had come from.

The driver cranks the door shut, engages the transmission and steps on the accelerator. The bus lumbers back onto the road and begins picking up speed. Some of the men twist around in their seats to see what they can see, but most don't. Palmer doesn't. He sits staring out the front window contemplating the fact that the man who had gotten off the bus eventually will be picked up by MPs and taken to jail and has completely fucked up his last day in Vietnam. An addict maybe, who doesn't want to leave the war, wants to stay here and indulge his vice forever. Like Omar. Maybe that was Omar. So long, Omar.

The driver accelerates across the flat asphalt-ribboned landscape and the men forget the incident, or don't talk about it anyway. The convoy turns down an access road and begins approaching a gate that will take them out to the airfield where a 707 is waiting for them on the tarmac. The buses pull up and park in a straight line. There is a wait while the officers overseeing this operation get off their buses and take up their observation posts before giving the order to open the doors and let the troops off. Maybe the security is not such a foolish thing after all, Palmer muses as he waits inside the conveyor growing hotter under the sun in the cloudless sky. Maybe men run off all the time, drug addicts, who knows? To even question security is finally pointless, as are all questions about the army. Hurry up and wait, that was the first annoying garbage that Palmer can remember really sticking in his craw back in basic. What a job though, herding millions of men around the world, in and out of planes and ships and wars. It's a miracle that anything gets done at all.

The driver cranks the door open, and the troops stand up and begin moving slowly and with military courtesy, almost as if they are savoring this final act, the men near the door climbing off first and then the troops in the rear shuffling forward with their duffel bags held in front of them. There's no talk, but Palmer can feel a kind of smiling anticipation emanating from everyone as they step down onto the concrete edge of the runway, the sunlight so bright out here where everything is concrete that it's almost blinding, and fifty feet away stands the 707 that Palmer had not gotten a very good look at when they pulled in because he was on the wrong side of the bus, but gets a good look now and is appalled. Painted along the side of the airplane in big block letters are the words *Flying Tiger Airlines* which strikes him as nonsensical, as if a crate from a traveling circus has shown up to fly them across the Pacific.

"All right, I want everybody to put your luggage on those dollies!" an officer shouts. Empty linked carts towed by small motorized vehicles have been parked near the busses. The men carry their luggage over and lay it down in neat military rows. Everything is going smoothly and according to schedule but for the minor snafu back there with the AWOL GI who is probably already in custody, Palmer supposes, absentmindedly tapping his chest for a cigarette and then remembering that he had decided not to smoke on the trip home. Do they allow smoking anyway? But he wants to keep his flames and embers and sparks to a minimum during the trip.

The enlisted men are told to wait until the officers have boarded the plane. More buses have arrived and the brass step off and walk right up a mobile stairwell and into the First Class section while the EM stand silently watching. When the last officer has skipped up the steps like an ambitious junior executive on the make and has entered the darkness of the doorway, the EM and noncoms are told to form a line and prepare to embark.

Palmer looks around the airfield, the landscape so sun-shot that the air itself seems white, the sky faded, the bowl of blue pale above his head, the heat intense out here with long mirages wavering and flickering in the distance. They are far from the control tower, there are no buildings at this end of the runway, there's nothing beyond the perimeter fence but weeded red earth. He looks around as the line shuffles forward, looking at everything even though there isn't much to see. Seems like there ought to be more. Then he's at the stairwell and plants a foot on the bottom step and lifts himself off Vietnam and makes his way up the mobile stairwell which sways a bit from the weight of the troops ascending and pouring into the blackness of the arched doorway leading into coach.

He expects the air inside the plane to be cold but it is the same temperature as the tropical air outside, the door of the jet standing open until the last troop has filed on, then closed quickly by a stewardess. Palmer has never liked to sit by airplane windows but wants to sit by one now, working his way down the aisle toward the last empty rows because it seems everybody wants to sit by a window.

He edges into a row near a wing and plants himself on the narrow seat and immediately buckles his seatbelt prior to the pilot's order out of habit, like a good luck charm, like an illusion. At least he won't go tumbling all over hell when the plane careens into the sea. The troops stow baggage in overhead racks, khaki uniforms in front of him now instead of the jungle green of last year, the flight to Alaska, Yokota, Bien

Hoa, he's been more places than he ever will be again in his life and he knows it.

The stewardesses are wearing bland gray skirts and jackets. They move up and down the aisle keeping their smiles fixed as GIs crack jokes with them. The women probably get good at deflecting wisecracks, but then soldiers, even soldiers coming home from a war, are trained to be courteous, and anyway nobody is going to say anything inappropriate with their buddies bristling with envy as a man gets the attention of one or another of these women who look not unlike nurses at evacuation hospitals, and in fact are not unlike them at all. Tall white women working in a service industry.

The wait for the plane to begin moving is long, but that's nothing to these men; long is relative. The engines start up, rendering mute the conversations. If only he didn't hate flying. This ought to be the happiest moment of his life. He looks out the window at the dry bright landscape. High above the ground now he can see a far horizon where the green of a rice paddy shimmers. Somewhere out there a water buffalo is dragging a hand-held plow. Somewhere out there Viet Cong troops are plotting assaults. Somewhere out there a cherry boy is walking toward his new billet. Palmer pulls out his paperback and opens it to a dog-eared page and tries to read but can't.

A gentle lurch, the GIs rock softly against the seatbacks as the plane begins to taxi out to the runway. Palmer closes his paperback, looks out the window which is like a TV screen, things drifting slowly past the glass, asphalt and earth, the plane rumbling, bumping and rocking, planes were meant to fly, it feels nonsensical to ride in a walking bird.

Then it happens as it always does, the plane suddenly accelerating, the ride smoothing out, the cushion pressing into Palmer's back as he glances out the window and sees the blurred asphalt and fencing and weeds, the slingshot sensation drawing near, the plane is moving too damn fast, no stopping it now, the bastard can't hold onto the earth any longer and the nose rises and the wheels give a last thud and leave the runway and the coach erupts with earsplitting cheers like you'd hear at a parade, with whistles and applause and garrison caps chucked toward the ceiling, with pumping arms and clenched fists like you'd see at a parade.

The stewardesses seated at the front of the plane must hear this on every takeoff, and probably like it a lot. But who wouldn't? Who doesn't like a parade? This is their parade, their victory residing in their very existence, their lives thrust like bullets into that false blue medium, ranks of buckled bodies cheering to beat the turbine squall screaming from the wings.

Palmer peers through the window, looks down at the shrinking landscape, looks out at the horizon broadening and bending with every gain in altitude and velocity. He takes a deep breath to make his eardrums pop, then exhales and leans back against the cushion and tells himself that there is nothing he can do now but relax and read his paperback. The plane will just have to fly itself. His job is finished. His war is over. Phil will be home by Christmas.

The End

CPSIA information can be obtained
at www.ICGtesting.com
Printed in the USA
FSOW01n0852010218
44045FS